LIGHT *of the* MORNING STAR

ABOUT THE AUTHOR

Dash Parsons was born in Wales. He has lived and worked in the UK, Cyprus, and the Middle East. He now lives in Queensland, Australia, with his wife and two children.

Light of the Morning Star is his debut novel.

DASH PARSONS

LIGHT
of the
MORNING
STAR

PERGAMOS

Pergamos Publishing
PO Box 1015
Buddina
QLD 4575
Australia
Email: pergamospublishing@icloud.com

Cataloguing-in-Publication details are available from the National Library of Australia.
www.trove.nla.gov.au

ISBN 978-0-646-87220-9

Cover picture by ArtDiktator/istockphoto.com
Cover design by Dash Parsons

To Caroline

For everything

Never attempt to win by force what can be won by deception.

Niccolò Machiavelli
The Prince

A lie that is half-truth is the darkest of all lies.

Alfred Tennyson

When it comes to bullshit... bigtime, major league bullshit... you have to stand in awe of the all-time champion of false promises and exaggerated claims... religion.

George Carlin

Religion (is) a universal obsessional neurosis.

Sigmund Freud

The greatest trick the Devil ever pulled was convincing the world he didn't exist.

Roger "Verbal" Kint
The Usual Suspects

1

Captain Arkadi Ben Ari sat in absolute darkness on a hard and uncomfortable chair. His stomach felt hollow and painfully cramped, his head was almost too heavy to lift, his mind was clouded, and his breathing laboured. There was something in his mouth, soft and stringy against his tongue. He tried to spit out whatever it was, but it didn't move. He could vaguely feel something wrapped around the lower half of his face. He tried to shout, but with the gag and a peculiar dryness in his throat, all he could manage was a muffled cough.

The floor was soft against the soles of his bare feet. He tried to stand, but he was unable to move. His legs felt weak, but his lack of strength was not what prevented him from standing. He felt fabric rub against the skin of his arms, thighs, and ankles and realised he was naked and bound to the chair. His heart pounded. He could feel it in his chest and temples. He twisted against the bindings. Gently at first, but when the bonds didn't slacken, he squirmed more violently, making his blood pump quicker and his headache worse.

He had, of course, endured torture before, during his military training—several times. In a sense, it was voluntary. You signed up for military service, and undergoing torture survival training was part of it.

But this was different.

He didn't volunteer for this.

Whatever *this* was.

Panic rose in him, like the bile in his throat, which he was sure he'd choke on. He struggled to loosen the bonds again, but the throbbing in his temples intensified, and the pounding of his heart was almost painful. He might burst a blood vessel or suffer an aneurysm if he continued. Wouldn't that be something? The hero of the Alexandroni Brigade, a survivor of numerous military skirmishes, found dead on a chair with his balls on show.

If he were found at all.

He needed to relax and slow his breathing. He closed his watery eyes and took slow, deep breaths through his nose, which had mercifully been left clear. Breathe in for four seconds, hold for four, exhale for another four, and repeat as necessary—a technique he learned during his training. Slow everything down, then refocus.

When he inhaled, Ben Ari smelled jasmine and sweat—his sweat, he realised. A ceiling fan, droning slowly on what sounded like its lowest setting, did nothing to ward off the late spring heat. Or maybe it was just his fear burning him up.

As his breathing returned to something resembling normal, Ben Ari opened his eyes again. He blinked hard twice, and his eyes finally cleared. All he could see in the darkness was a vague shape in front of him, wide and boxy, roughly as tall as the chair's seat. Was he still in his room at the Market Hotel or elsewhere? Somewhere his captor could do unimaginable things to him without discovery.

He struggled to free himself again with a muffled scream of frustration, but the more he moved, the tighter the bindings seemed to get. Sweat ran down his forehead into his eyes. It stung as the Mediterranean used to when he swam in it open-eyed as a child. The chair rocked as he twisted from left to right and back again. His momentum forced the chair over as he swung back to the right. His head and right shoulder took the brunt of the fall, and despite the floor being carpeted, the impact sent a shockwave of pain through him. He thought the blow might have dislocated his shoulder.

As his panic intensified and his breathing quickened, he again used the calmative breathing technique the army taught him. It took him longer to compose himself this time, but as his breathing finally slowed, he attempted to recall what happened before he woke to this predicament. After a moment of blankness, he remembered.

Ester.

He'd booked Ester a few days earlier through an escort service he used whenever he was in the city. He'd requested a tall brunette who wouldn't object to rough sex. Having been on active duty for the last six months in various shitholes to the north, he needed a good hard fuck. The service had told him that Ester would be very accommodating.

In preparation, Ben Ari had showered and changed into clean clothes, then called reception and ordered a chilled bottle of Smirnoff, a bucket of ice, and two large shot glasses. Five minutes after room service had brought everything, Ester had arrived wearing a black cocktail dress. Ben Ari remembered thinking that even though Ester was probably not her real name, she lived up to its meaning. Ester meant *star* in Hebrew, and she'd shone with extraordinary brightness.

He'd stood back to let her in and then offered her a brimming glass of vodka, which she'd accepted and swallowed in a single gulp. He'd done the same and then poured them another double slug. They'd made small talk. He'd told her he was in Tel Aviv to receive a medal from his superiors for exceptional service during the war against the Arabs the year before. She'd pretended to be impressed. Then, she'd commanded him to sit on the edge of the bed. He remembered becoming hard before she'd laid even a finger on him. She'd climbed onto the bed behind him and unbuttoned his shirt. And then something sharp drove into his neck, and everything had faded to black.

Ben Ari snapped back, realising what had happened.

Ester had drugged him.

Bitch!

He attempted once more to break free from the chair. He was sure he could feel some give in the fabric around his arms, but as one

3

shoulder was trapped against the floor, his movement was even more restricted than it had been when he was upright. His heart felt like it would explode from his chest. He tried to shout again, but his rage escaped with a stifled grunt. He shut his eyes and let his head drop to the floor, resigned to the fact that he was entirely at Ester's mercy.

As his sobs became quiet whimpers, something shifted behind him—a curtain moving in the downdraft of the fan, perhaps?

No.

Someone was in the room with him.

Ben Ari raised his head and swivelled it, straining to see behind him. It was pointless. His captor was behind the chair, and Ben Ari couldn't twist his head far enough to catch sight of them. His breathing became erratic again, and he thought he might start to hyperventilate. He heard the snick of a lighter's flint wheel. As the unmistakable scent of cigarette smoke reached his nostrils, he suddenly had an overwhelming desire for a Camel.

Fingers touched his face, and Ben Ari recoiled in shock—a reflex response. The fingers pulled down the gag, then reached in and removed whatever was in his mouth. He heaved in great gulps of air.

'Ester?' he rasped, his throat as dry as bark in summer. 'What is this? Let me out of this.'

No movement. No reply.

'What the hell is going on?' His rage built, and he squirmed against the bindings. 'Ester, this isn't funny. Cut me loose, you fucking whore, and I promise I'll only cut out one of your eyes.'

'Ester's not here.'

Ben Ari stiffened. The voice wasn't Ester's. It wasn't even a woman's voice. It was a man's. Deep and calm and unfamiliar. He spoke Hebrew, but Ben Ari could tell it wasn't the man's native tongue. There was something else underneath. English, perhaps? Not that it mattered.

'Where is she?' Ben Ari demanded. 'Who are you?'

Without warning and making no sound of exertion, the stranger hauled the chair upright with such force that Ben Ari thought it, and he with it, would topple over again. Instead, it teetered and then settled. The man brushed past him, and a moment later, a thin column of pale light appeared ten feet in front of him. It widened quickly, and he realised the man was opening a curtain. As the moonlight flooded in, he could make out his surroundings. In front of him was a bed. On the other side of the window was a balcony, and beyond that, the sea, a shard of silvery-white on a rippling swathe of blackness. In the corner was a desk, and draped over a table lamp on it was a military cap.

His cap.

He was still in his room at the hotel.

Knowing where he was, though, was a small comfort.

The stranger looked out toward the ocean and took a long draw on his cigarette. He was taller than Ben Ari—at least a few inches over six feet. He wore a dark suit and a shirt of a similar colour, and although he couldn't yet fully make out the man's face, Ben Ari could see enough to know the man's skin was the colour of night.

'Who are you?' he asked again while trying another futile attempt at breaking free. 'How long have I been here? What do you want?'

The man took another, longer draw from the cigarette. Without turning back from the window, as if talking to the sea, he said, 'My name is Gideon. I'm here because I made a promise to a friend. And you've been unconscious for two days.'

'What? Two days? What is this? What friend?' Ben Ari spat out his words in rapid-fire.

'You wouldn't know him. His name is Sultan Haddad.'

Ben Ari knew some Arabic. The Israeli military required a rudimentary understanding of it, particularly of someone of his rank. As with Hebrew names, Arabic names often—or at least used to—reflect people's occupations. He frowned, trying to recall what he knew.

'Haddad?' He searched his mind for a few moments more. 'A blacksmith?'

'Of sorts.'

'So what?' he said, glaring at the back of Gideon's head. 'The name means nothing to me.'

'I know. I said you wouldn't know him.' Gideon took another pull on his cigarette. 'How old are you, Arkadi? Thirty-one? Thirty-two?'

'I'm thirty-one. What does that have to do with anything?'

'My friend Sultan had a nephew, although he thought of him more like a son. His name was Khaled. You wouldn't have known him either. He'd just turned thirty when he died. You're older now than he will ever be.'

Ben Ari's rage and irritation started to surge, both with still being bound to the chair and having to play this ridiculous game. 'And what does any of that have to do with me?'

Gideon turned from the window, and the moonlight gave Ben Ari his first look at the man's face. He was perhaps fifty, give or take a few years, and a ragged scar ran down the right side of his face, from his forehead to his cheek, stopping just above the line of a neatly cropped beard. His right eye appeared to have been undamaged by whatever had made the scar, and it, along with the left eye, shone with a bright, peculiar silvery-grey light.

'Tantura.'

Ben Ari felt his left eye twitch minutely. Given the darkness and the distance between them, he didn't think Gideon would have seen it.

'There it is,' said Gideon. 'The penny drops.'

'I was following orders,' Ben Ari said, attempting to conceal his alarm at the stranger's sharp-sightedness and knowledge of his military exploits.

Gideon nodded slowly.

'By the end of your rampage through Tantura and the other villages in the north, you and your troops had killed dozens of people and injured and made homeless hundreds, if not thousands more. Did you know the village was ready to surrender?'

'I was following orders!'

'Were you ordered to destroy the buildings in those villages with innocent civilians, elderly and physically incapable of leaving, still inside of them?'

Ben Ari glared but said nothing. Probably, there was nothing he could say that this man would listen to.

'No,' said Gideon softly. 'I didn't think so. That's on you. The nephew, Khaled, lived in Haifa. Before it fell, Khaled took his family out and made for the safety of Fureidis. On the way, he made a detour to Tantura to try to persuade his grandmother to leave the village. He was still there when you and your thugs attacked the place. The grandmother was sick. She'd been unable to walk and couldn't leave her house. Reports from survivors who fled the village say that when you were demolishing the houses with mortars and heavy machine-gun fire, Khaled had stayed by his grandmother's side so she wouldn't die alone and terrified.'

Ben Ari struggled in his chair. He could feel the fabric around his wrists tightening and the heat of rage and fear burning inside him.

'Khaled had a son,' said Gideon. 'His name's Ali. He's nine years old now. A beautiful little boy. And smart, too. He'd wanted to go to Tantura with his father, but Khaled had insisted the boy go with his mother. Thankfully, the boy and his mother made it to Fureidis, where Khaled's uncle—my friend Sultan—took them in.'

'So that's what this is? The uncle of some poor dead Arab has paid you to hunt me down and kill me?'

'No. Sultan doesn't know I'm here. I haven't seen him since we moved him, the boy, and the rest of his family to London last year. But I did make him a promise, and now I'm fulfilling that promise. Regrettably, it's taken me longer than I'd hoped, but... you know... all good things.'

'How did you find me?'

'Is that important?'

Ben Ari shrugged as if it didn't matter, but he believed he could walk away from this. And when he did, he would find whoever betrayed him and remove their tongue. And their eyes. And their ears, now he thought about it. Hear no evil, see no evil, speak no fucking evil.

'It wasn't that hard,' said Gideon. 'The organisation I work for trades in many things, the most important of which is information. We have people in most major cities, including Tel Aviv. We also engage with certain other organisations who funnel information to us or who can assist us in our activities.'

Ben Ari sighed, piecing it all together.

'Like the escort agency,' he said.

'Like the escort agency. We pay it, and others like it, for information. We've found that nothing loosens a person's tongue better than a belly full of alcohol and a good-looking woman or man in their bed. The agencies feed us the info its clients let slip to their escorts, and we use it to our advantage.'

'Blackmail and extortion.'

'Sometimes, but not always. And not in your case. You are the prize this time, Arkadi. It took me some time to learn that you were in command at Tantura, but once I had your name, it went on watch lists at all the hotels and escort agencies in Tel Aviv and Jerusalem.'

'I'm sure you think you're very clever.'

'I received two telephone calls in the last four days,' Gideon said, ignoring the jibe.

'Lucky you. Clever *and* popular.'

'One from the hotel to tell me you'd be here, and the other from the escort agency confirming you'd booked a companion. I couldn't ask one of the agency's girls to come here and drug you, so I had one of our operatives come instead.'

'Ester.'

'Ester.'

'So, what do you want from me? Money? Is that it? Compensation for your friend's loss?'

Gideon grunted, stubbed out the cigarette in an ashtray on the desk, and turned again to the sea. 'It's not about money, Arkadi.'

'What then?'

'Today's the anniversary of Khaled's death,' said Gideon, fingering aside one of the net curtains. Ben Ari now saw they were torn, which explained what Gideon had secured him to the chair with and probably what was in his mouth. 'Did you know that? Of course you did. You were there. Poetic, I think, that you'll die on the very same day, a year later.'

Despite his fear, he refused to shout for help. He wouldn't give this man the satisfaction of seeing him afraid.

'You don't have to kill me,' he said, keeping his voice as calm as his thundering heart and the adrenaline coursing through his veins would let him.

'I've taken many lives over the years, Arkadi. *Many* lives. These days, it's infrequent and largely professional, and I usually try to do it quickly. Painlessly. But I'm not going to be merciful today, Arkadi. Today, I'm going to take pleasure in it.'

Gideon continued to stare out the window for five seconds, then spun back from the window, strode around the bed, and crouched in front of him so that their faces were level. The swift invasion of his personal space startled him, and he recoiled. As the men stared at each other, Gideon reached behind his back and pulled out a knife.

Ben Ari pulled away again as he eyed the blade. It was almost the length of a man's forearm and shone with the same peculiar brightness as Gideon's eyes. He thought he might piss himself.

'What are you going to do with that?'

'I'm going to make you suffer, Arkadi. I could just slice your throat and wrists open, but that's too quick a death. And too painless. You'd just feel like you're falling asleep. I could feed you your fingers, toes, and testicles and let you bleed out while you choke on yourself, but frankly, that's very messy, and I don't want to go anywhere near your... well, I would call it your manhood, but you're more coward than man.'

'You have me drugged and then tie me to a chair, and *you* call *me* a coward?' Ben Ari spat at Gideon. 'Cut me loose, and we'll see which of us is the coward.'

'I spent some time in China many years ago,' Gideon said, wiping spittle from his scar. 'While there, I learned a skill many Chinese considered an art form. Something called *Lingchi*. Usually, it was reserved for those who had committed only the most terrible crimes. It was considered so barbaric that it was officially banned at the turn of the century, but it's still occasionally practised by those who favour its particular challenge.

'What are you talking about?'

Sweat ran into Ben Ari's eyes again. He tried to blink away the sting, but it was pointless. The salty fluid kept pouring from his forehead, the burn on his eyeballs unabating. He just wanted to give up and beg this man to release him. But he wouldn't do that. He would let this bastard play his stupid game, and then, when he was free, he would kill him.

Gideon casually ran the knife over the forefinger of his free hand, and it drew blood, which he wiped away with his thumb. Ben Ari didn't know whether it was the sweat in his eyes, adrenaline making his mind deceive him, or a trick of the light, but he was sure he saw the cut heal, leaving not so much as a blemish on Gideon's skin.

'Wha—'

'The challenge is to keep the victim alive just long enough to complete the process,' said Gideon. 'It has various translations. *Lingering death. Slow slicing.* The most common, though, is *death by a thousand cuts.*'

The repeated threat of death brought Ben Ari back into focus.

'You're crazy! And you're a dead man! You're fucking dead!'

'And how you do propose to accomplish that, Arkadi? You're not going to leave that chair alive. And nobody is going to avenge you. The hotel conveniently has no record of you staying here. Your superiors have already sent someone to look for you, given that you failed to attend the medal-giving ceremony. They left here without argument or care. They didn't even ask to look around. As far as the military is concerned, you've simply vanished. Maybe you've had enough of trawling through dusty shitholes killing innocent people. Maybe you ran away with a lover. They don't know, won't care, and won't look that hard for you.'

Ben Ari roared. Who the hell was this Arab-lover to imprison him and threaten his life?

'Here's what's going to happen,' said Gideon calmly. 'First, I will show you the moment my friend Sultan discovered his nephew was dead.'

'What?'

'You're going to feel everything he felt. The anger. The pain. The overwhelming sense of emptiness and loss. Then, when Sultan's grief has consumed you, and you feel every ounce of his agony, I'm going to start cutting. Tiny little cuts. Like papercuts. Not very deep, and each no longer than a centimetre, but every single one will hurt.'

'You're insane!'

'I'm going to start on your torso. Your chest, your sides, and your stomach. Then I'll move on to your arms, starting at your armpits, moving up to your shoulders, and then down to your fingertips. Then I'll go to work on your legs. I'll work slowly from your hips to the soles of your feet. Your sweat will seep into all those cuts and feel like an open flame against your flesh. You'll be in agony, and at some point, before I've finished, you'll black out. I'm going to wake you up, and I'm going to keep cutting. Cut, black out, wake, repeat. And then, at the end, when you're sitting in shit and piss and drenched in blood, I'm going to take a photograph of your corpse, and I'm going to give it to Sultan, so he will know I have fulfilled my vow to him.'

'I'm going to fucking kill you!' Ben Ari boiled with rage. With another futile struggle, he could feel his entire body ache. He was furious, terrified, and on the verge of releasing his bowels and bladder.

Gideon smiled and looked intently into his eyes. As the Israeli glared back, he saw Gideon's irises turn from their bright, shining silvery-greyness to burning orange. The amber hue seemed to ripple outward from the pupils as if they were pools into which someone had cast stones.

'What *are* you?' he asked.

Saying nothing, Gideon continued to stare into his eyes. He felt a pressure build inside his head as if someone had opened his skull and was jabbing their fingers directly onto his brain. It made him nauseous. He started to see blurred images in his mind's eye.

'What are you doing to me?' he asked numbly.

Gideon didn't answer.

As the images in his head sharpened, he saw a middle-aged man sitting on a wooden chair in what looked like the kitchen of a dilapidated house. People surrounded him, some with their hands on his shoulders. Tears streamed down the man's dirt-covered face. He wiped them away with a large, calloused hand, but they kept coming. They would not stop.

'So, an old man cries,' he said with some effort. 'So, what?'

Gideon continued gazing into his eyes. In his mind's eye, Ben Ari saw himself reach out with a black-skinned hand and touch the face of the man on the chair. Instantly, he knew the man was Gideon's friend, Sultan. After a few seconds, he could feel a tear roll down his left cheek. Then another. And then one on the other cheek. Single tears became a flood. He could feel everything that Sultan had. His body ached, and his heart pined as if it were he who had lost a nephew.

'How are you doing this?' he whispered, his voice almost catching in his throat.

'I was there,' Gideon said quietly. 'What you're seeing, I saw. What you're feeling, I felt. The loss. The feeling of complete devastation. I felt it all as if I were Sultan himself. And it's only right that you now feel it, too.'

'I can't—'

'This is what you did, Arkadi. *You.* This is the consequence of your actions and those of your thugs.'

'I was following orders.' A whimper this time, all defiance having abandoned him.

As Gideon's eyes returned to the colour of slate, the pressure inside Ben Ari's head subsided, and his nausea disappeared. He began to feel normal again.

'How did you do that?' he asked.

'My kind calls it a *push.*'

'Your *kind*?'

'Now that you've felt Sultan's anguish,' said Gideon, ignoring the question, 'it's time for you to feel a different kind of pain.'

Before Ben Ari could cry out, Gideon put the cloth back into his mouth with an expression that was part grimace and part satisfaction, pulled up the fabric gag, and started to cut.

2

Ellie Hansen dragged herself from her belly to her hands and knees and gingerly brushed her forefinger under her nose, which sent a shockwave of agony up behind her eyes into her brain. Her finger was smeared with blood and snot when it came away from her face. She wasn't surprised—she was reasonably sure the blow she'd just received had broken her nose—but her stomach lurched, and her throat filled with bile anyway. She swallowed it down and cleared her nose with a hard snort that shot another searing pain through her. Then she sniffed in, spat a mouthful of phlegmy blood onto the floor and wiped her mouth with the back of her thumb.

Ignoring the pain, she concentrated on calming herself. In her peripheral vision, she saw the blur of a foot speed toward her planted hand. It seemed to travel in slow motion, but she knew she'd get crushed fingers if she didn't move quickly. She jerked her hand away, and the foot stomped harmlessly beside her. It came back in a fast kick toward her doubled-over torso, so she transferred her weight to her knees, then raised both hands and grabbed the foot as it flew toward her ribcage. She twisted it and pushed with a loud grunt, sending her attacker off balance.

She quickly refocused, hauled herself onto the balls of her feet, and stood up to her full height. A thick clump of her raven hair, matted with blood and sweat, impaired her vision. She brushed it away from her eyes and felt the wet smear of blood across her face as it moved.

Her assailant gripped a black baton in his right hand—the telescopic kind used by police forces everywhere. There was a streak of dark crimson a few inches from the top of the baton, where it had struck her nose.

'You just don't stay down, do you?'

'Fuck, no,' she said, sucking blood through her teeth.

'I told you, I want everything you've—'

Ellie launched herself at the man with a savage roar. She threw a fast punch at his face, which he deftly blocked with his forearm. He curled his arm around the outside of hers, trapped her wrist in his armpit, and, with the heel of his hand, pushed her elbow the wrong way in a move she knew could snap the joint. She cried out and spun, trying to lever herself out of his grip. He turned with her, both locked in an elaborate, violent dance.

The baton came in fast again toward her head. She lashed out sideways with the heel of her foot and stomped down on the man's knee. He howled and loosened his grip on her wrist for a split second, which was all she needed. She grabbed the end of the baton and twisted it out of the man's grip, then fell into a crouch and clubbed the man's thigh, just above the knee she mashed. He bawled and dropped onto his back. She stood, took a step back, and then, with a war cry full of rage, launched her leg forward, aiming it squarely between the man's legs. He managed to cover himself with his hands an instant before she struck.

'Jesus, Ellie,' he said. 'The balls? Really?'

'You said you wanted everything, Lars.'

'Maybe keep a little in reserve next time. Help me up, will you?'

Ellie grabbed his outstretched hand and helped him get to his feet.

'Okay,' said Lars, rubbing his knee and thigh. 'I think we're done for tonight. I know I am.'

They took a step back from each other and bowed as a mark of respect and gratitude, forgiveness for the other's actions, and, as each of them had injured the other, a sign of apology.

'Sorry about going for the balls,' she said as they stepped off the grey training mats.

'Don't be. If there's only time for one move in a real-life assault situation, always go for the balls. Or the... you know... if it's a woman.'

'Lovely.'

She stepped over to the low bench on which her gym bag lay and pulled out her water bottle. She took a couple of long gulps and tossed the bottle back into the bag.

'And sorry for the mess on the mats, too,' she said, untying her black wrist straps. 'If you get me a mop or a cloth and some disinfectant, I'll clean it up before I go.'

Lars waved dismissively.

'I'll deal with it,' he said. 'I'm technically responsible for the mess, after all.'

Ellie was silently grateful.

'So, when do we start knife training?' she asked.

'Christ, Ellie. You've only been on offensive strikes for six weeks, and we only started on blunts last week. You're coming on well, but I don't think you're ready for the good stuff just yet.' He pointed at her face and moved his finger in a circle. 'Do you?'

She pulled a black hoodie and a white hand towel from her bag and dabbed sweat from her forehead and blood from her cheeks and mouth. As she gently touched the towel to her nose, an explosion of pain shot across her face and everything went black, lit only by a thousand pinpoints of different coloured lights. She sucked in a breath through gritted teeth.

'Fuck! Maybe not.'

'Let me take a look at that,' said Lars. Stepping close, he cupped her face in his palms and gently rubbed his thumbs along the sides of her nose. Her eyes welled up again. 'I don't think it's broken, but it's probably best to get it properly checked.'

'If it is, I'll be sending you the medical bill,' she said, blinking her vision clear and shoving the towel and wrist straps into the bag.

'Health care in Copenhagen is free. And I thought your flatmate was a nurse. Can't she fix it for you?'

'Maybe, but I'll still be sending you a bill.'

'Will a bottle of Danzka cover it?'

'That'll do nicely,' she chirped.

She shrugged on the hoodie, zipped up the bag and slung it across her shoulder, then leant in and gave Lars a tight hug and a double-pat on the back.

'Thanks, Lars.'

'I'll see you next week.'

'Yep.'

As she reached the dojo's door, he reminded her to get her nose checked at the hospital and to put a bag of frozen peas on it as soon as she got home. Without turning, she raised one arm in the air to acknowledge him and, with the other, shoved open the door and walked out into the chill night air.

Ellie shivered and fought back a gag reflex as she crouched on the foul-smelling carpet in the corridor outside her apartment, fumbling in her bag for the key to her front door. It had rained heavily on her way home, and even though it was only a short walk, her clothes and hair were now soaking, and she felt frozen to the bone. There was nothing worse than January rain. Even snow wasn't as bad. A strip light flickered above and behind her with just enough frequency to become nauseating, and when she could not immediately put her hand to her keyring, she felt like kicking the door open.

'Thank fuck,' she murmured as her fingertip found the metal loop of her keyring.

The door to her apartment had no handle—just an old Yale-type spring bolt lock set into the door at chest height that unlocked with a key twist to the right. She opened the door, pulling the key out as it swung away from her, then heeled the door shut once she was inside. With the lights off and the curtains in the main living space closed, the apartment was almost pitch black.

'Zin?'

No response.

She called out again, then remembered her flatmate, Zindy Lindberg, was on a late shift. She flicked a switch on the wall next to the front door, and a warm orange-yellow glow washed over her from a line of unshaded Edison bulbs that zigzagged across the apartment. She immediately felt better.

The three-bedroomed apartment Ellie shared with Zindy was on the top floor of a six-storey building on Westend. They'd furnished it in a way some would graciously call eclectic, others would less kindly describe as thrift-shop-throwback, and she preferred to call retro-chic. It was clean and bright and almost always smelled like springtime, thanks to Zindy's cleaning regime. While she would, if asked, humbly say it's not much, it was their sanctuary away from the craziness of everyday life. She loved the place, and she was grateful for it every day.

She hung her keys beside the door and headed to the open kitchen to find some painkillers. As she passed the red metal sideboard, she turned on her old click-wheel iPod and the Marshall amp-styled speaker it was connected to, then scrolled through her playlists and settled on *Soft Grunge*, thinking that some low-energy nineties rock would suit her mood the best. She set the play mode to shuffle, turned the speaker's volume down from five to three, and shivered again, violently. Painkillers could wait, she decided. She needed to dry off and change into something warm and comfortable, so she headed toward her bedroom and the apartment's one bathroom. Out of habit, she dumped her gym bag beside one of their two sofas—this one made of worn brown leather.

She shrugged off her clothes as she walked. She was naked when she reached the bathroom but already felt warmer, no longer covered in soaking fabric. She dropped her wet clothes into the laundry basket and wrapped herself in a towel she took from a heated rail mounted to the wall. The chill in her bones vanished almost immediately, like sinking into a steaming hot bath but without the sting. The towel was old, but it didn't feel flat and rough. Instead, it felt soft and fluffy, like new. God knows how Zindy managed to keep them like that. She gave her messy bob a quick but gentle rub, taking care not to go anywhere near her face, and stared at herself in the mirror. No sign of bruising yet, but it wouldn't be long, she thought. She went to her bedroom and rummaged around in her chest of drawers until she found a pair of grey cotton off-brand tracksuit bottoms and a blue Berghaus fleece top, which she carefully pulled over her head.

When Ellie finally got to the kitchen, she opened the freezer compartment of their pastel blue Smeg fridge. As Eddie Vedder sang from the sideboard about a trapdoor in the sun, she dug around for a bag of peas or something as malleable. She found nothing useful, so she grabbed the ice cube tray, a half-full bottle of Danzka vodka, and an upturned tumbler from the draining board next to the sink. She shuddered as she poured herself a giant, ice-free slug of vodka. She was unsure whether it was a delayed surge of adrenaline from her fight with Lars or a residual chill in her bones. Suddenly, she felt like she had spun around and upside down a thousand times and barely managed to get her head over the sink before she vomited.

When she was sure she'd finished throwing up, she gulped down the vodka. She poured another, set it aside, and pulled a plastic First Aid container from a high cupboard next to the sink. She fumbled around in it, past a box of Band-Aids, a roll of self-adhesive bandages and a bottle of TCP, and found a packet of Panadol Extra.

She washed down two painkillers with the second shot of vodka and wiped her mouth, carefully avoiding her nose. She decided against putting the box back into the cupboard—she'd probably need more pills again later, anyway. Instead, she poured a third, more generous measure of vodka and made an ice pack with a clean drying cloth she took from a drawer, twisting the plastic tray to release the more stubborn cubes. As exhaustion enveloped her like a heavy coat, she plucked two cubes from the pile and dropped them into her vodka, then took the ice pack and her vodka and navigated her way around the small round dining table to the nearest sofa—this one, perpendicular to the leather one, was made of red fabric. She slumped onto it with a groan.

Every muscle in her body ached. With the flaring pain in her nose, She'd forgotten about the other places Lars had landed blows. There were more than a few. Her ribs, especially, felt like a horse had kicked them. She probably should have gone to the hospital. She might have a concussion or, worse, a broken nose and ribs. Fuck it, she thought. She was too tired, and it was raining outside. As long as she could sleep pain-free, she'd be fine, and she'd go and get checked out in the morning.

She pushed her legs underneath the large, distressed-wood coffee table that sat equidistantly between the two sofas and stretched herself out like a cat, extending every fibre within her. She held the stretch for a few seconds, almost relishing the discomfort—knowing she'd earned it doing something worthwhile, something important—then sat up slowly and glanced at her watch, which told her it was eight-thirty. She drained her vodka in two gulps, using her teeth to catch the ice, then slowly rotated to put her head on one arm of the sofa and her feet on the other and carefully placed the ice pack onto her face. It stung and drew tears to her eyes. She let out a long, lung-emptying breath and listened to the rain beat down on the roof above.

Ellie woke to the thud of a door slamming. She was lying face-up on the sofa. The front of her neck was wet, and something cold and soggy covered her face. She panicked, grabbed the thing on her face, and hauled herself upright, for which her head rewarded her with a hefty thump.

In one hand was a cloth, soaked through, and in the other was an empty glass, and she realised she must have dozed off with the ice pack on her face. Her head throbbed again. Probably best not to move too quickly after a whack to the face and three large vodkas.

'Ellie? Holy shit!'

She looked blearily at the voice, and a blurred figure came into focus as it moved toward her.

'Zindy. Hey.'

She and Zindy had been close friends since school and had moved in together a couple of years after graduating. Like her, Zindy was twenty-eight but was a little taller. She had bright blue eyes and a shock of purple in her otherwise short, spiky, bleach-blonde hair.

'What happened to your face?' Zindy asked.

Evidently, the bruising had already begun.

'I walked into a police baton.'

'What?'

'One of my sessions with Lars.'

Zindy crossed to the sofa, knelt in front of her, and cupped her face as Lars had done earlier, feeling for the slightest abnormality or misalignment.

'Well, it doesn't look or feel broken, but that bruising will get worse. Have you taken anything for the pain?'

'A couple of Panadol and one or three of these,' Ellie said, raising her glass.

'I'm guessing that wasn't water.'

'And you'd be correct.' She squinted at Zindy. Something about her was different, and it took her a second to figure it out. 'That's new.'

'What? Oh, yeah. I got bored with having just one.'

'Looks good,' she said honestly, admiring Zindy's second eyebrow piercing.

'Thanks. Do you want me to take you in?'

'Do you think I need to go in?'

'Did you black out when it happened or shortly afterwards?'

Zindy reached inside her coat into a pocket of her work uniform. She pulled out a small penlight, clicked it on, and shone it across Ellie's eyes.

'Nope. Conscious the whole time until I got home and crashed here. And that is not uncomfortable at all,' she said, squinting and looking away from the light.

'Okay. Your pupils are responsive enough. It's worth getting an X-ray and a full concussion test done, but as the skin's not broken, you're not bleeding, and you didn't immediately lose consciousness, you can probably wait until tomorrow.'

'Works for me.'

'I'm on a shift in the afternoon, but I can take you over in the morning.'

'You don't have to do that.'

'One,' said Zindy, counting on her fingers, 'if I don't take you, you won't go. And two, we might be able to use my backstage pass to get you seen quickly. No point hanging around in gen-pop if you don't have to.'

'Awesome. Thanks, hon.'

'What time d'you take the painkillers?'

'Around eight-thirty. What time is it now?'

'Just after twelve.'

'Shit. I need to get to bed. Help me up, will you?'

Zindy stood up, taking Ellie by the hand as she did so. She helped her get to her feet and held her by the shoulder while she steadied herself.

'Thanks, babes,' said Ellie.

She headed toward her bedroom, collecting her gym bag on the way.

'You sure you're okay?' Zindy called after her.

'I'll be fine. I just need some sleep.'

'Okay. I'm going to bed, too. But if you need anything or start to feel sick or have more pain, just shout, yeah.'

'Okay.'

Ellie closed her bedroom door, dropped her bag at the foot of the bed, and crossed to the window. She closed the blackout curtains, slumped heavily onto the bed, and pulled out her phone. As she unlocked it, there was a knock on her door. Before she could answer, Zindy walked in, holding a glass.

'Don't get excited,' said Zindy, handing her the glass. 'It's just water. It'll help you rehydrate after your one or three whatever they were, and I figured you'd be okay to take some more painkillers by now.'

Zindy held out her hand, palm up. Ellie took the pills, washed them down with the water, and returned the glass.

'Thanks, hon,' she said.

Zindy winked and left, closing the door behind her. Ellie raised her phone again and navigated to the list of recent calls. The number she wanted was at the top of the list.

Jakob Nørgard's number.

She hovered her thumb over it and then glanced at the time displayed in small numbers at the top of the screen. Fourteen minutes past midnight. Too late to call.

'Shit.'

She silenced the phone, scrabbled at the side of the bed for its charging cable, then plugged it in and placed it face-down on the bedside table. She was too tired, sore, and, apparently, drunk to change out of her clothes, so she flicked off the bedside lamp. The room became pitch black, and within seconds, she was asleep.

3

She stands beside a shaky wooden bench in a garden. It's not Ellie's garden or any other she's been to. It's Shimon's garden. She's unsure of how she knows this. All she is sure of is that this isn't her time or her body.

As before, it's Marta's.

She cleans the wooden plates from which she, Shimon and her husband Yehuda ate dinner and thinks about what Yehuda told her moments ago.

The strangeness of it all.

Yehuda had been debating the future with Yeshua and others from their group. He appreciated and even agreed with some of what they'd discussed, but some of it—such as Yeshua's repeated suggestion that he would go to Jerusalem—he disapproved of.

He'd told her that he'd gone with Yeshua and a few others to one of the olive groves, as Yeshua had said he wanted to talk further, to those few specifically, about his plans. They'd taken a jar of wine and some bread and fruit. They'd not long been in the grove when figures had come out of the shadows on all sides. They were the temple guards of the Sanhedrin, and they were there to arrest Yeshua.

Yeshua didn't resist and ordered the others not to fight. He thought it had been part of Yeshua's plan. Before they dragged him away, Yeshua had stepped close to him so that their cheeks were touching and whispered to him that he knew. That was all he said—that he knew. And *then Yeshua had kissed him on the cheek.*

A rustling in the bushes at the end of the garden brings her back from her thoughts. She peers into the darkness but sees nothing except the shadows of tree trunks. A movement catches her eye, but she hears a loud crash and raised voices from within the house before she can investigate. She rushes back inside to see four people dressed in black and wielding ugly-looking swords. They're wearing black scarves around their heads, and their mouths and noses are covered, but she can tell from their eyes and voices that they're all men.

She feels strong hands grip her shoulders from behind. Someone has come in from the garden through the rear of the house. The intruder flings her against a wall. She bangs her shoulder and falls to the ground hard. When she looks up, she sees two more attackers.

The six invaders now have Yehuda and Shimon surrounded. One of the men lunges at Yehuda, who sidesteps quickly and slices through the man's stomach with his sword. The man goes down and crawls back to make way for his comrades. She hears one of the men tell Yehuda it would be easier if he didn't fight. She thinks she recognises the voice, but the man's identity escapes her. Yehuda curses back at him, and she sees the attacker's eyes crease. Under the cloth that covers the lower part of his face, he's smiling, she thinks.

The man charges at Yehuda with a snarl that's more animal than human, and his eyes, she sees, are black with fury. He swings his blade with speed she has never before seen. When the man's sword is only a hand's width from her husband's face, it stops in a shower of sparks and with a grinding sound of metal on metal.

Shimon has managed to get his sword in the way. She almost cries with relief. He puts his hand on the blunt spine of his blade and pushes it toward the invader, fending off the man's attack. He swings his sword so quickly that it is just a blur to her eyes. The attacker howls as Shimon strikes a blow to the left side of his head. The man rips away the scarf covering his head, and she sees that Shimon has sliced off the top of the man's ear. Refocusing, she sees the man's face for the first time and recognises him. It is Kepha, Yeshua's rock. He sees her looking at him and glares back at her with fury in his oddly black eyes.

Kepha flies into a rage and slices at Shimon, cutting him on the arm with which he holds his sword. Shimon snarls with pain and anger and drops his sword. Kepha steps forward and kicks him hard in the genitals. He crashes to the floor, and Kepha kicks out again, this time to Shimon's face.

She cannot take any more. She runs back through the house and goes outside into the garden. She grabs a knife from the bench where she'd cleaned the plates and rushes back into the building. Two invaders hold her husband by his arms, and another man has his arm around her husband's neck. Desperate to help, she does the only thing she can think of. She jumps onto the back of the nearest attacker and, with one arm around his neck for grip, she reaches her other arm around and plunges the dagger into his chest.

The man yells, grabs her hair, and throws her away from him. She hits the wall again, and her vision fades to black as she drops to the floor.

When she wakes up, the attackers have gone. Shimon is lying in a pool of blood, his dagger sticking out from his chest.

Yehuda is gone.

They have taken him.

4

SUNDAY

Ellie sat on a grey plastic chair in the radiology department's waiting area. On a low coffee table in front of her was a pile of magazines, most of which were several months out of date and were of no use to her unless she wanted to learn how to hang chintzy curtains or tune a Toyota Supra, neither of which she did. She was slightly hungover and exhausted from broken sleep, and the dull peppermint walls seemed to be closing in on her by the minute. The place made her skin itch, but mercifully—probably due to the floor covering being thin grey carpet and not linoleum—it was devoid of the throat-clogging stench of disinfectant that seemed to seep out of every other surface in the building.

She hated hospitals. They were supposed to be places that gave you comfort but seemed invariably decorated in ways that made you feel nauseated. And, if recent statistics were accurate, you were more likely to become sick in a hospital than to be made well again in one.

A doctor named Anders approached from a door beyond the reception counter. When they'd arrived earlier, Zindy had persuaded him to see Ellie in between his other patients. The guy obviously found Zindy attractive, and it was just as evident that she knew this and had unashamedly used it to her—or rather, Ellie's—advantage. A tuck of her hair behind her ear, a light touch on his forearm, a tilt of the head, a coy laugh. Ellie had chuckled as she'd watched the show and then feigned moral outrage when Zindy had said she'd promised Anders a date in return for squeezing her in.

'Well, the good news,' said Anders, 'is, there's no fracture or misalignment, the CT scan shows no clouding on the brain, and all the other red flag tests—hearing, reflexes, coordination, memory, and vision—were clear, too.'

'What's the bad news?'

'I strongly suggest you take a break from your martial arts classes.'

'For how long?' asked Zindy.

'Two weeks. Three would be better.'

'Three weeks?' Ellie said. 'Anders, that's—'

'You've taken what was, given the extent of the bruising and swelling, a serious knock to the face, Ellie.'

'You should see the other guy.'

'Oh? How does he look?'

'Better than me. Although I did almost give him elephant balls.'

'Ouch,' he said, chuckling. He looked at his watch. 'Look, I have another patient I'm late for, so I need to get going. I'm serious about taking time off from your sessions, Ellie. While there's no break, and the scan was clear, you could still experience bouts of dizziness, headaches, and mental fatigue in the next week or so. Participating in any full-contact sport, or even doing something more than mildly exertive, could make you feel worse and delay your recovery. What you need is a few weeks of rest.'

'Okay.'

'Really, Ellie. You must take it easy. Proper rest.'

Ellie felt like a teenager who'd been grounded.

'Fine,' she said petulantly.

'Well then, you two are free to go.'

They stood up and thanked him. Ellie winked and teasingly tapped his arm. He smiled back coyly and disappeared through the double doors that led to the treatment rooms.

'Okay,' said Ellie, checking her watch. 'It's almost one o'clock. I need something to eat and a big fucking drink. You coming? It's on me.'

'My shift starts at four. I can't turn up smelling of booze, but—'

'That's what Tic Tacs are for.'

'Bu-ut, I should be okay for one small glass of wine. And I can walk it off after lunch with a quick shop. Mama needs a new outfit for Saturday night.'

They stood outside the café they'd gone to for lunch, which had consisted of sandwiches made with fancy bread, and a bottle of Pinot Grigio, consumed mainly by Ellie. As they loitered on the pavement, their coats buttoned high against the cold, she rubbed her arms and exhaled a breath that immediately turned to mist.

'You'll probably be asleep by the time I get home tonight,' Zindy said, thrusting her hands into her pockets. 'Keep taking the painkillers every four hours even if you feel you don't need them. At least for the rest of today.'

'Don't worry, hon. I'll be on those *and* the natural kind.' Ellie raised the plastic bag she held, containing two bottles of Frederiksdal Sur Lie *kirsebÊrvin*—a medium-sweet cherry wine she'd bought in the café before they had left. 'And hey, thanks for today.'

'No probs. I got something out of it, too, so winner-winner.'

'You're such a slut.'

'Yeah. Anders could be a lucky boy.'

They both laughed hard, which gave Ellie a brief stab of pain. Then they hugged and said their goodbyes, and Zindy strode off toward the Frederiksberg Centre to look for a new outfit for her date with Anders. Ellie watched her go, then breathed in deeply through her nose. The cold bit at her airways. She fished her phone from her jeans, unlocked it, went into the recent calls list, and tapped the number at the top of the list.

The number she'd almost called the previous night.

Jakob's number.

She put the phone to her ear and shrugged against the cold while waiting for the call to connect.

'Hey.'

'Hey. Are you coming over tonight?' she asked.

'Yep.'

'What time, do you think?'

'Not until after seven, probably.'

'Okay. I've got some wine. Can you pick up whatever you want to cook?'

'I'm cooking, am I?'

'Yeah. Sorry. I don't feel like doing it tonight.'

She heard him breathe out a *for fuck's sake* sigh. She knew he'd be tired after work and probably wouldn't want to cook, but she certainly wasn't in the mood to do it.

'Okay,' he said, *'but if I'm cooking, I get to pick what we watch on TV.'*

'Deal.'

'Curry okay?'

'Very.'

'Okay. I'll see you later, then. Love you.'

'Yeah.'

She hung up and smiled. Not responding with, 'I love you, too,' was a private thing of theirs, on the basis that doing so—which, for her and Jakob, had become typically automatic—devalued its meaning. The *say yeah and hang up* thing was something new she'd heard about from a friend, and was a great source of amusement for her.

She decided to walk home instead of taking the bus or the metro. Even though the journey home was short, she didn't relish the prospect of being cooped up on stuffy public transport and thought some fresh air would probably help keep at bay the post-lunch hangover she already felt coming on.

She strolled unhurriedly through the streets, occasionally pausing to window shop and check her phone for messages, even though she wasn't expecting any. Halfway home, she dropped into a café and found a comfortable armchair beside the large front window. She divided her concentration between watching passers-by and reading a battered English-language copy of Neil Gaiman's *American Gods* she'd picked up in her local library. Eventually, as her third chai latte went cold, she glanced at her watch. It was almost five o'clock, so she casually gathered her things and left.

Next door to the café was a charity shop she'd visited many times. The place always had some cool stuff for sale—jackets, books, quirky artwork. She considered going in but decided that one, she ought to get home and have a nap before Jakob came over, and two, that going in might be dangerous, as something usually came out with her whenever she ventured into the place. Resolute, she turned and resumed her journey home. After taking a few steps, she stopped.

'Fuck it.'

Twelve minutes later, she came out of the charity shop with a wide grin and a black, beaten-up leather biker's jacket. Feeling better than she had at the start of the day, she headed home.

Ellie woke to a loud, persistent buzzing from near the apartment's front door and a vibration in the front pocket of her jeans. She brushed her hair away from her face, which sent a flash of pain through her, then carefully rubbed her eyes and rolled off the sofa. She pulled out her phone and saw she'd forgotten to un-silence it after leaving the hospital. She'd missed two calls from Jakob.

Shit.

She also saw it was just past eight in the evening.

Double shit!

The buzzing near the front door continued, so she quickly crossed to the door and pressed a button on a wall-mounted intercom next to it.

'Hello?'

'It's me.'

It was Jakob, and he sounded frustrated.

She released the intercom button and pressed another that unlocked the building's main door on the street. Then, she opened the apartment door, left it ajar, went to the kitchen, and took a box of extra-long matches from a low drawer next to the fridge. As she walked around the apartment lighting candles, the scent of scorched match heads and burning wax calmed her. She heard the door close and the soft squeak of boots on the hardwood floor.

'Hey,' Jakob said from behind her as she lit a candle on the coffee table next to the sofas.

This is *not* going to be fun, she thought. She steeled herself and turned around.

'Holy fuck!'

'It's fine, Jakob. I'm okay.'

'You don't look okay.' He put down his motorcycle helmet and backpack, stepped forward, and gently touched the side of her face. 'What happened?'

'Lars landed a lucky blow.'

'With what? A hammer?'

'Police baton.'

'What?'

'I asked him to.'

'You asked him to hit you in the face with a police baton?'

'No, I...' She knew he wouldn't like what she was about to say, but she wasn't going to lie to him. 'A few weeks ago, I asked him to include weapons in our sessions, so now we're using blunts, as he calls them. We've been using them for a couple of weeks with no problems. I just lost my concentration this time, that's all.'

'Jesus, Ellie. Why the hell do you want him to use weapons? Are you using them, too? Am I going to get a call from Zindy or the hospital telling me you've been stabbed in a knife fight?'

'Jakob, it's not—'

'No?'

He pushed his hands through his scruffy dark hair, and his eyes began to fill.

'Is it broken?'

'No. I went to the hospital this morning and got checked out. No break and no concussion. Zindy pulled some strings to get me seen quickly, and she got a date out of it.'

'Whoop-de-fucking-do for Zindy.'

'Hey, come on. She didn't have to help me. And she deserves a bit of fun.'

Jakob scoffed.

'You sure you're okay?'

'I'm fine, Jakob. The doctor said I'll have some bruising and swelling for a few days, and he suggested I take a break from my sessions with Lars for a few weeks so—'

'You'll get no argument from me there.'

'So I can fully recover. But I'll have no lasting damage.'

He picked up his backpack and walked to the kitchen.

Ellie followed.

'I can't be bothered cooking, so I picked this up instead,' he said, pulling a knotted plastic bag from his pack and placing it on the counter. 'Spring rolls to share, chicken and cashew nuts for me, and green goat curry for you.'

She stood beside him and ran her hand up and down his back. She knew the goat in her green curry would be chicken, but she played along nonetheless.

'Sounds good to me.'

'I know you love those sessions, but can't you just stick to kicks and punches like normal badasses? Do you have to use blunts?' He punctuated the word *blunts* with air quotation marks.

She laughed and went about fetching bowls, cutlery, and a couple of oversized wine glasses. As he untied the bag and pulled out plastic containers full of food, shee got a bottle of wine from the fridge and grabbed an angel-wing corkscrew from an adjacent utensil drawer. She drove the corkscrew into the stopper without removing the bottle's foil wrapper and pushed the corkscrew's arms groundward. The cork came out with a soft pop.

'I *do* love them,' she said, pouring them generous measures of wine, 'and lately, I feel like the only things keeping me sane are you and those sessions.'

'I know, babe.'

She passed him a glass of wine and clinked hers against it. He took a mouthful, kissed her on the cheek and began scooping food into the bowls.

Ellie loved watching him at work in the kitchen. Cooking was a form of therapy for him. Not that he needed therapy, but it helped him wind down after long days of hard work and everyday bullshit. And even though he wasn't strictly cooking right then, she could see the tension in him dissipating.

'Can I do anything to help?' she asked.

'Yeah, why don't you stick some music on?'

'Done.'

She returned his kiss with one of her own, then went to the sideboard, turned on the speaker and the iPod, scrolled through her list of albums, and clicked on Massive Attack's *Mezzanine*. As she returned to the kitchen, Jakob grinned and topped up their glasses.

'This cherry stuff is deadly,' he said.

She beamed broadly. She knew the wine would help soften his annoyance over her training mishap with Lars.

'Alright,' he said, handing her a bowl. 'Let's get it on.'

They went to the sofas. While the red one was closest, they went to the leather one. Ellie had learned from experience that wine stains were not easy to get out of fabric sofas, so it was now a rule in the apartment that all food and any drink that was not transparent must be consumed on the easier-to-clean leather sofa.

They put everything on the coffee table, then retook their glasses and eased onto the sofa, careful not to spill their wine. Jakob leaned on the arm, and Ellie snuggled into him. They sat silently for a minute, each enjoying the other's closeness without feeling any immediate need to talk.

'Why didn't you tell me about your face when it happened?' he eventually asked, his tone calm and quiet.

'All I wanted to do when I got home was sink a few vodkas to ease the pain and turn off. I crashed out until Zindy came home just after midnight. I almost called you when I went to bed, but I thought it was probably too late by then. Besides, there's nothing you could have done, and I didn't want you worrying about it.'

'I guess that makes sense. Are you going to work tomorrow, or did the doctor give you a pass?'

'No, he didn't. I'm going in.'

'You sure you're okay to go? Dag would probably give you the day off if you asked her.'

'I'll be fine,' she said, leaning forward. She put her wine glass on the coffee table and picked up her bowl of curry. 'I'll take a load of Panadol with me. Plus, I've got a client that I can't reschedule.'

'Fair enough,' he replied, reaching for his food. 'But, if you start to feel sick or anything, just tell Dag you need to—'

'Okay, mum.'

Jakob chuckled.

For the next twenty minutes, they ate their food and talked about work and life. They talked about everything except her dreams, for which she was thankful. After eating, they watched TV for a while, occasionally pausing to comment on the show or refill their wine glasses.

Eventually, Ellie said she was tired and wanted to go to bed. Jakob asked whether he should make a move to go home. He lived a short walk away on Tøndergade, so he could leave his motorbike outside her apartment and collect it in the morning, as he had done many times before.

'No,' she said. 'You should stay over.'

He stood and offered his hand, which she took. She turned off the television, and he gently pulled her off the sofa. He put his arm around her, and they headed for her bedroom.

'You know I'm not going to bang you with...' He left his sentence unfinished but circled his forefinger in the air around Ellie's face.

'Fuck you,' she said, giving him a playful nudge.

Ellie closed the bathroom door before pulling the cord to turn on the overhead light. She crossed to the sink, gripped its sides, and stared at her reflection in the square mirror above it. A sheen of sweat covered her, and strands of her tousled hair stuck to her forehead and face. She looked terrible. And that was without the purple, swollen face.

'What's going on with you?' she whispered to her reflection.

She removed her toothbrush from a plastic beaker on the glass shelf under the mirror and filled the cup with cold water. She left the tap running, emptied the beaker in one gulp, filled and drained it again, then topped it up once more and drank half. As the icy water slid down her throat, she leaned, one-handed, on the basin and closed her eyes.

After a few moments, she blinked away the fog that was setting in, then finished the rest of the water, put the beaker back on the shelf, and dropped the toothbrush back into it. It settled with a muted clatter. She grabbed a hand towel from a metal ring on the wall and took another look at herself while she soaked it in cold water.

She looked utterly exhausted, which was precisely how she felt. Drained of almost every ounce of energy she imagined could be contained within her. And she knew it wasn't an after-effect of taking a whack to the face. It was something else. She leaned toward the mirror and studied her eyes. Jakob had told her once he loved their colour. They were usually a piercing green—bright, striking, and, according to Jakob, full of life and mischief. At that moment, though, she thought their light might have dimmed a little recently.

'What the fuck is going on with you?' she said again, louder than before. This time, her voice trembled, and she cursed herself for being so weak. She slammed her hand against the side of the basin. 'Damn it!'

Ellie covered her face with the cool water-soaked towel, which provided little relief. She could feel something bubbling inside her that the cold water couldn't wash out. Anxiety, maybe? Fear? A sense of helplessness? Or something else?

Despair overcame her. She felt new wetness on her cheeks, and what started as a whimper became a shoulder-jerking weep. She bent her head down to the sink, cupped her hands together, and scooped some still-flowing cold water up to her face. She did that again and then once more. When she straightened up, Jakob's reflection stared at her in the mirror. She jumped with alarm and almost screamed.

'Jakob, you bastard!' she said to his reflection.

'Sorry,' he said softly, gently placing his hands on her shoulders. 'Just checking you're okay.'

'Fuck. No, I'm sorry. I didn't mean to wake you up.'

'It's okay, babe. I was awake, anyway.'

'You're a bad liar.'

He stepped closer to her, wrapped his arms around her in a tender bear hug, and hunkered down to kiss the back of her neck. She reached up behind her and ran a hand through his hair.

'Another dream?' he asked.

'Yep. I had a new one last night. Had it again just now.'

'Really? Shit, Ellie. Why didn't you tell me? What did you see?'

'Can we talk about it tomorrow? I'm fucked, and I just want to get back to sleep.'

'You sure?'

'Yep.'

'Okay.' He hugged her a little tighter and nuzzled the back of her head. 'Come on. Let's get back to bed.'

Jakob pulled the cord to turn off the overhead light, then took Ellie's hand and led her to her bedroom, which, with the blackout curtains still drawn closed, was lit only by the ambient light from the hallway. He was in bed by the time she closed the bedroom door. What little light was in the room was swallowed entirely by blackness. As she blindly inched around her side of the bed, her foot caught on something bulky. She lost her balance and bashed her shin on the bedframe.

'Ow, Jesus!'

'What?'

'I just tripped over my gym bag.'

'You're such a dick.'

Ellie stepped over the bag, dropped onto the bed, and pulled the duvet up to her ears. She turned onto her side and put her back to Jakob, who snuggled in behind her, then she slid an arm out from under the duvet toward the bedside table, fumbled for her phone, and thumbed the *Home* button. Over the home screen photo of her and Jakob—a selfie she took of them on the back of his motorcycle, helmetless—stark white numbers glared at her.

It was four-seventeen in the morning.

5

MONDAY

Ellie sat at the circular table between the kitchen and the sofas, absent-mindedly swirling a spoon through a bowl of cornflakes. The apartment had a balcony overlooking Saxopark, just deep enough for a small square table and two wooden chairs, and when the weather was good enough, she would sit out there for breakfast, but today was not a good weather day.

Jakob brought two large mugs filled with steaming coffee to the table and put one down in front of her. He put the other down at the seat to her left, went back to the kitchen, and returned holding a knife, a tub of spreadable butter, and a plate on which were two slices of well-done toast. She suspected the bread would only be cooked on one side so the undersides would still be soft, the way his grandfather used to make it under his old gas grill.

He sat down, and she knew, even without looking up from her breakfast, that he was watching her. He was worried about her. Over the past few weeks, her dreams had frequently woken her at night, and he'd been at her place for at least half of those. They'd already spoken several times about the dreams—why she was having them, what they were about, and what they could do to stop them—but they hadn't reached any significant conclusions or devised any practical solutions. It was clear to her that her suffering was also taking its toll on him.

'I'm gonna get soaked going to work,' he said, watching the rain bounce off the balcony's concrete floor.

'Uh-huh.'

He took a piece of toast from the plate and thickly buttered it.

'So, tell me about this new dream.'

Ellie felt her shoulders sag. She didn't want to talk about it but knew it was unavoidable. Jakob wouldn't want to drop it. He thought discussing it would help. Maybe it would. Probably not. Perhaps it was easier just to tell him and have some breathing space.

'Okay,' she said. 'It was pretty similar to the last three.'

'You were the same woman again? Marta?'

'Yep.'

'And?' he asked, liberally buttering the second slice of toast, which he folded over and took a large bite of.

She briefly shut her eyes and concentrated. She wanted to relive the dream in her mind's eye in as much detail as possible. As she described what she had seen—the fight in Shimon's house, Marta being thrown to the floor, and Yehuda being abducted—Jakob remained silent, for which she was grateful, as she didn't want to lose her stride.

'Fucking hell!' he said when she finished recounting the vision.

'I know. What the fuck, right?'

'What do you think it means?'

She shrugged.

'I have no idea,' she said softly.

Jakob took the empty toast plate and his coffee mug to the kitchen sink. Ellie went to the pedal bin, scraped milk-sodden cornflakes into it, then joined him at the sink and passed him her cereal bowl and empty mug. They washed up in silence, like automatons. One scrubbed and handed over, the other took, dried, and put away.

She was distracted and tired, and she dropped the mug. She caught it by the handle, although not before it struck the edge of the worktop and cracked on the rim.

'Fuck,' she said. 'Fuck!'

'Hey,' Jakob said softly, gently taking the mug from her and putting it on the worktop. 'It's okay. It's just a mug.'

'*You're* just a mug.'

'Nice.'

'For putting up with my shit.'

'Yeah, I know what you meant,' he said, smiling.

'I think I need to do something about this crap now. Three times this week already, four last week, three the week before, and I've lost count of how many before those. And now they're getting worse. I can't take it anymore, Jakob.'

'What do you want to do?'

'I think I'll speak to Suzi and get the name of that therapist she saw a while back.'

'You sure about that? It might drag up all that Lina shit for her. It took her ages to get over that.'

'Yeah, I know. I really don't want to, but what's my other option? Find a random shrink on Google? Suzi was a wreck before she went to that therapist, and within a few months, she was pretty much back to her old self again. I need that kind of help, Jakob.'

'Okay. If you do make an appointment, I'll come with you if you like.'

'No, it's fine. You don't need to. You've got too much on at work. And don't therapists have that whole confidentiality thing? You probably won't be allowed in, anyway. She'll make you stand outside on the curb.'

'What? No, she won't. They have waiting rooms in those places.'

'I remember Suzi saying she used to go to the woman's home. I bet she won't even have a waiting room. And she definitely won't want you dirtying up the place with your greasy hands and oily boots.'

'Good point,' said Jakob, finishing the lukewarm contents of his coffee mug in one long gulp.

'Besides,' Ellie continued, 'I doubt whether Goat will give you the time off, anyway.'

'Yeah, you're probably right. He *is* more of a grumpy bastard than usual at the moment.' He swilled his mug through the water in the sink, gave it the once-over with the washing cloth, then put it upside-down on the draining board and pulled the rubber plug from the basin. He took the drying cloth from Ellie and dried his hands. 'You going to call her today, then? The therapist?'

'I guess so.'

He drew her in close. She could smell the coffee on his breath, but she didn't mind it. He slung his arm around the back of her neck and kissed her softly on the lips, careful not to brush his nose against hers.

'She was Swedish, I think,' she said.

'Who?'

'Suzi's therapist.'

'Oh, right. Look, I'm sure we'll get this shit figured out, babes.'

She smiled weakly, desperately hoping Jakob was right.

He unwrapped himself from her and looked at his watch.

'I gotta run,' he said, kissing her again before heading out of the kitchen. 'I have to pick something up from my flat before going to the workshop. Let me know how you get on with Suzi. And please,' he said, pointing to Ellie's face, 'take it easy today, okay? If you start having headaches or get dizzy, just come home.'

'I will.'

Not long after Jakob left, Ellie filled an oversized cup with green tea and went to the leather sofa. As she lay semi-upright and listened to the rain, she wept. Softly at first, but it became a wrenching sob that made her whole body ache. After a few moments, she sniffed hard and wiped her eyes—both of which made her wince—then sat bolt upright and slammed a fist on the coffee table. She would not let this—whatever *this* was—take over her life.

6

Most mornings, the team working at Double D's tattoo studio arrived between nine thirty and ten to get the place ready to open at eleven. Ellie got there just before half past eight. After she'd broken down in the apartment, she needed to escape it, so she'd put on her usual work clothes—all blacks and greys, brightened only by her oxblood Doc Martens and a few bangles—and wrapped herself in a thick coat and left for work early.

Double D's—named after her boss, Dagmar Dico—occupied a unit on the first floor of an old but stylish building on Bredgade, above an upmarket gallery. Ellie went through the building's wrought iron gated entrance on the street and opened the communal front door to the upper floors. Placing her takeaway triple-shot long black on a narrow, waist-height wooden shelf, she picked up and rifled through a pile of mail and fliers from the floor. She took everything addressed to the studio—a few bills, the day's edition of the local newspaper, a brown envelope with a government seal stamped on it, and the latest plastic-wrapped issue of *Inked* magazine—and put everything else back on the ground.

After wearily climbing the stairs to the first floor, she unlocked the studio's door and went in. The lights were off, and the place was quiet, so she guessed she was the first to arrive. Locking the door behind her, she went to the reception counter and flicked on the radio, then put all the mail on the counter for Dagmar, took her coffee and the edition of *Inked*, and headed to her workstation—one of three in the studio. She slumped onto the reclinable dentist-style chair at her station with a grunt and looked around the place. With its light beech floor, pale blue walls, comfortable waiting area, and tons of natural light flooding through the unit's four double windows, it was more like a hair salon than a tattoo studio. There were even plants dotted around the place. It was a place she felt safe—a second home.

She took a sip of her coffee, wishing a shot of whisky was in it, then closed her eyes and let out a long breath of exasperation. She remained like that for a few moments, hoping the tension gripping her entire body would soon dissipate.

'You're here early, babe,' said a female voice beside her.

'If you were trying to sneak up on me,' Ellie said, her eyes still shut but her head turning toward the voice, 'you failed. Miserably.'

'Really?'

'I heard you come in, even over Buckley,' she said, gesturing to the song on the radio. 'You're not as quiet as you think, you know.'

'You saying I'm fat?'

Ellie opened her eyes.

'Sooz, you're built like a breadstick. So, yeah, you're totally fat.'

Suzi Matsutoya was one of the studio's other two resident tattooists. She was a year younger than Ellie, and they had much in common, not least their taste in music, films, and tattoos. Next to Zindy, Suzi was her closest friend. Japanese by descent, her family had lived in Copenhagen for three generations. She stood there, coffee in hand, wearing a pair of mirrored Ray-Ban sunglasses.

'What the fuck happened to you?' Suzi asked, sliding the sunglasses to the top of her head, which pushed her long mahogany-tinted hair away from her face.

'Huh?'

She had somehow forgotten about the bruising across her nose and under her eyes, but the shock on Suzi's face and the swiping gesture Suzi made with a pointed finger reminded her.

'Oh. Training with Lars a couple of nights ago. I got smacked in the face.'

'With what? A chair? Looks painful.'

'Yep.'

'Broken?'

'Nope'

'You sure about that?'

Ellie opened her mouth to explain that she'd already been to the hospital when a suspicion distracted her. She squinted at Suzi. 'Why are you here so early? You're never in before Dag.'

Suzi dropped into the chair at her workstation and took a packet of Dunhill Switch from a pocket of her red leather jacket. She opened the pack and pulled out a stick of chewing gum. Smoking in workplaces was banned in Denmark, so Suzi carried gum with her cigarettes for when the urge to smoke struck at work or in a public indoor space.

'Jaz and I had a fight last night,' she said, popping the gum into her mouth. 'I slept on the sofa. That fucker is *not* comfortable to sleep on. I didn't want to be there when she woke up. Thought we could both use some space to cool off.'

'What did you fight about?'

'The TV.'

'The TV?'

'I know. It's ridiculous, right? But that's how it started. She wanted to watch one thing, and I wanted something else. I gave in, but she sat there stewing about it, so I told her to say whatever she needed to say. Vent, don't resent, right? But then it escalated into me apparently always getting my way because it's my flat. Anyway, it just got worse after that. A lot of shouting and name-calling. Then she stormed off to bed. So, I got hammered and crashed on the sofa.'

'Sounds pretty crappy. What are you going to do?'

'Fuck knows. I don't want to think about it right now.'

'You can stay with Zindy and me for a few days if you need to,' Ellie said. 'I'm sure Zin wouldn't mind. And no sofa. The spare bed's already made up.'

'Thanks, babe, but I'm not letting her boot me out of my own flat. If anyone needs to leave for a few days, it's her.'

'Okay, but the offer's there if you change your mind.'

Suzi winked at her. 'How come you're here so early, anyway?'

'One of those shitty dreams woke me up again last night. Or rather, at half-four this morning. Jakob and Zindy left early, and I didn't want to stay in the flat alone. Besides, I've got that guy coming in at nine-thirty.'

'What guy?'

'That sleeve job. The one he designed himself, with the weird tribal-gothic thing going on.'

'Oh, *that* guy,' said Suzi, lifting her coffee to take a sip. Ellie cringed internally at the thought of chewing gum-flavoured coffee, or should that be coffee-flavoured gum? 'So, what are you going to do about these dreams?'

Ellie shrugged and shook her head. She was conflicted about needing to resolve her problem but reluctant to stir up painful memories in her friend by asking for her former therapist's details.

'You should go and see Doctor Carlsson. She really worked magic on me when Lina died.'

To the surprise of both women, Ellie burst into tears.

'You're a fucking legend,' she spluttered through a flood of tears and snot. 'You know that?'

'Huh?'

'I was going to ask you for her details,' she said, wiping her eyes and, more carefully, her nose. 'But I wasn't sure how to do it. I didn't want to drag up bad history for you.'

'What? Don't be an idiot. You absolutely could've asked.'

She kept crying, partly because she felt bad about possibly unearthing difficult memories for Suzi, but mainly out of despair and desperation.

'Hey,' Suzi said. 'I'm okay. I carried a lot of survivor's guilt after the crash, but Doctor Carlsson was amazing. And I really am okay, babes. Honestly.'

Ellie nodded, and as she calmed herself, Suzi pulled out her phone and thumbed the screen a few times.

'Just texted you her number.'

'Thanks.'

'Are they really that bad?'

'Getting that way, yeah.'

'Shit. Sorry, hon.'

'Do me a favour, will you, and spot me one of those,' Ellie said, nodding to Suzi's cigarettes and pulling out her phone. 'I think I may need one in a minute.'

7

'You're bloody late!'

'Sorry,' said Jakob, removing his crash helmet. 'I had—'

'I don't pay you to be late. Or sorry. I pay you to—'

'Goat!' he snapped, eyeing the Jack Daniel's clock on the wall above the workshop's office. It read eight-thirty-three. 'I'm three minutes late. Ellie's still dealing with all this weird dream shit, we're both exhausted from lack of sleep, and I'm working overtime without pay to get the Zed finished in the ridiculous fucking timeframe you've agreed with the client. So, today of all days, give me a fucking break, okay!'

'Oh. Okay then, lad. I'll stick the kettle on then, eh?'

Jakob sighed.

'Yeah, thanks.'   •

Goat waved—a gesture Jakob took to mean *don't worry about it*— and headed toward the office in the corner of the workshop. Billy *Goat* MacKenzie was a bearded, heavily tattooed Scot who moved to Copenhagen fourteen years earlier with Natasja, his half-Danish, half-Scottish wife. He was also Jakob's boss and the owner of Goat's Customs—a small motorcycle workshop behind the Q8 petrol station on Sønder Boulevard. Goat's Danish was passable—even though he retained the lilt Scots often fail to lose when speaking a language other than their own—but in his workshop, he stuck to his native tongue. That was fine with Jakob, whose English was better than Goat's Danish, thanks to the excellent Danish education system and a couple of years travelling in his early twenties.

As Goat disappeared into the office, Jakob wheeled his custom Royal Enfield to the parking area in the far corner of the garage. The parking bay was large enough to hold fourteen motorcycles across two rows. Thanks to a couple of notable custom motorcycle builds that had made it into the international motorcycling press and television shows, the workshop was busier than ever, so the back row was already filled with customers' bikes, and there were three machines—including Goat's new Triumph Bobber—in front. He turned his bike and reversed it onto the front row into the bay furthest from Goat's bike. The last thing he wanted was for something to happen to Goat's pride and joy—a scratch here or a dent there—and for him to get the blame.

He stowed his helmet and jacket on a metal rack bolted to the wall next to the parking area, pushed a kink from his lower back, and took a deep breath, relishing the smell of petrol, oil, and exhaust fumes. No matter how clean you kept a workshop, you could never eliminate that smell. Next to the scent of Ellie's hair, it was probably his favourite smell.

A few moments later, slow, melancholic acoustic music began pumping from speakers mounted high up in the workshop's corners. As Jakob wrestled on his oil-covered overalls next to his workbench, Goat strolled back with a broad smile, a mug of tea in each hand and a rolled-up magazine in the hip pocket of his overalls. He set a cup down on the bench and lifted the other in a *cheers* gesture.

'Thanks,' said Jakob, picking up the mug and taking a sip of the steaming tea, wincing as he did so. He pointed his finger in the air. 'Cash?'

'Yeah.'

'Sorry, Goat.'

'Well, Johnny's not for everyone.'

Jakob chuckled.

'No,' he said. 'About earlier.'

'Nae bother, lad. You want to talk about it?'

'I wouldn't even know where to start. Last night Ellie had another vision or dream or whatever the fuck we're supposed to call them. Worse than the last lot. She's—'

'What are you two lovebirds cooing about?'

The question was mumbled, and when Jakob turned around, he saw why. Goat's other employee—whom everyone called Chewie, but whose actual name was Demir Candemir—strolled toward them, holding a can of Coke and what looked like a greasy fried egg sandwich—a large mouthful of which he was chewing on.

Chewie was a second-generation Danish Turk who, at twenty-nine, was three years younger than Jakob. People called him Chewie partly because he was rarely seen without some form of food, but mainly after the character in the *Star Wars* films because of how tall, lumbering and hairy he was. In Goat's words, he was a cocky bastard but gifted by God when it came to working on motorcycles. While, like the other two, Chewie owned a motorbike, he lived only a short walk from the workshop and rarely rode it to work, which is why neither Jakob nor Goat had heard him arrive.

'Nothing,' said Jakob.

'Well, not exactly nothin',' Goat said. 'I was just gonna tell Jakob about the new build we've got comin' up after the Zed.'

'Anything good?' asked Chewie, around his mouthful of mashed egg and bread.

'Aye, you could say that.' Goat took the magazine from the pocket of his overalls and unrolled it. It was a copy of *Custom Classics*. He tossed it to Chewie. Faced with a choice of dropping either his Coke or his sandwich to catch it, he chose to release neither. The magazine hit him in the chest and fell to the floor.

'Good work,' Jakob said.

'What? You think I was going to sacrifice my breakfast to catch it?'

'Those guys,' Goat said, pointing to the magazine on the floor, 'want us to remodel a Norton Commando 961 for their fifteenth-anniversary cover shoot.'

'Sweet,' Chewie said.

Jakob looked at him and frowned, his mind making a quick calculation about the direction in which he'd approached them. 'Did you go to the toilet with that?' he asked, nodding to the sandwich.

'Damn right, I did. Can't leave anything lying around out here with you two infidels lurking about.'

'So,' said Goat, picking up the magazine and giving the other two a *don't interrupt me* look, 'we've got to finish the Zed by the end of this week. Then it's a straight roll-on to the Commando. The mag wants it done in seven weeks, so I want it done in six.'

'Of course you do,' said Jakob. 'Any ideas?'

'Aye, some.'

Chewie, almost choking on another mouthful of now-cold egg and sticky bread, asked, 'Who gets the Norton?'

'You do, lad. Jakob can finish the Zed on his own. It's only paint, wiring, and some bits and bobs left. You and me get to start brainstorming on the Commie today, and once we've agreed on the design, it's your project.'

'Awesome.'

'Don't thank me just yet, son,' Goat said, tapping the magazine on Chewie's shoulder. 'You're going to be beggin' me to fire your hairy arse before we finish.'

An hour and a half later, while Jakob was testing an LED light strip he was planning to install on the rear of the Zed—their short name for an old 1973 Kawasaki Z1 they were customising—his phone, perched near the edge of his metal workbench, rang and vibrated simultaneously. He didn't usually take calls at work, so he ignored it. It skittered around violently for a few seconds and then tumbled off the bench. He scrambled to put down the LED strip without breaking it, lunged for the phone, and slammed his ribs into the handle of a bench-mounted vice.

'Shit!' he said, wincing.

As he caught the phone, he glimpsed the caller ID, which told him it was Ellie, so he answered.

'Hi, babe,' he said. 'You okay?'

'Yeah, I'm okay. Feeling a bit fried. Sooz gave me the number of her therapist. Got an appointment booked for tomorrow morning.'

'Jesus, that was quick. What time?'

'Eleven-thirty. She's away for two weeks from Saturday afternoon but has a couple of free slots this week. I wasn't sure I could wait until she gets back, so I thought I'd just get it done.'

'You need me to come with you? I can pull a late tonight to get the hours in. I'm almost done with the Zed anyway, and I'm sure Goat will be okay with it.'

'No, it's fine.'

'Okay.' He winced again as he nursed his rib cage. 'You want to do something tonight? See a film, maybe? The Empire's showing a re-run of The Lost Boys.'

'Yeah, sounds great. Can I stay at yours afterwards? I could use a night away from my apartment, too.'

'You're on. I think I'll be done here by seven-ish, so shall I pick you up at eight? I've already checked the showtimes, and there's a screening at nine, so we could have a drink at the bar next door first.'

'Okay.'

'Awesome. Just take it easy for the rest of the day, okay?'

'Yep.'

'Love you.'

'I know,' she said before hanging up.

Jakob chuckled, sparking off a fresh burst of pain through his torso.

8

TUESDAY

Ellie stood nervously on the pavement outside a tall, slim, pastel yellow townhouse on Overgaden Oven Vandet, a quiet brick-surfaced street running alongside a stretch of canal in the trendy area of Christianshavn. She'd rather have been at work, where she was supposed to be. She and the other tattooists at Double D's worked five days a week—including Saturdays—so they had Sundays off and a weekday, which changed on rotation. Her day off was meant to be the following day. When she'd asked Dagmar if she could change her day off and had explained why, Dag had suggested that she take a couple of personal hours for the appointment with Carlsson and keep her day off as scheduled. When Ellie asked whether she was sure, Dag hadn't hesitated. 'Absolutely,' she'd said. 'Take as much time as you need,' she'd said.

Her appointment with Doctor Carlsson was at eleven-thirty. She glanced at her watch for the second time since arriving outside Carlsson's house. It was eleven-twenty-seven. She'd been standing on the pavement, stamping her feet to keep out the cold, for nine minutes. Not because she didn't want to be too early, but because she was trying to muster the courage to go in. Because to go in meant meeting the therapist, and meeting the therapist meant she was crazy. Didn't it?

Screw it, she thought. Just get some fucking balls!

She locked her orange crash helmet in the storage compartment of her Lambretta scooter—also orange—and half-unzipped her new-but-old leather jacket, did the same with the grey hoodie she wore underneath it, and took a deep, steadying breath of crisp winter air. Then she trudged up the four concrete steps to the front door, rang the doorbell, and stepped back onto the pavement. Partly out of politeness—one should never crowd a doorway—and partly because she half hoped the doctor wouldn't be at home, and being slightly further away from the front door meant she was closer to a quick getaway.

The front door opened after what agonisingly felt like an hour but was probably only seven or eight seconds. In the doorway stood a woman she recognised as Doctor Carlsson, having googled the therapist after getting her details from Suzi. She thought it odd that Carlsson herself would come to the door but remembered this was the woman's home, and she probably didn't have a receptionist. She put Carlsson in her late fifties or early sixties, but she looked good for it. She was taller, with hair the colour of milk chocolate, and a warm, welcoming smile. Ellie liked her immediately.

'You must be Ellie,' she said.

'Oh, yes. Sorry. I'm, uh—'

'Early? Or wishing you'd turned around before I answered the door?'

Carlsson gave her a warm smile.

'Both, actually.' She chuckled nervously.

'I'm Maja,' the therapist said, pronouncing it *Maya*. 'Why don't you come in?'

'Thanks.'

Ellie walked back up the front steps, and Carlsson stepped aside to let her through. The entrance hall was warm and smelled of cinnamon and freshly baked bread. If that was a ploy by Carlsson to calm her patients, it went some way to working. On the dark timber floor was a deep-piled rectangular rug that matched the light beige walls of the hallway—earthy tones, meant to engender a sense of warmth, comfort, and safety.

Three doors led off from the hallway. The nearest one, on the left, was open, as was the one at the end of the hall facing the front door, which could have been the kitchen. The middle door, also to the left, was closed.

'Just in there,' said Carlsson, gesturing to the open door on the left as she closed the front door.

Ellie stepped to it.

Carlsson asked if she would like a cup of tea and reeled off the names of several types, some of which she'd never heard of.

'Uh, peppermint would be great,' she said. 'Thanks.'

'Go on in and take a seat on the sofa. I'll be there in a moment.'

As Carlsson disappeared toward the back of the house, Ellie entered the front room. More warm, earthy tones surrounded her. The walls were slightly darker than those in the hallway, and upon them hung a collection of black-and-white photographs in square ebony frames depicting scenes of trees, smooth waterfalls, and rolling fields.

She scanned the rest of the room. It had what she imagined the typical home office would have. A fancy swivel chair behind a desk—glass-topped and supporting an iMac computer, a Rolodex, a landline phone, and a notebook—a four-drawer filing cabinet and a short square table with a printer on top. It also had a sand-coloured fabric sofa set against the wall opposite the door, above which hung a beech-framed wall clock.

The only concession to colour in the room was a high-backed, deep ruby armchair between the desk and the sofa. It faced the couch but was angled, she presumed, to afford the therapist the best position to observe her patients.

As she waited for Carlsson to return, she inspected the photographs. There was something ethereal about them that she initially couldn't identify. Then she realised that everything in them that should have been green—or, at least, a black-and-white version of what was ordinarily green—was ghostly white.

'They're infrared.'

Ellie started and spun her head. The pictures captivated her so much that she hadn't heard Carlsson enter the room.

'Sorry,' said Carlsson, passing her a light green mug. 'I didn't mean to startle you.'

'No, it's okay.' She warmed her hands on the cup, took a quick sip, and gestured to the photos. 'I've never seen anything like these. Did you say they're infrared?'

'I did. My husband's work. He's a commercial photographer by trade—portraiture for magazines, that kind of thing. The landscape stuff is his hobby. He says he's dabbling with infrared, but I think it's excellent work.'

'They're amazing.'

'He's in Iceland at the moment, on a photographic tour. I'll pass on your compliments when he gets back.' Carlsson gave her a few more moments to look at the photographs, then gestured to the sofa and suggested she make herself comfortable.

She sat with her knees together and one upturned hand resting on them, cradling the mug of tea. Were it not for the hot drink, it was almost like she was sitting in a headmistress's office.

'First of all, Ellie, I'd like you to relax. Today is just for me to establish whether I can be of help. So there'll be no head-shrinking today. I promise you.'

'Okay. Thanks, doctor.'

'Please, call me Maja.'

'Okay.'

As Ellie took another sip of tea, Carlsson reached to put her own mug on the desk, picked up the notebook, and slid a pen from its spiralled spine.

'So,' she said, flipping open the notebook, 'you mentioned when you called that you've been experiencing a recurring dream.'

'Dreams, plural. For almost two months, I guess. Initially, they were fairly infrequent, with the first occurring every five or six nights for the first couple of weeks. Then a new one started. That repeated more quickly than the first. Maybe every four or five nights for a week or so. Then a new one. Every time a new dream starts, its frequency increases. Now I have them every night.'

'What can you tell me about them?'

Ellie inhaled deeply, held her breath for two seconds, and blew out hard and loud.

'Well, they all seem to be from a woman's perspective. It's the same woman each time, but it's not me. Her name's Marta. It's like I'm inhabiting her.'

Carlsson wrote something down. Marta, she thought. Or crazy.

'And what are they about? What are they showing you? Can you remember anything specific about any of them?'

'I could probably run through every detail of each of them.'

'Why don't you just give me the highlights?'

'Okay. In the first, I—as Marta—was at a wedding. Her sister was the bride. Many people were there, including Marta's husband, although she stayed away from him as if their relationship was a secret or something. I remember Marta feeling a deep love for that man and pure loathing for the man who'd married the sister. He acted like some magnanimous host but was just an attention-loving poser.'

More writing.

'The next was Marta in a dark room with her husband. Just the two of them. He was standing behind her, and his arms were around her belly. There was a gentleness to how they were with each other and how he held her. There was a lot of love there.'

She paused as Carlsson scribbled once more.

'The third,' she said, when she saw Carlsson was ready to continue, 'was a dinner at another man's house. Marta's sister was there with their brother and with the sister's new husband. And Marta's secret husband who, I think, was there under the guise of being a friend of the guy who owned the house. It was supposed to be a celebration. The brother had been away. But not on holiday or a journey of some kind. It was like he'd been excluded from the group and accepted back in. But then things got weird. The sister's husband started insulting everyone, especially Marta's husband. It ended badly, with the brother and sister taking the side of the sister's husband and the three of them leaving angry.'

More notes.

'And now this latest one.'

'What can you tell me about it?'

Ellie described the dream in which Marta's husband, Yehuda, had been abducted.

'That's quite a recap,' said Carlsson, jotting down more notes.

'Yep. And the weirdest thing is that they're not happening here, now.'

'What do you mean by that?'

'They're happening in a different time and a different place.'

'Different in what way?'

'Well, everything seems old. The houses, and the clothes people wear. Not old, actually. Crude. Simple. There's no modern technology of any kind. The people are foreign. Middle Eastern, maybe? Olive-skinned, dark-haired. It all seems very... biblical. And...'

'And?'

'The language. Everyone, including the woman I inhabit, talks in Hebrew or Arabic. Maybe even a different language. I don't know what it is, but I can understand it. And I can speak it. Fluently. In the dreams, that is.'

'Okay. Anything else?'

Ellie hesitated. The only details left to tell were the names of everyone in the dreams. But should she go that far? What if Carlsson thought this was all a practical joke? That she was deliberately wasting the therapist's time for kicks?

'Ellie?'

She knew she didn't have a choice. If she wanted Carlsson's help, she had to tell her everything.

'Their names,' she said.

She rattled off a list of names, which Carlsson wrote down without comment. The therapist then appeared to think for a moment, jotted down something else, then closed her notebook and looked at her silently.

'That looks like it was painful,' Carlsson said eventually.

Ellie pursed her lips and nodded.

'How did it happen?'

'Self-defence classes.'

'Really? How did that come about?'

'I was attacked about seven months ago after a late work shift. The guy had a knife. He didn't hurt me, but I couldn't defend myself, so he took my bag, which had my wallet and phone and house keys and a load of other stuff in it. It really shook me up. And getting cards cancelled, passwords changed, and everything replaced was a pain in the ass. I decided I didn't want to be a victim again, so I started taking the classes.'

'So, one of your classmates landed a lucky blow, did they?'

'Not exactly. I'm taking private lessons with Lars, the trainer. I asked him to beef up the sessions a few weeks ago. We started with kicks and punches, which aren't usually part of self-defence training, and we've recently progressed to blunt instruments.'

'How long ago would you say you modified the training?

'About six or seven weeks ago, probably.'

Carlsson checked her notes.

'So, around the same time you started having the dreams?'

The question hit Ellie like a slap in the face. Was it possible that she'd been having these violent dreams because her sessions with Lars had become more intense? Or was it the other way around? Was she pushing things with Lars to deal with the dreams? Surely, they were not connected? She shook her head, puffed her cheeks, and blew out.

'Shit.'

'It could be entirely coincidental, Ellie. There's nothing to suggest they're related. Not yet, at least. But we can explore that if you decide you'd like to come back for some formal sessions.'

She brightened momentarily, pleased that Carlsson could be of help. But that feeling was quickly replaced by frustration for needing help in the first place. Carlsson glanced at her watch.

'Why don't we leave it there for today?'

Ellie agreed, relieved that the session—because that's what it was regardless of what Carlsson had said at the start—was over.

'Full disclosure, Ellie... I'm by no means an expert on dreams, but I'd like to help you if I can. Are you able to come back again this week for a full session?'

'This week?'

'Well, as I explained on the phone yesterday, I'm away for a couple of weeks from Saturday, so it's either this week or after I get back.'

Ellie considered this, still conflicted about what it would mean to start seeing a shrink properly—what it would say about *her*. But she knew she needed Carlsson's help. And she knew she couldn't wait another two weeks for that help. There was no way she'd be able to cope.

Fuck it.

'Okay,' she said. 'Let's do it.'

'Great.'

Carlsson got up and went around the desk. She pushed the office chair away, moved the computer's mouse around and clicked a few times. Ellie guessed the iMac was only in sleep mode and not password-protected, as the therapist started clicking away almost immediately, probably on the computer's calendar application.

'I can come any time tomorrow, as it's my day off,' said Ellie. 'Failing that, I can come either of the other two days so long as we're done by ten, as I need to be at work by ten thirty.'

'Right, let's see. We're in luck. I have an opening tomorrow afternoon at two. Will that work?'

'Yep.'

'Excellent.'

She clicked again and then typed on the keyboard. Finally, she came around the desk to Ellie, who was now standing.

'Thanks for today.'

'No thanks necessary, Ellie.'

'No, they are. Chatting through all this with someone who isn't my boyfriend, flatmate, or workmate has helped a lot. It's not that they're unsympathetic, but they're probably all sick of it, and I feel like I'm burdening them more and more.'

'I wouldn't count them out. People who love us stand by us. You might be able to lean on them more than you think you can or should.'

Ellie shrugged, unconvinced, and made her way out of the room. As she opened the front door, she thanked Carlsson again.

'I'll see you tomorrow,' the therapist replied.

Ellie smiled, zipped up her hoodie and jacket, and bounced down the concrete steps onto the pavement. She pulled out her phone and called Jakob. He answered on the sixth ring.

'How'd it go?' he asked.

'Great, actually.'

'Really?'

'Yep. It felt good to talk to someone I haven't bored with all of this shit yet.'

'You haven't bored anyone with it, babe. You do know that, right?'

'I know.'

He was silent for a second. She suspected he didn't believe her and that he thought *she* thought she was burdening everyone with her dream shit. And he was right. She did believe she was a burden. But who else could she turn to?

'So?' he probed. '*Come on?*'

'It was just a *getting to know me* thing. To see if she can help me. And by *can,* I suspect she meant *wants to.*'

'*And can she?*'

'Not sure if she can, but she does want to. So, we've got our first real session tomorrow afternoon.'

'*Awesome.*'

'I feel like going out again tonight. But just a quiet one. Just you and me. You fancy that?'

'*Yeah, I do, actually. Where do you want to go?*'

'Dunno. Café Noir, maybe?'

He was silent again, for longer this time.

'Jakob?'

'*Uh, yep. Sounds good.*'

'Are you okay? You seem a bit distracted.'

'*I'm getting the evil eye from Goat. He's glaring at me over the top of his giant mug of builder's tea.*'

'Ah, okay. I'd better let you get back to it, then. Shall I meet you at Café Noir at eight-thirty?'

'*Yeah, that's perfect. And it'll be on me.*'

'Awesome. I'll book a table. See you later.'

'*Yeah, see you later. I love—*'

She hung up and chuckled. Another gag she'd heard about from a friend. Hang up before your significant other finishes their *I love you.*'

During the day, like most coffee shops, Café Noir sold cappuccinos, lattes, and espressos and a selection of pastries, sandwiches, and light snacks. After six in the evening, though, it transformed into a wine bar and restaurant.

Inside, the bar counter took up three-quarters of one wall, leaving enough space at the end closest to the front windows for the café's resident three-piece band and a couple of round glass-topped tables, each with two chairs with red wooden frames and crisscrossed wicker seats and backs.

Along the entire wall across from the bar was a berry-red leatherette banquette, in front of which were square, round, and rectangular tables capable of seating groups of two or four people variously, all with red-framed wicker-clad chairs on the side nearest the bar. The dark timber floor was framed by walls the colour of merlot, and the dimmed low-hanging ceiling lights and wall lamps gave the place a cosy, intimate feel, even at the busiest times. One of the things Ellie loved about the place was that it didn't discriminate against its customers. It was as accepting of scruffy university students as affluent bankers and lawyers dressed in expensive suits.

The place was busy, with over half of the tables occupied, but the conversations around them were at volumes low enough for her to hear the band's guitarist singing about how she had a bowling ball in her stomach and a desert in her mouth. She spotted Jakob standing at the bar, staring at his phone and looking smarter than she'd seen him in some time. Dark blue jeans, a matching shirt and a grey three-quarter-length woollen coat. She thought he scrubbed up well. He'd probably even polished his boots. While she was six minutes early, she'd guessed he would already be there. They both had a thing about not being late, especially when meeting each other.

On the bar in front of him were two bottles of Carlsberg, droplets of condensation giving away how cold they were. She walked over. He was still looking at his phone and hadn't seen her yet. She walked past him, flicked his left ear, and stepped to his right. His head swivelled to the left. With nobody at his left shoulder, he spun his head around the other way and found her beaming at him.

'That wasn't childish at all.'

'No? I'll have to try harder next time. You look amazing.'

'As do you,' he said, taking in her jet-black ensemble of leather trousers, Cashmere turtleneck, and trench coat. 'Like a hot ninja.'

'Yeah, complete with natural makeup,' she said, gesturing to her facial bruising.

He bent toward her, cupped her jaw in his hand, and kissed her. It was a long, lingering kiss. Not a raunchy *take me to bed* kiss. An *I love you, and I've missed you all day* kiss. And it turned her on. She'd recently felt that they'd lost some of their connection. Partly because that can happen in any relationship over time, she guessed. But mainly because of the dreams and how they had been affecting her—affecting them. Her doubts evaporated with that kiss.

'What was that for?' she asked when Jakob let her come up for air.

'Because.'

'Because of what?'

He shrugged.

'Just because,' he said.

He put his phone on the bar, picked up the two bottles of beer, and handed one to her. She took it and clinked it against his, and they each took a long gulp.

'So, how'd it go with Carlsson?'

'It was good, actually. We talked about the dreams, and she asked me about my face, which made me realise that I asked Lars to step things up in training around the same time the dreams started.'

'Really? Does she think the two are connected?'

'She said it could be a coincidence, but I'm not convinced. I think, on a subconscious level at least, that getting more hardcore with Lars is my way of dealing with all of this shit.'

'Could be. Anyway, I've got something that I guarantee will cheer you up.'

He reached for his phone, unlocked it, and held it up so she could see the screen. She squealed with delight.

'Metallica?' she said. 'No. Fucking. Way!'

Jakob grinned.

'At the Royal Arena in July. It was either them or Sheeran two weeks later,' he said..

'Uh, no, thank you.'

'I thought about getting the *Devil's Dance* package but couldn't stretch to the sixteen thousand kroner per ticket, so I just went for general admission. Hope that's okay.'

She hugged him and kissed him on the lips. A long, lingering *I love you, you have no idea what you have just done for me* kiss.

'Jakob Nørgard, you're on a spending spree. Dinner tonight, the concert. What's going on?'

He shrugged and, for a moment, looked uncomfortable.

'Things have been shit for you lately,' he said, 'and I'm sure I haven't helped much with that, so I wanted to do something that might cheer you up or take your mind off things. Or something. I don't know.'

Ellie smiled and took his hand.

'You're an idiot. Just being there for me is more than enough. You do realise that, right?'

He shrugged again.

'I feel a bit useless, to be honest,' he said.

'It's lucky you're good-looking, then, isn't it?'

'Nice. Shall we go stuff our faces, then?'

Ellie nodded, and Jakob motioned to the Maître D' that they were ready to sit. The woman smiled and gestured for them to follow her, which they did, beer bottles in hand.

9

She peers through the crowd, finding gaps between heads wherever she can to catch glimpses of him. She can feel his pain. She can feel the burning in his legs and the sting of cuts on his knees from falling. She can feel the throbbing ache of shattered cheekbones hidden behind the matted, blood-soaked hair plastered across his face and the excruciating pain of splintered wood digging into his shoulders, cutting them almost to the bone.

And she relishes it.

Here is the man who'd ordered the abduction of her husband. There is no doubt in her mind that he was responsible for it.

Yeshua.

Shimon, disguised under a hooded cloak, walks in front of her, slowly but firmly clearing a path for her. She knows he can also feel Yeshua's pain but senses it differently. He doesn't feel the man's physical pain. Instead, he senses Yeshua's anger. The hatred, burning like an inferno, for having to humiliate himself like this to further his cause.

Someone in the crowd on the other side of the street throws a rock at Yeshua. It hits him on the nose, breaking it. He stumbles and falls to his knees. The noise from the crowd is unbearable. Some cheer and clap, some moan in sympathy, some shout at the man to get up, and others, in a frenzied bloodlust, throw more rocks at him.

A man with skin darker than hers stumbles out from the crowd on the other side of the street. She doesn't recognise him. He looks back to

66

where he came from, and she thinks he hasn't come forward voluntarily. She sees a Roman centurion pointing his spear at the man, and she realises the soldier probably pushed him out of the crowd. The man squats down and places himself underneath the T-shaped cross, taking its weight on the top of his back, then heaves it onto his shoulder. Straining under its heaviness, he slowly stands and begins to take small steps forward.

The mob goes wild. Roars of apoplectic fury drown out cheers of encouragement. Another person throws a rock. It hits the man in the chest. He falters for only the briefest of moments, then carries on bravely.

Two more men come forward from the crowd. They are both known to her. Taoma and Kepha. Thanks to Shimon's blade, Kepha now wears a bandage on his left ear. They look for some part of Yeshua to hold where they won't hurt him, but there is no part of him not cut or broken or bruised. They gingerly roll his broken body onto its side, and as they turn him, she sees a crisscrossed pattern of blood and deep cuts on his back, where his captors had him whipped before sending him on his way through the crowd. She almost pities him but then remembers this was his doing. It was his choice.

Another man runs out and places a sheet of sand-coloured muslin on the ground next to Yeshua. It's her brother, Elazar. Her stomach lurches, and she vomits a little, but she manages to catch it in her robes and discreetly drops it into the dirt. Elazar quickly retreats into the crowd, probably out of fear of getting stoned himself.

Taoma and Kepha gently lay Yeshua onto the muslin, each standing at opposite ends of the sheet. They wind their fists into the corners of the fabric, heave up his limp body and follow the dark-skinned man who carries the cross.

10

WEDNESDAY

'If you don't mind me saying,' Carlsson said, handing Ellie a large cup of green tea, 'your face looks much improved from yesterday. Remarkably so, in fact. How are you feeling?'

Ellie leaned forward on the sofa in Carlsson's front room, in the same spot she'd occupied the day before. She felt bone tired, but the morning sun had warmed her face on the ride there, giving her a much-needed boost. However, her anxiety about this being her first official session had not melted away. Carlsson sat in the ruby armchair and took up her notebook, which was wedged between the arm and the seat cushion.

'Thanks,' she said. 'Yeah, I'm doing better. I thought I'd be purple and swollen for at least a couple of weeks, but the swelling's already going down, so it's easier to breathe, and the bruising's clearing up, too. It's weird, but I'm not complaining. The worst part has been people staring at me. Especially when I've been out with Jakob. When they see me, they look at him with barely disguised anger and disgust, like he's been smacking me around.'

'That can't be easy for either of you.'

'Thankfully, it won't last. And I don't really care what they think of me. I just feel bad for him.'

Carlsson smiled, tilted her head almost apologetically, and held her gaze for a few seconds.

'What?' Ellie asked.

'I looked up the names you gave me yesterday.'

Okay, she thought. Straight down to business. Probably just as well, considering this session wasn't free like yesterday's.

'And?'

'It looks like you were right about the locational setting of your dreams. Most of the names are Middle Eastern variations of common western names—possibly even the historical root names of the modern variants. But they're not Hebrew or Arabic, as you thought. They're Aramaic.'

'Which is?'

'Practically a dead language these days. But, along with Hebrew and Greek, it was thought to have been spoken by Christ and his contemporaries. And that leads me to consider that your theory about the characters in your dreams being biblical could be correct. Particularly...'

'What?' Particularly what?'

'As I understand it, much of the New Testament was originally written in Greek. What we read now is the modern translation of that. So, to establish whether the characters you're seeing are actually those from the Bible, we'd need to look at the modern versions of those names and translate them back to old Greek. As far as I could tell from the online Aramaic translation site I found—which I trust as far as I can fly—the western forms of Marta, Shimon and Mariam are Martha, Simon and Mary. All unremarkable now and likely to have been so back in the day.'

'But?'

'But, the modern variants of Yehuda and Yeshua are Jude and Joshua. Work those back to the old Greek, and you have—'

'Judas and Jesus.'

'Yes.'

'Yeah,' said Ellie. 'I'd guessed as much. To be honest, I had considered not telling you the names in case you thought I was just here wasting your time or something.'

'Why would I think that?'

'I don't know. It's just...'

She slumped back on the sofa. Carlsson watched her for a moment, clearly waiting for her to elaborate. When she didn't, the therapist pushed.

'What, Ellie? What are you not telling me?'

'I had a new dream last night.'

Carlsson flipped back through her notebook until she found the page she wanted. She studied it quickly. 'Judging from the progression of those you've already had, I'd say they're increasing in their regularity.'

'They're exhausting, is what they are.'

'Can you remember anything about it?'

'I always remember. Everything.'

'Okay, so why don't you run me through it?'

Ellie took a sip of her tea, then breathed in deeply, let it out slowly, and began describing the dream she had the night before of Yeshua's journey through the crowd, carrying the T-shaped cross. Carlsson listened intently without writing notes.

'He was a real mess, and he was in a lot of pain. It was almost as if Marta could feel it. And she felt good about it.'

'She felt good about it?'

'Yeah. And I mean, *really* good. It's like she was enjoying seeing him hurt. She hated him. I felt what she felt, and it was like I hated him too and liked that he was in pain.'

Now Carlsson did scribble something. Probably sadist, she thought.

'Why did Marta hate Yeshua?' Carlsson asked.

'Because she thought he was responsible for Yehuda's abduction.'

Carlsson sat quietly, appearing to consider something.

'Okay,' she said eventually. 'So if we assume these characters you're seeing *are* Christ and his inner circle, then what you're saying, based on your earlier dreams, is that not only was Jesus married—which I know is a popular theory these days—but also that he was behind the kidnapping of Judas Iscariot, who was also his brother-in-law. I don't recall much from my religious education at school, but I don't remember anything about Judas being abducted. I thought he committed suicide.'

'I don't know. Am I saying Christ was married? Am I saying he had Judas kidnapped? I mean, am *I* saying that? If I am, it's not me. It's what these damn nightmares are showing me.'

Ellie squeezed her temples. She rubbed around the outside corners of her closed eyes and accidentally brushed her nose. She swore with the pain of it. While her face's puffiness had somewhat subsided, it was still sensitive. Then she felt a lump growing in her throat. She desperately didn't want to start crying in front of Carlsson.

'I don't understand it,' she said, almost a whisper. 'I don't understand why I'm seeing them or why they seem so... real. I'm pretty sure I'm about to lose my mind.'

'What you're experiencing, Ellie, are dreams of a non-self-character—someone who plays a part in a story with which you're familiar. They're not uncommon. Research has shown that when a person has such dreams, the character they inhabit can have the same cognitive skills that a person would have in real life. They talk, walk, make decisions, and in some cases, even have their own consciousness—one entirely independent of the person having the dream. It's probably the main reason they seem so fluid and so realistic.

'They're usually triggered by something. An event we experience, or perhaps something we read or see. And sometimes, frustratingly, that trigger could be entirely unrelated to what we experience in the dream. For example, the story of Christ's walk to Golgotha is well-known, taught to almost all children in this country. I think I can safely presume that you haven't been to a public crucifixion, but something may have sparked your memory of that story. And that memory is now manifesting in a particularly vivid manner. Have you seen any films recently that have depicted scenes similar to those you've seen in your dreams or read any books or articles that might be related, even tenuously?'

Ellie shook her head.

'Are you especially religious? Have you been going to church lately or reading the Bible?'

'My grandparents were Catholic, but they never forced their beliefs on me. And the last time I went to church was for my grandfather's funeral fourteen years ago. So, no, I'm not religious. And, like you said, we didn't learn about kidnappings, dinner arguments, and beheadings growing up, so how do I see visions of events I've never been taught about?'

'Well, as I—'

'And they're never fluid. Nothing changes. This Marta has always done the same things in every recurrence of whatever dream I have. She says the same things. She does the same things. And everything else that happens is always the same. It's almost as if each dream is a film I'm watching over and over. There's never been a different version of the same dream. Things only change when a new dream starts.'

Ellie could feel herself becoming hot with anger and despair.

Carlsson nodded slowly, sipped her tea, then fell silent and stared into her mug. She looked like she'd drifted off. Ellie was about to give her a verbal nudge when she looked up.

'If the dreams are as linear and repetitive as you say, and show you events you have no prior knowledge of, then perhaps one–if not the only–explanation for what you see could be the resurgence of life memories, which *would* more likely be unchanging.'

'But that's impossible. Isn't it? How can I have a memory of a place I've never been? Or a time I've never lived in?'

'It would be impossible for you, as your current self, to have experienced, in real terms, what you've seen in these dreams, yes. But there are abundant theories about past lives and the transference of memories through successive lives.'

'You're saying I used to be another person? I used to be Marta?'

'It's one possibility. Although I must admit, I don't personally subscribe to theories surrounding reincarnation, which is what we would call this if these are true memories.'

Ellie digested this for a few seconds. Like Carlsson, she didn't believe in reincarnation, but what else could it be? She inhabited the same person in every dream. Characters in those dreams consistently performed the same actions and said the same things. If what she'd seen weren't memories of a past life, the only reasonable explanation was that she could control the speech and actions of everyone in her dreams to such a degree that every recurrence matched those before it. Which was impossible, right? She *was* going crazy. Unable to stop herself and no longer caring about breaking down in front of Carlsson, she burst into tears.

Not a tiny weep.

A full-flowing torrent.

Carlsson picked up a box of Kleenex tissues from the side table beside her chair, leaned forward, and offered it to Ellie. She took a tissue, then thought better of it and plucked out three more.

'Thanks.'

Carlsson quickly glanced above Ellie's head. Looking at the wall clock, no doubt. Less obvious than checking her watch.

'I know you're frustrated, Ellie. And to be honest, I'm somewhat vexed myself. I've had patients who've had recurring dreams—they were drowning or falling or were in a car crash—but it was usually only the generalities of the dreams that repeated, not the specifics. What you're experiencing—the precise repetitions in each vision—intrigues me greatly. In our next session, I'd like to delve deeper into what you see. If we can do that, we might be able to determine why this is happening.'

'Okay, and how do we do that?'

'With past life regression therapy.'

'You mean hypnotherapy.'

'Yes.'

Fuck no!

'Uh, no. I don't think so,' Ellie said.

'Could I ask why not?'

'Well, first, I don't think I want to give up control of myself. And second, the last two dreams I've had were pretty violent, and, to be honest, I'd rather not relive those voluntarily.'

'Both valid points. But hypnotherapy doesn't require you to give up control, Ellie. It's not like you see on those TV shows where the hypnotists make people do silly or embarrassing—'

'What about Hardrup?'

Palle Hardrup was a man convicted of murder in the 1950s, along with Bjørn Schouw Nielsen, after what had become known as the Copenhagen hypnosis murders. A film based on the murders came out in 2018. Ellie had seen it. The two men had been cellmates at Horsens State Prison, both serving time for treason. Sometime after their release, Nielsen had hypnotised Hardrup to commit a bank robbery, during which he shot and killed two of the bank's staff.

'Nobody can make you do anything your subconscious mind doesn't want to do,' Carlsson said. 'It will only do what it knows you want to do or what it believes you *need* to do—even if you don't consciously realise you need to do it. Nothing happens that you, consciously or subconsciously, don't allow. A part of you is always in control. As for Hardrup, given his relationship with Nielsen, I suspect he was entirely open to whatever Nielsen suggested.'

Ellie considered this for a few moments. What were her options? Have the hypnotherapy or let the dreams continue? She wasn't sure she had a choice.

'Look, I understand your reluctance to revisit the violent dreams, but if we're to get to the bottom of what you're experiencing, hypnotherapy is probably the best starting point.'

'And you're sure it's safe?'

'Perfectly.'

'Okay,' she said resignedly.

'And there's something else I'd like to suggest, which I'm not sure you'll like but which I think may be helpful.'

What now? she thought.

'Given the religious nature of your visions,' Carlsson continued, 'I think it might be worth you speaking to a friend of mine. A priest. He may be—'

'A priest? What do you want him to do? Perform an exorcism? I don't think fobbing me off to—'

Carlsson raised her hands in a calming gesture, and she begrudgingly fell silent.

'I'm not fobbing you off, Ellie. I want to do everything I can to help you. I've only suggested you talk to my friend because, given the specifics of your dreams, he may be able to offer some insight. I want to continue our sessions here, in my office, and I'd like him to join our next session. Would you be open to that?'

Ellie said nothing.

'I know it's completely unorthodox, and ordinarily, I would never suggest something like this to a patient, but I've known this guy for a long time. He's not just an acquaintance. We're good friends, and I trust his judgement. All I ask is that you allow him to sit in on the next session and offer any opinion he might have.'

She still wasn't entirely convinced. She weighed up her options—get help or not—and after a few seconds of contemplation, she agreed.

'Okay,' said Carlsson. 'I'll make a call later.'

'Shit!'

Jakob clenched his fist and extended his thumb like he was hitchhiking. Scored down its centre was a hair-thin two-centimetre cut, at the top of which was a small globule of blood. It didn't look too bad, despite feeling like he'd sliced the entire thumb off. He pushed at the cut with his other thumb to wipe away the blood, which was a mistake. The thin slice opened to a gash, and the droplet of blood turned into a rapid flow.

'Fuck!'

With his customary oversized mug in hand, Goat ambled over from the other side of the workshop, where he'd been replenishing the coffee vending machine in the customer waiting area.

'What's up, big man?' he asked.

Jakob displayed his thumb, and Goat took a step back, his face paling. He hadn't taken the Scot to be the queasy type, and seeing the look on his face made getting cut almost worth it.

'Oh. Well, that's what you get for tryin' to fix the wiring *after* it's on the bike.'

'Thanks,' he said. 'Helpful.'

Goat shrugged and smirked and took a gulp of tea. 'I'll get the first aid kit,' he said, slapping him on the shoulder, then whispering, 'You fuckin' pussy.'

'I heard that.'

'You were meant to.'

Jakob headed for the bathroom to wash the cut. It stung more than he expected it to. Enough to bring tears to his eyes. He reluctantly squeezed the gash open under the running tap. If he'd sliced the thumb with a blade, he might not have been so concerned, but he'd been pulling wires through a loom, and his hand had slipped on the plastic coatings and slid across the bare wires, so there could be metal fibres in there which would need to come out.

He looked at the cut and almost vomited into the sink, more from adrenaline-induced nausea than the sight of his blood flooding away down the plughole. He ripped a couple of paper towels from a wall-mounted dispenser, gingerly patted the thumb with the first, and then wrapped the second around it to prevent further blood flow, which, while unlikely, was still worth the effort.

When he got back to his workbench, the first aid kit was on it, and a piece of *Hello Kitty* notepaper was taped to it, on which was a scruffily written message.

Here you go, princess. If you need someone to kiss it better, ask Chewie. XOXO.

As he grunted a chuckle, his phone rang from the back pocket of his overalls. He fished it out with his uninjured hand. It was Ellie. He accepted the call and wedged the phone between his shoulder and ear, keeping both hands free to fix his thumb.

'Hey, babes,' he said, opening the first aid kit. He took out a Band-Aid, three gauze patches, a tube of Savlon antiseptic cream, and two butterfly stitch strips. 'How'd it go with the doc?'

'*Okay.*'

'Just okay?'

'*Well, she'd googled all the names I'd given her.*'

'And?'

'*And, I was right about it being Jesus. The new dream I had last night pretty much confirmed that anyway.*'

'What? You had another one? Why didn't you call me?'

'*What, at three in the morning when it woke me up?*'

'Come on, Ellie. You know you can call me when—'

'*And it turns out the guy I saw kidnapped is probably Judas like I thought.*'

He removed the paper towel from his thumb, and for a microsecond, he thought the bleeding had stopped. It hadn't.

'Shit,' he said, more in response to the continuous blood flow than Ellie's revelation about her dreams.

'*Yep. So, we talked about all that, but we're no closer to solving the problem.*'

'Well, it's probably going to take a few sessions with her.'

'She reckons they could be memories of a past life or something.'

'Really?'

'She also said she wants to try hypnotherapy in the next session. Past life regression therapy, she called it. Oh, and she also suggested we rope in a priest.'

'Fucking hell, Ellie! For what? An exorcism? Will I have to change my phone ring to *Tubular Bells* and stand over your bed chanting, "The power of Christ compels you"?'

'That's what I said. About the exorcism. But no, Carlsson reckons that a priest might have a different perspective because the dreams are about biblical shit, and lucky me, she's got a priest pal who might be able to help.'

As Ellie kept talking, he finished dressing his thumb and clumsily wrapped the Band-Aid around it. Focussing on affixing the plaster, he zoned out of the conversation.

'Jakob?'

'Huh?'

'Can we stay at yours tonight? I need another break from my place. Is that okay?'

'Yeah. Sounds good.'

'You okay? You're not quite with me.'

'Sorry,' he said, sticking down the edges of the Band-Aid. 'I just sliced my thumb open doing some wiring. I'm just wrapping it up, and it hurts like fuck.'

'Ouch!'

'Yep.'

'Shit, I have to go. My next client is here.'

'Okay, babe. I'll see you later.'

11

As the sun set, Father Frederik Sigvardt closed his den's heavy brown curtains, dimmed the lights, and settled into his leather armchair. He was nursing an aggressive headache, which he tried to soothe away with a snifter of Hennessy and by curling his socked toes on the thick pile rug at the foot of his chair. As Bruce Springsteen quietly sang from a small Denon stereo system on the mid-level shelf of a mahogany bookcase that took up an entire wall, a vibration of plastic on wood grabbed Sigvardt's attention. His silenced Nokia—a dumbphone he believed it was called these days—was bouncing around vigorously on the side table, its screen aglow.

Damn it.

Reluctantly, he picked up the phone and answered the call without reading the caller ID. The great thing about Church-owned mobile phones was their numbers were kept unlisted and, therefore, usually inaccessible to spam callers, which meant this call was either from someone within the church or from somebody to whom he had personally given his number.

'Sigvardt.'

'Fred, it's M.'

'Hello!' Sigvardt said happily, recognising Maja Carlsson's voice. 'How are you, my dear?'

'Coming down with a cold, I think, but otherwise not too bad. How are things with you?'

'Exhausting. Grethe and I have decided to take a trip to southern Europe to celebrate my sixtieth and her retirement from the RDO. I've spent the last two hours scouring the Internet for reviews of hotels along the Mediterranean coastline and compiling a list to show Grethe when she gets home from rehearsals. So now my head hurts, and my eyes ache.'

'Sounds very exciting, though.'

'Yes, but I'll be glad when it's all decided on and booked. Is Erik back yet?'

'No. He'll be there for another couple of days. He's having an amazing time, he says, but he can't wait to get back. It was two degrees yesterday.'

'Ha! It's not much warmer here.'

'True, but I think he misses his home comforts. You know Erik. He's a sensitive soul.'

'That he is.'

'Fred, I know this sounds terrible, but as much as I'd love to catch up properly, I'm afraid this isn't a social call. It's a professional matter. I wouldn't usually come to you with something like this, but it's such an odd case, and it has me stumped.'

Sigvardt shifted in his chair.

'Colour me intrigued. Please, continue.'

'I have a patient. Her name is Ellie. She's been having unusual dreams for a couple of months or so. Initially, they were infrequent and appeared to be fairly benign. But they've been increasing in frequency recently, occurring every couple of days now, and the last two she had were quite violent.'

'That sounds awful. And how do you think I can help?'

'Well, she says they're all from the perspective of a woman named Marta. And they all seem to be about characters from the New Testament. Specifically, Christ and his followers. The latest vision was of Christ's journey to Golgotha.'

'Religious dreams aren't that uncommon.'

'*She's even had a dream about the abduction of someone who appears to be Judas Iscariot.*'

'Iscariot wasn't abducted.'

'*That's what I said, but I think this is less about the accuracy of her dreams and more about the fact they're happening and what I— hopefully we, if you're agreeable—can do to help her.*'

He listened as Carlsson explained how she and Ellie had discussed the nature of the dreams being linear like films constantly replaying, how they had talked about trying hypnotherapy at their next session, and that she'd suggested asking him to meet Ellie, given the dreams' religious content.

'I see,' he said.

'*She's understandably worried about the whole situation, Fred. Not least by the fact that I've suggested I speak with you. The last thing I want is to make her feel like I'm abandoning her to some Church-led witch hunt.*'

'I understand completely. Look, I'm not an expert on such things, but I'd be happy to meet with her. When is your next session with her?'

'*We haven't arranged that yet. I told Ellie I'd talk to you, and we'd try to schedule something that suits your diary. She's available weekdays until ten in the morning and any time on Wednesdays. The only problem is that I'm away for two weeks from the weekend, so it's either this week or when I get back. Frankly, Fred, this is troubling her so much that I'd rather do this before I go away. I know that's short notice, but...*'

'Well, I've got meetings all day tomorrow, but I could see you on Friday morning. Will that work for you both?'

'*I'm free then. I'll check with Ellie and get back to you to confirm. Would you be okay to come to my place? I think she'd feel more comfortable with that rather than us coming to you. Neutral ground.*'

'Of course.'

'*That would be great. Thanks, Fred. I'll owe you a large bottle for this. It's still Hennessy, yes?'*

'Ha! You know me way too well.'

'Hennessy it is, then. I'll text you later once I've checked with Ellie.'

'Alright.'

The two exchanged goodbyes. Sigvardt hung up first, placed his phone back on the side table, screen-side down, and tuned back into Springsteen, who sang of devils and dust.

Two hours later, as he cradled his fourth brandy of the evening, his phone vibrated briefly. It was a text message. He remained still for a few moments, deciding whether to bother reading it, then remembered Carlsson had promised to send him a text about meeting with her patient. He picked up the phone. The screen had already gone dark again, so he thumbed the numerical pad clumsily, knowing that pressing any of the buttons would illuminate the display. The message was, as he had anticipated, from Carlsson.

`On for Friday at 9am. Thanks Fred.`

He sighed, knowing that he should respond. He held the phone in two hands, used his thumbs to press the two buttons required to unlock the phone, and typed his reply. Despite the simplicity of his message, he needed to retype some of it twice—tiny keys and old, drunken fingers didn't work well together. Finally, on the third typing, it was ready.

`Great. See you then.`

12

Gendarme Vasco Ruggeri sat at his workstation in the Vatican's Operations and Control Room, deep within a cluster of administrative buildings north of Saint Peter's Square. He sipped black coffee from an off-white mug and cast his eyes over each of the twenty variously-sized screens attached to the far wall opposite him and the bank of three monitors directly in front of him.

As he watched the main screen wall, flashing in his peripheral vision caught his attention. It was an alert message on one of his workstation screens, stating that the Vatican's communications monitoring system had raised a Priority Four flag.

Like the *Echelon* system used by several government agencies worldwide, the Vatican's system—codenamed *Prophet*—monitored electronic and voice data across all Church-owned email accounts, landlines, and mobile phones. It kept its virtual eyes and ears open for a range of specific keywords—referred to as hot words by the Vatican's security forces—which, when used in a particular order or frequency, could suggest a threat to the Church, either physically, ideologically, or otherwise. Like any global organisation, the Catholic Church had its interests and its people to protect, and it did that, amongst other means, by utilising the latest in communications technology.

'Dannazione!' he said. *Damn it!*

He pressed the space bar on his keyboard, and the flashing alert message disappeared. An information box opened in its place. It provided a unique reference number and a time and date stamp for a few minutes earlier. It also confirmed the communication was audio—a phone call to a Church-owned number attributed to one Father Frederik Sigvardt based at Saint Ansgar's Cathedral in Copenhagen. Finally, it advised why the system had raised the alert—the hot words *Christ*, *Golgotha*, *Iscariot*, *dreams*, *abduction*, and *violent*. *Prophet* had not, however, identified the name or phone number of the person who had made the call.

Ruggeri sighed with frustration. Priority Four alerts were usually only triggered if one or more of the communicating parties used hot words that, while not constituting a direct threat to the Church, could still be significant. While the Vatican didn't consider alerts of that level serious, the flagged communication would still need to be read or listened to and then escalated to a senior Gendarmerie office for assessment and, if appropriate, further investigation. In the ever-constant struggle to remain relevant in a modern society that worshipped money, social media status, and technology more than God, the Church embraced every opportunity to investigate incidents that could endanger its continuing significance. All of which meant Ruggeri now had some actual work to do.

A triangular *Play* icon flashed on his screen. He took a set of headphones from a drawer under his workstation and plugged them into an audio interface on his desk. Then, he grabbed his mouse, clicked on the icon, and began to listen.

The flagged communication was a phone conversation between Sigvardt and someone who identified herself simply as Em. In it, they discussed someone called Ellie, who was having strange dreams. He listened with a lack of interest but decided, mainly to cover his back, that it was important enough to escalate. He opened his internal email account, started a new email message, and typed *bag* in the *To* line. Before he could type anything more, the email software automatically completed the recipient's name.

As he typed, a quiet beep and the *shoosh* of something brushing across the thin carpet tiles broke his concentration. He looked up to see a colleague enter the room. He wasn't sure if personnel from an external agency could strictly be called colleagues, but he afforded them a degree of professional courtesy regardless.

The colleague in question was Interpol officer Nina Weiss. She was from Austria or Switzerland—he could never remember and didn't care. He did know, though, that he found her attractive despite her cold, mechanical demeanour. Maybe she was German. She was there because, besides being the Gendarmerie's central security hub for the city-state, the Operations and Control Room also served as one of Interpol's one hundred and ninety-two National Central Bureaus.

The door closed behind Weiss with a soft click. Ruggeri nodded as she made her way across the carpet, and flashed her a muted smile. She disliked the guy. He was always courteous enough, but something about him made her cringe. Her workstation was identical to his and was landlocked between it and a flanking wall, so she had to walk behind him to access it. When she reached him, he pulled his chair in to let her through. As she passed behind him, she noticed the alert on his screen and the string of hot words it had flagged.

'Thanks,' she said. 'That looks interesting.'

'Probably not. It's only a P-four. A telephone call from some therapist to some priest about some patient dreaming about Christ. It's very... how do you say it? Mundane? But it still needs to be reported, so I'm sending it to Baglioni.'

'What will he do with it?'

'Either log it and forget about it or kick it upstairs and forget about it.'

She knew that by kicking it upstairs, it would eventually reach a cardinal named Peter Barjona, responsible for the department that physically investigated the more serious *Prophet* alerts. She mentally noted the reference number in the information box on the screen and continued to her workstation.

Given how closely Interpol and the Gendarmerie worked together, all Interpol officers in the Vatican had access to *Prophet*, which was already running on her computer in a minimised window. She rescaled the window to half its full size, clicked in the *Search* box, and typed the reference number she'd memorised. The details immediately appeared in an information box, including the associated *Play* icon.

She fished her headphones from her workstation drawer. Unlike Ruggeri's, they were noise-cancelling—a set she'd personally brought in. She plugged them in, turned them on, and double-clicked the *Play* icon. She listened to the telephone conversation between Sigvardt and the therapist, then listened to it again.

So far, all she'd done was listen to an audio file on a system she legitimately had unrestricted access to. Nothing the video recordings from the wall-mounted dome cameras behind her would show as a violation of protocols, and nothing the Vatican's cyber security team, based in another windowless room, might consider a risk to the Church or the Vatican specifically. No firewalls were breached, no systems hacked.

Everything was above board.

She looked over at Ruggeri. He was too wrapped up in writing his email to pay her attention. She took a long breath, then simultaneously pinched and held the + and - buttons on the headphones' volume control unit, activating a miniature digital recorder housed in the right earpiece. She replayed the audio file of the priest's conversation with the therapist. This time, every word was recorded onto a removable micro-SIM housed underneath the battery compartment in the left earpiece.

As the headphones recorded the telephone conversation, she reviewed the information box. *Prophet* recognised Sigvardt's details, but there were none for the woman who'd called him—probably because her phone was likely not Church-owned and possibly because her number may have been unlisted. She clicked on Sigvardt's name, and the screen displayed all his details, including his home and work addresses.

She fiddled with the top button of her shirt. Contained within it was a miniature camera made of plastics and polymers that were undetectable to the body scanners she had to pass through each day upon entry to the building. The camera's lens had a wide field of view, and the sensor inside it was of a high enough resolution that it would capture an image of the screen that could be resized and read easily on a laptop's screen or even a desktop monitor. To be safe, though, she took four photographs of her screen to ensure that at least one picture captured everything she needed.

Later, after she finished her shift, she would check the recording and the photographs at home and send them by encrypted email to the man she reported to. A man based far from Rome and not connected with Interpol or the Vatican. She closed the information box, and all other screen data relating to the P-four alert *Prophet* had raised, opened her Interpol email program, and began her usual work of the day.

13

FRIDAY

Ellie sat on the sofa in Carlsson's front room, hugging a large mug of sweet black coffee. No tea for her today. She needed something more robust, and in the absence of a shot of whisky or vodka, coffee would have to do. She'd been early again, so Carlsson had put her in the front room, then disappeared. The morning sun came in through the windows but did nothing to warm her or lift her spirits. Her stomach churned, and she thought she might vomit. She wasn't usually anxious, but something about meeting the priest unsettled her. She took a large swig of coffee, which, despite the two spoons of sugar she'd dumped into it, tasted more bitter than usual. She hoped it wasn't a bad omen.

She heard the doorbell ring, Carlsson's footsteps on the timber floor in the hallway, and then muted voices—Carlsson's and a man's. She couldn't hear what they were saying, but she could make out the tone, and it sounded friendly. There was even some laughter.

The door opened, and she stood up, which she briefly thought was ridiculous. This guy was a local priest, not a head of state. But she was nervous, and, despite having a few rough edges, she was still a good person, and standing up was the polite thing to do.

Her stomach heaved again. She realised she was clutching the coffee mug so tightly that her knuckles had turned white. She relaxed her grip and took in a lung-filling breath. Carlsson came into the room first, with a broad smile on her face, still chuckling. They must have had a joke in the hallway. So, the therapist hadn't lied when she said she was good friends with this guy. Ellie's stomach churned a little less.

The man who followed Carlsson into the room wasn't what she'd expected. He wore dark brown boots, smart indigo jeans, and a chocolate-coloured fur-lined leather jacket with thick patches of the same leather at the shoulders and elbows. Under the coat were a black shirt and the trademark white dog collar. She knew it had an official name, but she was fucked if she knew it. He was roughly the same age as Carlsson, if not a little older, and he was also a little taller. His hair was thin and receding. It looked well-cut but scruffy as if he'd just smoothed it with his hand instead of combing or brushing it. The motorcycle helmet he held explained it all.

A biker priest.

Interesting.

'Ellie, this is Father Sigvardt.'

'It's a pleasure to meet you, Ellie,' Sigvardt said, holding out his hand. 'And please, call me Fred.'

'You too,' she said, taking his hand. 'I think.'

She allowed herself another quick body scan of him, and he must have noticed because a look of amusement passed over his face.

'You weren't expecting me to be a motorcyclist?'

She was embarrassed. She had a picture of this guy in her mind before she'd even met him and, she knew, had probably already judged him unfairly, at least subconsciously. And worse, he saw it and called her on it.

'Not many people do,' he continued. 'That's part of the fun I get when I turn up like this to weddings and christenings. And especially funerals. People give me the best looks at those.'

An almost imperceptible crinkle touched the corner of Sigvardt's mouth, and at that moment, his eyes seemed to catch a little more light. Ellie decided she liked this guy.

'Maja's told me—' He broke off and looked at Carlsson. 'Sorry. I should have asked earlier. Are you Maja or Doctor Carlsson in these sessions? I don't want to break any ground rules.'

'Maja's fine, Fred,' she said, gently touching his arm.

'So, as I was saying, Maja told me you're a bit nervous about my coming here today. I can understand that. After all, the last thing you want is me calling in the black van to whisk you away for an exorcism.'

'You don't actually still do those, do you?'

Another tiny crinkle at the corner of his mouth. He looked at Carlsson and gestured to the high-backed chair.

'Of course,' said Carlsson, mirroring the gesture. 'Do you want some tea, Fred?'

'I'd love some. Chamomile, if you have it.'

Carlsson glanced at Ellie and gave her a slight nod. 'Back in a second,' she said.

Sigvardt took off his jacket, placed it over the arm of the ruby chair, and sat down. He moved around in it for a few moments.

'Oh, this is incredible,' he said. 'Super comfortable. I think I'll have to get myself one of these. My old leather thing is lovely, but it's too bloody lumpy.'

Ellie raised her eyebrows at him.

'What?' he asked.

'Uh, *bloody*?'

'Oh, that,' he said, with a dismissive wave. 'You didn't expect a priest to curse?'

'I'm learning very quickly not to have any expectations about priests.' She gave him an exaggerated look up and down.

He grinned. 'I wasn't always a priest and old habits die hard. I even listen to Springsteen. A guilty pleasure I never quite managed to deny myself.' He shuffled again in the chair and patted its arm. 'I think I'll have to get myself one of these and get rid of my lumpy *bloody* thing.'

She laughed.

'What do you ride?' she asked.

'You know motorcycles?'

'What? You didn't expect a chick to know bikes?'

'Ha! Touché. I've got a Royal Enfield five-hundred.'

'You should talk to my boyfriend, Jakob. He'd love you.'

'He's a biker, too?'

'Bikes are in his blood. He rides an Interceptor at the moment. Works over at Goat's Customs.'

'I've heard of that place. It's supposed to be very good.'

'They do the usual mechanic stuff as well as custom jobs, so next time your Enfield needs servicing, take it there and tell them I sent you. They'll do you a good deal. And if they don't, you let me know.'

'Thank you, Ellie. I will. So, if you don't mind me asking, what do you do for a living?'

'I'm a tattooist. I work in a studio on Bredgade.'

'Double D's?'

'How would you—'

He rolled up his left sleeve. On the inner side of his forearm was an elaborate tattoo of a cross, riddled with Celtic filigrees.

'Dagmar did that for you?' she asked, surprised.

'Lord, no. She's far too young to have done this. I had it done a few years before I took the cloth. I wasn't particularly religious at the time but crosses like this were all the rage then. I got it done by Dagmar's grandfather, Henrik. A big bear of a man and an excellent tattooist. Won a few awards, too. Dead now, regrettably. He had a studio down on Abel Cathrines Gade. Dagmar apprenticed under him. She was known as Double D even then.'

'And you've kept track of her all this time?'

'Actually, I'm cheating a bit. Your studio is right across the street from where I work.'

'You're from St Ansgar's?'

He nodded, and she laughed heartily.

'It looks like you two are becoming well-acquainted.' Carlsson had returned. She held out a large mug to Sigvardt, which he took with a nod of thanks.

'Indeed, we are,' he said, giving Ellie a wink and a wide grin. 'Ellie, I want you to know that I will help if I can, but I'm not a specialist in these matters. Not by any stretch. I want to make that clear at the outset. If I'm able to offer an opinion, I will. But there's no guarantee of that.'

'I understand that, and I appreciate you taking the time to help.'

'Okay. So, shall we get started then?' he asked, looking at Carlsson, who had taken a seat on the sofa next to Ellie.

'So, a little background to start with,' said Carlsson. 'Ellie first came to me earlier this week. She's been suffering from dreams for around two months or so which, as I told you on the phone, appear to have some religious context. Specifically about Christ, and people associated with him. They're occurring with increased regularity, and the last two have been more violent in content than the others.'

'Violent, how?'

'One looked like the abduction of someone we think could be Judas,' Ellie said, 'and the other was Christ's walk with the cross.'

'Yes, Maja mentioned you'd dreamed of Iscariot's abduction. You do know that he wasn't abducted, don't you? He went off into the scrubland and hanged himself.'

'I've explained to Ellie about dream triggers,' Carlsson said. 'Events that may cause us to have dreams, even without us consciously realising it. And I've also told her that those dreams may not reflect reality or what we think we know. They could manifest in any number of different ways.'

'Quite.'

'However—and here's where I need you to suspend your disbelief a little further, Fred—we discussed in our session on Wednesday that what she's experiencing may not be dreams in the strictest sense.'

'What do you mean?'

'Well, I suggested to her that she's having dreams of a non-self-character, in which she inhabits an entirely different person who can walk, talk and make decisions in its own way. But she explained that the actions of the woman from whose viewpoint she experiences the dreams never change in any recurrent dreams. It's as if she's watching a film. She sees the same thing each time she has a recurrent dream.'

'Really? There's never any variation?'

'Nope,' said Ellie. 'Everything happens the same way every time. Until I have a new dream.'

'So,' Carlsson continued, 'a tentative theory we have is that what she might be seeing are memories.'

'Memories?'

'Yes.'

'Are you suggesting that Ellie's having recollections of a past life?'

'I've been quite clear with her that reincarnation is not a theory I personally buy into, and I suspect you'll say the same.'

'I would,' said Sigvardt.

'However, I do think I owe it to Ellie to at least try to help her, which is why I asked you to join us. I know you don't subscribe, but with the dreams being biblical in context, you might see or think of something we don't. Anything is better than nothing.'

Sigvardt looked at the women in turn. Ellie was desperate, and she was sure her face gave that away. She glanced at Carlsson, whose expression was hopeful. When she looked back at Sigvardt, she could see uncertainty in his eyes. He was going to say no. She could feel it in her gut.

'Alright,' he said. 'How do you want to do this?'

Carlsson smiled. Ellie exhaled heavily and realised that she'd been holding her breath. She was partly comforted that Sigvardt was open to helping her but overshadowing that relief was the feeling that things would worsen somehow—that digging deeper wouldn't stop the dreams but would unlock even more nightmarish visions.

'In our last session,' said Carlsson, 'I suggested that we ought to try past life regression therapy.'

'You're talking about suggestive hypnosis,' Sigvardt replied.

'Yes. I want to place Ellie into a heightened state of focus and have her guide us through whatever she sees. She'll be responsive to verbal cues and will be able to respond to us.'

'Okay.'

'And, hopefully, we'll gain some insight into what's happening.'

Sigvardt looked at Ellie. Her uneasiness with the idea of hypnotherapy must have been evident because he asked, 'Are you sure you're okay with this, Ellie?'

'Not really. But if it's going to help, I need to do it. Right?'

He glanced at Carlsson, who nodded.

'Ellie, have you had any new dreams since our last session?' she asked.

'No.'

'So, Christ carrying the cross was the last one you had?'

'Yep.'

'Have you had that one since we last saw each other?'

'Yeah, last night.'

'Okay. I'd like you to try and recall what you saw. Would you be okay with that? I know it was more violent than some of your earlier dreams, and I don't want to unsettle you unnecessarily, but if you're able to recall it in as much detail as possible, it may give us something useful.'

Ellie shrugged. She wasn't looking forward to what was coming next, but if she wanted to stop the dreams, or at least understand why she was having them, what choice did she have?

Carlsson got up from the sofa and went to her desk. She grabbed her office chair and pulled it around the desk, its wheeled castors making it easy to move. She positioned it next to the ruby chair where Sigvardt sat and faced it toward the sofa. Then she went to the sash windows and closed the curtains. The room darkened but didn't go pitch black.

'Before we begin, Ellie,' she said, 'I want you to know that you'll be completely safe during this process and remain in full control of your thoughts, actions, and yourself. And whenever you want to return to consciousness, simply open your eyes.'

'Really? It's that easy?'

'It's that easy.'

Ellie exhaled deeply. As long as she was in control, she'd be okay.

'Now, take off your boots and lie down with your feet at this end.' Carlsson gestured to the end of the sofa closest to her chair so that Ellie's head would be at the other end and more easily observable by both Carlsson and Sigvardt.

She complied.

Softly, Carlsson told her to relax her body, straighten her legs, and put her arms by her sides. Then she began to speak slowly, in hushed tones, inviting her to enter a state of conscious listening and unconscious observation, ignoring all distractions. After a short time, Carlsson said she was happy that Ellie was where she needed to be.

But she wasn't.

She was somewhere else.

14

It's the middle of the night when she makes her way to the city's outskirts with Shimon, and despite the warm breeze, a chill grips her body. It's been five days since they took Yehuda. When Shimon told her that he'd found out where they'd taken him, she'd pleaded until her throat was sore for him to take her there. He'd been reluctant, of course, claiming that it would be too dangerous even for him alone, and he couldn't guarantee that he could protect her. She'd told him she didn't care and that he must take her to her husband.

They silently take an indirect route to where he'd said they needed to go, seeking cover behind the largest rocks and the thickest trees they find. While the waning moon illuminates their path, their journey across the rocky scrubland has been difficult—she's jarred her ankle twice since leaving the city gates behind.

As they creep along, she hears hushed voices in the distance. Shimon has heard them too, and gestures for her to hunker down behind the broad trunk of an old olive tree. This is the place. She knows it must be so. She holds her breath, afraid that even the slightest exhalation would give away their presence. Shimon gently touches her wrist. She knows he can sense her anguish and fear. He makes a slow, breathe-in, breathe-out motion with his left hand, and as she watches it, she feels her chest begin to rise and fall to the same rhythm.

He smiles. He points to his chest, his eyes, and then in the direction of the voices. He's telling her he's going to take a closer look. He points *at her and then to the ground.*

Stay here.

She nods her agreement.

The time that he is gone—in reality, only moments—is an agonising eternity. He returns, his face grave and sad. She shakes her head, a gesture of enquiry. She wants to know what he's seen. His head drops for a few seconds, and when it comes back up, his eyes are full of tears. He shakes his head and reaches out to take her arm and lead her away. She shrugs him off and shakes her head once, firmly.

No!

She must see for herself.

She creeps forward, careful not to step on any loose rocks or fallen twigs that might crunch or snap underfoot, giving her away to whoever is ahead of her. The hushed voices grow louder as she inches onward.

She comes to the edge of a small clearing. Within it are four men. Three are squatting and playing a game with dice. The fourth is standing at the far side of the clearing with his back to them. He bounces on his heels a few times, wipes a hand on his long tunic, and returns to his associates. It looks like he was urinating.

She expects to find her husband bound by his hands and feet, tied to the trunk of a tree. But when she sees the body hanging from the tree by the neck, she's struck by a horror she has never known before. The person suspended there, twisting in the breeze, is unrecognisable. His clothes are shredded and blood-soaked. Through rips in the cloth, she can see deep lines of red scored into his skin. Someone has lashed him with a whip or a branch. Her gaze drifts down his body, and she can see that his hands are bloodied and contorted. They've broken his fingers. Her eyes travel further, and she sees that his feet, covered in dusty, syrupy blood, have been crushed, probably with rocks or hammers. Finally, she looks back at the man's face. Despite the mask of congealed blood, hair and dirt, and the shattered nose and crushed, bloodied cheekbones, she recognises him.

It's her Yehuda.

Why have they done this to him? What is his crime? To love humankind and to want to liberate them from the shackles of religious tyranny? How could that be a crime? Desperate and pain-wracked, she is about to howl into the night air when his body moves.

Just the wind, she thinks.

Then it moves again, and then a third time. She goes to move closer, but Shimon, who has silently moved up beside her, grabs her wrist and silences her with a cautionary gesture—a single finger raised to his mouth. But she cannot be quiet. Will not. She must let her husband know she's there for him and damn the risk to herself for doing so. If they catch her, let them hang her next to her husband so she may die by his side.

Before she can pull away from Shimon's grip, two new figures come to the edge of the clearing on the far side. They remain in the shadows, unseen. The man who'd been urinating approaches them and nods, and the others stand up. They cluster together and speak in muted tones, too quiet for her to hear.

One of them walks to a rolled-up piece of dark cloth on the ground, tied at each end with twine. He squats down, unties the strings, and rolls open the fabric. When he stands again, he holds a long, thick sword. He goes to the tree from which Yehuda hangs and swings the blade above her husband's head. Nothing happens for a few moments, then the rope crackles and snaps, and his body thumps to the ground.

Another man kicks him in the stomach as he lies on his side on the ground. The man kicks him a second time, then again, and again. Before the man can land the fifth blow, Yehuda stirs. He spits a mouthful of blood on the dirt, then draws his knees up to his chest and slowly rolls onto them. His forehead is planted on the stony ground as if he's praying, but she knows he wouldn't be. He rests there for a few seconds and then, with clearly incredible effort, pivots at the waist and hauls his torso upright. She watches as he glares at each of his captors through scratched and swollen eyes.

And then his gaze comes to rest on the figures in the shadows.

The unseen figures come into the clearing, their faces illuminated enough by the moonlight for her to recognise them. One of them is Kepha, the bastard who'd led the attackers that invaded Shimon's house and took her husband. He wears a bandage on his left ear where Shimon had sliced it. Good. She hopes it will become infected, although she suspects that will be unlikely. The sight of the other man turns her stomach.

It's her sister's husband.

Yeshua.

If she didn't know who he truly is, what he truly is, she would be terrified to see him risen from the grave. But her husband had told her everything—about himself, his father, Yeshua, and the others. And the ongoing struggle and seemingly irresolvable divide between the two sides.

Yeshua crouches in front of her husband and gently lifts his face. She can hear what he says. His words drip with venom. He says it's poetic that her husband will die on the same day that he has risen. Then he stands and gestures to the man with the sword. The man obediently hands over the weapon. Yeshua takes the blade and walks to Yehuda's side, his back to her. As he raises the sword, she hears her husband tell him, in a pained, hoarse voice, that this will not be the end.

The sword falls.

As Yehuda's head rolls in the dirt, it's all she can do to hold back the vomit that has come up to her throat. She gags and swallows it back down noisily. Yeshua must hear her because when her eyes clear and she raises her head to look back to the clearing, she sees that he's looking in her direction. He's smiling as if he knows she or someone else is hiding there, and it seems he cannot care less that someone has seen him and his cohorts torture and execute her husband.

Why would he? He's the saviour. The Messiah. Who would believe he is capable of such a thing? Who would trust her word over his?

Her final thought as Shimon drags her away is that even in the darkness, she recognises the tree her husband had hung from as a purple-flowered Eurasian tree. One that she had, until then, regarded as a pretty tree, but from now on, would be one that she would associate only with one thing.

Death.

15

Ellie slid into a state of silent blackness. After what seemed like an age, a faint murmur broke through the quietness—a vague hum that seemed to come and go. She realised someone was talking but couldn't distinguish the words or who spoke them. As the fog in her mind dissipated, the murmuring became clearer. Someone was calling her name. She didn't want to open her eyes. Not yet. She wanted to go back under, but not to where she'd just been. She wanted to go somewhere else, somewhere with only blackness.

With nothingness.

'Ellie, can you hear me?'

It wasn't going to work. She was back now, and she wasn't going under again. Feeling soft, comfortable fabric beneath her, she opened her eyes unhurriedly and glanced around. She was back in Doctor Carlsson's front room. The curtains were open. Carlsson was leaning forward in her desk chair looking worried. Sigvardt's red chair was empty.

'Are you alright?' asked Carlsson as she regained her composure.

'Yeah, I think so. Did it work?'

'Not exactly.'

'What do you mean?'

Sigvardt returned, holding a glass of water, and also appeared concerned. He handed her the glass. She thanked him as she took it and then drank a sip of the cold and refreshing water as he sat back down in his chair.

'You went completely under,' Carlsson said. 'You were unresponsive to anything either of us said to you.'

'Shit.'

'Can you remember anything you saw or experienced while you were... wherever you were?'

Ellie shook her head and shrugged.

'Just take your time with it.'

She breathed deeply through her nose, then took another sip of water and let it wash over her parched throat. The other two looked at her expectantly. Carlsson seemed calmer now, but Sigvardt was cleaning under the fingernails on each hand with the thumbnail of the other, clearly still agitated.

'It was an entirely new dream,' she said eventually, knowing she couldn't stall any longer.

'Already?' Carlsson asked, surprised. 'That's a rapid progression from the last one.'

'Yeah.'

'What can you remember of it?'

'I didn't say anything when I was under? I thought you were going to guide me and have me tell you what I was seeing.'

'I did, but, as I said, you were unresponsive. You were completely immersed in the vision.'

'That's never happened to me before. Having a dream when I haven't been asleep, I mean. At least, I don't think it has.'

'I wouldn't consider *that* the unusual aspect of this, Ellie. With hypnotherapy, you should still be aware enough to communicate and accept suggestions. What's curious here is that we lost that connection with you. It's as if the dream completely took over so that you could see whatever it needed to show you without interruption.'

'Holy fuck.'

Carlsson winced and looked at Sigvardt.

'No offence, Father,' Ellie said.

'None taken,' he replied, with a smile and a dismissive wave.

'So,' Carlsson said, 'do you think you'll be able to walk us through what you saw?'

Ellie inhaled so deeply it almost hurt, then started to describe, in precise detail, what she'd just seen.

'That's absurd!' Sigvardt proclaimed.

He was familiar with the more popular conspiracy theories surrounding Christ—magician and con artist, time traveller, husband of Mary Magdalene and progenitor of the royal bloodlines of Europe, and even that Judas Iscariot had died on the cross in his place. He usually brushed those off as nonsense. Never had he heard of Christ being the executioner of Judas or even being directly involved in his death, and it angered him for some reason unknown to him.

'That's not only ridiculous, it's blasphemous!'

He shot out of his chair, glaring at Ellie, who looked from him to Carlsson, clearly seeking her intervention. Carlsson reached up and placed a hand on his arm.

'Fred—'

He shook her off, paced to the windows, and stared out at the street, clenching and unclenching his hands and taking deep breaths. His insides churned at the thought of Ellie's allegations against Christ.

'Christ wasn't a kidnapper or a murderer,' he protested, turning back to the room. 'Yes, he was driven, perhaps even aggressively committed to his cause. And yes, he was known to have a temper. But I cannot believe that he was capable of such terrible things as you've described.'

'I'm not saying I believe it, Father,' Ellie replied with a tremor in her voice, and what he could see might be the start of tears in her eyes. 'I'm just telling you what I saw.'

'It could mean absolutely nothing, Fred,' Carlsson said. 'Especially within the context of what the Bible tells us. Everything that Ellie has seen could simply be manifestations created by her unconscious mind using familiar figures to convey to her a message.'

'Which would be what?'

While he was sympathetic to Ellie's plight and was painfully aware of how distressed she was, her accusations—for that's what they were, whichever way one looked at it—rankled him.

'I don't know,' Carlsson said.

'Do you believe that whatever she's seeing is purely symbolic? Some sort of allegorical representation of something yet to be interpreted?'

'I don't know, Fred. It's entirely poss—'

'Or do you think it could be more likely that this is another one of countless attacks on the church? Intended to weaken an organisation that, despite its many faults, only wants to serve as a beacon of hope in a world that becomes more morally bankrupt by the day?'

'I'm not saying it's anything yet, Fred. Frankly, it's all highly unusual. But I do think that Ellie's concerns are genuine and that she's here for our help, and I also believe that storming around in a rage isn't doing anyone any good, so why don't you sit down and we can all try and discuss this a little more rationally.

'What do you intend to do, Ellie? Pose as a new prophet and start a cult?'

'That's enough, Fred,' Carlsson warned.

'Or hold the church to ransom? Extort money from the church to keep silent?'

'Father Sigvardt.'

Carlsson's tone was quiet but firm.

Sigvardt could almost feel his blood pressure hitting a point of no return. The last thing he needed was to suffer an aneurysm. And he knew he must give Ellie the benefit of the doubt and his support. Regardless of what she'd said, it would be unchristian of him to do otherwise. He took a few deep, calming breaths and slowly lowered himself back into the chair, pushing against its tall back once he sat down.

'So, what do we do now?' Ellie asked as if his outburst hadn't happened. A ripple of shame flowed through him. She was far more charitable than he.

Carlsson looked at him.

'Fred, if we ignore whether what Ellie has seen is or isn't what's commonly believed to be true—'

He went to interrupt, but Carlsson held up her hand and stopped him.

'Not everyone is religious or believes what the Bible says,' she continued. 'Plenty of people have their doubts about the veracity of the book. You know that's the case, and I thought you accepted that people are entitled to believe what they want.'

He stiffened and then sagged back into the chair, resignation trumping indignation.

'And,' she went on, 'I'm sure Ellie doesn't have a grand plan to take down the church.'

'Of course,' he said quietly, ashamed of his eruption. 'I *do* believe that people are entitled to think what they want. That's the point of our God-given free will. But sometimes, that belief and its practice don't always meet.' He turned to Ellie. 'I'm sorry, Ellie. I'm supposed to be helping you, not attacking you.'

'It's okay.'

'No. It's not. You're not the first to come to me with a revelation about the Church or the Bible. Usually, I can contain myself when I hear such things, but what you've just told me goes beyond anything I've ever heard. I honestly don't know what came over me. I know many aspects of the Bible are likely to be either purely symbolic or flagrant exaggerations. But because of my faith in Christ as a healer and a preacher of kindness and forgiveness, what you said about him killing Judas was... well, it was almost as if it were an attack on me, personally. Does that make any sense to you?'

'Really,' Ellie said, smiling. 'I get it.'

'So,' said Carlsson, looking back and forth at Ellie and Sigvardt. 'The rate at which new dreams occur seems to be increasing. That much appears clear. The questions are, why are they happening, what's the significance of their religious context, and why the increased rate of occurrence? Any ideas on the first two questions, Fred?'

Sigvardt felt lost in the wilderness, with no compass to guide him home.

'I honestly don't know. Let's take the second question first. What's the religious significance? The only explanation I could accept is that, regardless of whether you consider yourself a religious person, Ellie, these characters are familiar to you. Your subconscious mind has chosen to use them to convey whatever message it needs to. I'm afraid I can't accept your theory that these are memories of a past life. If you seek acceptance of that notion, I think you're better off visiting the local Hindu temple.'

'You don't think it could even be possible?' Ellie asked.

'No. I'm afraid I don't. Apart from the fact that it's contrary to scripture—Hebrews nine twenty-seven, should you wish to look it up—and that it would devalue Christ's manifestation after the crucifixion, I can't see how it would even make sense. If God intended for our souls to occupy new bodies upon death, why would He have given us bodies at all? Why not just let our souls exist without the need for physical shells? The Hindus believe that our souls are continuously reincarnated until we achieve enlightenment, at which point we're released from that cycle and the material world. But that theory doesn't even make sense. How can we learn if we have no clear, persisting memories of our past lives? The only concept I can readily accept is that of ultimate resurrection—we get one shot at life, and if we get it right and we're deemed worthy by God, He gives our souls new, immortal bodies after the end of days.'

'Sure, because that's way more believable than people having past lives.'

He caught the sarcasm in Ellie's voice and chuckled.

'That's a fair comment.'

'So, if we don't agree on why the dreams have a religious theme or why I'm having them in the first place, where do we go from here?'

He shifted in his chair, knowing that she would probably not welcome what he was about to suggest.

'Well, as I've said before, and as my inability to add anything positive today demonstrates, this is not my field. However, I do have a colleague who may be able to help. Truth be told, I've only met him once, briefly. His name is Leonard Byrne. From Dublin, I believe, but now based in London. He's a bishop and, if I recall correctly, also a clinically certified psychiatrist. This *is* his field. I believe he started in religious counselling, but now he specialises in religious dream interpretation. He's the Vatican's top man in this area. With your permission, Ellie, I'd like to contact him.'

She was quiet. He could sense her resistance, and he knew what she must be thinking—another priest to accuse her of blasphemy.

'Honestly, Ellie,' he said. 'I realise this is difficult for you, and I'm sure you don't want to be pushed around from person to person trying to find answers, but I'm at a complete loss and, frankly, I'm not sure what—'

'Okay.'

'Okay, I should stop my snivelling and shut up, or okay, you're happy for me to contact him?'

'I'm starting to lose my shit with this stuff, Father, and at this point, I'm ready to look at all options short of a lobotomy.'

'I think we also ought to continue with our sessions, Ellie, regardless of whether Fred's colleague can help,' Carlsson said. 'Are you happy for those to continue?'

'Like I said, Maja. All options.'

'In that case,' said Sigvardt, 'I'll contact Leonard tonight.'

'*I need to get really fucking drunk.*'

'It didn't go well with the priest, then?'

When Ellie called Jakob, he was in the middle of adjusting the front brake callipers on the Zed, which was still on the hydraulic lift. Needing both hands for the job, he activated the phone's speaker function and placed it on one of the lift's runners.

'*Not really,*' she said. '*I had a new one.*'

'What? So soon? How?'

'*I don't know. The same way I've had all the others, I guess. It just happened. Maja did the hypnotherapy to help me recall things I'd seen in the last one, and the new one just popped right in there. And, she said I was completely unresponsive to her while I was out of it, which shouldn't have happened, apparently.*'

'Shit. What was it about?'

'*It was fucking weird. But, first things first, before I forget. The priest rides an Enfield.*'

'Okay.'

'*He's heard of Goat's place, so I told him to go and see you guys the next time he needs a service, and you'll do him a good deal. His name is Frederik Sigvardt.*'

'Oh-kay. So, the dream?'

'*Yeah, so Maja did her thing. It was so weird having two strangers watch me go to sleep. I felt very uncomfortable. But then I was Marta again, like always. I was creeping around outside of the walls of whatever town it was. Jerusalem, I guess. It was at night. I was with that guy, Shimon. We came across a clearing in the trees, and I saw...*'

She drifted off. Jakob remained silent, giving her the space to get wherever she was going in her own time. Pushing would only slow her down or black things out of her mind.

'*It was fucking horrible, Jakob. A group of men were standing around a guy they'd hung from a tree. The guy was Judas. They'd whipped him and beat the shit out of him. He was a real fucking mess.'*

'Fuck.'

'I felt her pain, Jakob. Every ounce of it. Like it was my own. It was so real. It was like it could've been you up there on the tree.'

'Jesus Christ.' Jakob put down his torque wrench and leaned with both hands against the lift.

'Oh, he was there, too.'

'Huh?'

'He and another guy—Kepha, who'd had his ear chopped when they kidnapped Judas—were there. I didn't see them at first. They stayed hidden in the shadows. But when they turned up, the others chummed up to them, and they all started chatting. Then, one of them takes this giant sword out of a blanket and chops the rope Judas was hanging from. Judas drops to the floor, and then another guy starts kicking him. It was fucking barbaric.

'Then Judas gets on his knees. How he managed it, I have no idea. It must've taken so much effort, but I think he wanted to face Jesus. I think he wanted to look him in the eye.'

'You do realise that none of this makes any sense, right? I mean—'

'I know, Jakob! I know how fucking ridiculous all of this sounds!'

He paused for a second, remembering that she was barely holding things together and that what she needed from him was patience and support, not to be criticised or second-guessed. 'So, what happened next?'

She fell silent again. This time he did push, albeit gently.

'Ellie?'

He heard her sigh on the other end of the line—a deep sigh, like she'd had enough, like she didn't want to keep talking about it.

'Ells?'

'Jesus came out from the shadows, squatted in front of Judas, and taunted him. And then he took the sword from the guy who'd cut down

Judas. He held it up, and then Judas spoke to him. He said it would not be the end.'

'End of what?'

'Dude, really?'

'Okay. So, then what?'

'Then, Jesus cut Judas's head off.'

'What the fuck?'

'Yep.'

'Holy shit, Ellie.'

'Yeah. The priest wasn't impressed. He went nuts and called me a blasphemer. I thought he was going to have a stroke or something. I reckon if he'd have had any holy water with him, he'd have thrown it all over me and let me burn.'

'Bloody hell.'

'He calmed down eventually and was pretty cool after that.'

'But it was only a dream, right? There's nothing to say any of it happened the way you've seen it?'

'That's what Maja said. Probably more to calm down the priest than anything. But...'

'What?'

He picked up the torque wrench again and resumed his work on the bike's brake callipers.

'I dunno. None of this makes any sense. One minute I think it's all just some weird bullshit, and the next, I start thinking it might all be true.'

'But it can't be, right? Not that last one, anyway. I'm no God-squadder, but I'm fairly sure Jesus didn't cut Judas's head off with a huge sword. Or with anything else. I think I'd remember being taught that.'

'That's obviously what the priest said. But honestly, I don't give a shit, Jakob.'

The wrench slipped out of his greasy hands as he tightened a bolt on the callipers, and it fell to the ground with a clatter.

'*Have you got me on speaker?*' she asked.

'Yeah. I'm in the middle of something I need two hands for.'

'*That's what she said.*'

'Nice.'

'*Can you take me off speaker for a minute? I don't want the guys hearing any of this.*'

'Goat's in the office with the door shut, and Chewie's gone out for what he calls his union-mandated coffee break, but okay. Just a sec.'

Jakob grabbed a cloth and wiped his hands, then deactivated the phone's speaker and wedged it between his ear and shoulder.

'How's that?'

'*Better. Thanks. Sorry, I just... I'm freaked out enough, and I know they already know what's been going on with me, but I just don't want to broadcast it, you know?*'

'It's okay, babes. I get it.'

'*Chewie does know there's no union for independent bike mechanics, right?*'

'Probably not, although the fact he doesn't pay any union subscriptions should be a dead giveaway. So, what happens now? What does the priest think about it?'

'*He's at a loss, which doesn't surprise me. He did say at the beginning that dream interpretation isn't his thing. Even after he'd calmed down, he still looked upset. Not angry upset. Sad upset. I think I may have shaken his faith a bit.*'

'Doubtful. You know those Catholics. They're hardcore believers. You could tell him that God's some sort of malignant being who enjoys human suffering and only put us here to fight each other so he and Satan could watch and place bets, and he'd still be right there every Sunday conducting his masses.'

'*Maybe. He's going to contact a colleague of his. Some guy in London. Apparently, he's some kind of magician when it comes to this shit. The Vatican's official dream whisperer, or something.*'

'So, he does think there's something to these visions, then?'

'Fuck knows. I think it's more that he knows he can't help me personally and feels bad about that, so he doesn't just want to walk away and let Maja deal with me on her own. Anyway, fuck it. I don't want to talk about it anymore today. I just want to get fucking obliterated tonight. I'm thinking Rust, or maybe Vega.'

'How about Dante's? Hellenbach's playing.'

'Yeah, that works. Maybe you should ask Goat and Natasja to come along. And Chewie. I'll ask Sooz if she wants to come. I know she could do with a decent night out.'

'Ooh, that might not be a good idea. Asking Suzi, I mean.'

'Why not?'

'Come on. You know Chewie's got a thing for her.'

I know, but she doesn't swing that way.'

'I know that, and you know that, and even Chewie knows it, but he's got some fucked-up notion that he'll be the one to turn her. So it could get messy.'

'It'll be fine. God, you're such an old lady.'

'I'm sorry. I missed that. My hearing aid's on the blink.'

'Funny.'

'I don't think I've got any going-out clothes at yours, so I'll need to head back to mine after work. See you at Dante's around, what, eight-ish?'

'You're on.'

16

Father Sigvardt sat in the armchair in his study with his laptop perched on his thighs. He stared at the screen and blew out hard. His email program was open, but the *New Message* window on the screen was blank. The cursor flashed impatiently at him, serving only to frustrate him. A few minutes ago, he'd closed the room's heavy curtains to shut out the distracting sodium glare from the streetlights, but he still couldn't concentrate. He pinched the bridge of his nose and exhaled forcefully again.

'Just write it, you old fool,' he muttered.

He struggled with a battle of conscience versus faith. He wanted to help Ellie. He *had* to help her. Everything in him that made him a good man told him so. But everything that made him a priest argued against it. He found it difficult to reconcile the events she described with what his faith told him was true.

He knew, and would happily admit to anyone, that there were likely many historical inaccuracies in the Bible—the four canonical gospels alone were evidence of that. And he knew that those who'd collated it in the early part of the first millennium might have purposefully omitted some, if not many, truths. But to think that parts of the New Testament might have been blatantly and shamelessly fabricated—and worse, that Christ was a murderer—was a crushing prospect. It couldn't be so. His faith told him it couldn't be so. And how could he question his faith?

And yet.

Damn it!

He slammed his laptop shut and put it on the side table next to him, then bolted up from his chair, almost overturning it, and stormed out of his office, his mind and heart conflicted. He left his apartment, stormed down the common corridor, heaved open the building's heavy main door, and stood at the top of the three shallow steps that led down to the pavement.

He inhaled deeply through his nose, the cold winter air chilling his nostrils and biting at the back of his throat as he swallowed. He took more frosty air down into his diaphragm and held it for a moment, then blew it out through his mouth and watched it turn to mist and dissipate.

Why was he so reluctant to contact Byrne? Of what was he afraid? That one young woman claimed to have visions that contradicted the Church's teachings? So what? Throughout history, plenty of people had fabricated stories—and done worse—to discredit the Church, yet it had survived. And it would continue to endure. Wouldn't it? What harm could one woman's dreams do?

He shivered, gulped down another lungful of cold air, and then went back inside. Once back in his apartment, he walked past his office and made for the living room. Along its far wall, behind a beige three-seater sofa with billowing armrests, was a long, low wooden sideboard. He reached for a half-full bottle of Hennessy that sat on a silver tray atop the cabinet and poured himself a three-fingered measure into a heavy-bottomed tumbler from the same tray. He rested against the sofa's high back and drank a finger's worth of the honey-coloured brandy, which burned as it slid down. Despite his beliefs, he couldn't let Ellie down. He'd promised to help her, and that's what he would do.

He pushed himself off the sofa, poured another finger of brandy into his glass, and trudged back to his study. Once there, he slumped down in his chair, put the tumbler on a coaster on the side table, and grabbed his phone, having decided out on the street that a call might be better than an email. He clumsily unlocked the phone and scrolled through his contacts list, hopeful that he'd taken and saved a number for Leonard Byrne when they'd met.

He had.

He sat motionless for a few seconds, staring at the screen, then took another nip of the brandy and held the warm liquid in his mouth for a few moments before swallowing. Leaning back in his chair, he closed his eyes and savoured the tingle in his throat, then allowed his head to clear, and made the call.

17

Relaxing at home after an early finish at the cathedral, Bishop Leonard Byrne had just poured himself a large glass of Jameson whiskey and was about to put on some Einaudi or Bjørnstad when the phone in his study rang.

He sighed heavily.

He wasn't in the mood to deal with any more work issues, but curiosity and the persistent ringing drew him into the study. When he reached the phone, its screen identified the caller as Frederik Sigvardt. The name was vaguely familiar to him, and his phone's contacts list wouldn't contain the number if he hadn't met or spoken with this person at some point in the past, so he answered the call.

'Leonard Byrne.'

'Leonard. Good evening. This is Frederik Sigvardt. In Copenhagen.'

He tried to picture the face that belonged to the voice. He closed his eyes to help his recall, but the visage of this Sigvardt failed to materialise in his mind's eye.

'I apologise for calling you out of the blue, Leonard, and I'm hoping you remember me. We met in Berlin in August last year, outside the Axica building. I arrived on that rented Triumph.'

A memory flooded into his mind, making him smile.

The biker priest.

'Frederik. Of course. We were so engrossed in our conversation about motorcycles that I was almost late for my speaking slot.'

'*I hope I haven't caught you at an inconvenient time.*'

'Not at all.'

'*Excellent. While I would enjoy some more motorcycle talk, I'll get straight into it if that's okay with you.*'

'Of course.'

'*Leonard, I need your assistance and guidance in a delicate matter.*'

He patiently listened as Sigvardt told him about Ellie and her dreams. She wasn't the first person to have dreams depicting biblical figures, and she certainly wouldn't be the last, yet the Danish priest seemed oddly shaken.

'I see,' he said when it sounded like Sigvardt had reached the end. 'And I'm sensing this jarred with you, Frederik.'

'*Naturally, I cannot believe such a claim. While, as a pragmatist, I can accept that the books of Matthew and Acts appear to contradict one another with their descriptions of how Iscariot died, neither they nor any other book in the Bible tells us that he was decapitated, and certainly not by Christ. I must admit, Leonard, that Ellie's claim angered me. It felt almost like a personal attack on my faith. And I'm ashamed to say I didn't behave particularly well toward her when she recounted the dream.*'

'I can understand that, Frederik. What this Ellie described to you is so at odds with what we know of Christ that it would naturally be difficult to accept. But it doesn't necessarily mean anything.'

'*Indeed. And I've promised her that I will help in any way I can. Hence this call to you. I've explained to her that dream interpretation is a speciality of yours. If anyone can help explain why she's having these visions and, most importantly, help stop them from continuing, it would be you. Would you be willing to speak with her? I'm sure I can arrange for her to visit with Maja at a time convenient for you to have a face-to-face conversation over Skype, Zoom, or whatever is de rigueur these days. I would, of course, also be present.*'

Byrne sat back in his chair and ran his hand over the greying bristles of his ginger beard. He was all too aware there had long been speculation over the accuracy of the Bible. Particularly since the discovery of documents like the Dead Sea Scrolls and the Nag Hammadi Library—a collection of thirteen codices containing over fifty early Christian texts and gnostic gospels, most notably the Gospel of Thomas and the Gospel of Truth. Detractors of the Church claimed such documents were deliberately left out of the Bible, as they were unhelpful to the Church's goal of establishing and maintaining its orthodoxy.

More recently, there had been the discovery of a book in Turkey, believed to be between fifteen hundred and two thousand years old, containing the gospel of Christ's disciple Barnabas. Controversially, Barnabas asserted that Judas Iscariot had taken Christ's place on the cross. That book was with the Vatican for authentication and further study and would most likely never see the light of day again. But Christ being responsible for the capture of Iscariot and personally executing the man? That was indeed preposterous. Wasn't it?

'Leonard?'

He felt tempted to tell Sigvardt there was little he could do to help, and that the best thing would be for Ellie to continue with hypnotherapy and perhaps a course of medication. But professional curiosity and the vague memory of a strange rumour he'd heard while in the corridors of the Vatican over three decades earlier pushed him in the other direction.

'I'd be happy to help, Frederik.'

'Thank you, Leonard. I'm very grateful, as I'm sure Ellie will also be.'

'I'll be on my way out shortly, so perhaps we could correspond in the next day or so by email to make the necessary arrangements for a Skype call?'

'Of course. And, again, thank you. Goodnight, Leonard.'

'Goodnight.'

Byrne placed his phone on the desk and exhaled heavily. He felt a knot in his gut and wondered whether getting involved was a good idea.

18

Three minutes after Father Sigvardt had spoken with Bishop Byrne, the Vatican's *Prophet* program flagged the call as a Priority Four communication. The associated alert appeared on the central screens of the three active workstations in the Operations and Control Room. Ruggeri was operating the first workstation. A Gendarme named Nico Esposito—a native Roman and his best friend since they both joined the Gendarmerie Corps four years earlier—crewed the second station. A Russian Interpol officer named Maxim Lazarev was running the third. He suspected Lazarev could be ex-Spetsnaz, but he didn't have the guts to ask. A second Interpol officer should have been piloting the fourth desk. He'd overheard Lazarev on the phone earlier, and it sounded like the Russian's colleague would be coming on shift late. Lazarev had not looked overly upset about that.

He looked at the alert on his screen.

'I'll take this one,' he said to Esposito, knowing that while Lazarev would also have noticed the alert, he would only look at it if one of the two Gendarmerie operators suggested that he should.

'Be my guest.'

As he clicked on the alert to open the details, the security lock on the door to the room beeped, the door flew open, and a man swaggered into the room. His name was Miguel de Falla. He was the Interpol officer who should have been on shift an hour and a half earlier, and Ruggeri knew why Lazarev hadn't been bothered about him coming in late. De

Falla was a blowhard Spaniard who thought too highly of himself and whom Ruggeri would prefer to spend as little time with as possible.

He turned his attention back to his central monitor. An information box provided the reference number, a time and date stamp for three minutes earlier, and confirmation that the communication had been a phone call between two Church-owned devices—one registered to a Bishop Byrne in London, the other to a Father Sigvardt in Copenhagen. A cog in his brain turned, and the caller's name struck a chord with him.

Sigvardt.

The same priest received a phone call a few days ago about some woman having visions.

He plugged his headphones into the socket on his desk, clicked on the *Play* icon, and listened to the phone conversation. Then he replayed it. He sat back in his chair, puffed up his cheeks and blew out hard.

'Nico, come and listen to this,' he said.

'Is it important? I'm in the middle of something.'

Ruggeri glanced over and saw that his friend was reading a news article on his right-hand monitor that appeared to be about a former president of the United States.

'Forget that orange idiot. Come and listen.'

Esposito wheeled his chair across from his workstation, took the headphones, and clicked the *Play* triangle on the central screen.

'Mio Dio! That's pretty serious. I take it you're going to escalate?'

'Escalate what?' asked de Falla, the Interpol agent nobody liked.

'It's an alert,' said Esposito. 'It seems Land Rover isn't going to make the Popemobile anymore. Kia's going to build it.'

'You're an idiot.'

'I know you are, but what am I?' Esposito muttered, quietly enough for the Spaniard not to hear him.

Ruggeri chuckled.

'You're such a child,' he said to his friend.

'That I am. So, is that going to Baglioni?'

'Yeah. I'm sending it on now.'

Ruggeri entered his email software, opened a new message box, and keyed his supervisor's name in the *To* line, which automatically completed after he'd entered the first three letters. Then he clicked on the main message space and started typing, his fingers travelling quickly over the keyboard. He reminded Baglioni of the alert he'd sent a few days earlier, connected to the phone call Sigvardt had received from the therapist. Then he explained that Sigvardt, having now met the woman experiencing the dreams, appeared to consider the matter serious enough to have escalated it to Byrne, who, according to Vatican records, was one of its dream interpretation specialists.

He summarised the conversation between Sigvardt and Byrne, attached the audio file to the email, and clicked the *Send* button. The email disappeared from his screen and began and ended its journey almost instantaneously. He logged the alert in the system's database, as was required, and then closed the alert window, the information box, and the database in which he'd logged the alert. His central monitor was now back to its regular appearance of a blue background and the blacked-edged white and yellow shield logo of the Gendarmerie Corps.

In a room in another part of the Vatican's vast complex, Vice Commissario Fabrizio Baglioni was entrenched in a security protocols meeting with his counterpart in the Swiss Guard. His phone vibrated, and the screen lit up to display a preview of a newly received email. The subject line held a single word.

Urgent!

He apologised for the intrusion, opened the message, and quickly read its contents. His pulse quickened. He apologised again, rose from his chair, and left the room. He pulled a set of corded earbuds from his breast pocket, connected them to his phone, and played the audio file.

Twin lines of sweat trickled down his forehead and the back of his neck, partly because the corridor was hot and partly because he now had to forward this to someone he disliked dealing with intensely.

'Merda!' *Shit!*

He pulled up his phone's contacts list and scrolled for a name. When he found it, he pressed the number, held the phone to his ear, and waited.

Within a few seconds, the dialling tone stopped.

'*Yes, Vice Commissario?*'

It was him.

Cardinal Peter Barjona.

Across the Tiber, Interpol officer Nina Weiss had just perched on the edge of a steel barstool at a high round table outside a bar on Piazza del Fico, a quiet backstreet walled by peeling four and five-storey townhouses. The bar was on the ground floor of the same building as her small apartment.

It was her day off. She'd spent most of it as she usually spent her free time—wandering around Rome, taking photographs. She wasn't into the usual tourist-style photos. She wasn't a *happy snapper*. Her passion was candid street photography—stealthily capturing everyday life in the city—and occasionally a bit of abstract architectural stuff. Not a professional photographer, but by no means an amateur, she would describe herself, if asked, as an enthusiast.

She only ever went to this particular bar to have one or two drinks after a shift at work or a long day walking around the city. She never got drunk there or at the retro American cocktail place across the street. If she ever went on a big night out, which was rare anyway, she'd make sure it was in another part of the city.

Don't shit where you eat, as they say.

She unlaced and kicked off her walking shoes to relieve the pressure on her feet and savoured her first long draw from a large glass of cold

Beck's beer. Halfway through her second lengthy gulp, she heard a muted chime from her sling pack, which sat unzipped on the steel table next to her new Fujifilm camera. Despite the many stories of tourists' bags, cameras, wallets, and phones getting stolen from chairs and tables in broad daylight in some parts of the city, she wasn't worried about having her stuff on display. She was on a backstreet rarely visited by tourists and, therefore, bag snatchers. And she carried a gun—one not issued by Interpol. Despite the image Hollywood liked to portray of the agency, Interpol was predominantly an information hub used by police forces around the globe, and its agents were mostly unarmed administrative operatives. She'd received the gun from another organisation. One to which her loyalties truly lay.

The chime from her phone sounded like the active sonar of a submarine, and she immediately knew what she'd see on her phone's screen. She'd programmed that specific sound for one thing only.

Alerts from *Prophet* in relation to Father Frederik Sigvardt.

After she'd listened to the therapist's call to him a few days earlier, she'd set up a command instructing *Prophet* to send her any further alerts linked to communications made or received by him in which the names of the therapist or her patient were mentioned, and then delete any record of *Prophet* having sent anything.

She fished one of two phones out of her bag and briefly thumbed the disc on the front. Not long enough to unlock the device, but just enough to lighten the screen, which had already returned to black. And there it was. A green banner with white text. A message from a sender identified as Bar Italia.

Your pizza is ready.

It would appear innocent enough to an onlooker, but it meant something entirely different to her.

Information.

A lead.

A potential discovery.

She thumbed the disc on the phone again, this time for slightly longer and with more pressure. Usually, with that model of iPhone, more pressure on the button would activate Siri, the phone's voice-controlled virtual assistant. On her device, though, the disc would read her biometrics and activate an encrypted communication and database system. The background picture on the home screen—a black-and-white abstract photograph of the Heizkraftwerk Mitte power plant building in her home city of Salzburg—dissolved into thousands of pixels and disappeared. The encoded system materialised in its place.

There was only one item in the communications portal. The subject line read:

```
Priority Four Alert—Sigvardt.
```

She pressed the phone's screen where the alert was displayed. It opened, confirmed it was linked to an audio communication, and provided the names of the caller and the recipient. It identified the caller as Sigvardt. The recipient was someone called Leonard Byrne. The audio file *Prophet* had flagged was attached to the alert. She plucked a set of wireless earbuds from her bag, switched them on, put them into her ears, and then played the recording.

Weiss stiffened as she listened. Not because what she was hearing was unbelievable. In fact, it was the opposite. It was a story with which she was more than familiar. Had her placement within Interpol and the Vatican's security centre finally paid off?

She recalled the training she had received from her employers—her *real* employers; how to infiltrate *Prophet* without being detected, how to beat polygraph testing, how to survive more mentally invasive techniques of information gathering, and how to live a lie. But she was a believer, as were generations of her family before her, and she believed any potential risk to her was worth it.

She listened to the file a second time and then thumbed and swiped her way to a list of contacts. There were only three listed. She pressed the first one, listed as HQ, put the phone to her ear and waited for the call to connect. It did so almost immediately.

'It's Weiss.'

'*Yes, Nina,*' said a digitised voice, its gender indeterminate, but one which she knew didn't belong to the person she needed.

'I need to speak to him.'

'*He's indisposed.*'

'It's urgent. I've received another alert. I've found something.'

Silence came at her from the other end of the call.

She drummed her fingers impatiently on the tabletop.

More silence, then, '*Wait a moment.*'

19

The sixty-inch television mounted to the wall of the south-eastern corner office was tuned to a news channel alternating between its main stories of a possible recession, a legal battle between a tech firm's CEO and a social media platform, and a looming war between China and practically everyone else. The man watching the broadcast sighed heavily. Nothing ever changes, he thought. He drifted off, focusing on a point beyond the TV screen. A knock on his office door brought him back. He picked up the remote for the TV and muted the sound as his assistant came in, her palm covering the mouthpiece of a cordless phone.

'Simon, I have Nina Weiss. She said, and I quote, "It's urgent. I've received another alert. I've found something".'

Simon nodded and stood up from his plush swivel chair. His assistant handed him the phone and left the office, closing the door behind her. Once the door was shut, he lifted the phone to his face.

'Nina.'

'Simon. Apologies if I've disturbed you.'

'No apology necessary. Always happy to take your call. What have you got for me?'

Weiss summarised the phone conversation between Father Sigvardt and Bishop Byrne, then remained silent as he considered what she'd told him.

'Send the recording,' he said finally.

'Understood.'

126

'And, Nina?'

'*Yes?*'

'Excellent work.'

He ended the call before she could respond, then placed the phone on his desk, walked to the window, and looked through a thick pane of multi-layered polymer glass that was bombproof and bulletproof and covered in a tinted film that eliminated ultraviolet transmission. From his vantage point, on the sixty-eighth floor of 875 North Michigan Avenue, formerly known as the John Hancock Center, he could see most of south Chicago and the vastness of Lake Michigan to the east. He exhaled, watched the white triangular sails of yachts and the choppy wakes of day cruisers on the lake, and wondered how useful Weiss's information would be.

He was, in effect, the chief operating officer of an organisation founded in Jerusalem over two thousand years earlier. To those aware of their existence, they were known as the Sicarii.

The Sicarii operated in the shadows. When conducting physical operations, its personnel preferred to work under the cover of darkness. When making financial transfers, it did so through a web of discreet accounts identified by numbers rather than names, held in countries where banks weren't required to report their clients' activities. When buying or selling real estate, vehicles, or other tangible assets, it conducted the transactions through shell corporations, usually within other shell corporations.

The group owned, had infiltrated, and had well-placed support in governments, organisations of faith, and corporations at the forefront of advances in computer technology and communications development, medical research and development companies, transportation firms, and weapons manufacturers worldwide. And its investments, directly in its business dealings and through speculation on the global stock markets, the mining and selling of cryptocurrencies, and the trading of NFTs, had made it incredibly well-funded.

The Sicarii had around fourteen hundred operatives spread across the globe. Most, primarily from families who'd worked for the organisation for generations, performed intelligence-gathering, digital espionage, armouring, logistics, and the like.

And then there were those like Simon.

Two hundred and twenty-three of them.

They were the warriors.

They were the hunters.

He inhaled deeply and shoved his hands into the pockets of his trousers. A tingle of excitement ran through him, and his irises flickered briefly from a warm brown to gold and back again. Usually, he kept his emotions on a tight leash, but he allowed himself to feel the electricity of anticipation for a moment. That electricity spiked when he heard a ping from the oversized computer monitor on his desk.

An email.

The email, hopefully.

He lowered himself back into the chair behind his desk and moved the wire-free mouse to wake the monitor from its standby mode. The screen went from black to cobalt. The window for his email program was in the middle of the screen, at half-size. Weiss's email had arrived. He opened it and double-clicked on the audio file attached to it.

His irises flared again as he listened to the conversation between Sigvardt and Byrne, and the prickle down his spine, more intense than it was moments earlier, made him shudder. Weiss had sent him a lead that seemed more promising than any the organisation had obtained in years. If this Ellie woman was what he thought she might be, Cardinal Peter Barjona of the Vatican would most likely hold the same view, would no doubt contact both Sigvardt and Byrne, and would almost certainly send a team to Copenhagen to pick the woman up.

He had to move quickly now.

First, he had to instruct some of his spies to be ready for and report on any move by the Vatican to send people to Copenhagen or London.

Then he would have to dispatch a hunter to Copenhagen. He clicked on the icon to compose a new email, and in the *To* line, he typed three names.

Hermes, Mercury, and Iris.

They were three of a particular group of spies Simon called his Messengers, of which there were seventeen in total, all given code names after the messengers of mythology. Like him, they were something more than human, and because of their particular abilities, they were the best suited to be deeply embedded into the structures of all the major religious faiths. And even some of the minor ones. Because all the faith groups, regardless of the differing belief systems they marketed, were also secretly looking for what the Sicarii sought.

The spies he was about to email were entrenched in the three rapid response teams commanded by the cardinal, Barjona. If Barjona ordered any of those teams to move, one of the three Messengers would immediately know.

He swiftly typed his instructions to the Messengers and clicked on *Send*. His instructions were simple enough—the Sicarii had identified a target in Copenhagen whom he would send a hunter to retrieve, and the Messengers were to report any activity or communications related to Copenhagen or London, specifically in connection with the parties he'd also listed.

He stood from the chair and returned to the window, then swept a strand of hair away from his forehead, closed his eyes, and rolled his shoulders back. It had been a long time since they were this close. Over a millennium, in fact.

He fished a rose gold Omega *Olympische* fob watch from his waistcoat pocket and checked the time. It was a chronograph made in 1932, given to him in the same year by an adversary who knew what Simon was. The adversary had sent it to him with a mocking sense of irony.

Time always turns, even for his kind.

It was almost one thirty in the afternoon local time, which meant it was late evening in Europe, where his hunter was. Not that it mattered. The people in their organisation didn't work according to time, they worked according to requirements and imperatives. He gave the watch's winding mechanism a couple of twists and replaced it in his pocket, then turned back to his desk and pressed the intercom button on a dark grey telephone console.

'*Yes, Simon?*' piped his assistant's voice through the intercom's speaker.

'Get me Gideon.'

20

Gideon brushed the rain off himself, unbuttoned his coat, turned down its collar, and took in the minimalist simplicity of Sabre Technologie's trapezoid, two-storey foyer. Located on Avenue Raymond Poincarè, the building housed the Paris-based weapons company's headquarters. He'd visited the building several times and was familiar with its layout, but, as he always did, he took a few seconds to note the most pertinent details—how many staff were in the lobby and where exactly they were. He doubted many employees would be on duty at this time in the evening, but it was always worth checking.

A long, chest-height reception counter was set against the back wall in front of him. Behind it stood a middle-aged receptionist. To the right of the reception desk, crewing an airport-style security station—replete with a body scanner, X-ray machine, conveyor belt and retractable fabric barriers—were two male security guards. The first guard, who stood in front of the body scanner, was a stubby pitbull of a man, with a thick neck and a shaved head. The second, seated at the screen of the X-ray machine, was slimmer, with thick dark hair and the pockmarked face of a man who had likely suffered from rampant acne in his teens. He couldn't tell whether Acne was taller than Pitbull, but he didn't think he would lose any money if he bet on it.

He walked to the reception desk, and the receptionist greeted him with a half-hearted smile. By the time he'd covered half the distance from the front doors to her desk, he'd already read her name tag.

'Good evening, Fabienne,' he said.

For the briefest moment, an expression of confusion and something that looked a lot like dread spread across the receptionist's face, which amused him a little. He knew his scar unsettled people, and sometimes—such as now—people could forget even the simplest of things, such as the fact they wore a name badge, to which he pointed, putting the woman's fears to rest. Her shoulders dropped slightly, and she exhaled, clearly relieved.

'Hello, sir,' she said in stilted English. There was a quiver in her voice which she coughed away. 'How can I help you?'

'I'm here to see Katerine Clément.'

'Can I have your name?'

'Gideon.'

The receptionist typed away on her keyboard, her eyes checking the screen as she did so. 'I'm sorry, sir, but I don't see your name on our system. Are you sure you have the correct appointment time?'

'I'm positive.'

'And you're sure also you have the correct day?'

Gideon nodded.

'Could I have your family name, please?' she asked. 'Your... uh... surname, I think you say in English?'

'I don't have one.'

'You don't have... oh, then I'll try your first name again. Perhaps I mistyped the first time. You said it was Gideon?'

She enunciated each letter to ensure she had the correct spelling. He nodded as she went. She glanced between her monitor, her moving fingers, and the security station. Movement in his peripheral vision caught his attention. He scanned sideways slightly and saw that Pitbull had taken a couple of steps away from the body scanner. He guessed his interaction with the receptionist was taking too long for the man's liking.

'I'm very sorry, sir,' she said, still looking at her screen, 'but I'm

132

afraid I can't find you on the system. I've checked against the schedules for yesterday, today, and tomorrow. You're not on any of them.'

'No. I wouldn't be. I don't have an appointment.'

Fabienne looked up from her screen, puzzled. 'Then—'

Gideon held her gaze, and she inhaled loudly. A reaction, he knew, to the rippling change in colour of his grey irises to a fiery orange. More movement behind and to his side. Pitbull must have heard her loud gasp and was now on alert and slowly moving toward them. Gideon looked back at her and hardened his focus. He watched her face slacken as she felt the strange sensation deep within her skull of the pressure of something forcing its way into her head, pushing on the soft tissue of her brain.

He spoke the words *keep calm* in his head, knowing that she would also hear them in hers. Fabienne, eyes glazed over in a fog of confusion and compliance, her mind dulled, nodded. Pitbull appeared at his side. He glared at Gideon and then looked at the receptionist.

'Problème, Fabienne?' he asked.

Gideon intensified his focus on the woman.

Tell him, Not at all. Everything is fine.

'Pas du tout,' she droned. 'Tout va bien.'

Pitbull looked at him again and held out his hand.

'Identification,' he said.

'You don't need to see that,' Gideon replied, turning to him, his eyes still glowing like fire.

The guard's face contorted briefly as if he were about to belch, then he hiccupped and a sliver of vomit trickled out of his mouth and down his chin. In Gideon's experience, it wasn't uncommon. Nausea that accompanied a *push* was often too much for some people to handle, especially if they had weak stomachs or were susceptible to motion sickness.

'After I leave this building,' he said, his gaze drifting between the guard and the receptionist, 'neither of you will remember this encounter.

You will not remember me. Do you understand?'

They nodded in unison.

'You will come with me to the security station,' he said to Pitbull, 'and you'll carry out your duties as you normally would. If your friend over there asks about our conversation here, you'll tell him everything's fine, and your lovely colleague here simply made a mistake in her initial search of the system. Do you understand?'

'I understand,' Pitbull slurred robotically in heavily accented English.

'Clean yourself up first.'

The guard fumbled in his trouser pockets for a handkerchief, but his hands came out empty, so he cupped a hand, rubbed it across his chin, and then wiped it on his trousers.

The two men turned away from the reception desk and headed toward the security station. Acne was watching them, presumably curious about what was going on but not yet interested or worried enough to leave his post. When they reached the security station, Pitbull handed Gideon a small rectangular plastic tray.

'Remove your belt and all items from your pockets and put them into this.'

He removed his wallet and phone from the inside pockets of his suit jacket and a neatly folded white handkerchief from his trouser pocket and placed them all into the tray.

'That is all?' Pitbull asked flatly.

'That's all,' he said, handing the tray back.

'No belt?'

'No belt.'

The guard grunted, put the tray onto the conveyor belt, and walked through the body scanner. It chirped brightly, having sensed the metallic items attached to his belt—a bunch of keys, a can of what was probably pepper spray, and a pistol which Gideon recognised as a Taser X26P stun weapon—and whatever metallic objects were not visible.

When the light above the scanner turned from red to green, Gideon walked through. It chirped again. Pitbull signalled for him to stop, then approached Acne. The guards had a mumbled exchange in their native French, which he heard and understood perfectly. Acne asked what had happened at the reception desk, and Pitbull replied as Gideon had instructed him to. The exchange ended with Acne handing Pitbull a device the size of a shoe, which Gideon recognised as an electronic detection wand.

'Arms up and out to the side.'

He obeyed. The guard waved the wand up and down his body, skimming a few inches from the surface. The device squealed when it reached his left wrist.

'Show me,' said Pitbull. 'Slowly.'

With his right hand, Gideon pulled back his sleeve and shirt cuff, exposing his watch.

'Rolex. Fancy. Take it off,' the guard said, reaching out to take the watch.

He complied again, and Pitbull scanned him once more. This time, there was no squeal, so the guard gave him his watch and held out the tray containing his other effects, which had gone through the X-ray scanner without issue. He took his things out of the tray and replaced them in their respective pockets, then Pitbull stood to one side and gestured for him to continue to his destination unaccompanied. With the building's extensive security camera network recording his every move within the rest of the building—a fact of which he was aware but unconcerned—there would be no need to keep human eyes on him.

Before moving on, he walked over to Acne, who stood and slowly moved his right hand to the Taser clipped to his belt. He looked into the guard's eyes, entrancing him with his amber gaze.

'After I leave this building, you will not remember me,' he said. 'Do you understand?'

Acne nodded dumbly.

Gideon turned and headed for the lift. He pressed the call button, and the door opened almost immediately. The car inside was softly lit and had marble floor tiles similar to those in the lift lobby and the main foyer. He stepped into it and pressed the button for the fifth floor.

'Yes, of course, Minister. I'm greatly disappointed that I won't be able to attend.'

Katerine Clément reclined on a dark brown, soft leather couch, taking what she hoped would be the last call of the evening. She gazed at the large black-and-white photograph that hung on the opposite wall of her office. It was of her at Mount Everest's base camp—a reminder that one could accomplish anything with enough determination, and a message to everyone else that, as CEO of Sabre Technologie, she was almost definitely made of tougher stuff than them.

'And you're sure you cannot reschedule your other appointment?'

'I wish I could, but it's with the Russian ambassador.'

'Levchenkov?'

'Yes. The delightful Mr Levchenkov. I'm sure I can say without offending you, Minister, that of the two of you, I'd rather risk upsetting you than him.'

'Indeed. In that case, I wish you the best of luck.'

'Thank you for understanding.'

'Good evening, Mademoiselle Clément.'

'Good evening, Minister.'

She put her phone face-down on her lap, relieved to have finished the conversation, then reached forward and took a large glass of Bordeaux from the rosewood coffee table in front of her. She sighed heavily, then leaned on one arm of the sofa, looked out of the window, and thought, Why does everything always have to be so goddamned difficult?

'Hello, Katerine.'

Clément spun around. Her phone dropped to the floor, and she spilt almost all her wine onto the purple rug at her feet.

'Jesus!' she said, sweeping a few strands of her long butterscotch hair from her face.

'Not quite.'

'What are you doing here, Gideon?'

'That looks like it was a waste,' he said, pointing to the almost empty glass.

'Chateau Ausone, 2013. So yes, it was a waste.'

'My apologies.'

'You can buy me a new rug if you're that sorry.'

'I couldn't help overhearing your conversation. It sounded awkward.'

'The Interior Minister is throwing a gala dinner. I had to decline her invitation. Prior engagement. Not that I wanted to go anyway. I hate ministry parties, and she's a bore. And you didn't answer my question. What are you doing here? What do you want?'

'Why would I—'

'Don't insult me, Gideon. You only ever come here when you want something, which, granted, is rare enough. But never just to catch up. Never just for fun.'

By fun, she meant sex. They'd slept together almost twenty years ago when she was in her early thirties and just starting to climb the corporate ladder. It happened only once. A vigorous—bordering on violent—encounter both had enjoyed but which they'd vowed not to repeat. Her vow had been half-hearted. His, she realised later with disappointment, hadn't been.

He came further into the room and closed the door behind him. She raised an eyebrow playfully.

'Don't get excited, Katerine. We agreed—'

'I know what we agreed, darling, but that doesn't mean I can't try to change your mind, does it?'

He approached the sofa and sat down next to her. She looked at his eyes, the scar, and the creases on his face. In the two decades they'd known each other, she had aged—well enough by most standards, she thought—but he hadn't. That wasn't a shock to her. She knew what he was. While she'd taken lovers since him, none had compared, and she wondered what it would be like now and, almost without thinking, placed her hand on top of his.

'I told you, Katerine. I'm not here for that.'

'It's always business with you these days, isn't it?'

'Anything else is too complicated.'

'It doesn't have to be.'

'It is.'

Clément shifted with irritation.

'Alright,' she said, withdrawing her hand. 'What exactly *do* you want?'

Gideon held her gaze.

'You've betrayed us, Katerine.'

'What?'

Her pulse quickened briefly. She knew he would have sensed it because she knew what he was capable of.

'You know you can't lie to me,' he said.

'I have no idea what you're talking about, Gideon.'

She stared into his eyes, looking for some indication of belief, but instead, she saw his irises lose their grey shine as they slowly phased to burning amber. She inhaled and steeled herself. Then she felt a pressing sensation inside her head. Having felt Gideon's *push* on three previous occasions, she was all too familiar with the feeling. On one occasion—when they'd slept together—it was a welcome sensation that allowed her to let go of her inhibitions. The other two times were less pleasant.

Before his mind could get a grip on hers, she dropped her wineglass and sprang from the sofa with a speed she didn't know she was capable of. She vaulted the desk, putting it between them, and fumbled around until her hand found what she needed. She drew a small black pistol from a holster bolted to the desk's underside. A Ruger LC9s—a slim, lightweight and compact weapon loaded with eight low-recoil 9-millimetre bullets. Despite its size, it would be more than sufficient to put a couple of holes in his face.

'You're making a mistake, Gideon.'

'I don't think so. What did they pay you?'

She shook her head.

'Ah,' he said. 'They haven't paid you anything. They promised you something, didn't they?'

Clément said nothing, but she knew her eyes and a throbbing pulse gave away the truth as much as her trembling hand gave away her fear.

'What did they promise you, Katerine? Inclusion in the ranks? Protection? You know they won't give you any of that, don't you?'

'If you're here, then clearly not.'

He shook his head slowly. 'You're a fool, Katerine. I thought you were smarter.'

The gun in her hand began to inch downward as if someone had grabbed the end of it and was slowly but firmly pulling it toward the ground. Gideon's irises blazed with fire and fury, but she knew this wasn't him. He wasn't pulling the gun down. She was letting it drop. She knew any fight now was pointless.

'What did you give them?' he asked softly.

'Will you let me live if I tell you?'

'No. But I can promise you'll die quickly and relatively painlessly.'

'Relatively?'

'Everything's relative.'

'And if I don't tell you?'

'I'll take a peek inside your head, find what I'm looking for, and then pull your mind apart. You'll go home this evening as if this conversation never happened, and when you wake up tomorrow, your sanity will start to decay. You'll start to rave. To anyone who will listen and to plenty who won't. You'll rave about the Sicarii, me, and those you sold us out to. People will consider you hysterical. Manic. Nobody will want to know you. They'll cast you out. You'll live, but you'll want to die. And so, at some point in the not-too-distant future, you'll kill yourself. And it won't be an easy death. I'll plant that little seed in there. It will be slow and painful. Drowning, maybe. Or perhaps you'll slowly poison yourself. Rat poison in your muesli every morning. Or you might hang yourself and shit whatever is left of your dignity on your living room floor.'

'You're a fucking psychopath, Gideon,' she spat.

'I'm a man on whom the secrecy and survival of my organisation depend. I take my responsibility seriously, and I take any betrayal personally.'

Clément's heart fluttered again. How many bullets could she unload into him before he could stop her? Or should she simply give up? She sighed heavily, laid the Ruger on the desk and slumped resignedly into the expensive ergonomic chair behind her.

'Tell me,' Gideon murmured. 'Everything.'

Four minutes after Gideon left the building, Clément stepped out of the lift and into the main lobby. The soft ping of the lift and the click-clack of her Christian Louboutins on the marble floor announced her arrival to the security guards, who turned toward her. She felt a knot in her stomach as if she hadn't eaten for days. Her arms hung limply by her sides. In her right hand was her Ruger. The guards looked puzzled— understandably so, she thought—but whatever training they had was good enough to take over, and they drew their Tasers and aimed for her chest.

'Mademoiselle,' said the short, stocky guard. She didn't even know his name. 'Please put the weapon down.' It was more of a request than a command.

She remained still, her grip on the pistol firm.

'Mademoiselle Clément, put your weapon down now!' A command, not a request. From the other man this time. The one with bad skin.

'Mademoiselle,' said the first guard, 'if you don't—'

She drew up her arm with a speed that clearly surprised both guards. She didn't rotate it at the shoulder. She didn't lock in a straight line. She didn't point the gun at the guards.

Instead, she bent her arm at the elbow and pointed her weapon toward the ceiling. The gun travelled skyward until its muzzle kissed the soft underside of her face, between her neck and chin.

The guards pleaded with her in unison to put the weapon down. It was all they *could* do. She knew enough about Tasers to understand that if either man shot her, the electrical charge released into her body could cause a muscle spasm so powerful that her trigger finger might contract, and she would kill herself. Or, rather, whoever tased her would kill her. And neither of the guards would want that kind of trouble.

They pleaded again.

A wave of serenity suddenly came over her, all pain and torment gone.

'Elyonim,' she murmured.

And then she pulled the trigger.

The bullet went through her tongue, her nasal cavity, and her brain. It kept going and exploded through the top of her skull, sending shards of bone and globs of grey matter into the air behind her.

She was dead before her body dropped to the floor.

21

There were twenty or so people in the basement wine bar on Rue Washington, most of whom were in groups of two or more, all deep in conversation. Only three people sat alone. Slow jazz music wafted from small cube-shaped speakers mounted in various high spots around the place, barely loud enough to be heard over the multiple conversations.

Gideon sat at a small square table in a dark corner, his back to the wall. In front of him was a plate on which lay a half-eaten blue steak. There were no side dishes or accoutrements. Next to the plate was a heavy-based tumbler containing a large ball of ice and a generous measure of The Dalmore 21 single malt whisky.

As he raised a steak-laden fork to his mouth, he felt a mild vibration on the back of his other arm. It was his phone, nestled in the pocket of his suit jacket, hung across the back of his chair. Ignoring it, he put the fork into his mouth, eased the chunk of steak off it with his teeth, and started to chew.

The vibrating persisted.

He put down the fork, swallowed the steak, and reluctantly fished his phone out of his jacket. The screen identified the caller as Simon. He sat back in his chair and answered the call.

'This is Gideon.'

'*I need you in Copenhagen.*'

'When?'

'*Now.*'

'Would you mind if I finish my steak first?'

'Where are you?'

'Paris.'

'Clément.' It was a statement, not a question.

'Yes.'

'How?'

'I suggested that she step down in the least painful way and gave her two options. Which she takes will be up to her.'

'You suggested?'

'Strongly.'

'Was it entirely necessary?'

'She betrayed us,' he said, his voice low. 'And without intervention, she'd do it again. Consider it a message to her successor, should you decide to keep Sabre retained, which I would strongly urge against, by the way.'

'When?'

He glanced at his watch.

'Depending on which choice she makes, she could already have done it. Given who she is, it will undoubtedly make the international news, so you should be able to see it for yourself.'

Simon exhaled loudly on the other end of the line.

'Traceable?'

'I should feel insulted that you even have to ask.' He lowered his voice even further, knowing that Simon would still be able to hear him even if he whispered. 'But no. At least not by ordinary methods. If anyone were to check the camera system, they'd find it inexplicably stopped recording while I was in the building, and none of the staff will remember seeing or speaking to anyone during that time other than each other.'

'So, why are you still in Paris? I would've thought you'd want to be clear as quickly as possible, despite how clean it may have been.'

'There is, or *was*, nothing else in the pipeline so I thought I'd take a couple of days to myself, and here's a good a place as any.'

'Can I leave you to make the arrangements for getting to Denmark?'

'Of course. What's the assignment?'

'A woman named Ellie. Last name unknown. No address for her, either. The primary focus for information-gathering should be a Father Frederik Sigvardt. We do have an address for him. The woman's therapist is a secondary source, should the priest not have any useful information. One Doctor Maja Carlsson. We currently have nothing on her. I'll have all the available details sent to you shortly.'

'Understood.'

'If this Ellie woman is genuine, Gideon, we can't afford any mistakes.'

'No.'

'Alright. Let me know when you're in the air.'

The line went dead, and Gideon put his phone face-up on the table. He sat back in his chair and looked around the bar. Nobody was looking at him, directly or indirectly. He was a dark man in a dark suit in a dark corner. He was practically invisible. He looked at the remains of his steak and found that he'd lost his appetite. Whether from the anticipation of a new mission—or, more accurately, the continuation of a long-ongoing one—or because of memories long ago buried, he wasn't sure.

He picked up his phone again, unlocked it, opened his contacts list, and scrolled to the name he wanted. He thumbed it, held the phone to his ear, and waited for the call to connect.

'This is Jacques.'

'I need a pickup.'

'When and where?'

'Immediately. I'm at Vinopoli.'

'Okay.'

'I also need you to call Enrique. Tell him to prepare the jet and file a flight plan for Copenhagen. It'll be an immediate departure upon my arrival at the airport.'

'*You're leaving Paris already? I thought you were having some downtime.*'

'Plans change, Jacques.'

'*Ils font toujours.*' *They always do.*

He ended the call and slipped the phone back into his jacket. He took a sip of the whisky, swilled it around in his mouth before swallowing, and then finished the rest in a large, single gulp, savouring the burn as it went down his throat. Finally, he stood up, took his wallet from his jacket and pulled out two hundred euros which he placed under the plate of half-eaten steak, then slipped on his jacket, returned his wallet to it, and made for the exit.

22

Laguna, an upscale bar in the Psyri district of Athens, was packed with the after-work crowd, reluctant to return to their homes until they'd fully decompressed after the day's trials in the office or the studio or wherever they worked. Thomas Jäger, who wasn't a local but who'd visited the city more times than he could remember, sat at the long mahogany bar, a packet of Marlboro Red cigarettes and a silver Zippo lighter on the counter next to his left hand. Engraved on the lighter were the words ME SERVUM TUUM FACERE VOLUNTATEM TUAM—*I am Thy servant to do Thy will*. Beside his right hand sat his wallet, his phone, and a tumbler containing an oversized ice cube and two shots of Don Julio 1942 tequila.

He ran a hand over his stubble and took a sip of the smooth tequila as he contemplated his reflection in the bar's mirrored backdrop. His unkempt mop of black hair, worn leather jacket and faded jeans gave him the look of someone who'd been sleeping in his car for a few nights, which couldn't have been further from the truth—it was nothing but plush hotels and gourmet dinners for the top agents of Christ.

His attention turned to a large high-definition television on the wall behind the bar tuned to an international news channel. A female news presenter sat on one side of a split-screen, with the other side showing the arrest of an elderly couple in an airport. The footage was narrow and shaky, and he thought it had probably been filmed on a bystander's phone. An elderly British couple, the presenter said, had been arrested at a security checkpoint in Dubai airport after authorities discovered what appeared to be rounds of ammunition in the woman's handbag. The police later released the couple after they'd established the shells were, in fact, a collection of bullet-shaped perfume pendants the woman had purchased while on holiday.

Idiots, he thought.

He got up to remove his jacket, the bar's heat having worked its way into him, and was bumped into by a business-suited man staggering his way to the toilets. The man was in his early thirties, with thin, greasy, centre-parted hair and a nose that looked like it had been broken more than once. A brawler, but a bad one.

'Des to, vlákas,' the man drawled. *Watch it, idiot.*

Thomas drew himself up to his full height, standing around three inches taller than the drunk.

'Sorry, man,' he said.

'Ah, an American. The world's peacekeepers. Get out of my way, fuckhead.'

'Fuckhead? Really?'

The drunk grabbed Thomas's jacket with his left hand and then pulled his right arm back, winding up to hit him. As he threw the punch, Thomas effortlessly blocked it with his left forearm, then grabbed the man's wrist and pulled it up over his head with such strength that he forced the man to tiptoe.

'You don't want to do that,' he said. He reached for his wallet with his free hand, opened it and showed it to the drunk. Contained within a clear plastic sleeve inside was an identification badge. Probably the man was too drunk to read all the small print on it. But he wouldn't be able to miss the words CORPS OF GENDARMERIE OF VATICAN CITY next to the photograph of Thomas, nor underneath them, capitalised in red ink, the words RAPID INTERVENTION GROUP.

'Fake, asshole.'

'As fake as this?'

He pulled his jacket open to reveal the butt of a pistol holstered underneath. The blood drained from the drunk's face, and Thomas let go of his wrist. The man rocked back on his heels and reached for the bar to steady himself.

'Look, I—'

'Bathroom's that way. I suggest you get yourself cleaned up and then get yourself home. Or to the next bar. Or any place that's not here.'

As the drunk staggered off, Thomas reached for the tumbler again. As he did so, his phone's screen came alive. He waited two seconds, then answered the call.

'Peter,' he said.

'Where are you?'

'Athens. Why?'

'I need you and your team to mobilise immediately. You're going to Copenhagen.'

'Do we have any assets on the ground that can deal with whatever it is?'

'We do, but this is too important to leave to them. They will have orders to assist you, but the operation's yours.'

'Instructions?'

'I'll give you more information once you're in flight.'

'Understood. I'll call you once we're airborne.'

'Thomas.'

'You don't need to say it.'

He disconnected the call and thumbed his way into the phone's messaging application. He began a new message, added two names into the *To* box, and typed:

```
Meet me at Pegasus ASAP.
```

He sent the message, then downed the last of the Don Julio, shoved his cigarettes, lighter and phone into various pockets, and took fifty euros from his wallet. He put the money on the bar with a nod to the bartender and pocketed his wallet. As he turned to leave, he bumped into the drunk from before, who was returning from the bathroom.

'Skata!' said the man. *Shit.* 'Man, I'm—'

Thomas put a finger to his lips, gesturing for the man to be quiet. He sidestepped the drunk and made for the exit.

Forty-five minutes later, a white Toyota Landcruiser pulled to a stop next to a one-storey terminal building at a private airfield on the outskirts of Athens. Above the frosted glass entrance doors was a gold-coloured stylised picture of a winged horse, and underneath it were the words PEGASUS EXECUTIVE AIR, also in gold.

A colossus of a man climbed out from the Toyota's back seat. He hauled a duffel bag behind him, slung it over his shoulder, slammed the door shut, and ran a hand through his salt-and-pepper hair. The duffel bag's strap had bunched the shoulder of his army-style jacket and exposed a black tattoo that crept around the base of his neck. He straightened his coat, brushed himself down, hitched up his black jeans, and went into the terminal building.

Inside, facing the door, was a tall reception desk staffed by a male receptionist in an expensive charcoal-grey suit.

'Good evening, sir,' the receptionist said in accented English, with a broad smile that showed off a set of teeth so perfect, they could have been fake. 'My name is Andreas. And you are?'

'Seth.'

Andreas made a show of checking a list, which Seth knew was pointless given that he and his two colleagues—likely already inside the lounge—would be the only passengers on this flight. Andreas looked up from the list, smiled again, and directed him through a frosted glass door to the lounge. It had leather armchairs and sofas, a well-stocked bar, and a hot and cold buffet. It also had male and female toilets and a bank of four private showers. Soft piano music wafted from speakers set into the ceiling, and a widescreen television in a corner above the bar showed a muted news channel.

A young woman stood next to the buffet table, picking up pieces of sushi with her fingers. She was around five-nine and had black, tousled hair cut into a bob tapered up at the back. She wore dark green cargo pants and a grey denim jacket.

He watched as she popped a piece of *ebi nigiri* into her mouth and then, almost absent-mindedly, wiped her hand quickly on the front of her cargo pants. She froze for a moment, seeming to sense his presence.

'Hey, big man,' she said through a mouthful of shrimp and rice, without looking around.

'Rebekah.'

He dropped his duffel bag onto an armchair and approached the table. As she reached out for another piece of sushi, he glanced sideways at her and saw the familiar grey and black head of a snake tattoo peek below the cuff of her jacket. She turned to him. The smattering of freckles under her lime-green eyes moved as she wrinkled her nose at him.

'Rough party?' she asked.

'Huh?'

She pointed to a dark stain on the sleeve of his jacket.

Seth grunted. 'Coffee. Someone bumped into me about a minute before I got Thomas's text, and I haven't had a chance to change.'

'You let 'em get away with it?'

'I did. And I'd probably be nudging her awake for breakfast tomorrow morning if I didn't have to haul my ass up here *toot sweet*.'

'Aww. Poor baby.'

Rebekah laughed, slapped him on the shoulder, and headed toward the bar. He took a plate from the buffet table, quickly loaded it with a couple of steak sandwiches, and followed her. The bar was a self-service affair similar to those found in most business and first-class lounges in commercial airports worldwide. It operated on the honour system—help yourself but don't abuse it.

She found a tumbler and poured herself a double shot of Johnny Walker Blue Label, into which she dropped an almost perfectly shaped cube of ice. She made a sweeping gesture with her arm, offering to make him whatever drink he wanted. He pointed to her hand, so she gave him her drink and started to fix another for herself.

'Where is he?' he asked.

'Outside, getting his fix.'

'You know where we're going?'

'Nope.'

A flicker on the television caught Seth's attention. The change of one news story to another. While he couldn't hear the details, the title of the news story and the photograph of a woman superimposed next to the newsreader gave him enough information. The title bar read CEO OF FRANCE'S LARGEST WEAPONS FIRM COMMITS SUICIDE.

'You hear about this?'

Rebekah looked around, and her eyes widened. Clearly, she hadn't. The scene on the television changed to high-quality footage from one of Sabre Technologie's security cameras. It showed Katerine Clément walking through the building's main lobby and two security guards, with their weapons raised, confronting her. The guards had their backs to the camera, so their faces, presumably showing confusion and panic, weren't visible.

But Clément's was.

It was serene. Like a millpond early in the morning. Or the eye of a raging hurricane.

Seth glanced around for the television's remote. Not immediately able to see it, he paced to the television and thumbed a button on its side to increase the volume, in time to hear Clément say only one word.

Elyonim.

Holy shit, he thought.

'Holy shit,' Rebekah said.

A door on the other side of the lounge opened, and Thomas stepped through it, holding a packet of Marlboro in one hand and his lighter in the other. He took a cigarette from the pack and put it in his mouth, then opened the Zippo and lit it by rolling the flint wheel against his jeans. Before he could light the cigarette, a polite but irritated voice interrupted the music through the overhead speakers.

'I'm sorry, sir, but may I remind you again *that smoking is not permitted anywhere inside the building.'*

Visibly frustrated, he closed the lighter.

'Fucker', he muttered, walking to the bar.

'Thomas,' said Seth.

With the cigarette still hanging from his lips, Thomas smiled and then clasped a hand on the giant's shoulder.

'Rough party?' he asked, nodding to the stain on his jacket.

'It could've been.' He motioned to the television. 'You seen that?'

'Yeah. I heard about it earlier.'

'Why'd you think she did it?' Rebekah asked. 'Blackmail, maybe? Or extortion?'

'Clément was at the top of her game, running one of the largest arms companies in Europe,' Thomas said. 'She would've made enemies, sure, but I doubt there was any human problem she couldn't deal with.'

'You think the Sicarii are behind this?'

'It's likely. I expect Peter will look into it. Right now, she's not our concern. We have a mission.'

'Guessed as much. Where are we headed?'

'To the land of the little mermaid.'

'Disneyland?' asked Seth.

Thomas looked at him blankly.

'Denmark, you moron,' said Rebekah.

'We leave in five minutes,' Thomas said. He nodded at Seth's jacket. 'You'll need a new wardrobe. You can't walk around looking like that.'

'I've got a spare in the bag. I'll change on the plane.'

Thomas turned back to the door he came in through. As he disappeared through it, Rebekah tucked her hair behind her ear, stared vacantly at a point on the far wall, and drummed her fingers haphazardly on the top of the bar. Seth swallowed his whisky in one giant gulp—ice cube included—then headed for the door Thomas had used.

'You coming?' he asked Rebekah, holding the door open.

She knocked back the rest of her drink, using her teeth to hold back the ice cube, then walked over to him and stepped out into the night.

23

The early afternoon sun shone through the tall windows of Simon's office, but the intensity of its glare was kept at bay by the layer of solar-reactive film on the glass, which darkened as the sun got brighter. Simon sat on a steel-framed brown leather armchair, one leg resting on the knee of the other, with a tall glass of club soda and lime in one hand and his mobile phone in the other. It had been twenty-one minutes since he'd issued instructions to his Messengers, and it was only a matter of time until one or more of them sent him a report.

Good or bad.

He took a sip of his drink and impatiently tapped the side of his phone.

Then it came.

A double-ping.

A text message.

He swivelled his wrist so that he could see the phone's screen. The message was from Mercury, one of his seventeen Messengers, and it contained only three words.

`Heading to Copenhagen.`

He knew where and with whom all his Messengers were embedded, so he immediately understood the implications of Mercury's message. Cardinal Peter Barjona of the Vatican had sent his best tracker, Thomas Jäger. He unlocked his phone and typed a response to the message.

```
Noted. Gideon also. Liaise with him point-to-
point but keep me updated when safe to do so.
```

He pressed the *Send* icon, and the message *swooshed* into the ether. Then he started a new message, added Gideon's name as the recipient, and typed.

```
Mercury is heading from Athens to Copenhagen.
Advised to liaise directly with you.
```

He didn't need to elaborate on the broader implications, as Gideon was also aware of who all the Messengers were and with which organisations they were entrenched. He sent the text, then reclined against the plush leather, tilted back his head and closed his eyes. If he were a praying man, he might have been inclined to do that, but praying to a God who wouldn't answer was pointless.

24

Gideon sat silently in the front passenger seat of the bronze BMW X5, contemplating his next few moves. His driver, Jacques, had skilfully slithered through Paris's evening traffic and was skirting around a high chain-link security fence topped with razor wire surrounding Le Bourget—an airport eleven miles from the centre of Paris that claimed to be the busiest in Europe devoted solely to private aircraft.

The journey through the city centre had been frustrating. While he loved many things about Paris, mid-town traffic wasn't one of them. It was the same as in any metropolis, but the French seemed to be largely terrible drivers technically, inconsiderate of other road users, and generally impolite.

Jacques Garidel, a Paris-based tech wizard, armourer and general fixer, was one of the rare exceptions. Garidels had worked for the Sicarii for eleven generations. They prided themselves on their professionalism and courtesy, even during the darker moments of some of the work they were required to do. In his mid-sixties, Jacques was a shaggy-haired, barrel-chested bear of a man with a hearty laugh who almost always conducted himself with decorum. He'd lost his composure only once on the journey to Le Bourget, near the Stade de France, after having to swerve violently to avoid a pastel yellow Fiat 500 driven by a myopic driver with no sense of direction. He'd slammed a meaty hand onto the car's horn and yelled out a flurry of expletives that would have made a rig worker blush.

'You kiss your grandchildren with that mouth?' Gideon had asked.

'Only after I've washed it out with a good brandy.'

Gideon had chuckled.

It was good that people like Jacques had families—a support network that couldn't always be provided from within the organisation. People like him had no such network, but then, they didn't need them.

Did they?

As he turned back to look out of his window, his phone chirped to announce the arrival of a text message. He pulled out his phone. On its screen was a message from Simon.

'That's going to complicate things,' he muttered, more to himself than to Jacques.

'What's the matter?'

'Peter has sent Thomas to Copenhagen.'

'Oh. Not good.'

'No.'

He knew from experience that Thomas Jäger was one of the Vatican's best, and he always worked with two others. The fact that one of those team members was a double agent for the Sicarii was irrelevant, as the standard rules of engagement for Messengers would apply—if you're with an opponent, you *are* the opponent.

Mercury would maintain their cover unless it became essential to break it, which meant Gideon may still have three people to contend with in Copenhagen. The mission was more important than the individual, so Mercury keeping up appearances could still prove difficult, if not deadly. He disliked it because it put all Sicarii agents at risk, including those operating undercover, but it was a policy he understood and accepted.

He drew a long breath through his nostrils, rubbed the bridge of his nose, and replied to Simon.

Understood.

Still looking at his phone, he felt the car slow down. He glanced up and saw they were rolling up to a security gate, located around one hundred and fifty metres from the terminal building. There was a sturdy-looking hut on their side of the gate, and he could see two guards inside. As the BMW pulled to a stop, one of the guards came out and strolled toward the car, his hand resting on the butt of a pistol cradled in a belt holster.

Jacques turned on the cabin lights, then lowered his window. With his hand still on his weapon, the guard approached Jacques's door, pointed at him, and held out his hand.

'Passeport,' he said.

Jacques opened a compartment in the centre console and retrieved a slim, dark blue leather case, on the front of which was the Mont Blanc star logo. Inside the case was a French diplomatic passport. It was fake—one of many high-quality forgeries he possessed. As he handed it to the guard, Gideon pulled his own counterfeit document from his jacket—this one seemingly issued by the United States—and passed it to Jacques, who kept hold of it.

The guard deftly opened the Frenchman's passport with one hand, the other still resting on his weapon. He looked back and forth between Jacques and the passport several times, then handed it back.

'Le sien,' he said, pointing to Gideon. *His.*

Jacques handed the passport over, and the guard went through the same routine, throwing Gideon the customary suspicious glances that those with even minor levels of authority are inclined to give foreigners as if to say that their onward journey was entirely at his discretion. He wouldn't have known that one phone call from Jacques to a high-level airport official on the Sicarii's payroll would have them through the gate and himself unemployed in under thirty seconds.

Fortunately for the guard, it didn't come to that.

He handed back Gideon's passport, then turned back to the hut and gestured to his colleague, who'd been watching closely. The sentry in the cabin reached for something out of sight, and the security gate eased open.

Jacques slid his window back up, passed Gideon's passport back to him, and rolled the car through the gate.

'I'm going to need some help,' said Gideon.

'Who?'

He didn't respond. Instead, he tapped the screen of the infotainment system embedded in the BMW's dashboard, which he knew was linked to the contacts list in Jacques's phone. He navigated his way to the phone menu, then into the contacts, and scrolled until he found the number for Enrique Sesta, their pilot. He pressed the number, and the dialling tone chimed from the car's speakers.

'Jacques, tout va bien?' While Enrique was a Spaniard, he spoke French almost as well as his native tongue. *Everything okay?*

'Enrique, this is Gideon.'

'Gideon. How can I help?' Enrique's English was better than his French.

'I need you to revise the flight plan. We'll be making a detour to London before heading to Copenhagen.'

'Understood.'

'Do it quickly and get the engines hot. We've just come through the airport's security gate. I want to be wheels-up as quickly as possible after boarding.'

'Will do. However, we could be waiting on the apron for a few minutes while we get departure clearance from the tower.'

'Noted.'

Gideon ended the call.

'London means Cain,' said Jacques.

He looked at Jacques but said nothing.

'You know I have much love for Cain, Gideon, but if he goes up against Thomas and his team, it could get messy.'

'I know. But if I do have to engage Thomas, there's no one I'd rather have with me. And perhaps messy could be useful.'

Jacques grunted.

'Besides,' Gideon continued, 'it's possible they'll have help—assets based in Copenhagen or somewhere close enough to get there quickly. Probably only one or two, but enough to be a problem if I have to deal with them and Thomas's team on my own.'

'We don't have anyone up there?'

'No.'

'You want me to tag along instead of Cain? I'm available, there's enough equipment in the back of the car for both of us, and it means you won't have to detour to London.'

'You're not bulletproof, Jacques.'

'Neither is Cain, technically.'

'He's as good as.'

Jacques nodded.

Gideon unclipped his seat belt as the car rolled to a stop next to a sleek, matte black and grey private jet idling on the tarmac. It was a Bombardier Global 7500—a seventy-million-dollar missile capable of carrying up to nineteen passengers in the utmost luxury further and faster than any other private aircraft on the market.

'Thomas's team is travelling from Athens, so I should have enough time for the detour. If it comes to it, I'll have Enrique drive us once we're in Copenhagen and stand in as backup if we need him. He's weapons-trained and more than competent.'

'That he is, but he's not bulletproof, either.'

Gideon nodded and gave Jacques a solemn look. Then, he unlocked his phone, which was still in his hand, went into the messaging application, began a new text, and started typing.

New target. In Copenhagen. Pick up some essentials from Hussein. Nothing ostentatious. Then meet me at Northolt.

He sent the text, locked his phone, and turned to look out of his window once more. Jacques was right, and there was no way of avoiding it. This *was* going to get messy, with or without Cain.

25

On the southern edge of London's Soho, halfway up the lower end of Shaftesbury Avenue, wedged between an Italian restaurant and a place that sold bubble tea, was a black, windowless façade. Unlike its neighbours, there was no signage to advertise any business there, so to the casual observer, it might look as if the place was abandoned and derelict.

Two pairs of solid, windowless wooden doors were set back in separate alcoves. The doors in the left-hand nook had no locks or handles or otherwise obvious way of being openable. There was no intercom panel or noticeable camera by which someone could announce their presence. All of which reinforced the illusion that the building was deserted, or at least that side was. In reality, the doors gave access to a luxury apartment that occupied the first and second floors, protected by a sophisticated security system activated by movement, pressure, and heat, and with windows that were triple-glazed, ultraviolet-resistant, and bombproof.

On the wall of the other alcove at eye height was a small square plaque, black with nine white concentric circles on it, in the centre of which was a pinhole camera and below which was an intercom and an electronic card reader. This entrance led to a private members' club that occupied the floors above the apartment and spanned the adjacent buildings on each side. It was a private club not only in its membership philosophy but also in how it operated. It had no website or social media accounts and never publicly marketed itself or its events. Instead, it relied almost exclusively on word of mouth, and potential members had to be referred by three existing members. To its members, the club was known as Nine, and like the apartment below, it was owned by the Sicarii.

The club's jazz and blues lounge occupied half of the fourth floor. On a small stage at one end of it, the house band was playing mellow renditions of other artists' songs. Felicity Harvey sat on a tall leather-backed chair at the corner of the bar. She cradled a thick-bottomed tumbler of Grey Goose on the rocks and was trying to enjoy a slow, smooth jazz version of *Everybody Wants to Rule the World*, but the man standing around the bar's corner was making that impossible.

He was an unattractive man, pockmarked and chubby, easily in his mid-fifties, with too much gel in his hair and too much alcohol in his fat belly. A chunky, unlit cigar took up almost all the left side of his mouth, and his shirt's open collar displayed a thick, gaudy gold chain nestled within the fatty rolls of his neck. Next to him stood an identical man with slightly less gel, jewellery and fat, and an overweight shaven-headed guy with a patchy ginger beard.

'Come on, Felicity,' said the fatter twin in an East London drawl that spilt around his cigar. 'Why won't you join us?'

She sighed and remembered the club's rules for employees who wished to refuse unwanted attention from members who thought their annual membership fee of fifty thousand pounds entitled them to what she and her colleagues described as *full benefits*—be firm but be polite.

'I've already told you, Mr Georgiou, it's been a long shift, and I'd just like to decompress, alone, before I head home.'

'And I've told you, Felicity, to please call me Theo.'

'I'm sorry, but club rules and my respect for our patrons prohibit that level of informality.'

'Now that ain't very friendly, is it, luv?' said the guy with the patchy beard.

'Why don't you just come over and join us?' the thinner twin asked. 'You don't even have to have another drink. Just bring that one. If you wanna leave after that, then fine.'

She looked briefly at each of their grinning faces. Tweedledick, Tweedledumbfuck and the Cheshire Twat, she thought. She weighed up whether standing her ground was worth the effort. Theo, the fatter twin, was the member. He had money, but it wasn't old money. She knew that much. She guessed he'd most likely made it at least semi-legitimately— probably in real estate or something just as mundane—but, with the swagger, the gelled-back hair, and the gold jewellery, he and his brother clearly considered themselves as East End gangsters. The Krays for the digital age.

Yes. It was absolutely worth it.

'Look,' she said, frustration now edging its way through the politeness. 'I went off the clock ten minutes ago. I just want to wind down before I go home, and I'd like to do that in peace. So, please, just leave me alone. I don't want to have to go to management with a harassment complaint, but I will if you persist in bothering me.'

Theo's face clouded over. He left his place at the bar, walked behind her, and wedged himself between her and someone hunched over the bar a metre to her right. He got close enough to her that she could feel his hot, foul-smelling breath on her ear and neck.

'You think,' he whispered, his voice laced with venom, 'that management is going to give a fuck about you with all the money I pump into this place? The second you go to them, you'll be out on the street like the little whore you are.'

'I'm going to tell you one more time, Mr Georgiou. I. Am. Not. Interested.'

The bartender, observing the exchange from the other end of the bar, came over.

'Everything okay here, Flix?'

'Yeah. Thanks, Jan. I can handle this. I'm about to leave anyway.'

Jan nodded and moved on to serve another member.

'Maybe we should just leave it, Theo,' said the thinner twin. 'I'm meeting the missus for dinner at eight-thirty, and you know Mel. She'll skin me alive if I'm late.'

'Shut up, Nicky.'

Felicity made to stand up, but Theo grabbed her wrist and pulled her toward him.

'Stay and finish your drink,' he said. 'Or do *I* have to call someone from management?'

'Let go of me.'

She tugged her arm away strongly enough to loosen his grip, but he'd drawn her to him with such force that his arm travelled backward, uncontrolled, into the person standing behind him.

'Watch yourself, pal,' Theo said over his shoulder, then roughly grabbed Felicity's forearm.

'Ow!' she said, wincing.

'I don't think you understand—'

'You know what? I've been as polite as I can be, but now you've gone too far. So, get your fat, dirty fucking paw off me.'

She pushed his chest with both hands, and he stumbled backward. There was a loud snarl behind him, deep and guttural, like a wild animal's.

'What the fuck?' he said.

He spun around. Towering over him was a man with long shaggy brown hair and an unkempt beard. He wore a navy suit and a crisp white shirt, accentuating a muscular frame. Peeking above his shirt collar, on both sides of his neck, were the black swirling lines of tattoos, and around his neck was a thin dark cord laced through a collection of what were possibly carved pieces of wood, but which looked like they could be the petrified ears of small children. Down the left side of his suit, creeping onto the shirt, was a dark, damp stain. Raw aggression seethed out of him, and a strange aura surrounded him that seemed to shimmer like a heatwave and yet chill the air simultaneously.

'Cain,' Felicity said. 'It's okay. I can handle these guys.'

Theo looked from her to the giant she'd called Cain.

'Yeah, candy cane,' he said boldly. 'She can handle me, so sit back down and finish what's left of your fuckin' drink.'

Cain stepped forward and placed a hand on his chest.

'Come on then, fucker,' Theo taunted. 'One of you, three of us.'

The bartender called out to Cain and swirled a finger in the air. He paused and glanced around, more with his eyes than his head. Theo got the message, too.

'That's right, you fuckin' caveman. Witnesses. And there's cameras all over the place, too. You try anything, and I'll take you to court with video footage to prove it.'

Cain growled again, quietly. Felicity thought she saw his irises ripple from green to the colour of congealed blood and back again but then decided she probably imagined it. The bar's lights were low, and her Grey Goose was her second double since finishing her shift. She'd gulped down her first as soon as her stint ended—a balm for already having to deal with Theo and his cohorts for almost an hour beforehand.

She touched Cain's arm and nodded. She would be fine. Two of the club's security personnel were now hovering around, so she thought it unlikely that the three drunk idiots would give her any more aggravation. Cain glared once more at Theo then pushed past him and headed for the emergency stairs.

Cain shoved the exit door at the bottom of the fire stairs and came out of the building at its rear, onto St Anne's Churchyard. The grounds were quiet, with no one else in them that he could see or hear. He set off across the stone-slabbed pathway that led around the nearest manicured square of grass and managed to take eighteen or nineteen strides before the exit door burst open behind him.

'Oi, Mongo! You think we're finished?'

He ignored the shout.

'Oi, cunt! I'm talking to you!'

He took a few more steps, and then something hard struck him on the back of the head and landed with a dull thud on the walkway. He looked down and spotted a fist-sized rock. One of the men, probably the one called Theo, had hurled it at him. He ran his fingers across the spot the rock had struck, and they came away slick with blood.

He hadn't left the club because he was concerned about witnesses, video footage, or the authorities. There were ways of dealing with those problems. But the last thing he wanted was to explain himself to Simon about a public altercation on Sicarii ground like a child who'd misbehaved. And by walking away, he'd given the three men the opportunity to be physically capable of doing the same. That the men had followed and assaulted him now made them fair game. And down here, in the relative darkness of the churchyard, there were no cameras or onlookers, and they were on neutral ground.

These idiots were on their own.

Concealing his rage, Cain slowly turned around, grabbed the rock, held it up, and crushed it to dust. He knew this unsettled the three men even without seeing their wide eyes and gawping mouths. He could hear their hearts thumping. He wasn't concerned with the two sidekicks, but he wanted to know what was driving Theo.

As with others of his kind, he could read a person's thoughts. He took a step forward and focused on Theo, whose face contorted slightly with the pressure he applied deep inside his brain. The thug unconsciously gave him everything he needed to know. He was desperate to be respected. To be taken seriously. To be thought of as the alpha. He didn't seem to understand that alphas don't showboat and bully and attack for no reason. They protect and provide for and fight only when necessary.

'You disrespected me in front of my brother and my friend and that bitch,' Theo yelled, bravado masking the dread Cain sensed in him. 'Nobody puts their hands on me.'

Cain took a few more steps forward and *pushed* into Theo's mind. The pressure he exerted caused the man to double over and vomit. As Theo wiped his mouth and chin with the back of his hand, head still between his knees, Cain *pushed* again.

You should've left the woman alone. And you should've left when I gave you the chance to walk away with your lives.

Theo spun back to the other two men.

'Did you guys hear that?'

'Hear what?' Nicky asked.

'Gaz?'

Gaz, the ginger-bearded friend, shrugged and shook his head.

'Him,' Theo said. 'I heard him. In my head. You didn't hear him?'

The other two men looked at Theo vacantly. He turned back to Cain.

'What the fuck are you?'

Cain grinned, showing him long white, fang-like canine teeth. For a few seconds more, Theo was motionless. Then, fumbling, he pulled a switchblade from his jacket. He thumbed the metal button in its handle and the blade sprung out.

'I'm gonna give you a facelift, you fuckin' freak.'

'Jesus, Theo. Just put that thing away, and let's go. You've already caused enough grief tonight.'

'Shut the fuck up, Nicky.'

'Yeah, come on, Theo. Let's leave it, yeah?'

'Gaz, I swear to God, if you don't get in here and help me take this dickhead, I'm going to start on you when I'm done with him.'

Theo paced forward and took a backhanded swing. Cain easily veered back enough to avoid the blade, then stepped forward and slapped his face hard. It took the thug a couple of seconds to recover from the shock of it and then he began lashing out erratically. Cain slapped him again as his arm wrapped around to the left. Theo roared, furious. Cain knew that slapping him in front of his brother and friend would be more embarrassing than being punched. It would make Theo his bitch.

'Come on, you fuckin' mutant,' Theo bellowed. 'I'm gonna cut your fuckin' eyes out.'

He reversed his grip on the knife so the blade pointed toward the ground, allowing him to punch and then slice in a single motion. He swung frantically, stepping forward with each punch, curling his wrist each time to angle the blade toward Cain's face. Each blow missed, as did each slicing curl that followed it.

After the sixth or seventh punch, Cain launched himself with a speed that Theo couldn't accurately have judged even if he weren't enraged and intoxicated. He slammed his forehead onto Theo's nose and kicked him between the legs with such force that the man's feet left the ground. Theo let out a piercing scream as if he were a boy whose voice hadn't yet broken. He dropped the knife and collapsed to his knees, one hand cupping his testicles and the other over his ruined nose, blood pulsing through the gaps in his fingers.

'Jesus fucking Christ,' Gaz yelled, pulling out his own knife. A big, ugly thing, one side of the blade smooth and the other jagged like a saw. He lunged, swinging left and right, hitting nothing but air. Then he tried a long jab which Cain sidestepped and countered by grabbing and lifting the thug's wrist.

While Theo lay sobbing on the floor, curled up in a ball, Nicky grabbed his knife, launched himself toward Cain, and tried to stab him in the stomach. Cain shifted his position, putting Gaz between them and using him to block Nicky's every thrust. Then, bored of the dance, he shoved Gaz forward, and both thugs went sprawling onto the floor.

Nicky pushed himself to his hands and knees. 'I'm going to gut this fucking wanker,' he whispered to Gaz. 'Let's take him together. He won't be able to take us both at once.'

Gaz nodded. Having heard Nicky as if he'd spoken aloud, Cain readied himself. The two thugs sprang up and charged at him. Nicky lunged first, thrusting his knife hand forward.

'You're fuckin' dead!' he shouted.

Cain dodged the blade, then grabbed the man's forearm, twisted it, and pulled it skywards. He drove the heel of his palm into the bone of Nicky's elbow, pushing it the wrong way with such force that the joint snapped and the bone broke through the skin. Nicky began to wail and kept wailing until he thumped him in the temple and knocked him unconscious.

Having watched Cain so devastatingly incapacitate his two friends, Gaz lost control of his bladder. He took hold of his knife's blade and hurled it at him. To his apparent surprise and Cain's, the throw wasn't only on target, but the knife hit him tip-first. The blade sank deep into his shoulder.

He roared and launched himself at Gaz. He grabbed him by the throat, pulled the knife from his shoulder, and brought it down toward the man's head in an arc. Gaz lifted his left arm to defend himself, and the blade slid clean through his forearm, shattering the bone as it passed through.

Cain shoved him to the ground as he screamed, then glanced at the other two. Nicky was still out cold. Theo was still curled into a ball but had gone quiet. The only one making noise now was Gaz. Cain knelt next to him, put his hand over his nose and mouth, and kept it there while he struggled for air. After a few seconds, he stopped thrashing and lay still. Cain didn't need to check for a pulse to know if the man was still alive. He could hear his heart beating. It was faint and weak, but it was there.

He stood up, straightened his clothes, and poked a finger through the hole in his suit jacket. The wound underneath was already closing, but the suit was unsalvageable. As he looked at the chests of his assailants, all rising and falling erratically, his phone chirped. He pulled it from his ruined jacket. A banner on the screen told him he'd received a text from Gideon.

He unlocked the phone, read the text, and checked his watch. Knowing how long the flight from Paris to London took, he calculated that Gideon hadn't given him much time to get to Hussein's and then the airport. He grunted, then headed for the churchyard's exit, leaving the thugs where they lay, alive but undoubtedly permanently disfigured.

26

Cain slowed his charcoal Mustang to a crawl as he turned onto Connaught Street. After the fight in the churchyard, he'd gone to his apartment underneath the club and picked up some clean suits and shirts, figuring he'd change on the plane to Denmark. It had started raining heavily after leaving his apartment, and with no umbrella in the car, he hunted for a vacant parking space as close as possible to Hussein's place.

He found one next to a large refuse skip which sat underneath a yellow plastic chute attached to a tall scaffolding tower. No good. Renovations or repairs of some kind were underway at the property there. As one of only thirteen hundred and fifty-nine of the original Boss 429s made, he'd owned the Mustang since it first came out of the Ford factory in 1969, and he wasn't going to risk falling debris damaging the car to avoid walking too far in the rain.

He spotted another free space further up the street and made for it. After parking, and with swift, fluid movements, he switched off the engine, exited the car, shut and locked the driver's door, and bolted for the cover of the scaffolding. From there, he dashed to the end of the street where it met Edgware Road and turned right. After a few yards, he stopped under the maroon awning of a small coffee shop and rubbed the rain from his clothes.

The café's single door was nestled between two large windows, all held in place by maroon wooden frames that looked and smelled freshly painted. On the pavement underneath the canopy were three round wooden tables, each with two wooden chairs. Two old men sat at one of the tables, puffing fragrant shisha through hookah pipes. A much younger man occupied one of the other tables drinking what was probably Turkish coffee judging by the size of the cup, and delicately holding a piece of crumbly baklava between his thumb and forefinger. An arc of gold lettering on each window said CAFE HADDAD.

A small bell rang as Cain went inside. It was empty of customers—smoking shisha wasn't permitted indoors—and the uncluttered serving counter was unattended, but a young woman in a peach-coloured hijab appeared within seconds.

'Mr. Cain,' she said, her accent Middle Eastern with a London lilt. 'I haven't seen you in some time.'

He smiled and nodded once.

The woman's name was Zainab. She was the café manager and the niece of Hussein's wife, Amal. She took care of the legitimate side of Hussein's business topside. Hussein's domain was downstairs.

She didn't say anything to him about the hole in his jacket or the bloody stain around it, and he didn't expect her to. On the wall behind her were two telephones—a white one on the left, the other a dark olive colour. She picked up the olive-coloured phone. It had no keypad or rotary dial on it. It was a direct link to a single phone somewhere else. She remained silent for a few moments, spoke quietly into the handset, and then turned back to the counter.

'You can go straight down,' she said.

He walked around the counter into the café's back rooms, opened a creaky wooden door and descended a dog-legging staircase to a dimly lit but well-organised and spotlessly clean basement containing numerous boxes of various materials, colours and sizes. He went to the wall on the far side of the basement. On it was a faded poster in a dusty frame. He pulled it, and it swung open like a small door. Behind it was a recess the size of a shoebox, and sitting within the cavity, angled at forty-five degrees, was a hand-sized rectangular black glass panel. To the right of the hole, set flush on the wall, was another rectangular plate slightly larger than a magazine, its top slightly below his eye line. At the bottom was a circle of holes that looked like an intercom speaker.

He placed his left hand on the angled panel and squatted enough to align his face with the one to its right. As the large panel glowed with a green light that scanned his face, he exhaled deeply into the ring of holes. Then the hand plate lit up with lines of similar green lights that scanned the underside of his hand in several directions, and an ultrathin hypodermic needle dropped from above it and speared the back of his hand, causing him to wince slightly.

It was a sophisticated biometric access system that verified a person's retina, irises, fingers, palm, blood, and breath. To gain access to what lay beyond, a user had to be alive and conscious and their biological data recognised by the system. He heard a series of beeps, and a section of wall opened away from him with a soft click. He pushed it and walked into the void.

In contrast to the basement, the room beyond was a well-lit space lined with clean, white panelling. On three sides were aluminium workbenches, atop two of which sat four computer workstations. On the third workbench were three long black cases that looked like oversized heavy-duty travel cases. Against the walls, between the workbenches, were numerous computer-aided machines used for drilling, milling, boring, grinding and shaping. It was a high-tech blacksmith's forge.

A bald, thin man in a dark brown cardigan sat hunched on a tall stool at one of the workstations, his back to the door. There was a soft, slow clicking as his fingers moved over the keyboard.

It was Hussein Haddad.

Hussein was the son of Ali, whom the Sicarii had moved to London in 1948, shortly after the murder of Ali's father, Khaled, at the outbreak of the Arab-Israeli war. At the time, Ali's great uncle, Sultan, worked as an armourer for the group. Israel had become an unsafe place for Arabs, so the Sicarii had arranged for Sultan and his family—including Ali and his mother—to migrate to London. As a cover for his work, Sultan had opened the coffee shop—the same cover he'd used in Israel. Upon his death, his work passed to Ali and then to Hussein when Ali became too arthritic to continue.

He coughed into a handkerchief and, without turning around, said, 'I thought you *Hashashin* were supposed to be silent.'

Cain focussed and projected his thoughts into Hussein's mind.

Hard to be silent with that clunky entry system you've got, old man. What are you doing over there? Updating your online dating profile?

'Ha! Amal would feed my balls to me in a bowl of *shorbat adas* and tell me they were dumplings if I were even to breathe in another woman's direction.'

Cain chuckled.

'And less of the old man,' continued Hussein, wagging a finger in the air.

He slid off the stool, steadying himself with a metal walking stick. When he turned around, Cain was stunned. Hussein had always been a big man, physically and figuratively, and had always seemed younger than he was. But in the few months since his last visit, Hussein appeared to have aged twenty years. Arthritis, and lung cancer, courtesy of a lifetime of smoking his favourite double-apple-flavoured shisha, had shrunken him down to a shadow of the character he used to be.

'My God, don't you ever age?'

The virtues of a healthy diet of red meat, dark spirits, and hot-blooded women.

Hussein laughed hoarsely. It was a joke they'd shared many times. He hobbled over, patted Cain on the shoulder, and then pointed at the bloody hole in his jacket.

'You need anything for that?'

Cain shook his head.

Already good as new. He smiled and looked around the workshop. *Things have changed in here.* He referred not only to some of the newer pieces of high-tech equipment but also to Hussein himself.

'Well, if—'

Hussein interrupted himself with a severe coughing fit that shook his entire body. As Cain reached out to steady him, the men heard the soft, unmistakable click of a gun's hammer drawing back.

'Getting easy to sneak up on you these days, old man.'

The two men turned in the direction from where the voice had come. In front of them stood a tall, slender woman in a black tee shirt, light blue jeans with holes in various places, and a pair of combat boots. Her long blue-black hair was tied back in a ponytail. On the top of her head was a pair of safety glasses, and in her left hand was a gun that looked like it belonged in a science fiction film.

Shouldn't talk to your father like that, Layla.

"Who said I was speaking to him?' she said, frowning slightly due to the pressure of Cain's *push* inside her head.

There's just no respect from the young today.

Layla's frown turned to a wide smile.

I wasn't expecting to see you here. Thought you were still in Chicago.

'Three years over there was enough. Plus,' she said, nodding to Hussein, 'I couldn't let Dad have all the fun here, could I?'

Cain nodded, understanding the meaning of what she'd said. Hussein was sick, and she needed to be here for him. She put the safety glasses and the gun on the nearest workbench and walked over to the two men. She gave Cain a tight hug and Hussein a gentle squeeze on the shoulder.

You look... good. What are you, now? Twenty-nine? Thirty?

'You don't stand a chance, old man,' she said, smiling. 'But I'll take the compliment anyway. And I'm thirty-eight.'

He nodded to the gun.

SIG Sauer MPX K semi-automatic pistol modified with a sound suppressor and laser sight. How's it handle?

'Not too bad in there,' she said, nodding to the room she'd come from—a thirty-metre, fully soundproofed shooting range that stretched underneath the row of properties to the south of the café. 'I need to get it out in the open for a decent field test, though.'

'I need some tea,' said Hussein. He picked up the handset of a green wall-mounted telephone and waited for it to connect to its twin upstairs. 'Zainab, could you please bring some tea downstairs? Lemon and ginger, I think. Thank you, dear.'

Cain observed again how starkly he'd aged, then looked back at Layla.

'What do you need?' she asked.

Gideon and I are heading to Copenhagen within the hour, so whatever you've got that's ready to go. And nothing too crazy.

'Ha! That's Gideon talking.'

He smirked.

How'd you know?

She went to the workbench the travel cases were on, unlocked the metal clasps of the nearest one, and gestured to it.

'For Gideon,' she said. 'I've made some updates to his usual pack.'

He opened the case and grinned like a child unwrapping presents on his birthday. Before him lay an assortment of weapons and accessories, set neatly into a slab of dark grey foam.

'The twin tantos are now black carbon steel, as are the two wakizashis. All pretty much indestructible and more than sharp enough at the tips to punch through Kevlar if thrust with enough force. The guns—'

Glock 19s. Gen-five. Double-stack magazines with fifteen rounds in each. The—

'Nineteen,' she said. 'I've given him extended mags. You, too.'

Cain grunted his appreciation.

'The shoulder holster is a combo rig made with a new graphene and Kevlar weave. It takes all the toys. I've modified the pistol slots to take the guns as fitted with the suppressors in the case. There are storage clips for three additional magazines on each side. Fast loaders. The swords slot upside down into the fibreglass scabbards moulded into the holster's backplate. Likewise, the knives. All fully concealable under any suit jacket.'

Ammunition?

'The usual,' said Layla, taking a small box from the case. She opened it, pulled out a bullet, and held it up. 'Nine-mil subsonic. One-forty-seven grain. And, as always, untraceable.'

Cain was impressed and smiled his approval. At that moment, there was a soft beep. Zainab had arrived on the other side of the workshop door with the tea.

'Would you mind?' Hussein asked him, nodding at the door. 'She probably has her hands full with the tray.'

The exit process was identical to the entry procedure—a safety feature to entrap unauthorised persons within the room if they somehow managed to access it. He went through the routine and stepped out of the workshop, then took a tray of cups full of steaming tea from Zainab, nodding his head with gratitude as he did so. On returning to the workshop, he placed the tray on the top of a clear workbench and turned back to Layla.

And what do I get?

'Take a look,' she said, gesturing to the middle case.

Its contents were almost identical to Gideon's, but instead of the two-foot swords were twin curved knives, each around sixteen inches long, slim near the hilts and fatter at the sharp ends. They were kukris—his favourite close-combat weapons.

'The kukris slot into the shoulder rig upside-down, just like Gideon's *wakis*,' said Layla. 'Their grips, and those of the tantos and his swords, are made of ridgeless G10, so you can reverse your grasp without compromising grip.'

Cain took one of the kukris from the case. He held it loosely by its grip, checking its weight and feel in his hand. Then he deftly reversed his grip so that he held the knife like an ice pick. He twirled it so the blade's edge faced away from him and slashed the air with an upward movement. Finally, he balanced the knife on his forefinger to locate its balance point. Then, with another flourish, he replaced it in the case. His lips spread into a wolfish grin, and he looked at Hussein.

She clearly loves her work. You must be very proud.

'That I am,' he said, patting Layla's face gently, holding back another cough.

'Open that last case,' she said.

Cain obeyed, then stood back and whistled.

'That's a SIG M400 SWAT five-point-five-six. It's fitted with a Trijicon VCOG sight for improved long-range accuracy, and the screw-on suppressor should make it whisper quiet. Everything a good sniper needs.'

I'd love to, but I'm under orders, remember? Nothing too flashy.

'Fair enough,' she said, pulling a smaller case from a shelf under the workbench. 'But take this. It contains three frags, three flashbangs, and one remotely controlled explosive device. Probably overkill, but...' She shrugged as she trailed off.

Excellent work, Layla. Thank you.

'No thanks needed. That's my job.'

'So, what now?' asked Hussein.

Cain's face clouded over.

We hunt.

27

Northolt Jet Centre was located on the A40, thirty minutes west of Marble Arch. Known more commonly as RAF Northolt, it operated primarily as a military airfield, but since 2006, it had also served as an extension to London City Airport and catered for private jets, allowing up to forty civilian movements per day. The Sicarii, through a veil of shell companies, leased a section of apron set away from the main terminal building that gave the organisation an exclusive and secluded parking area.

Due to favourable tailwinds, the black and grey Bombardier jet carrying Gideon from Paris had touched down four minutes earlier than expected. Besides some minor turbulence over the English Channel, the journey had been uneventful.

As the plane rolled to a gentle stop on the Sicarii's private apron, Gideon stepped to the cabin door and pulled the release lever. The door swung down and he started to descend its built-in stairs before it had fully unfolded. As he reached the bottom step, he glanced up and saw Cain standing on the apron. When he'd crossed half the distance between them, he pointed at the bloody hole in Cain's suit.

'What happened?'

He felt a familiar pressure inside his head.

Nothing consequential.

'For you or them?'

Cain smiled darkly.

They may be sore for a while.

Gideon held out his hand. Cain ignored it, slapped him on the shoulder, and went back to his car. Ordinarily, no private vehicles were permitted beyond the parking areas on that side of the security fence, nor were passengers allowed to access the apron or exit the terminal without first having passed through the immigration gate within the terminal building. The Sicarii, however, had a long-standing private arrangement with a senior official at the facility, which not only granted them unimpeded pedestrian and vehicular access to their leased area but also meant that instead of having to go into the terminal building to complete passport control procedures, an immigration official would come out to them. It was all perfectly legal, except for the Sicarii's use of counterfeit passports.

A tall man in a fully buttoned black woollen overcoat and a charcoal scarf wrapped snugly around his neck approached them from the terminal building. He wore a sombre expression and held something small and black in his right hand. Gideon momentarily tensed, preparing to react if he had to, but then saw the device for what it was—a handheld scanner—and relaxed.

'Good evening, gentlemen,' the man said. 'Could I have your passports, please?'

'I'm in transit,' Gideon replied.

The man from immigration nodded, acknowledging there was no need to inspect his passport if he was getting back onto an aircraft. He then looked expectantly at Cain, who handed over a United Kingdom passport for one of his many false personae.

The man flipped the passport open, switching his gaze between the photograph within it and Cain's face. Satisfied, he held the passport wide open, scanned it, and handed it back.

'Thank you, sir. Have a good flight, gentlemen.'

As the man headed back to the terminal building. Gideon watched him for a few moments, then turned to Cain.

'Did you make it to Hussein's?'

Cain went to the back of the car and opened the boot. Gideon joined him and saw the two black weapons cases and the box of grenades Layla had provided. The two larger containers had pull-out handles and small rubberised wheels, like most ordinary travel cases. They also had centrally mounted carrying handles. Cain grabbed the top case, removed it from the boot, and motioned to the remaining boxes with his head.

Can you take those? I need to grab something from the front.

He made his way around to the Mustang's passenger side and opened the door. Leaning deep into the car, he pulled a black suit protector from the back seat, then slammed the door shut and locked it manually.

Gideon lifted his case and the box of grenades from the boot, then elbowed it shut and headed back to the jet. Enrique, their pilot, was standing at the bottom of the steps. He acknowledged Cain when he joined them, then wordlessly took his suit protector and the grenades, climbed the stairs, and disappeared into the jet. Cain turned to Gideon.

So, what's the story?

'We have practically no intel on the target other than a first name, the name of her therapist, and the name and address of a priest she's met. I'm hoping we'll get more information while we're airborne.'

Cain grunted and gestured to the plane.

Gideon climbed the steps ahead of him, and without turning or stopping, said, 'Thomas will be there.'

Fuck.

28

Cardinal Peter Barjona sat on the plush, black leather rear seat of his Bentley Flying Spur, which had pulled to a gentle halt on Victoria Street moments ago. He held a large iPad and was watching a piece on CNN about Chinese aircraft menacing Australian warships in the Philippine Sea. Upon leaving his London residence in Kensington, he'd deployed the privacy blinds so that he could watch the news without distraction. So far, they'd done their job, but he was unable to concentrate, preoccupied as he was with one thought.

Who the Danish woman, Ellie, might be?

On the tray of the full-length centre console that separated the two rear seats from each other sat a crystal decanter two-thirds full of Delamain Grande Champagne Cognac. In the cup holder sat a matching thick-based tumbler containing a generous measure of the expensive brandy. It was his second glass since getting into the car. Usually based in Rome, he believed the Italians did many things very well—clothes, cars, coffee, changing governments—but nobody made brandy like the French.

His driver, Markus, put the car into neutral, applied the parking brake, and tapped the button to activate the hazard lights. Peter lifted his tumbler, swirled the alcohol around it for a few seconds, then raised the glass to his nose and inhaled deeply. He savoured the aroma, swallowed the brandy, and placed the tumbler back onto the tray, knowing that Markus would remove the glass once he'd left the car and replace it with a fresh one. He straightened the rose gold signet ring on the small finger of his right hand and looked to his left. Markus had parked the car facing west, putting Peter's side of the car conveniently against the curb, adjacent to Cathedral Piazza—a public space, roughly trapezoid in shape and over fifty metres across. His destination sat to the south, on its far side.

Westminster Cathedral.

He opened the privacy screen on his window and peered out into the night. It was raining steadily, although the sky threatened to empty a torrent. He fished a pair of black, cashmere-lined leather gloves from the inside pocket of the grey wool and cashmere overcoat he wore, slid them on, and opened his door. It had only opened an inch or two before Markus hurriedly unbuckled his seatbelt.

'No, don't trouble yourself, Markus,' he said. 'Drive around to the cathedral's car park. Hopefully, the gates will still be unlocked and open. Then come inside through the rear when you're able.'

Markus acknowledged the command with a nod and passed a silver-handled umbrella back. Peter took it, slid out of the car, and slammed the door shut. The car rolled away immediately, almost silently.

He turned and marched across the piazza. It was almost empty except for a small group of pub-goers, a couple of late-working office drones running for cover from the rain, and a homeless man who sought shelter under an alcove next to a McDonald's. He was able to cross it quickly and unimpeded.

Westminster Cathedral, a building he'd visited countless times, had been constructed in the Victorian era in memory of the first Archbishop of Westminster, Cardinal Wiseman. In 1895, during its construction, it was dedicated to the blood of Christ. Since its opening in 1903, it had been the mother church of Catholicism in the United Kingdom, presided over by the incumbent Archbishop of Westminster. With its neo-Byzantine styling, its four crowning domes, and its tall minaret-style campanile bell tower, it had, in more recent times though, been mistakenly thought of by some, and to the Church's very public embarrassment, as a mosque.

As he approached the cathedral's tall oak and iron doors, Peter glanced up at the stone archway above it. Inscribed into it were the words DOMINE JESU REX ET REDEMPTOR PER SANGIUNEM TUUM SALVA NOS—*Lord Jesus, King and Redeemer, save us by Your blood*. It was a nod to Christ's sacrifice for the sake of humankind, to his return, and the blood he would shed in the battle at the end of things. He smiled, as he always did when reading it. But now, he thought, that time could be drawing closer.

He turned the large wrought iron ring-shaped door handle and pushed the door forward, stepping inside quickly. He shook off and then closed and furled the umbrella, wiped down the lower part of his body, and paused in the narthex. The cathedral's interior was a place of grandeur. Its belly was cavernous, and its nave—illuminated by lamped chandeliers giving off a warm yellow glow—was seventy metres from where he stood to the sanctuary steps. And at the far end hung a great crucifix, ten metres tall, painted bright red, and bearing the image of Christ. In the darkness of the vaulted ceiling, it seemed to levitate.

The building could hold roughly three thousand congregants, but now there were barely twenty people. There was no sermon or mass underway. Instead, the worshippers sat in quiet contemplation, either sending their prayers to God or simply escaping the rain outside. A young priest was making his way to each person. He spoke quietly to them, and after a few seconds, they each stood and made their way to the front door. Peter looked at his watch. It was just past eight o'clock.

Closing time.

He stood in the narthex for a few more seconds, then turned and walked swiftly and almost silently up the east aisle, unbuttoning his coat as he walked. He spotted the young priest again through a gap between the cathedral's towering columns. The man had finished speaking with people and was collecting small paper leaflets from the forward rows of the front block of pews. He looked to be distracted, deep in thought. He wasn't whom Peter was looking for, but he was a good start.

'Excuse me, Father,' Peter said.

Despite other people being in the cathedral, the priest was startled, as if the building were empty and he was alone. Peter raised his hands in a gesture of apology and then took a step backward, giving the priest some room.

'I'm sorry. I didn't mean to surprise you. I'm looking for Bishop Leonard Byrne. I'm hoping he's still on the premises and hasn't yet left for the day.'

The priest regained his composure.

'I'm sorry, but the cathedral's about to close to the public. Perhaps you could come back tomorrow? The bishop conducts the Saturday morning mass at eight, so you could catch him after that.'

'I'm afraid the matter is urgent, Father...'

'Oh, uh, Pius. Father Justin Pius. And I'm sorry, but I—'

'Father Pius, I really must insist.'

Before the priest could respond, Peter held up a hand, reached into his overcoat and withdrew a rectangular wallet. He opened it and showed it to Pius, who took two seconds to read and digest the information within.

It was a passport issued by the Holy See.

The young priest's face turned pale and then scarlet.

'Oh, dear God. Your Eminence. Please, accept my apologies. I had no idea...'

'It's quite alright.'

'No, your Eminence. It's not. I should've known.'

'Have we met before, Justin?'

'I don't think so, your Eminence.'

'And am I wearing my red cassock?'

'No.'

'Then how would you know who I am?'

The young priest blushed again. Peter had neither the time nor inclination to assuage the man's embarrassment, so he curtly asked whether Byrne was in the building. Father Pius, still visibly flustered, shook his head.

'Uh, no, he's already left for the evening.'

Peter exhaled a long breath of frustration. This exchange was becoming painfully tiresome.

'But you'll probably be able to catch him at home,' the priest continued.

'Which is where?'

'Oh. Just over the road, on Ambrosden Avenue.'

Ambrosden Avenue was a quiet street with Westminster Cathedral on one side and five seven-storey apartment blocks on the other. Each block was made of red brick and white stone and was conjoined to the next, giving the appearance of one long building. When Peter arrived at Byrne's block, an older woman was struggling to take a suitcase through the heavy front door. Peter trotted up the stone steps to the raised ground floor and held the door, for which she thanked him. Once she was through the door and on her way to the street, he stepped into the carpeted, musty lobby. There were only two apartments off it, which meant that Byrne's place—apartment 5, according to Father Pius— would likely be two floors up. He chose to take the stairs rather than the small, ancient-looking elevator.

When he reached the third floor, Byrne's door was to the left of the stairs. He knocked, and it took less than half a minute for the bishop to answer. Byrne was a couple of inches shorter than him and significantly broader. His auburn hair and beard were streaked with white, and his age-lined face wore the expression of someone who didn't want to be disturbed on a Friday evening.

'I'm sorry to intrude upon your Friday evening, reverend bishop,'

Peter said. 'I'm—'

'Cardinal Barjona,' said Byrne. There was a soft Irish lilt to his voice, and while it carried a note of mild surprise, he appeared calm and unworried. He held out his right hand to Peter.

'You know who I am?' Peter asked, shaking Byrne's hand.

'I do. I've seen you in the Vatican several times, at a distance. Please, come in.'

He stepped over the threshold into a warm and softly lit hallway. Soft piano music drifted from a room somewhere, as did the aroma of a cigar or possibly a pipe.

'You don't seem concerned that I'm here unannounced.'

'Should I be?'

Peter smiled.

'No,' he said.

'So, what brings you to my home?'

'Straight to the point. I admire that.'

'Well, it's Friday night, I was officially off the clock an hour ago, and I have dinner plans. If this were a matter important enough to ensure I'd be available, I'm sure your office would've called in advance of your coming here. However, as that didn't happen, I'm guessing that your visit is informal and won't require that I cancel my plans, so getting straight to the point is probably best for both of us, wouldn't you agree?'

Peter pursed his lips and nodded once.

'You received a phone call earlier,' he said, 'from a Father Sigvardt in Copenhagen, concerning a young woman he's recently met named Ellie.'

'That's correct. How—'

'We're the Vatican.'

Byrne smiled wryly.

'Of course,' he said.

'We believe the woman could be a person of significant interest to us.'

'What kind of interest?'

'Her visions are very... specific. As you will have gathered from Sigvardt, they hint at the possibility that certain events as laid out in the Bible may not be completely accurate.'

'She certainly does have an intriguing take on things.'

'We're concerned that if these visions come to the public's attention, they could damage the Church, so we want to investigate the matter fully and, if appropriate, ensure this young woman remains discreet.'

Byrne looked thoughtful for a moment.

'Your Eminence,' he said, 'With the greatest of respect, if you don't want to tell me the real reason you're interested in this woman, that's fine, but please don't come to my home and lie to me, and think that I'll believe you. I'm not an idiot.'

Peter considered Byrne's words for a moment. He'd forgotten that the bishop was a certified clinical psychiatrist and that it was part of his job to listen to people's stories and, where necessary, distinguish fact from fiction.

'Why would you think I'm lying to you?'

'Perhaps lying is too strong a word, but I sense you're not being entirely transparent. It would, I'm sure, take more than the unsubstantiated dreams of a young woman in Copenhagen to harm the Roman Catholic Church. It's come up against and overcome worse in its time. There's another reason you're interested in her.'

Peter smiled.

'You're very intuitive, Leonard. And correct.'

'But you're not going to tell me, are you?'

'I will. But not yet. Ellie will need an explanation, and I'd rather not repeat myself, so if you can wait until she arrives, I'd appreciate your patience.'

'She's coming here?'

'To London, yes. I have a team travelling to Copenhagen as we speak. I'm hopeful they'll locate Ellie quickly and without issue, and I want them to bring her here.'

'Why?'

'Well, for one, I have further business in London, so it makes sense for them to bring her to me here instead of taking her to Rome to await my return there.'

'And?'

'And you are here. As I understand it, she's aware of you. You've been recommended to her by someone she presumably trusts, so you being present when I talk to her might ease any concerns she may have.'

'And what story will your team give her for whisking her away in the night?'

'There is an organisation directly opposed to us and what we stand for. And as much as Ellie is of interest to us, she'll be of much greater interest to them if they were to learn of her existence.'

'Who are they?'

'They're known as the Sicarii,' Peter said.

'The assassins?'

'You know of them?'

'Acts Twenty-One, if I recall my scripture correctly. A passing reference made by Luke when writing of Paul's arrest in Jerusalem. They still exist?'

'They do, and, as I said, they're against us and everything we stand for.'

'So, that's what your team is going to tell the woman? That a group of assassins is hunting her because she's had odd dreams. Are you sure that using scare tactics is the most appropriate way of persuading her to go with your people?'

'It may be the only way.'

Byrne looked simultaneously unconvinced and despondent.

'So, you *will* need me for the rest of the night.'

'No. 'Peter smiled and looked at his watch. 'My team left Athens an hour and a half ago. As I understand, it will take them another two hours to reach Copenhagen, plus an hour and a half from there back to London. So, accounting for travel time to and from airports and however long it will take them to locate the woman, we have a few hours until they arrive here. I can conduct some of my other business in the interim, so why don't we meet across the road at, say, half past midnight?'

He could see that Byrne wanted to argue. The bishop's dinner plans would likely include a few generous tots of Irish whiskey or whatever else he was partial to, and no doubt, he disliked the thought of having to return at least partially sober.

'I don't suppose I have any choice in the matter, do I?' Byrne said.

'None at all, I'm afraid.'

Byrne brushed his hands down his front.

'Alright,' he said, making no effort to hide his frustration. 'Twelve-thirty it is.'

29

Ellie stood in the entry line for Dante's with her hands in her pockets and her long, thick coat buttoned up to keep out as much of the night's chill as possible, but nothing helped keep the cold from her ears, which were becoming increasingly numb. There were around thirty people in front of her, but mercifully, they were inching forward, so she and Suzi would be inside and warming up in minutes. She glanced behind and saw the queue tailed back past the gelato place, the paint store, and around the corner onto Gasværksvej.

'Jesus, I hope Jakob's already inside,' she said, stamping her feet, 'or at least in front of us. Otherwise, he's going to freeze out here.'

'He's probably on his second drink by now, knowing how early he likes to be for everything.'

'He's not early for *everything.*'

'Too much info, babe.'

Ellie laughed.

'Besides,' Suzi continued. 'A little cold won't hurt him. He's a tough nut.'

'No, but it'll set his night off to a crappy start if he has to wait out here for too long, and that'll mean *I'll* have a shit night, which I really don't need right now. I just want to have fun and get so hammered that not even a fucked-up dream later will wake me up.'

'I'm sure he'll be fine. Like I said, he's probably already in there. Speaking of dreams, how'd it go with Carlsson and the priest today?'

While Doctor Carlsson was bound to confidentiality, Ellie wasn't and had been briefing Suzi after each session. Today was Suzi's day off work, so she hadn't had a chance to update her.

'Not great,' she said. She recounted what had happened, including the new dream she had. Retelling it meant reliving it, which isn't what she wanted to do, but she figured that getting it out might be cathartic.

'Holy shit!'

'Yep. It's getting too much, Sooz. First a therapist, then a priest, and now some church dream whisperer. Next, they'll be carting me off to Rome in a straight-jacket and a Hannibal Lecter mask.'

The two women were laughing as they reached the front of the line and were greeted at Dante's heavy oak double doors by two giant, sombre sentinels in long, thick coats whom Ellie knew were named Torben and Victor. With their shaved heads, bushy beards, and matching scowls, they could have been twins but were not. Torben waved the women in with a slow sweep of his thick arm.

Before stepping inside, she looked back along the queue to see if she could spot Jakob. If he was there, she couldn't pick him out. Then she scanned what she could see of Vesterbros Torv, the brick-paved square between Dante's and the wide main road of Vesterbrogade. On warmer evenings, the space would be busy, and it would be impossible to pick anyone out, but there were only a handful of people in it now, mainly smokers taking their final draws before going into Dante's or one of the other bars on the square. He wasn't among them.

She cursed silently, crossed the threshold, and went to the first of two counters to pay her and Suzi's entry fees. She could feel the faint thump of music from elsewhere in the club in her bones and through her feet.

'Where are we supposed to be meeting everyone?' Suzi asked, shrugging off her coat and handing it over to an attendant behind the second counter.

'I have no idea,' she said, passing over her coat. 'I guess we just float around until we find them.'

They took their cloakroom tickets and made their way along a short narrow corridor, at the end of which was a staircase heading upward and an open doorway leading further into the floor they were on.

'Inferno first?' asked Suzi.

'Nah. I doubt it's Goat's scene down there. It's definitely not Jakob's. Chewie's a dark horse, though. He might like that stuff.'

Suzi laughed.

'Paradiso it is, then,' she said, heading upward.

The stairs came out within an arched alcove of the club's main floor. As she always did when she came to Dante's as if she were preserving something of the building's past, but without really knowing why, Ellie thought of how the place was so starkly different from when she'd first come here.

She'd been four or five years old, and it had been a church then. But a group of local bar owners bought the building a few years ago when the Church of Denmark began closing and selling off its churches due to ever-decreasing congregations and perpetually rising running costs. They converted it into a rock club and named it Dante's, after the Italian poet and author of *The Divine Comedy*.

The ground floor was now home to the cloakrooms, bathrooms, and a small dancefloor and bar called Inferno which catered to those who loved the extreme subgenres of metal—thrash, black, doom, death, and the like. The main body of the church, on the upper floor where she stood now, had been named Paradiso and was home to more mainstream rock and metal.

When the place was still a church, the congregants would reach *Paradise* by ascending the twenty stone steps from the public square and entering through the now-defunct twin double oak doors far to her right. These days everyone came in at ground level, through what used to be the priests' entrance, and worked their way up, either through or past *Hell*, to get there.

She quickly scanned the room. It was busier than she expected, but even so, and despite the distraction of the thumping music and the flashing lights, she guessed it wouldn't be hard to find Jakob and the others they were meeting, given how open most of the place was.

To her immediate right, running the length of the alcove that used to be the east aisle, was a long bar made of black wood. Her eyes drifted across the faces of people waiting to be served and as many of those behind them as she could see, but there was no sign of Jakob or the others. She could see across the room up to the arched balcony above what used to be the west aisle. As with the gallery immediately above her, there was a line of blue-baized pool tables up there. She could see people gathered around the tables through the arched openings, but none she recognised.

In the west aisle at her level was another long bar. Between it and Ellie, occupying what used to be the nave, was the dancefloor. The old granite-tiled floor had given way to dark timber. At one end, built in front of the imposing former entrance doors, was a concealed fire exit corridor, accessible from both sides of the room, which utilised the old doors as emergency exits. In front of the fire corridor were four semi-circular booths, each with a round table and banquette-style seats upholstered in merlot-coloured vinyl, tall enough to hide their occupants when seated.

At the other end of the nave, at the top of eight or nine stone steps, was the apse, which had been cleared of the old altar and was now a stage used by bands that played on Friday and Saturday nights. High on the wall to the left of the apse was the old pulpit, currently occupied by the club's resident DJ, who had a Marilyn Manson number thumping through the club's speaker system. She smiled at the irony of a song about the antichrist playing in a building that used to be a church, and whose congregants now only worshipped the gods of modern life—music, drugs, sex, alcohol, and, worst of all, social media.

She pushed through the crowd toward the bar in the west aisle, looking left and right as she went but finding it impossible to identify

Jakob or anyone else she knew. When she got into the recess of the aisle, she nudged her way along the back wall of people waiting to order their drinks. There was still no sign of the others.

Besides the dancefloor, which she considered an unlikely prospect, there was only one more place to look. The balcony on the opposite side of the room, above where she'd initially entered Paradiso. She looked through the first archway but saw nobody she recognised. Where the second arch should have been was the box for the old Marcussen and Søn organ. The organ itself was gone now, but the ornate pipes it had once used were still in place and, like the walls of Paradiso, were painted crimson and black like the conduits of some demon's instrument. She eyed the third and final archway but didn't know the faces she could see through it.

Where the hell were they?

As she turned to Suzi to verbalise her frustration, she spotted Chewie appear in the first archway. She tapped Suzi on the arm and headed to the staircase for the east gallery. When she arrived upstairs at the pool tables, she found Chewie with Goat and his wife Natasja, waiting for a pool table to become free.

Jakob wasn't there.

She greeted the others with quick hugs, as did Suzi. Then, half-shouting over the music, she asked if he'd arrived yet, and received shrugs and headshakes in response.

'I'm going back to the bar,' she said, annoyed and concerned that he hadn't turned up yet. She pointed at Suzi and asked if she wanted a beer, to which Suzi nodded. Then she swiped a finger at the others, who answered by shaking their heads and holding up half-full drinks.

'I'll come with you,' Chewie said.

'You already have a drink.'

'Yeah, but I can part the seas on the way there and help you carry the drinks back.'

'My hero.'

On the main floor, she followed Chewie as he pushed his way through the crowd to the bar directly under their balcony. When they reached the front, she immediately caught a bartender's eye and ordered three pints of Tuborg—one for herself, one for Suzi, and one for Jakob, hoping he'd arrive before it went flat. And if he didn't, she'd have to drink it, and she was more than okay with that.

When she'd given her order to the barman, she turned to talk with Chewie, but to her amusement, and predictably, she thought, he'd abandoned her to chat up a dreadlocked and heavily tattooed blonde with breasts so large they might pop if anyone even whispered the word *pin* to them.

She chuckled. He was nothing if not confident. And relentless.

'One-eighty,' said the bartender, putting the last of three pint-sized plastic cups on the bar, each full of beer.

'Sorry, what?' she shouted, distracted.

'One. Eighty,' he repeated, holding up one finger and then eight fingers as he spoke each word.

She handed over a two-hundred-kroner note and, jostled from all sides, waited for her change, which the barman swiftly brought back. She tapped Chewie on the shoulder, who appeared unimpressed with the intrusion. She pouted mockingly and handed him a beaker of beer, some of which he deposited on the floor by squeezing too hard in the exchange.

'Shit!'

'Makes no difference to me,' she said. 'That's Jakob's.'

'Oops,' he said sarcastically.

Ellie grabbed the other two pints, and they both pushed back through the crowd to head upstairs to the others. When they got there, she handed a drink to Suzi, and Chewie put Jakob's beer down on a shallow wall-mounted shelf on which Goat and Natasja were leaning.

'What time are we expecting your other half?' Natasja asked her.

'We said eight-ish, but you know men.'

'Indeed, I do.'

Natasja looked at Goat and gave him a couple of gentle taps on the face.

'Hey, lass. I take exception to that.'

'Ah, bless,' said Natasja, patting him again.

'Alright, alright,' he said, all flustered.

All three women laughed at the tough guy who turned to butter in his wife's hands. Ellie was about to ask Chewie if he'd gotten the dreadlocked woman's number when the bar's speakers fell silent, and spotlights came on above the apse, illuminating a jumble of guitars, amplifiers, and a large drum kit. Four women, dressed mostly in black and with varying degrees of tattoo coverage, came onto the stage from its left to a cacophony of whistles, cheers, and claps. One approached the microphone in the centre of the stage as the others went to their instruments. Half of her head was clipped buzzcut short and dyed blonde, while the other was a long, wavy mop of dark cherry red. She tightened the lumberjack shirt tied around her waist and grabbed the microphone, sending a screech of feedback through the speakers.

'Hey, what's up, Dante's? We're Hellenbach.'

There were more shouts and whistles from the crowd.

'If you haven't been to one of our gigs before, we like to mix it up. Do some of our stuff, throw in some shit by other bands. That okay with you guys?'

Everyone in the place roared their agreement. Ellie and the others joined in, whooping and cheering.

'Awesome,' the singer said, then shouted, 'Reach out... and touch faith!'

As the drums and heavily distorted guitars came in, Suzi raised her arms and rocked her head.

'I love their version of this,' she shouted.

'Same,' yelled Chewie.

Ellie rolled her eyes. And so it begins, she thought.

She felt a hard push against her back. Probably just someone trying to get past her to watch the band. She'd done the same before, so she paid no attention.

Another shunt.

For fuck's sake, she thought, but she remained calm and refocused on her friends. She felt like shit but wasn't in the mood for trouble.

At the third shove, she lost her patience and her temper. She spun around to confront the pusher, shoulders tensed, her free hand clenched into a fist, ready to fight if necessary.

Standing there with a wide grin on his face was Jakob.

Her shoulders dropped, and she relaxed, much to the amusement of Goat and Natasja, who'd both seen him coming.

'Sorry I'm late,' he said.

'You almost got taken down, there, lad,' said Goat. 'I thought she was going to swing for you.'

'I don't doubt it.'

He threw an arm around Ellie's neck, playfully putting her in a chokehold. He kissed her on the forehead and then gave her a lingering, closed-mouth kiss on the lips.

'Get a room,' said Chewie.

Jakob released his lip-lock on Ellie and grinned.

'Where've you been?' she asked.

'Sorry, babes. There was some kind of incident on my street earlier. A mugging or something. It must've happened after I got home from work. When I left the flat to come here, the police were going door-to-door, so they stopped me on the street and questioned me for a bit. Did I live on the street, did I see anything, that kind of shit.'

'You mugging old ladies for their pension money, now Jakob?' said Chewie. 'You should ask for a pay rise.'

'Any pay rise he gets,' said Goat, 'will come straight out of your wages, sonny.'

Chewie's jaw dropped in feigned shock.

Ellie patted Suzi on the shoulder and nodded at the pool table they stood closest to, which was now free. Suzi took a pool cue from one of the men who had just finished playing and handed it to Chewie, whose face lit up.

'Don't get any ideas, Shorty,' she said. 'It's just a game of pool.'

She took a cue from a rack attached to the wall and rubbed a cube of blue chalk on its end. Then, she passed the chalk to Chewie and he did the same. He cradled his cue in the crook of his arm and rubbed his hands together.

'Prepare to be conquered,' he said, with a Germanic accent.

'What?'

'It's from that film, Red Sonja.'

She gave him a blank look.

'Schwarzenegger says it to Nielsen.'

Another blank look.

He looked at the others, who all mimicked Suzi.

'Fuck the lot of you,' he said, to a chorus of laughter.

'Come on, Arnie,' said Suzi, nodding to the pool table. 'Get conquering.'

30

The Vatican's pearl and obsidian fourteen-seater Embraer Legacy 650E was travelling at over four hundred knots twelve thousand metres above the Adriatic Sea. The atmosphere on board was mixed.

Rebekah was asleep on a sofa toward the back of the plane.

Seth was reclining in a seat across the aisle from Rebekah, busily making his way through a pile of food he'd found in the galley.

Thomas was sitting upright at a four-person table in the middle of the cabin, looking at an iPad. Like all modern business aircraft, the Embraer contained state-of-the-art communications technology that allowed passengers full connection to mobile phone networks and the Internet. Forty seconds earlier, he'd received a text message from Peter telling him two things. First, to check his email account. And second, that Peter was in London dealing with several matters and that Thomas and his team were to head directly there from Copenhagen once successful in their endeavour.

He chuckled to himself at Peter's use of the word *once*. Not *if*.

'No pressure,' he muttered.

He read the email displayed on his tablet. He read it again and then called for Seth, who, after swallowing a mouthful of cold chicken breast, got up from his seat and made his way forward, giving Rebekah a soft kick as he did so. She stirred and groggily got up to join the men.

'What's up?' he asked.

'We've got some intel,' said Thomas, turning the iPad's screen toward the others. On it was a transcript of the phone conversation between Father Sigvardt and Bishop Byrne, followed by the phone and address details for Sigvardt and the instruction to transport Ellie to London once acquired.

'Well, that's… interesting,' Rebekah said. 'It could be another wild goose chase.'

'Maybe. It doesn't matter if it is. We just have to do our jobs.'

'We've got an ETA of fifty-five minutes,' said Seth, looking at his watch. 'If we assume it'll take us no more than an hour to get from Copenhagen airport to wherever this priest is, that gives us two hours. Can we put anyone on him until we get there?'

'We have a couple of assets in Copenhagen. Peter's already given them instructions. One will pick us up. The other will conduct surveillance on the priest.'

'What if the Sicarii turn up?' asked Rebekah, 'or they get there before us?'

'Why would they?' Seth asked.

'They have the same intelligence capabilities we do, so it's not beyond the realms of possibility.'

'True,' said Thomas.

'Who do you think they'd send?' asked Rebekah.

The men looked at each other, then back at her.

'Gideon,' she said, slumping into the seat across the aisle.

Thomas watched Seth walk back to his seat, fishing his phone out of his front pocket as he went. Rebekah reclined her seat, brushed her hair back, stared into space and drummed her fingers on her cargo pants.

There was nothing to do now but sit and wait.

Thirteen hundred kilometres to the north, at roughly the same altitude as Thomas's Embraer, Cain was asleep in a reclined seat halfway down the Bombardier's cabin. He'd already changed into clean, undamaged clothes, kicked off his shoes, and wrapped his new jacket across the back of his seat.

Across the aisle, Gideon was awake. His jacket lay across one side of the mahogany table in front of him. His phone, a Macbook laptop, and the pistols and tanto knives Layla had provided were spread out over the rest of the tabletop. He'd checked and double-checked the moving parts of the guns and loaded, unloaded, and reloaded them. Then, more from habit than need, he'd started sharpening the already lethal blades of the tantos.

His phone vibrated with the arrival of a text message. He picked it up. The text was from Mercury.

```
ETA Copenhagen: 50 minutes.
```

He placed the phone back beside the laptop without responding to the message and pressed an intercom switch embedded into the arm of his seat.

'How long until we land, Enrique?'

'Just over thirty minutes.'

He powered up the laptop. The jet was Internet-enabled, so he searched for information about Carlsson and Sigvardt. Frustratingly, there was little on the therapist other than her professional website and a few articles she'd published. The search on the priest proved more fruitful, giving up his place of work, a brief biography of his time with the Church, and some personal details that, if necessary, could be used as leverage.

Once satisfied that he'd learned all he could, Gideon shut down the Macbook, reclined his seat, shut his eyes and smiled.

They were close.

31

At eighteen minutes past nine, the Sicarii's jet landed at Roskilde, an airport roughly forty minutes west of Copenhagen, used primarily for domestic taxi flights, private air travel, and the deployment of military troops. While the main international airport at Kastrup was closer to the city centre by around twenty minutes, it was easier to schedule a short-notice arrival at Roskilde, which is why Enrique, the pilot, had chosen it.

Gideon got up from his seat while the plane was still taxiing and slipped on the shoulder holster Layla had provided, which he'd already loaded with his guns, knives, and spare magazines. Then he pulled on his suit jacket and held out his hand to Cain, who, still seated, retrieved his passport and handed it over. He walked to the front of the cabin and, when the jet had slowed enough, released the catches on the door and opened it. As the plane rolled to a stop, he disappeared through the door into the night.

Cain stood and paced back through the cabin to a rack on which the weapons cases lay. He opened his case and removed the shoulder rig, which he loaded with everything from the container except the large kukri knives. Those he left in the case, as Gideon had done with his wakizashi swords. He shrugged on the holster, closed the case, and grabbed the box of grenades. On his way back up the cabin, he stopped at his seat and put on his jacket. Carrying illegal weapons was one thing, but showing them off unnecessarily, particularly at an airport, was not worth the trouble.

By the time he stepped onto the apron, Gideon was standing beside the rear right-side passenger door of a black, aggressive-looking car, having already opened the boot. The vehicle had been rented from an executive hire service by Jacques, their fixer in Paris. The fact that it was sitting on the apron and not waiting for them in the airport's parking lot was a testament to the man's influence and web of connections.

The car was a Jaguar XE. It was a sporty four-door sedan with a decent amount of power, room for three passengers in the back, enough boot space to contain a person—perhaps two—and was understated enough to offer them some level of anonymity. It was a good choice. There was no sign of the delivery driver, so he guessed they must have left the keys in it and headed either to the lounge to await their return or back to the rental firm's depot.

He placed the grenades in the boot, closed the lid, and went around to the front. He leaned against the bonnet and looked over to Gideon, who was now talking with an airport official. The guy had a face like a weasel—all teeth and no chin—and blinked excessively, which he put down to a nervous tic.

Unlike Northolt and numerous other transit terminals around the globe, the Sicarii didn't have immigration officials on its payroll in Denmark. It wouldn't be a problem, but he thought it was something the organisation probably ought to consider rectifying.

He noticed that Weasel's face went slack, and the light went out of the man's eyes. Gideon was *pushing* him. The man nodded, nodded again, then looked at Cain, then shook his head, then nodded again. He held out his hand, and Gideon gave him one of the passports. Weasel scanned it with a handheld device and then took a small, blocky item out of his raincoat pocket, which he pressed onto the passport. An ink stamp, he supposed.

He chuckled to himself. Gideon could easily have *pushed* the guy to let them through without completing any of the usual formalities, but even the Sicarii needed to follow the rules sometimes—to a point, at least. Persuading the man to let them through without the scan and the stamp would be simple enough but could raise questions back in the terminal. Why did he let people exit the plane and leave the airport without immigration clearance? Who were they? What is their destination in Copenhagen? To whom does the jet belong?

Those were questions they couldn't afford to have asked, and the last thing they needed would be a delay on exit—especially if they had their quarry in hand. So, Gideon had helped the guy do his job with minimal fuss and without the need to inspect their cargo.

After Weasel scanned, stamped and handed back the second passport, Gideon walked past Cain, gave him a brief nod and a genuine but minute smile that barely creased the corners of his eyes and mouth, and went to the jet's stairway, where Enrique waited.

'I don't think we're going to need you, Enrique,' he said.

'Are you sure? Another set of eyes could be useful.'

'No. Better for you to stay put. We may need to leave quickly on our return. I'll call you when we're heading back so you can request tower clearance and be ready for departure.'

Enrique looked relieved.

'Understood,' he said. 'I'll need to file a flight plan. I take it we'll be heading to Chicago from here?'

'Currently, yes, but that may very well change.'

The pilot wished his colleagues good hunting, then climbed the stairs and pulled up the door. Gideon returned to the car and got into the front passenger seat, which made Cain the driver—a scenario he was not unhappy with. He opened the driver's door and spotted the key fob on the seat, which he picked up and, after sliding into the car, dropped into one of the cup holders in the centre console. The Jaguar had a keyless start function, so he tapped the start button, and the big cat roared to life. Then he tapped the touchscreen in the dashboard and navigated his way into the GPS.

'Head for Saint Ansgar's Cathedral,' Gideon said.

He typed the church's name into the search box, and the navigation system returned a single match. He selected the address, and the digital screen behind the steering wheel changed to a map showing the route and giving them an estimated journey time of forty-two minutes.

Within minutes, they were heading north on Route 6. With Thomas and his team on the way or possibly already in Copenhagen, he wanted to put his foot down, but he had to obey the seventy-kilometre-per-hour speed limit. Getting zapped by fixed speed cameras was not an issue, as the shell corporation through which Jacques had rented the car would pay for those. But getting stopped by an enthusiastic traffic cop looking to fill their monthly ticket quota would be problematic.

He could feel the Jaguar's turbocharged engine straining, wanting to be let loose as if it were as frustrated at being reined in as he was. He tapped the steering wheel to apologise to the car, then looked sideways at Gideon.

What's the play when we get there?

'We find out what this priest knows.'

And if he doesn't know anything?

'He'll know *something*.'

32

Saint Ansgar's Cathedral was a slim, rectangular four-storey red-brick building on Bredgade. Constructed in 1842, it stood on the site of an earlier Catholic chapel. It was the mother church of the Roman Catholic Diocese of Copenhagen and, therefore, the rest of Denmark, Greenland, and the Faroe Islands. It sat perpendicular to the road so that its front door faced the narrow street. Set into the façade just over halfway up were five recesses, each over two metres high and each containing a statue made of zinc. They depicted figures from the Old Testament—Isaiah, Moses, David, Aaron, and Elijah. Above the sculptures in raised, gold-plated letters were the words CHRISTO REDEMPTORI SACRUM—*Christ the Sacred Redeemer.*

The cathedral was set back roughly two metres from the footpath, separated from it by a tall wrought-iron fence the colour of oxidised copper. To each side of the building, jutting out to meet the railings, were single-storey red brick entrances, each with a heavy, black wooden door.

Neils Ingmann looked at his watch. It was four minutes before ten. He was bored and hungry, and he needed to urinate. Parked thirty metres from the cathedral, on the opposite side of the street, he'd been sitting in the unlit cabin of his navy Audi A4 for three hours and fifteen minutes since receiving a phone call and several text messages from Cardinal Peter Barjona, who'd bypassed his superior and called him directly. His orders had been clear. He was to go to the cathedral and position himself unseen but with a clear line of sight to the building, conduct surveillance, and report all movements in and out to a team the Vatican was sending. He was not, under any circumstances, to leave his post. Not having the courage to refuse the cardinal, Ingmann had abandoned the plans he had made for the evening and driven straight to the cathedral.

Bredgade was a one-way street, so he'd parked before passing the cathedral so that his car faced it and had climbed into the passenger seat for a better view. Nobody entered or left the building for the first thirty-five minutes. Then, two and half hours ago, a priest had gone in alone. The priest's face matched the photo of Father Frederik Sigvardt that Barjona had sent him. In the fifteen minutes that followed, maybe thirty or more people turned up—male and female, from young children to pensioners, either in small groups or individually. The last of them had gone in just after seven-thirty. Nobody else had gone in since, and no one had come out.

He'd taken photographs of each arrival, including the priest, with his high-resolution Sony camera. The camera had a long lens and was tethered by a USB cable to a laptop on the driver's seat running a database incorporating a sophisticated facial recognition program. The program hadn't flagged any of the people Ingmann had snapped. Still, he'd nonetheless reported all of them back to headquarters.

But now he badly needed to piss.

He recalled the cardinal's order not to leave his position, but the pressure on his bladder and the imminent risk to his leather seats outweighed the requirement to obey someone who would never discover his disobedience, regardless of how powerful that person was.

Screw it, he thought.

He opened the door and left the car to find a place to relieve himself. There were a few parked cars between him and the cathedral, but he didn't like the idea of being interrupted mid-flow by a random stranger walking their dog.

Ten metres behind him, on the other side of the street, was a building fronted by scaffolding covered with an orange tarpaulin sheet that ran from the roof down to street level. It had a human-sized slit at ground level on the side facing him that would give him access to the hidden space beyond to urinate in private and allow him to peek out onto the street to continue his vigil undeterred.

He dashed to the scaffolding, snuck through the slit in the tarp, hurriedly unzipped his Levi's, pulled out his penis, and emptied his bladder. His manhood and the tips of his fingers tingled with relief. He'd left it so late that he almost didn't make it in time, and in his rush to get himself out of his jeans, he splashed urine over his boots.

'Damn it,' he murmured.

Less than a minute later, he was out on the street again. He wiped his boots on the back of his jeans and thumbed his key fob to unlock the Audi. While he'd known he would only be gone a matter of seconds and would have eye contact with the car the entire time, he hadn't wanted to risk leaving it unlocked with his equipment on show on the driver's seat. Before he could open the passenger door, a dark-coloured Jaguar crawled past behind him. He looked over his shoulder and saw a long-haired, bearded man in the driver's seat. The Jag slowed as it reached the cathedral, then pulled to the curb directly opposite its front door. Ingmann scrambled into the Audi and grabbed his camera as a man with black skin climbed out of the Jaguar's passenger seat. Even from this distance, in the dark and with the naked eye, the guy didn't look like a typical churchgoer. A businessman, maybe. Or a policeman.

Or something else.

'Shit!'

Ingmann flicked on the camera, and in the two seconds it took to start up, he twisted the barrel on the lens to achieve its maximum zoom and lifted the viewfinder to his left eye. He half-pressed the shutter button to focus the lens, then fully thumbed and held the button. Set to its continuous shooting mode, the camera captured five high-resolution images of the man as he crossed the road to the cathedral.

The man stopped at the curb and looked at the building, his head moving around as if he were examining it. Then he approached one of the side entrances. When he reached the door, he tried the handle, but the door remained closed. He shoved the door with his shoulder. It opened, and he disappeared inside.

Ingmann reviewed his photographs of the man, hopeful to have captured at least one useable image. He had one. It was a half-profile shot. Not great, but it would do. Straight-on would have been better. He cursed himself for not taking a piss earlier and Barjona for sending him there in the first place. He woke the laptop, clicked on an icon shaped like a camera, and the Sony's memory card library appeared on the laptop's screen. He selected the photo he wanted to use and hit the *Enter* key. The laptop's screen turned black, and white text appeared, advising him the picture was uploading.

Within a few seconds, one half of the screen lit up with the photograph he'd uploaded. The other half remained black. The photo enlarged until the black man's face filled the frame, and then a series of green dots appeared across the face, each joining to those around it by a green line until the face was covered in a mask of minuscule triangles. As the software mapped key points of facial structure, the word *Processing* flashed in white on the other half of the screen.

The uploaded photograph shrank to half its size, and a new picture, showing the same man in a different location, in daylight, and face-on, appeared alongside it. A green box flashed symmetrically over the two photographs, and a string of white text inside it confirmed a ninety-eight per cent match. The other side of the screen then displayed the details held on the man, including his name and the organisation he worked for.

Gideon of the Sicarii.

Holy shit, he thought.

In addition to Gideon's name and other basic information, such as his estimated age and physical attributes, the database provided details of his genus, known abilities, and kill count—officially two hundred and forty-one but presumed to be higher. According to the system, he was a *pusher* and a *reader*. He was also a *mover*. He could control people, read thoughts, and move objects using brainpower alone.

He was also—

'What the hell?' Ingmann murmured. His eye had moved back to Gideon's age. He knew some of the Sicarii operatives were centuries old, but he hadn't expected this. According to the data, the man was over six thousand years old. How was that even possible? He'd had learned during his training what Gideon and others like him were, but seeing it on the screen made it all the more real.

He held down three keys on the laptop's keypad and took a screenshot of the database, which was saved automatically to the computer's desktop screen. Then he brought up the computer's menu bar and opened his email application. Three of the texts he'd received from the cardinal were digital business cards providing the names, contact numbers, and email addresses of the Vatican's incoming team, all of which he'd immediately stored into his phone's contacts list, which automatically synchronised with his email program.

He started a new email, typed the letter T in the *To* box, and a list of possible recipients appeared. He scrolled until he found the name he wanted, then selected it.

Thomas.

He clicked in the *CC* field and began typing Barjona's name, which automatically completed after he entered the first three letters. Then, he keyed in two words in the Subject line of the message.

Copenhagen—Urgent!

He stared blankly at the screen for a few seconds, considering how best to phrase his email, but settled on writing nothing, deciding that the screenshot of the database page would hopefully convey enough information. He attached the screenshot file and clicked *Send*, confident he'd provided everything he needed to. Then he tapped the touchscreen in the centre of the dashboard. The Audi's media system was connected to his phone via Bluetooth. He navigated to a screen that showed his contacts list, found Thomas's name, and pressed it. The dialling tone came through the car's speakers and the call connected almost immediately.

'Yes?'

'Sir, my name is—'

'I know who you are. What have you got for me?'

'Someone's just arrived at Saint Ansgar's Cathedral. I've done a facial rec and got a positive ID. I've emailed you the file.'

'Hang on.'

The line at the other end went quiet, but Ingmann thought he heard someone say, 'How the fuck did they beat us there?'

'Okay,' said Thomas. *'You are to observe only. If you can listen at close quarters, all the better. But do not get made. And for fuck's sake, do not engage. You won't be able to handle him. Is that understood?'*

'I don't think I'll be able to get any closer without being spotted. His car is parked directly opposite the cathedral's entrance, and there's another man with him. Long hair, beard. He stayed in the car. Gideon broke into one of the building's side entrances, and if I follow him, his partner will definitely see me. I don't think I can even get a picture of the other guy without possibly blowing my cover. Their car is facing away from me, and I'd have to go past it to get a shot.'

'Okay. Stay in your car. The other guy is probably Cain. He's known to work with Gideon and is also somebody with whom you do not want to fuck. So when they leave, follow them. If the car leaves first, stay with that, even if Gideon is still in the cathedral. I want updates as and when necessary.'

'Understood.'

'And Neils.'

'Yes, sir?'

'Do. Not. Engage.'

Four minutes later, the Vatican's jet landed at Roskilde airport. It taxied to a section of apron set apart from the terminal building, and as it stopped, Thomas opened the cabin door. Rummaging in his pockets for his lighter and cigarettes, he descended the steps once they'd unfolded, and as his feet touched the apron, he lit a Marlboro, shielding the Zippo's flame from the drizzling rain, and took a deep draw.

Ten metres away on the wet tarmac was a dark grey Mercedes G-Wagon with heavily tinted windows, its idling engine growling. The driver's door was open, and a tall man in an all-black ensemble of turtleneck, leather jacket, and jeans stood wedged between it and the car's body. Thomas stuffed his lighter and cigarettes back into his pockets and headed for the car, watching the driver as he went. The man acknowledged him with a nod, and his eyes then went to Rebekah and Seth, who had deplaned and followed close behind. As they drew closer to the vehicle, the driver dislodged himself, walked around to the front of the car, and held out his hand, which Thomas took.

'Welcome to Copenhagen. I'm Rasmus.'

'Rasmus, I'm Thomas. This is Rebekah and Seth.'

'A pleasure. Do you have any baggage to transfer?'

'Only Seth's bag.'

Seth held out a large duffel bag. Rasmus took it with one hand, stumbled, and dropped it to the ground, its contents clattering together, metal on metal. Seth grinned and patted him on the shoulder. He tightened his grip on the bag's handle and walked off-balance to the SUV's rear.

He opened the car's rear door, then grabbed the bag with both hands and hauled it up and into the back, using his right knee to support and guide it on the way up. He managed to get one end of it up over the bumper and into the car's rear, but as he put his leg down to regain his balance, the bag fell to the ground with a loud, metallic clang. Seth went over, picked up the bag with one hand as if it were empty, and slung it in. Rasmus tried, unsuccessfully, not to look pissed off. Seth laughed and gave him a consoling pat on the back as he swung the rear door closed.

As Rasmus returned to his seat, Thomas climbed in beside him and fastened his seatbelt. Rebekah got in directly behind him, which left Seth positioned behind the driver's seat. He opened his door and squeezed himself in, grunting with dissatisfaction. Thomas noticed a smile form on Rasmus's mouth. As the four of them almost simultaneously pulled their doors shut, Rasmus put the car into gear and released the parking brake, and they pulled away and headed toward a security gate.

'You'll need to complete an immigration check before we leave the airport,' he said, 'but that shouldn't take long, given your credentials. And, I've received the information on Sigvardt and programmed the coordinates for his church and home addresses into the GPS. I've also looked up Doctor Carlsson. She has a professional website, which only provides a submission form as a means of contacting her. No address or phone number is given. I've searched the phone number *Prophet* logged against her call to Sigvardt, but it's registered to a post box held in the city's central post office.'

'Maybe she consults at home,' said Rebekah, 'and doesn't want to advertise her home address to every crazy in town, which is why her phone number isn't registered against her residence. She probably only gives that out once she's vetted whoever uses her website's contact form and, likewise, her home address once she's spoken with potential clients on the phone.'

'Most likely.'

'Forget the therapist,' Thomas said. 'Our only real lead is the priest. We focus on him.'

When they reached the security gate, Rasmus rolled the SUV to a stop, slid the transmission into neutral, and lowered his window. In the concrete security hut beside the exit, a guard and a weasel-faced

215

immigration official were deep in conversation. The official glanced at him, left the cabin leisurely, and approached the car's open window.

'Tre ankomster,' said Rasmus. *Three arrivals.*

The man from immigration held out his hand and asked for their passports. Everyone handed over their documents to Rasmus, who passed them to the official. Upon seeing the gold inlay on the front of the black covers—the crossed keys of Saint Peter and the papal tiara behind a coffin-shaped shield—the man blanched. He evidently recognised the documents as diplomatic passports issued by the Holy See.

He bent over and peered into the car to study each occupant in turn, then quickly returned to the hut. He spoke to the guard, who looked over the man's shoulder at the SUV, then flicked through all three passports in under ten seconds. He put them out of sight onto what was probably a counter, thumped each one, hurriedly returned to the car, handed them back to Rasmus, then bent down again and peered at Thomas.

'Velkommen til Danmark,' he said. *Welcome to Denmark.*

'Thanks, man.'

The official returned to the hut and looked back at the car for a few seconds. Then he spoke to the guard again, who reached for something Thomas couldn't see. The security gate in front of them rolled open slowly.

'So, where to?' Rasmus asked Thomas as he closed his window.

'We have eyes on the cathedral, and we know the priest is there, as are the Sicarii, so let's just head for the city. That could change on the way, so we may need to adapt as we go.'

Rasmus nodded, put the car into gear and drove out of the gate and onto a road that would take them to Route 6, bound for the city.

33

Hellenbach had finished their first set, and the DJ was back on. Ellie and her friends were still by the pool tables, but they'd given their table to a group of university students who'd patiently waited through three games for their turn. She gulped a mouthful of beer and turned to speak to Goat when Suzi nudged her.

'How's it going with you two?' Suzi asked, eyeing Jakob to ensure he was out of earshot and otherwise occupied. He and Chewie were talking animatedly about something. 'Other than all of the weird dream shit?'

'It's awesome,' she replied, honestly.

'He asked you yet?'

And there it is, she thought.

The marriage question.

They had been together for a little over two years. They'd met at a three-day motorcycle rally on the city's outskirts. She'd been on the Double D's tattoo stand, and he'd been her last customer on the final day. They'd connected instantly. He'd asked for her number, she'd given it to him, and he'd called her two days later.

'No,' she said, 'but we've been talking about it recently.'

While that was true, he still hadn't officially asked her yet. It was all hypothetical. But that was okay. She *had* told him there was no rush, even though secretly she wanted to get married before turning thirty.

Still, despite what she kept telling herself about there being no rush to marry or even get engaged, she sometimes wished he would get a move on and ask her. Partly because she wanted that commitment from him, but mainly so she could avoid conversations like this, with the pitying looks, the pats on the shoulder, and the numerous variations of 'Don't worry, hon, it'll happen.' Of course, *she* could ask *him*, but she was, despite appearances, a traditional girl at heart when it came to some things. Or maybe not. Maybe she just wanted to be asked.

'Talked about it? What the fuck is that?'

Ellie smiled. She could always rely on Suzi to take a brusque approach.

'You know,' she said. 'What it would be like if we did it, when and where we'd do it, where we would live afterwards. Stuff like that.'

'How very fucking romantic. Aren't you supposed to talk about all of that shit *after* he's proposed?'

'Maybe. I don't know.'

Suzi took a swig of her drink, swallowed it down, and beamed.

'How's the sex?' she asked. 'Please tell me there's still at least *some* spontaneity there, or does he want to talk about *that* first, too?'

'*That*,' Ellie said, 'is great. More than great. It's almost magical.'

She wiggled her fingers in the air.

'Really? He doesn't look that...'

'What?' She smirked. 'He doesn't look that *what*?'

'I dunno. Talented?'

Ellie laughed heartily.

'If I weren't so attached to him, and you weren't, you know, of the other persuasion, I'd let you borrow him for a night so you could find out for yourself.'

'Maybe we could...'

Suzi left the sentence hanging but raised three fingers and wiggled them.

'A three-way?' Ellie said. 'I'm not sure he'd go for that. He's very, um, conventional in many ways.'

'Aw, bless.'

'Plus, I reckon he'd say no to it even if he *would* be into it with you as the third. He'd be too afraid I'd want what he calls a devil's threesome in return.'

Suzi nodded.

'Two dudes instead of two chicks. Yeah, guys aren't into that so much. Probably has something to do with being afraid of not measuring up to the other guy or thinking it'd mean they're gay if their balls accidentally bang together.'

Midway through another gulp of her drink, Ellie snorted and sprayed beer into the air through her nostrils. Suzi looked with wonder and amusement at her for a second and then erupted into laughter. Then she did the same. It felt good to see her friend having fun, given the crap she was going through in her relationship. When Suzi calmed down, Ellie hugged her, placed her drink on the thin wall-mounted shelf and peered at Goat, whom she knew had been sneakily listening to their conversation.

'What?' he asked, eyeing her with suspicion.

'*You* what? You were earwigging.'

'Not really, lass. But let's just say that if Jakob comes into work one day walking funny and talking about how he's had a devil of a night, I'll know exactly what he means.'

She chuckled.

'Is there something you'd like to come clean about, Goat?' asked Suzi, stepping back slightly.

'What the hell?' shouted someone from behind her.

Everyone twisted to look. Standing there was an angry man with smooth skin, neat hair, and an expensive-looking navy shirt with a dark amorphous patch on the left side. He looked around Jakob's age and had three friends with him, all with the same baby-soft faces, tidy hair and upmarket clothes, all as conspicuous in the place as the first guy.

'You made me spill my drink, you stupid bitch!'

'I'm sorry,' said Suzi. 'It was an accident.'

'I don't give a shit what it was.'

Jakob took a couple of steps forward and put himself between her and the man. Ellie stepped in beside him.

'Calm down, Frandsen,' he said. 'She's apologised.'

'You know this guy?' Ellie asked.

Frandsen eyed him for two seconds and scanned the rest of the group, who had closed in. Then his eyes lit up, and his face contorted into a wide grin.

'Well, if it isn't the billy goat and his kids. Are you in here trying to find more customers to rip off?'

'We didn't rip you off,' Jakob said. 'You know that.'

'You overcharged me for shitty work. I'd say that constitutes ripping me off.'

'If you've got a grievance, you can file a complaint with the union,' said Chewie.

'Fuck you, you freak of nature,' Frandsen snapped. He looked back at Jakob. 'Your bitch friend here made me spill my drink. She needs to pay for a new one and cover the cost of dry-cleaning my shirt.'

'Like she said, it was an accident. She's not going to pay you anything.'

Frandsen stepped forward, closing the gap to under a metre. His three friends stepped in behind him.

'If she won't pay, you will.'

'Why is it,' said Suzi, 'that wankers like you think they can do whatever they want to everyone else?'

'Because that's how it works. We can do whatever the fuck we want because we're better than you.'

'You might be financially better off,' Jakob said, 'but fuckers like you are morally bankrupt and devoid of any positive personality traits. Frankly, I'd rather be a pauper than an entitled, stuck-up-my-own-ass, fake-friended cocksucker like you.'

'Who the fuck do you think you're talking to?'

'I want to say, an asshole.'

Frandsen's face clouded over. He pulled back his arm, winding up to punch Jakob, telegraphing the move so much it could have been happening in slow motion. When he lashed out, Ellie stepped in and blocked it with her forearm. In a move too fast for him to counter, she swung her forearm around, caught hold of his wrist, and twisted it so hard he had to double over to prevent her from pulling his arm from its socket. He screamed in pain.

'You need to calm down, Backstreet,' she said.

'Let go of me, you fucking cunt!'

One of Frandsen's three clones went for her, but Jakob took a quick step forward and kicked the guy between the legs. The man yelped and went down hard.

'I suggest,' he said to Frandsen, 'that you apologise to my friend and then pick up *your* friend and fuck off.'

'Fuck you!'

Ellie twisted his arm a few degrees. He cried out again.

'Okay, okay. Fuck!'

'Well?' she asked.

Frandsen looked at Suzi through water-filled eyes. 'I'm sorry. Okay? I'm fucking sorry!'

She looked at Suzi, who smiled and nodded. She let go of Frandsen's wrist, which he quickly pulled back and rubbed. He straightened, then looked at the two of his friends who were still standing and told them to pick up the guy on the floor. He went to step forward again, and Jakob put a hand on his chest to stop him.

'It's over, Frandsen. You need to leave.'

'Keep your eyes open, Nørgard.'

'Sure.'

Frandsen scowled at him for a second longer, then turned and headed for the stairs. His friends followed.

'I said I was sorry!' Suzi shouted, gleefully.

Without turning around, Frandsen gave her the middle finger. Once the four men had disappeared, Ellie and the others relaxed. Jakob raised his eyebrows, puffed his cheeks, and took Suzi's elbow.

'You okay?' he asked.

'Just about.'

'Nice move,' Ellie said to him.

'Likewise.'

'That fella's plums are going to be purple for a week,' said Goat.

'Who was that asshole?' Suzi asked.

'Knud Frandsen,' Chewie said. 'A trust fund baby with a new Harley he barely knows how to ride. Brought it in a few months back for a custom job. Goat gave him a quote, which he agreed to, and Jakob and I did the work.'

'Took us almost three weeks,' said Jakob. 'When he came to pick up the bike, he gave us a load of bullshit about poor workmanship and refused to pay. Goat told him we could restore the bike to its original condition and that it would probably take about six months, given our workload. The guy was furious. He threatened to call the cops, and Goat told him he absolutely should. He must have realised it was a no-win, so he paid his bill and took his bike.'

'Goat made him wheel it out of the shop before giving him the keys,' Chewie continued. 'The guy went mental. He was still swearing at us when he rode off. Fucking wanker.'

'Oh, *that's* the guy,' Ellie said to Jakob, who nodded and glanced at Goat.

'You might need to install some cameras in the workshop, Goat. I wouldn't put it past him to get nasty after this.'

'Not a bad idea, lad. I'll get on that first thing tomorrow.'

After a couple of seconds of anticlimactic silence, Ellie raised her beer cup.

'Well, here's to an awesome night.'

34

As simple in its internal design as its exterior, St Ansgar's Cathedral had an apse, a small choir, and a pillar-free nave. A column of pews ran down each side of its central aisle. Narrow benches were set along the flank walls, separated from the pews by a gap barely wide enough for a person to walk along. Its white walls were inlaid with blue and gold, and from the ceiling hung eight circular chandeliers, each holding numerous electric lightbulbs that gave off a warm, yellow light. Oil frescoes covered the dome and walls of the semi-circular apse at the far end. On the dome was the Holy Trinity—including Christ and his apostles—and the lower wall showed Mary encircled by saints.

Frederik Sigvardt stood between the front pews holding a mug of strong tea in one hand and a pencil in the other. He held mass each weekday morning and on Saturday evenings, led Bible study classes on Tuesday afternoons, and curated the occasional lecture or seminar from visiting colleagues on Wednesdays. He was not typically in the cathedral on a Friday evening.

But tonight was an exception.

He was leading a rehearsal for a night of choral recitals in five weeks, in which the choirs of all the larger churches in Copenhagen would be participating. The piece the Saint Ansgar's choir would be reciting was *Dies Irae* from Mozart's *Requiem*.

The song's title meant Day of Wrath and was about the day of judgement on which, according to the Bible, God would judge humankind for their sins. While Mozart's original work—and most modern renditions of it—had the choral section accompanied by an orchestra, Sigvardt had thought it would be an exciting challenge for the choir to perform it acapella.

And it was working.

Mostly.

Standing in two lines in front of the altar—adults at the back and children in front—the choir had already sung it in its entirety four times that evening and were nearing the end of their fifth and final run-through.

'Cunta stricte,' sang the women and the girls.

'Cunta stricte,' sang the men and the boys.

'Stricte discus surus!' sang everyone for the final line.

For a few seconds, the cathedral was almost silent. Only the creak of the chandeliers overhead and the whistle of a breeze under the front doors intruded. The choristers—younger ones shifting nervously or uncomfortably, older ones standing stoically—waited patiently for Sigvardt's judgement to be passed down upon them.

He felt a cloying sensation in the back of his throat. It could have been due to the incense that, burning or not, was ever-present in the cathedral but was most likely a lump forming from being overcome with joy and love and pride in the people who stood before him. He placed his mug and pencil on the pew to his left and clasped his hands.

'That was outstanding,' he said, barely getting the words out. He coughed to clear his throat. 'By far your best yet. Those harmonies are much closer. And the replication of the orchestral pieces is much, much tighter. I think the timing was a little off going into the second chorus, but we'll straighten that out next time.'

Two stars and a wish.

One of the younger choristers had suggested this to him the previous week after he'd led with a criticism. She had learned in school that when remarking on something that someone has done, you should say two nice things, and if it's necessary to make a criticism, make only one point and make it constructive.

A teenage girl in the second row raised her hand and spoke up without waiting for him to acknowledge her.

'Does that mean we're finished for the night, Father?'

'Yes, Trine, it does. I'll see you all here on Monday night. Seven o'clock sharp. Is that okay with everyone?' There was a unified murmur of agreement from the choristers. 'And don't be late again, Per Vonsild,' he said, with a stern glare that turned into a warm smile.

'No, Father,' replied a small boy from the front row.

After a minute or two of placing song sheets on the front pews, grabbing coats and backpacks, and parents collecting children who were too young to travel around town on their own at night, the choristers filed out of the cathedral, leaving Sigvardt alone. He leaned against the pew on his left, picked up his mug, took a gulp of his now-cold tea and closed his eyes. As much as he loved having a packed, bustling cathedral on Sundays, he loved the quiet stillness of the place more.

He breathed in deeply, savouring the pungent aroma of the incense in his nostrils, and jumped with alarm when a door banged. He quickly looked around but could see nothing except the flicker of the candles on the stands on either side of the front door. He collected the song sheets from the front pews and made his way down the nave to lock the front doors, snuff out the candles, and turn off the lamps on the chandeliers.

On his way back to the front, he heard a faint noise behind him. It sounded like the scrape of something on stone—a chair, perhaps, or a shoe. He paused and turned and watched the darkness for a moment but saw and heard nothing, so he continued toward the apse. Then the noise came again. Once more, he stopped and stared into the blackness, and once again, nothing.

'Is someone there?'

No answer.

Nervous, he quickly made his way up the nave to his private office.

He fumbled in his pocket and withdrew a large iron key, with which he unlocked the office door. He hurriedly went inside, closed the door, and rested his back against it. He took a few deep breaths, then chuckled at the absurdity of being scared in his own building.

His office was a small room, furnished with a large oak desk and three leather-seated wooden chairs, one of which he used at the desk, and the other two were for visitors, placed in front of the desk. On the top of the desk was a lawyer's lamp with a brass stem and a tilting shade of green glass, a push-button telephone, a blotter pad, and an in-tray. In the corner of the room opposite the door was a coat stand, on which hung a knee-length fawn woollen coat, a matching cashmere scarf, and a flat black cap.

The room's overhead light was off, but the desk lamp was on and tilted to face his chair. It threw a narrow circle of light into one corner of the room, but the rest of the space was in darkness. Despite his earlier nervousness, he left the overhead light off and went straight to his chair. When he sat down, he and it groaned in unison.

'I know how you feel,' he said, patting the chair's arm.

He opened the bottom of three desk drawers, reached in, and took out a small bottle of Hennessy and a glass tumbler. When he was in this building, he would only allow himself one drink at the end of the night, and tonight he'd make it a large one. He poured himself a generous slug of the brandy and put the bottle back in the drawer. As he picked up the glass and took a slow sip, there was a shuffle from the corner of the room. He peered into the darkness and thought he saw someone standing there, then realised it was just his coat on the stand.

'You're losing your mind, you old fool,' he murmured.

After a couple of seconds, he heard the sound again. This time, he tilted the shade of the desk lamp. Standing in the corner was a tall, black man in a dark suit. His heart jumped so hard he thought it would leap out of his throat.

'Who are you? What are you doing in here?'

'I apologise for startling you,' the man said in English.

'What are you doing in here?' Sigvardt repeated, also in English. 'This is a private area. And the cathedral is closed. You shouldn't even be in the building.'

'My name is Gideon. I'm—'

'I don't care who you are,' he snapped, despite having asked. The alarm bell in his reptilian brain had started to ring. 'I'd like you to leave. Now.'

'I don't wish to take up much of your time.'

Sigvardt reached for the phone on his desk, his hand quivering with adrenaline.

'If you don't leave now,' he said, 'I'm calling the police.'

'All I need is some information.'

'What information?'

'A young woman named Ellie, whom I understand you know. I need to know where she lives.'

Sigvardt faltered, his hand hovering over the telephone.

'Who?'

Gideon smiled. It wasn't a warm smile. It was the smile of someone with a cold heart and evil intent.

'Ellie. The young woman your therapist friend, Doctor Carlsson, introduced you to. The woman who's been having intense dreams about Christ and his circle. You spoke with Leonard Byrne about her on the phone.'

'Where are you from? Did Leonard send you?'

'No.'

'Rome, then? Someone above Leonard?'

Gideon shook his head.

Sigvardt couldn't comprehend this. If neither Leonard nor Rome had sent this man, how could he possibly know about Ellie and Maja and his conversation with Byrne? He had to shut this down. This man was dangerous.

'I'm sorry, but I really don't know anyone named Ellie.'

He looked into Gideon's eyes, hoping that his own eyes conveyed that he was telling the truth. He was ordinarily a terrible liar, so he tried to calm himself with slow and, hopefully, silent breaths and prayed to God that he wasn't sweating. Gideon seemed to consider his words for a moment.

'The inscription on the front of the building.'

He was put off-balance by Gideon's sudden change in direction but thankful for it nonetheless.

'What of it?'

'Do you truly believe he's a redeemer? Christ? Do you genuinely think he's a saviour? *The* saviour?'

'Of course. Why would I not?'

Gideon chuckled.

'We all have our crosses to bear, I suppose,' he said.

Sigvardt cleared his throat and sat straighter in his chair, his hand still floating above the phone.

'Now, I'd like you to leave, please,' he said. 'I really don't want to call the police, but I will if I have to.'

'I wish to be here no more than you want me here, believe me. I care little for your kind and churches even less. They make my skin itch. So, I will leave. As soon as you tell me where or how I can find Ellie.'

'My kind?'

'People with religion.'

Sigvardt sighed. He grabbed the phone's handset and picked it up, then put it to his ear and, with his free hand, went to press the keypad.

'Don't,' said Gideon.

'I've given you a chance to leave without a fuss, but you've left me little choice.'

'Please put the phone down.'

He ignored Gideon's command and pushed a button.

1.

'I'm warning you.'

1.

'You're not leaving me much choice, Frederik.'

He was briefly distracted by Gideon's use of his first name. It sent a chill through him, but he wouldn't give in to this man. He went to press 2 and was halted, his finger a hair away from the plastic button, by a deep, vicious snarl. His head snapped up to look at Gideon, who sprang from the far corner of the room to the desk—a distance of over two metres. It was almost as if the man dematerialised and reappeared simultaneously. He recoiled, surprised by the speed with which Gideon had reached him.

Gideon gripped the edge of the desk so tightly that his fingers splintered the wood. His lips pulled back tightly like a wolf on the attack, and his sharp canine teeth lengthened and dripped with saliva. Sigvardt saw that his irises were bright, burning orange.

Terrified, Sigvardt reflexively pushed himself away from the desk with such force that he fell backward out of his chair. He scrambled around on the floor, away from Gideon, until his back hit the wall. He clawed his way up it with one hand, the other scrabbling for the crucifix that hung from a long chain around his neck.

Gideon let go of the desk, stood upright, and approached him slowly. His eyes were still the colour of fire, but his grimace was gone, and his face was serene. When he was less than an arm's length away, Sigvardt thrust his crucifix into the man's face.

Gideon covered his face with his hands and screamed, a piercing wail that didn't seem quite human. It was like an animal howling in pain. It penetrated Sigvardt to his core.

Then the screaming stopped, and through Gideon's hands, he heard laughter. Quiet, low, and slow. Gideon removed his hands from his face, and his laughter continued for only a moment, then faded.

Sigvardt expected to see... what? A burn mark in the shape of a cross? He didn't know what, but he expected to see something with all the screaming Gideon had done. But, besides the ragged scar he'd come in with, there was nothing new.

'What are you?' he asked.

'Not what you think.'

'I don't... I don't understand.'

'You don't need to. All you need to do is tell me where I can find Ellie.'

Sigvardt moved along the wall, trying to put himself closer to the door. 'I've already told you. I don't know—'

'I hoped we could do this easily and with no mess.'

'What do you mean, no mess?'

'I normally do this kind of thing with a bit of intrusion into your mind—what we call a *read*. I'd work my way into your thoughts and root around until I find what I'm looking for. You'd feel a little queasy, but there'd be no lasting effects. That would be Plan A. But, as I said before, I don't like you church types, with your righteous indignation and sense of self-importance, and given that you've already wasted enough of my time, we'll go with Plan B.'

Gideon's hand lashed out in a blur. He grabbed Sigvardt's left wrist and forced it palm-down onto the blotter pad, then reached behind his back with his other hand and pulled out a black-bladed knife with a flat tip like a broad screwdriver.

'What are you going to do with that?' asked Sigvardt, unable to mask his distress.

'This is a tanto. It's very sharp. It can cut through a man's hand like a hot knife through... well, a man's hand.'

He howled as Gideon plunged the blade through the back of his hand and watched in horror as blood seeped out of the wound and ran down between his fingers onto the blotter pad. Gideon removed the knife, making him wail again, then took hold of one of his fingers and snapped it back, breaking the joint. He screamed again.

'I'm going to break one finger at a time until you give me what I've asked for. I'd think it'll be pretty tough to pull in your clutch lever with a broken hand.'

Sigvardt questioned Gideon with water-clouded eyes. How did this man know that he rode a motorcycle? Then it dawned on him. In his phone call to Byrne, he'd reminded the bishop of how they'd met—that Byrne had seen him arrive at the Axica building in Berlin on a rented Triumph. This man not only knew of his phone conversation with Byrne but must also have heard it.

'If you still haven't told me before I've broken all your fingers, I'm going to visit your sister,' Gideon said, pointing to a framed photograph on the wall behind the desk of Sigvardt and Grethe, both of them smiling, his arm around her. 'She plays with the Royal Danish Orchestra, doesn't she? Cello, I believe. I'm sure losing the use of her hands would leave her at a bit of a disadvantage.'

'She wouldn't care,' he said through gritted teeth and with all the strength and bravado he could muster. 'She's retiring.'

Snap!

Sigvardt screamed. Tears ran down his face, and his forehead was covered in sweat.

'Come on, Frederik. Where does Ellie live?'

'I've told you. I don't know any—'

Snap!

'Please! I don't know where she lives. I don't!'

He felt pressure on another finger, and he tensed up.

'Do you have any contact details for her?'

More pressure on the finger.

'No.'

'How did you arrange to meet her if you don't know how to contact her and you don't know where she lives?'

Sigvardt hesitated.

Snap!

He wailed again. His stomach lurched with the pain, and he almost vomited.

'It was all arranged through Maja. Her therapist. I met her at Maja's house.'

'And where can I find Maja's house? Before you answer, know that I won't come back here for you if you misdirect me. I'll come for your sister. And it won't be her fingers I break.'

'She lives in Christianshavn. On Overgaden Oven Vandet.'

'What number?'

Sigvardt, sobbing uncontrollably and ashamed of being so weak, gave Gideon the number.

'Thank you, Frederik. You'll no doubt want to call Doctor Carlsson and warn her that I'm coming. Don't. It won't end well for Grethe.'

Snap!

35

After his conversation with Thomas, Ingmann had climbed across the Audi's centre console into the driver's seat, wanting to be ready to leave when the Jaguar did, with or without Gideon. He was still charged with adrenaline when Gideon came out of the side entrance and walked back to the Jag swiftly, with purpose. Like he was on a deadline. Or someone's life was on the line. Or he was fleeing the scene of a murder.

'This can't be good,' he muttered as he grabbed his phone from the passenger seat. He unlocked it and quickly typed a message to Thomas, glancing between the screen and Gideon.

`Gideon's out, alone.`

He refrained from sending the message, wanting to be sure that whatever information he was about to fire off would be correct. Gideon got back into his car, and a few seconds later, it peeled out of the parking space.

As he watched the Jaguar pull out, movement at the door of the cathedral drew his attention. Sigvardt was leaving the building, clutching his left hand to his chest while holding a phone to his ear with the right. The priest's face was contorted in agony. He couldn't see clearly from this distance, but it looked like Sigvardt's hand was covered in blood.

Not my business to help him, he thought, but perhaps worth reporting. He speedily added to the message he had typed but not yet sent.

```
Sigvardt is leaving separately. Looks injured.
I'm staying with Gideon.
```

He sent the message, put the Audi into gear, and followed the Jaguar without a second thought for the priest.

As the big Mercedes SUV thundered along Route 21, Rasmus skilfully weaving it around cars travelling slower than they were, Thomas's phone chirped. He pulled it out. The screen was still lit and showed the text message from Ingmann, which he could read in its entirety from the preview without unlocking the device.

'Shit.'

'What's up?' Rebekah asked.

'Gideon's left the cathedral. So has the priest, who may be injured.'

'What do you want to do?' asked Rasmus.

'Depending on how badly Sigvardt is injured, he might go to a hospital,' said Rebekah.

'If the guy could walk out of there, the injury can't be that bad,' Seth said. 'And even if it is, he'll most likely go home before going anywhere else, if only for some initial medical care and maybe a drink for the pain.'

'Agreed,' said Thomas.

Recalling what Rasmus had said about having programmed the car's GPS with Sigvardt's addresses, he tapped the touchscreen, entered the navigation system, found the listing for the priest's home, and pressed the button to calculate and show the route. It told him they would be there in thirty-one minutes.

36

After leaving the cathedral, Gideon and Cain drove south. They crossed the inner harbour over Knippelsbro—a counterweighted, moveable bridge designed to open for river traffic—entered an area called Christianshavn via a wide street named Torvegade, and took the third right turn onto Overgaden Oven Vandet, which ran parallel to a canal. Sixty metres along, Cain slowed the car.

'That's it,' Gideon said, pointing to a house on the left that, under the illumination of the street lamps, was the colour of butter.

Cain looked for a vacant parking space on their side of the road. He'd already passed one and considered backing up to it but decided it would be better to turn the car around and point it back toward Torvegade. Odds were they'd have to go back to that street regardless of which part of town Ellie lived, and pointing in the right direction meant a quicker getaway.

He spotted an empty space thirty metres down on the other side of the road, so he accelerated hard to the end of the street, turned around, sped back, and smoothly slid into it.

They sat quietly for two minutes, with only the sounds of the engine and the heater breaking the silence. Even beings such as they felt the cold. He unbuckled his seatbelt, and as he opened his door, Gideon inhaled. He glanced back.

What?

'In and out, with no fuss. If that's not possible, just get it done quickly and quietly.'

Cain huffed.

Not my first rodeo.

He left the car and walked toward the house. Before reaching it, he went to the middle of the brick-surfaced road to better look at the property's façade. As he turned to observe the house, a faint, irregular ticking sound drew his attention. Pausing to listen more carefully and closing his eyes to concentrate, he let the ticking guide his ears. When he had a location dialled in, he swivelled his head lazily in that direction and opened his eyes. It was coming from a dark blue Audi parked in the space he'd passed earlier, and he realised the ticking was the sound of the car's engine cooling. Probably, it belonged to a resident who'd just come home from a long day at work.

He turned back to the house. It was a four-storey townhouse, three windows wide. Like its neighbours, it had a windowed basement that was half-below street level and half-above, which raised the ground floor half a storey. The windows on the raised ground floor appeared to be split centrally, which meant they were hinged on the frames and probably opened outward onto the street. If the front door proved too difficult a barrier, they would serve as a possible entry point, even if he had to pull himself up on the sills to make it through. The basement windows could also work, although his sharp eyes told him the window frames were thicker and broader than those above, so it might not be possible to push a knife blade in far enough to release a catch, and smashing a window would create too much noise. He'd worry about alternative entry points only if he couldn't get through the front door.

There were no visible signs of a security system—no alarm box or external security cameras—but that didn't mean the house wasn't protected. Plenty of people had clever home security gadgets, like tiny cameras that would activate on detecting the slightest movement and record onto computer hard drives, or motion sensors linked to applications on their phones that would alert them to the presence of an intruder.

Or dogs.

Cain liked dogs as much as anyone but wouldn't hesitate to kill one that was too loud or too eager to chew on his arm, leg, or throat.

He guessed that if the doctor practised at home, the front room on the ground floor would be where she'd take her clients. While a south-facing room to the rear might provide better direct sunlight, it would be unlikely that the doctor would want people walking through her house. Hopefully, the front room would also be where he'd find her computer and her client files.

Satisfied he'd seen enough outside, he climbed the steps. Set into the bottom of the front door was a rectangular letterbox slot. He crouched, put his ear to the slit, slowly opened it with his thumb, and listened for anything to indicate people or animals were inside. Then he whistled. Quietly at first, then louder, then louder still. His whistling was met with silence.

So, no dog.

He stood up, pulled a small black pouch from his jacket, placed it on the upturned palm of his other hand, and unzipped it. Inside was an assortment of small silver lockpicks with heads of varying sizes and shapes. He held the pouch with his thumb to prevent it from slipping off his hand, then removed two picks, zipped it up, and put it back in his jacket. He slid the picks into the lock, and with a few deft twists, he heard the barrel click. He turned the handle and nudged the door, which moved effortlessly and, more importantly, noiselessly. He eased it open enough to check above the door for a motion sensor or a camera.

Nothing.

He opened the door wide enough for him to get his head through and searched the ceiling in the hallway. No cameras. No sensors.

He whistled again. Not loudly enough to attract a human but enough to draw the attention of a dog that might not have heard him earlier.

Still nothing.

Satisfied it was safe to move into the house, he crossed the threshold and swung the door back into its wooden frame. He held onto it for a few moments, keeping the catch twisted so it wouldn't re-lock, and listened for the multiple beeps of an alarm system, conversation from the kitchen or the living room, or the noise from a television that might be on somewhere in the house.

The house was silent.

Ingmann lay across the Audi's centre console, his entire body hopefully invisible to anyone outside the car. He held his phone high enough that its camera lens cleared the top of the dashboard and allowed him to observe Gideon's partner through the phone's screen—which he'd darkened to avoid illuminating the car's cabin—without himself being seen. When the man had been looking directly at the Audi, he'd disengaged the phone's flash, zoomed in as far as the lens would allow, and taken three photographs. He'd quickly reviewed them, airdropped the most suitable to his laptop, and waited for the database to identify the man. As the computer processed the photo, he watched the man ascend the steps and break into the yellow house.

The laptop pinged. Its facial recognition program had matched the photo of Gideon's partner with one held in the database.

Thomas had been right.

It was Cain.

He read the information shown on the computer's screen. Cain had almost double the number of confirmed kills attributed to him than he recalled Gideon having. And like his partner, he was a *pusher*, a *reader*, and a *mover*.

'Holy hell,' he muttered. 'Who are these people?'

The database displayed another fact that caught his attention. Cain was also a mute. There was no explanation for why he couldn't speak, so Ingmann shrugged it off as irrelevant and pushed himself upright. He needed to call Thomas. With the Audi's electrics turned off, the Bluetooth was unavailable, so he grabbed his phone and made the call.

'*Yes?*'

'They've stopped. The guy I couldn't identify earlier has gone into a house. You were right. It's Cain. I'll send you the photo match from the database as confirmation.'

'*No need. We know what he looks like. You have an address for me, Neils?*'

He gave Thomas the address.

'*Okay. Stay with them.*'

Cain gently released the lock's catch, waited for the securing bolt's soft click into the metal housing in the door frame, and turned back to the dark hallway. He remained quietly on the parquet floor, listening again for any sounds indicating people were at home—voices, music, or even the sound of running water. There were none.

All the internal doors on the ground floor were open, and the rooms beyond them were dark, so he crept to the bottom of the stairs, gripped the handrail, and peered upward. The floor above appeared to be unlit, too. As for the storeys beyond that, he couldn't tell, but it wouldn't matter. If anyone were on either of the top two floors, he'd hear them moving and be out of the house before they could get anywhere near the ground floor.

He entered the first room on the left. Its overhead lights were off, but the curtains were open and warm golden light flooded in from the street. He'd been right. The room was a home office. He considered closing the door behind him but thought better of it for two reasons. First, if the occupants came downstairs or returned from an evening out while he was still in the room and found the door closed, having previously left it open, they might investigate. Second, if the door's hinges were poorly oiled, the door might creak and be heard by anyone in the house either now or when he opened it to leave the room. Either scenario would be problematic—more for the occupants than him. Nevertheless, they were both situations he'd rather avoid.

He glanced back at the desk. A red light was flashing on a telephone's base unit—an integrated answering machine, most likely. He stepped to the desk. The red light was an LED number display, flashing *1*.

A single message.

He reached for the *Play* button, then paused, turned the machine over, found and lowered the volume control, replaced the device and began the playback.

'*Maja, it's Fred*,' said the voice from the speaker. It was quiet, but he could hear the agony in it. '*I know it's late, and I apologise for that, but this is extremely important. I've just been visited by some strange... I don't even know what he was. He wanted to know about your patient, Ellie.*'

The talking stopped momentarily, but Cain could still hear pained breathing.

'*He didn't say why he was interested in her, only that he wanted to know where she lives. I told him I didn't know, which obviously I don't. He didn't believe me. Maja, he stabbed a knife through my hand and then broke all the fingers on it. And he threatened to hurt Grethe. I couldn't resist him anymore. I couldn't risk him hurting her. I'm sorry, Maja, but I had to tell him that I met with Ellie at your—*'

He pressed the *Stop* button. It wasn't what he needed to hear, but it was also not unexpected, despite Gideon's threat of harming Sigvardt's sister if he tipped off the therapist. He deleted the message and turned his attention to the computer. The screen was mainly black, but in the middle was a nebulous glow of bright light that continually changed colour. He tapped the space bar, and the screensaver disappeared, replaced by an unlocked desktop screen that required no access password.

Careless, he thought.

He brought up the menu bar and moved the cursor along it, looking for an icon for a contacts application. There was none.

Fuck!

Next to the computer was a black box. He opened it. It was a Rolodex. The therapist was old school. He smiled and quietly snapped his fingers, then skipped past the raised tabs marked A through D and went straight to E, hoping Carlsson filed her clients' contact details alphabetically by first name, not last. Otherwise, he'd have to look through every card in the box, which he had neither the time nor patience for.

He fingered past the card marking the start of the Es, then flicked each card forward. Ebba, Edele, Edina, Elisabet, Emmie, Erika, Eugenie, Evie. Thankfully, they were in first-name order, but there was no Ellie. He returned to the section marker and flipped through the cards again to ensure he hadn't missed any. He hadn't. A growl rose from deep within him as frustration took hold.

Then, a thought struck him.

Ellie wasn't the woman's full name.

It was a shortened version of her full name.

A nickname.

He swiftly rifled through the cards again and pulled out the one he wanted, then laid it on the desk, pulled out his phone and brought up the camera. He deactivated the flash—no point in drawing the attention of anyone out on the street, and there was enough light coming in through the windows from the streetlamps that he didn't think he'd need it anyway—and took a picture of the card. He checked the quality of the photo, then replaced the card and closed the Rolodex.

He'd got what he came for.

Time to leave.

As he circled back around the desk on the window side of the room, movement on the street caught his attention. An alarm bell went off in his head, so he planted himself flat against the wall between the room's two windows, sidestepped closer to the window on his left, inched his head toward the edge of the wall, and snuck a peek through the glass. He scanned the street but saw no one.

Then, he saw it.

He saw *him*.

There was a man in the blue Audi whose engine had been cooling. Perhaps he *was* a local who'd just come home and was now going back out again. But if that were the case, why was the guy sitting in the dark holding a camera? An astrophotographer, perhaps, checking his equipment before setting off on a trip out of the city?

Possible.

But unlikely.

The hairs on the back of his neck spiked.

He went for the opposite wall, careful to keep his body hidden, and paused at the door to listen again for sounds of life in the house but heard none. Then he was across the parquet and at the front door with a few quick steps. He opened it and snuck out, quickly but quietly closing it behind him. He glanced at the Audi as he jogged down the front steps to the pavement. The driver's seat looked empty again. He swivelled his head left and right but saw nobody on the street in either direction.

He strode back toward the Jaguar, got in, and looked at Gideon.

I think we have a shadow.

'What do you mean?'

There's a dark blue Audi up there, parked across the street from Carlsson's house. Before I went inside, I heard the engine ticking.

'So?'

Engines tick when they cool down. It'd just been shut off.

'Again, so?'

When I was inside, I saw movement on the street through one of the front windows. A guy was sitting in that car in the dark, holding a camera. *I was out of the place in under four seconds from then. He was gone, and the street was empty. I think he'd ducked down to avoid getting made.*

'Are you sure?'

Are you fucking serious?

'Okay,' said Gideon after a moment's pause.

I'd like to find out who the fucker is.

'As would I, but we could already be trailing behind. I'd rather not have any unnecessary delays.'

They don't know where Ellie lives, Gideon. If they did, Mercury would know, so we'd know. Even if Thomas hadn't explicitly shared the woman's address with the rest of his team, we'd know they know where to find her. He would at least tell the others that. And if they'd already been there or were on their way, we'd probably know that, too.

'Your point?'

We're in front. This guy is tailing us because they don't know where she lives and probably because we beat Thomas to Copenhagen. Either this guy's been on us since Roskilde, or he picked us up at the church, which is more likely. And he's updating Thomas on our progress until he lands or finds Ellie, whose full name, by the way, is Elisabet Hansen. We're doing their work for them.

'Not necessarily. They could've already found her and this guy is simply here as a distraction. If he is, it's clearly working. We need to move.'

Cain contemplated this briefly, then sighed resignedly. Gideon was right. He put the car into gear and pulled out of the parking space. As they passed the Audi, he slowed the Jaguar almost to walking speed and looked into the Audi. This time, the driver wasn't quick enough to hide. He locked eyes with the man until he was gone from his field of vision, then pushed his foot down, and they took off at speed, heading for Westend.

For Ellie's apartment.

As the Jaguar got smaller in his side mirror, Ingmann cursed himself for being so careless. He thumped his fist on the rim of the steering wheel.

'Fuuuuuck!'

He started the Audi's engine. It sounded as angry as he felt. He slammed the steering wheel three times, each harder than the last. The fury inside him burned hotter, and the anger rose higher.

He put the car's automatic transmission into drive and stomped on the accelerator pedal, turning hard to the left to avoid ramming into the vehicle parked in front of him. Once the car had squealed out of the parking space, he pointed it toward the end of the street, keeping the Jaguar's tail lights in his rear-view mirror.

At the end of the road, he spun the car around in a screeching one-eighty and pointed it at the Jag's back end. Then he pressed the car's touchscreen. Switching his gaze between the screen and the road to ensure he didn't hit any parked cars, he tapped Thomas's name and waited.

'They're on the move again,' he said when the call connected, politeness and deference abandoned in favour of expedience.

'*Is anyone with them?*'

'No.'

'*Okay. Stay with them.*'

Ingmann remained silent for a few seconds, unsure how to pass on his bad news.

'*There's something else. What is it?*'

'They made me.'

Silence from Thomas this time. Only for the briefest moment, but enough for him to know he'd messed up.

'*How?*'

'I don't know. I tailed them here perfectly. There's no way they could've noticed me.'

'*Did they stop?*'

'No, but—'

'*But what, Ingmann?*'

'But as they left, they passed my car, going slower than they needed to. Cain looked straight at me and didn't break off until he passed me.'

He heard Thomas breathe out hard.

'*Okay. They obviously know you're on them, so there's no point in being coy about it now. They left you alone, which means you're still in the game, so just keep on their tail and keep me updated.*'

'Understood.'

'*One more thing.*'

'Yes?'

'*No more fuckups.*'

The line went dead before Ingmann could respond.

'Fuck!'

As he refocused, he saw the Jaguar turn left at the end of the street. They were heading back into the city. As Thomas had said, he now had no reason to hang back, so he floored the accelerator, and the Audi sped forward.

He repeated Thomas's last instruction like a mantra.

'No more fuckups.'

37

Frederik Sigvardt's apartment was in a six-storey red brick building on Hindegade—a quiet street a few blocks from Saint Ansgar's Cathedral. Cars, vans, and SUVs occupied all the parking spaces on both sides of the road, so Rasmus pulled up alongside a dirty white panel van parked directly outside the building's front door. Seth and Rebekah got out and closed their doors behind them.

'Stay with the car,' Thomas said to Rasmus. 'We can't take the risk of leaving it double-parked and unattended, and four of us in there would be overkill.'

Rasmus nodded.

'And keep it running,' he continued, sliding out and pushing the door shut.

He pulled out his Marlboros and his Zippo, tugged a cigarette out of the packet with his lips, and thumbed the lighter's spark wheel.

'You really think we have time for a smoke break?' asked Seth.

Without replying, he lit up and turned half of the cigarette to ash in a single, long drag. He exhaled a cloud of smoke through his nostrils, then dropped the cigarette to the pavement and crushed it under his heel.

Seth grunted.

Rebekah chuckled.

He trotted up the building's two concrete steps to the front door. A metal intercom panel was on the wall to the left of the door. Above the speaker and microphone was a flush-mounted camera at roughly head height. Underneath were twelve buzzers in two vertical lines of six, each next to a rectangular nameplate protected by transparent plastic. The names were handwritten in varying degrees of neatness.

Sigvardt's name was neatly written in capital letters next to the buzzer for ground floor flat 1B. He pressed the buzzer and waited a few seconds. When there was no answer, he pushed it again and stepped back. When there was still no answer, he pressed again, holding the buzzer down for a count of three before releasing it. Unexpectedly, a woman's voice came through the intercom's speaker.

'Ja?'

It was a curt 'yes'. Not a 'hello' or a polite 'who is it?' She was flustered. Angry, maybe.

'Ms Sigvardt?' he said in English, looking directly at the camera, pulling back slightly so she could get a clear view of him. Having read the Vatican's database file on Sigvardt during the flight to Copenhagen, he knew that the priest had a sister but hadn't known they lived together. Maybe they didn't. Perhaps Sigvardt had called her, and she'd come over to care for whatever injury Gideon had inflicted upon him.

There was a brief silence from the intercom, then—

'Ja?'

This time, something else came through in her voice. Fear, perhaps?

'My name is Thomas Jäger. I'd like to speak with your brother.'

'You're American.' A statement, not a question.

'Yes, ma'am, and I need to speak with Frederik.'

'I'm afraid that won't be possible. We're about to leave for—'

'The hospital. Yes, we know.'

Silence.

'Ms Sigvardt, it's imperative that I speak with him.'

'I'm sorry, who are you?'

'I'm with the Vatican, Ms Sigvardt.'

'The Vatican?' There was a brief silence, then, *'Do you have any*

identification?'

'Yes, of course.'

He withdrew his identification wallet, flipped it open, and held it before the camera.

'What's this about?'

'It's about the incident with your brother earlier this evening at the cathedral.'

'What? How could you—'

'Ms Sigvardt,' Thomas said calmly, more to control his frustration than to assuage any concerns the woman might have, 'I must speak with Frederik, and it's not a particularly warm night tonight, so I'd rather do it inside. Could you please open the door? I promise I won't take up much of his time, but I cannot leave without speaking to him.'

The intercom crackled and then clicked off. He looked back at the others. Rebekah pursed her lips and shook her head. Then, a buzzer sounded, followed by a loud click. Sigvardt's sister had remotely unlocked the building's front door. He opened the door, walked down a short corridor, and found Sigvardt's apartment on the right. The door was already open a foot or so, and a slim woman with pure white hair tied back from her face was standing in the opening, with a look of frustration on a face that otherwise would have been striking. She looked past him and caught sight of Rebekah and then Seth, and her expression turned to one of apprehension.

'I didn't realise there were three of you.'

'We travel in packs,' said Rebekah with a smile. 'It keeps the pagans at bay.'

Thomas threw her a look to tell her that her comment was unhelpful. She shrugged it off.

'You said you're here about the incident that happened earlier?' asked Sigvardt's sister.

'We understand your brother has been injured,' said Seth.

'Injured? He'll be lucky if he doesn't completely lose the use of his hand!'

'Perhaps if we could come in,' said Thomas, 'we could talk to Frederik to establish exactly what happened.'

'As I was trying to tell you earlier, we're about to leave for the hospital.'

'We'll be as quick as possible.'

She peered at him. Suspicion was all over her face, and he could practically see the cogs working inside her head.

'How do you know about what happened?' she asked. 'And how is it... *why* is it that you're here so quickly?'

'I'll happily answer all your questions, Ms Sigvardt. But the longer we stand here, the longer it'll take for your brother to get the medical attention he needs. So, perhaps you can let us in so we can get out of your way as quickly as possible?'

She briefly stood her ground, then relented and moved aside to let the trio enter. She showed them into a living room softly lit by modern-looking lamps that stood in all four corners and warmed by a roaring fire that crackled in a cast-iron grate at the foot of a chimney flue set into the middle of the left-hand wall. Piano music drifted quietly from a small speaker on top of a wooden sideboard on the far wall opposite the doorway. In front of the cabinet was a long beige sofa, and hunched over on it, head bowed, and with a bloody bandage wrapped around his left hand and a balled-up handkerchief in his right, was Sigvardt.

On the floor next to him was an open bottle of Hennessy. There was no glass. Thomas walked to the sofa and crouched before the priest, who'd barely noticed them.

'Frederik? My name is Thomas Jäger. I'm with the Vatican's Rapid Intervention Group.' He opened his identification wallet and held it up. Sigvardt raised his head sluggishly. His face was almost colourless, through shock or loss of blood or both, and he looked notably older than his sixty years. He lowered his head again but said nothing.

'He was looking for Ellie, wasn't he?' said Thomas.

The priest remained silent as if he hadn't heard the question.

'Frederik, where can I find her?'

'Who?' asked Sigvardt, his head still bowed.

'Father, neither of us has the time to play games. You need to get that hand looked at, we need to find Ellie, and unfortunately, we can't let you leave for the hospital until we know what you know.'

'I don't—'

'We're aware of your phone conversation with Leonard Byrne. Because of that call, some pretty serious people are now hunting her, one of whom you met earlier. You don't have the time to hear why they want her, and I don't have the time to tell you. You just need to tell us what you told the man who did this to you.'

'He said his name was Gideon.'

'We know who he is.'

'And he was no man. He was... God only knows. He was something else.'

'We know that, too. Just tell us what you told him.'

'I didn't want to tell him anything, but the bastard stabbed my hand and broke my fingers. Then he said he would hurt Grethe. I couldn't take it anymore. The pain was—'

'Mother of God, can't you see he's in agony?' protested his sister. She gripped Thomas's shoulder and tried to pull him away. 'We must go to the hospital. Right now!'

'Ms Sigvardt,' said Seth, stepping over to her, 'we don't want to be here any longer than necessary, but this is bigger than your brother and his pain, so we'll keep him here for as long as it takes for him to give us what we need.'

She scowled at him, her eyes full of tears and anger. She went to unleash her fury on him, but Sigvardt waved his hand at her.

'It's okay, Grethe,' he rasped, looking at Thomas. 'Yes. He wanted to know where Ellie lives. I couldn't tell him because I don't know. All I could tell him was where I met her.'

'Which was?'

'Maja's house.'

'That would be Maja Carlsson? The therapist? You met her at her therapist's house?'

'Yes.'

'What's the address?' asked Rebekah.

Sigvardt hesitated.

'The address,' Seth pressed.

'It's on Overgaden Oven Vandet, in Christianshavn.'

Thomas grunted with exasperation.

'That's no good to us, unfortunately. Gideon and his partner have already been there and left. I'm guessing, one way or another, they found out where Ellie lives, and they're on their way there now.'

'What does he want with her?' Sigvardt asked. 'And why is a Vatican rapid action team involved? I don't understand any of this. What's going on?'

He winced again, coughed a mouthful of phlegm into his handkerchief, and cradled his hand against his chest. As his sister went to comfort him, Thomas's phone chirped. He stood up and pulled it from his jacket. Ingmann was calling.

'Yes, Neils?'

'They've stopped again. At an apartment building on Westend.'

'We're on our way.'

As he hung up, Sigvardt's sister turned to him.

'You told me before I let you in that you would answer all of our questions,' she said. 'So, answer them.'

He looked at Seth and Rebekah, ignoring the question.

'Gideon and Cain have stopped. It could be they're at Ellie's place.'

'Oh, dear God!' said Sigvardt.

Seth motioned to the priest and his sister.

'What about them?'

Thomas looked at the Sigvardts.

'We weren't here this evening, Frederik. Nor did you see what you think you saw at the cathedral.'

'But—'

'Look at me, Frederik. No buts. It's important you tell nobody. And if anyone asks how you injured your hand, you'll tell them... I don't know... that you were fixing your motorbike and your screwdriver slipped.'

Sigvardt looked at him blankly.

'Do you understand?' he asked, glancing between Sigvardt and his sister.

They both nodded back dumbly.

He turned to Seth and Rebekah.

'Let's go.'

38

The Jaguar's navigation system brought Gideon and Cain to a junction three-quarters of the way up Westend, presenting them with the option of turning right to head north or left to drive south. The northern route was short but narrow and one-way. If the building they sought didn't lie in that direction, they would be unable to turn around. Instead, they'd have to go through a narrow stone archway onto Vesterbrogade and circle back, potentially costing them valuable time.

Gideon pointed south.

Cain pulled out and kept the car at a crawl as Gideon scanned the terrace of five-storey, red and white brick and stone buildings on his side of the street. On Cain's side, there was only a long, six-foot brick wall interspersed with steel and wood gates providing access to the rear gardens of buildings one street over. They got to the end of the street without finding Ellie's building, so he swung the car around and powered back up to the T-junction, where he slowed down.

Beyond the junction, buildings lined both sides of the street. Like those to the south, they were all five or six storeys and made of brick and stone, but they looked decades older. Ellie's building was two up from the junction, on the left. There was a car-sized gap outside it, between a small white van and a line of diagonal spaces running up to the archway at the end of the road, the closest of which was occupied by three large black motorcycles with winged skulls on their petrol tanks.

Three bikers stood in the gap, holding bottles of beer. They wore blue jeans and black leather jackets and had hair of varying lengths and degrees of cleanliness. Over their jackets, they wore leather vests that bore badges and patches of skulls, flags, and the like. The closest of the men stood with his back to the car. In the middle of his vest was a winged skull patch that matched the logo on the bikes' petrol tanks. Above and below the skull were curved white patches inlaid with red lettering, identifying the club and chapter the bikers belonged to. Gideon didn't need to read them to know who these guys were. He could tell from all the winged skulls.

They were Hells Angels.

Cain sighed and nudged the car forward until its bumper almost touched the closest biker, who stubbornly refused to look around. His brothers-in-arms talked to him and laughed as they eyed the Jaguar with amusement. The guy's shoulders shook. He was laughing, too, probably thinking nobody would be stupid or brave enough to ask him to move.

He revved the engine to move the man on. The guy glanced over his shoulder and glared at him but stayed put. He tapped the car's horn. The biker started, then half-turned and scowled. Covering the right half of his face was a poorly done tribal tattoo. The guy sneered and gave him the middle finger, then turned back to his brothers.

'We need to move these idiots along,' Gideon said.

Cain grunted, inched the car forward, and nudged the back of the biker's legs. The man spun but stood his ground. He inched the car forward again, giving the guy two choices—move out of the way or have his kneecaps inverted. The biker, his face knotted with fury, stepped back and gave him enough room to park the car but did so leisurely enough to indicate that he, not Cain, was in charge.

Gideon exited the car and walked around the back, toward the pavement. Cain then got out, and the man he'd nudged stepped forward a few paces. He was as tall as Cain but broader. Above the left breast pocket of his leather vest was a patch that said 666. Having tangled with the Angels many years earlier, Gideon knew it wasn't a reference to the

Devil but the numerical representation of three Fs, which stood for Filthy Few Forever—the name given to the Hells Angels' enforcer squad. The other two bikers had similar patches. Over the guy's right pocket was a patch that read PRESIDENT.

He was the head of the local chapter.

'Gjorde du virkelig bare det, morfucker?' the biker said to Cain in almost a whisper. *Did you really just do that, motherfucker?*

Cain grinned cockily and shrugged his shoulders.

'I apologise for my associate,' said Gideon, who'd reached the pavement and now stood at the door to Ellie's building. 'We have urgent business here, and he became impatient.'

The biker glared at them, and then at the car. His face brightened as if all was forgiven and forgotten. 'Nice car,' he said in heavily accented English. 'This is a narrow street. I hope it doesn't get scratched.'

Cain pulled open his suit jacket to reveal the butt of one of the guns he carried in his shoulder holster. The biker looked at the gun and laughed. He reached behind his back and pulled out his own weapon, which had been tucked into the top of his jeans and concealed by his jacket. It was a large silver revolver that Gideon recognised as a Colt Python. The other bikers pulled out their weapons.

Cain took a few steps forward.

The lead biker did the same, their faces now mere inches from each other's.

'You think you can take all three of us?' he asked.

A deep, rumbling snarl escaped Cain's throat. Disconcerted, the biker backed off and stumbled into his comrades.

'Hvad fanden?' he said, fear and confusion taking him back to his native tongue. *What the fuck?*

Gideon guessed that Cain had also shown the biker his fangs or changed the colour of his irises. Or both.

'Cain,' he said, wanting to diffuse the situation. Tangling with these bikers would take up time they could not afford to waste.

As Cain turned, something down the street caught his attention. He motioned to Gideon, who looked and saw a navy Audi parked on the opposite side of the road, beyond the junction. The driver was sitting upright, watching them. Having been spotted outside the therapist's house, he must have given up trying to hide. He heard Cain's voice in his head.

We've still got our tail.

'It doesn't matter,' he replied, his eyes fixed on the Audi. 'As you said earlier, if *he's* following *us*, probably it means we're ahead, and all they can do is play catch-up. Can I trust you to play nice out here?'

He looked at the bikers. They had all tucked their guns behind their belt buckles—presumably for quicker access—but had retreated slightly, most likely fearful of whatever Cain had just shown of himself and confused by Gideon's one-way conversation with him. Cain looked back at him and grinned.

Absolutely. I'll channel my inner Swayze.

'What?'

You know. Patrick Swayze. Road House. Be nice until it's time to not be nice.

Gideon groaned, then turned and walked to the half-glazed, white-framed double door of Ellie's apartment building. He grabbed the silver metal handle, twisted it, and pushed. The door remained shut. Electronically locked, he supposed. A small intercom panel was set into the wall to the right of the door. He decided against using it and instead twisted the door handle again and pushed hard enough to force the lock.

The bikers, who had now put more space between themselves and Cain, watched this, dumbfounded. Their leader shouted and started walking toward the building.

'Hey, that's my building, motherfucker. I'm going to make you pay for that.'

Gideon turned around, showed his fangs, and snarled at the biker—a vicious, feral growl full of menace. The biker stopped dead in his tracks, and Cain, leaning casually against the side of the car, pushed himself off the Jag and stepped closer to the guy. The biker raised his hands and stepped backward, his nervous gaze flitting between them both.

'Cain,' Gideon said.

Cain glanced at him.

Yes?

'Be nice.'

Until it's time to not be nice.

Gideon exhaled loudly, entered the building, and walked hurriedly but almost silently across the linoleum floor of the ground-floor hallway. It was poorly lit and smelled of fried food, mould, and fresh vomit. He passed two apartments, numbered 1A on the left and 1B on the right, and headed for the end of the corridor where, next to a door marked 1C, was a staircase that doubled back on itself as it disappeared upward.

He recalled from Cain's photograph of the therapist's Rolodex card that Ellie lived in apartment 6C. Having noted the layout of the apartments on the ground floor and assuming each level was the same, he guessed that her flat was directly above him, probably on the top floor. There was no elevator, which meant he'd be walking up.

He took the steps three at a time and arrived on Ellie's floor in under a minute without losing breath or breaking a sweat. He turned toward the door for apartment 6C and noticed a glass spy hole set into it at head height.

Damn.

Cain was most likely correct that their shadow in the Audi meant that Thomas had not yet located Ellie. What would be the point of having them followed if he were ahead of them? Moreover, neither of them recognised the man as one of his usual team—all of whom the Sicarii were aware, as much as the Vatican was aware of the Sicarii's overt operatives. That would suggest that Thomas was either still in the air or elsewhere in Copenhagen and hadn't beaten them to Ellie.

But Cain could be wrong.

Thomas or one of his team could be standing on the other side of that door, gun drawn, eye to the spyglass. They'd see Gideon before he saw, heard or sensed them, giving them a distinct advantage.

Bullets go through old doors.

Even Mercury, the Sicarii spy within Thomas's team, would shoot at him—if only for appearance's sake—and even bullets that are shot to miss a person can accidentally hit them.

The peephole could still be problematic, even if there were no Vatican people inside. Despite Gideon's smart attire, his facial scar always gave people reason for concern, and when people had a preview of him through a door, they became less inclined to want to open it.

He flattened himself against the wall, slid along it, and took position on one side of the apartment door. He drew a pistol from his shoulder holster, softly pulled back the gun's top slide to load a bullet into the chamber, then took a suppressor from a slot in the holster and screwed it on. He put the weapon back in the holster, pulled out its twin, performed the same ritual, and then re-holstered it.

He leaned in toward the door and listened, ensuring his head didn't pass beyond the doorframe. He could hear music playing within the apartment. It was loud and sounded like old rock music. The band's singer was a woman—Joan Jett or Pat Benatar or someone of that era. He straightened, his back still against the wall, and rapped his knuckles low on the door. This time, he listened for the sounds of movement or conversation or changes in the music's volume. Or the readying of weapons.

He heard none of those things.

He knocked again to be sure and heard only the music, no change in volume. He calculated that Thomas probably wasn't in the apartment, but *someone* was.

Ellie, hopefully.

At shoulder height on the door frame was a doorbell. He stood side-on to the door, hiding his scar, and pressed the button for a second.

There was a buzzing sound inside, which he gauged was marginally louder than his knock, but the music stayed on, and the door remained closed. He buzzed again, but again, no one answered. Finally, his patience frayed, so he held the button again, this time for a count of five.

Zindy sat on the leather sofa, painting her toenails with a new shade of bright purple gloss to match the streak she'd dyed into her blonde pixie cut. She'd wanted to join Ellie at Dante's but was pulling double shifts to earn extra money for a winter-sun getaway and had an early start the following day, so she had instead opted for a night at home with some vintage rock, a few large vodka and sodas, and some pampering—the ultimate evening of self-care.

She ignored the buzzer for as long as she could, but when the idiot at the door held it down, she launched herself from the sofa, stopping at the red cabinet to pause the iPod and begrudgingly silence The Runaways. Before she reached the door, there were five loud knocks from the other side.

'Jesus Kristus, hold fanden på!' she shouted. *Jesus Christ, hang the fuck on!*

She was about to twist the door lock when she stopped herself. She wasn't expecting anyone, and if it were someone she knew, they would have used the intercom outside the building or called her phone, which had not, as far as she'd noticed, rang, vibrated, or lit up. She peered through the spyhole and saw a suited black man standing side-on to the door. He didn't look like a junkie or someone who was there to burglarise the apartment. He looked like... what?

Zindy panicked.

What if the guy was a cop, there to tell her something had happened to her brother, one of her parents, or Ellie? They didn't phone people to give them news like that. They told people face to face. Even at night, the police would send someone—the human touch.

Shit.

She didn't want to open the door, but she had no choice. Her reptilian brain had gone into overdrive, making her think the worst might have happened to someone important to her. But she still needed to be cautious.

She flicked the steel door limiter into place and opened the door the two inches the clasp would allow. The man in the hallway turned to face it, and when she saw the scar on his face, her heart thumped, and she failed miserably to stifle a gasp. It was all she could do not to close the door again.

'What do you want?' she asked boldly, hoping the guy didn't pick up on the tremor in her voice.

'My name is Gideon,' he said in English. 'I'm looking for Ellie.'

'What do you want with her?'

'You're not Ellie.' A statement, not a question. His grey eyes bored into her with an intensity that made her feel simultaneously uncomfortable and drawn to him.

'No. I'm Zindy, her flatmate. I'll ask you again. What do you want with her? You the police?'

'No. I'm not with the police. It's a private matter, but it's important.'

When she had leapt off the sofa, she'd taken her phone. Now, as she eyed Gideon, who apparently wasn't a cop, she held it behind the small of her back and unlocked it with her thumb on the *Home* button.

'Do you know where I can find her?' he asked.

'No.'

'Can I come in and wait for her?'

'No, you fucking can't. Why don't you come back some other time? Or give her a call.'

'Unfortunately, I don't have—'

She slammed the door shut—as much, at least, as a person *could* slam a door on a two-inch limiter—and raised her phone to look for Ellie's number. Her whole body shook, like whenever she went through the always-cold pre-swim sanitising showers at the public swimming pool. There was something about this guy that made her blood freeze. Who the hell was he, and what did he want with Ellie? As she turned to walk back to the living room, another shiver gripped her. Suddenly, there was a loud, resounding crack of wood breaking. She whirled and saw the doorframe had shattered, splinters had flown everywhere, and the door was hanging from only the top hinge.

She screamed and almost dropped her phone.

Gideon stood in the doorway. Everything about him appeared calm. And then she noticed his eyes.

They were the colour of orange fire.

With her phone still barely in her hand and still displaying Ellie's number, Zindy fled to the only room in the apartment with a lock.

The bathroom.

She slammed the door closed, engaged the lock, and sank to the floor. She pushed her back against the door and her feet out in front of her. The trunk of the washbasin was too far away to brace herself against, so she drew her legs back up and planted her feet flat on the tiles, hoping her bare skin would give her enough grip. With trembling hands, she thumbed Ellie's phone number and put the phone up to her ear. After three seconds, the call connected.

'*Hey*—'

'Ellie, it's—' she said, reverting to her native Danish.

The door shuddered.

'I'm not going to hurt you, Zindy,' Gideon said from the other side of the door.

'*I'm too busy and important to take your call right now, so leave*—'

'No!' she cried. She waited for the tone. 'Fuck! Ells, it's Zin. There's a —'

The door shuddered again.

'Zindy,' said Gideon from the other side of the door, 'I just need to find Ellie.'

'There's a guy here, Ellie. He's broken into the flat. He's looking for you. Don't come home. Do not come home! Call the—'

The door burst inward, propelling her across the tiled floor with such force that she struck the sink's pedestal and dropped her phone. As she scrambled toward the bath, her hand found the phone. She put her hand over it, hoping Gideon hadn't seen it.

'Give me the phone,' he said.

'Fuck you!'

He seized her wrist, took the phone from her, ended the connection to Ellie's number, and shoved the device into his trouser pocket.

'Why is it always this difficult?' he asked.

Unable to speak now, she gulped air past a lump that had formed in her throat. Gideon hauled her to her feet. Her shoulders burned in his vice-like grip, and his gaze bore into her, his irises like tiny fires. She felt an odd pressure inside her head, which made her queasy. A strange paralysis overcame her, and she felt her body start to relax.

'It's an interesting look you've got. What is that? Punk chic?'

'Fuck you!' she said for a second time, almost robotically.

'That's not very nice.'

He paused and gazed with a fierce intensity into her eyes.

'I want to know where Ellie is.'

'No.'

'Where is she, Zindy?'

'No!'

She felt the pressure in her head increase. Her limbs weakened, and she thought she might vomit. What the fuck was this? What was he doing to her? She tried to resist, but she felt herself wanting to tell him— *needing* to tell him.

'Where is she?'

'Dante's,' she said. 'I think she's at Dante's.'

'Which is what?'

'It's a club on Vesterbros Torv. I think she's there with Jakob and some friends.'

'Jakob?'

'Her boyfriend.'

Gideon released her, and she crumpled to the floor. She clawed at the side of the bath and heaved herself up to the rim. With the strength in her arms returning, Zindy clambered around the tub to the toilet. Her head barely made it into the bowl before she vomited. It came out fast and hard and was almost transparent, given that the contents of her stomach consisted only of vodka and soda water. She pulled a length of toilet paper from the roll that hung on a metal holder next to the toilet and barely had time to wipe her mouth before Gideon hauled her up again.

'Let's go,' he said.

Cain leaned casually against the rear flank of the Jaguar on the pavement side, facing Ellie's building, his hands in his pockets. Six metres to his right, on the other side of their motorcycles, the three Hells Angels stood huddled together on the road, glaring at him and occasionally laughing to show they weren't afraid. They talked in hushed voices, but he could hear them perfectly. Full of bravado, they were discussing the various ways they would hurt him and Gideon if given a chance. Their heartbeats and their use of their bikes as a protective barrier told a different story.

He smirked to himself.

Suddenly, the front door to the building wrenched inward, and Gideon came out hauling a woman by the arm. She saw the bikers and called out to them as she struggled against his grasp. Gideon, giving only a sideways glance to the bikers, tugged her toward the Jaguar's pavement-side rear door.

'Zindy,' said the alpha biker. 'Hvad sker der?' *What's going on?*

'Soren, hjælp mig.' *Soren, help me.*

Cain wondered briefly how the woman would have known the man and then remembered the guy had said he lived in the same building. Perhaps they were neighbours. Or maybe he was her boyfriend. Or her dealer.

Gideon opened the car door, shoved her in, slid in beside her, and jerked the door closed behind him. Soren pulled his Colt from his belt and stepped toward the car. Before he could pull the trigger, Cain snarled and lunged at him. His jaw clamped around the biker's gun hand, paralysing it. He bawled with pain and dropped the gun. Cain released him, and he inspected his hand. In it were two circular holes, both dripping with blood. Cain glared at him when he looked back up, his irises blood red and his canines extended. Soren staggered backward and slumped against the wall of the building.

'Hvad fanden?' one of the other bikers shouted, drawing his weapon. *What the fuck?*

Before the man had a chance to raise his gun, Cain crossed the distance between them, grabbed his wrist, and pulled his arm from the socket with a sickening pop. The biker howled and crumpled to his knees. He shoved the man's shoulder with his foot, and he tipped sideways onto the pavement.

He looked at the third guy, who backed off with his hands raised in surrender. Life over duty was always the true coward's choice, he thought. Soren, who appeared to have recovered his senses, roared at the biker who'd backed off. He threatened to strip him of his patches—a fate worse than death for an Angel—and pulled a large Bowie knife from inside his right boot. Then he bellowed and lunged at Cain.

Cain deftly countered the attack, swiping the brute's knife hand to the side and kicking him hard in the testicles. Soren went to his knees, tears streaming down his cheeks, and Cain struck him hard with a roundhouse punch to the temple. He dropped heavily and ungracefully to the pavement. The biker who'd surrendered rushed over to him and pressed two fingers against his carotid artery, and a look of relief passed over his face when he found a pulse. Satisfied his club president was still alive, he went to help his other brother, who'd managed to stand and was cradling his limp arm in the other, his face contorted.

Cain took a breath, recomposed himself, and returned to the car. He opened the driver's door, got in, and started the engine.

'Good work,' said Gideon.

Cain looked around to the back seat, first at Zindy and then at him.

Be nice until it's time to not be nice.

He turned forward, fastened his seatbelt, and swivelled the car's rear-view mirror to see Gideon's reflection. He recalled the biker calling out the woman's name.

That's not Ellie.

'No,' said Gideon. 'This is Zindy, her flatmate.'

Zindy looked confused, probably wondering why Gideon appeared to be having a conversation with himself.

'Who the fuck are you people?' she asked.

So, where to?

'She says Ellie's at a place called Dante's. Apparently, it's a club off Vesterbros Torv.'

Cain looked up Dante's in the car's GPS and pressed the button to calculate the route. After a couple of seconds, it returned the result.

She's right. We should be there in three minutes. And we still have our tail.

Gideon glanced through the Jag's rear window. The Audi was still across the street, its driver making no effort to hide.

'Forget about him. The most he can do right now is provide intel to Thomas or whomever he's reporting to. He'll only become relevant if he puts himself between Ellie and us.'

Cain grunted, repositioned the rear-view mirror, put the car into gear and made for Dante's.

39

They arrived at the public space in front of Dante's almost three minutes later, just as the Jaguar's GPS said they would. Cain slowed the car, drove across a cycle lane, pulled onto the pavement, and parked illegally beside a large stone fountain nestled between two low brick walls that snaked around the bases of two tall, bare trees. Zindy silently lamented the absence of traffic wardens this late at night but hoped an overly zealous police officer might stop and take an interest in the car.

He switched off the engine, unbuckled his seatbelt and twisted around to look at her and then at Gideon. She'd become quiet and knew that was probably all too obvious. No doubt they'd think she was contemplating the best way to escape—which she was, but what else was she supposed to do? Just lead them to Ellie?

Fuck that!

She stared at the headrest of the front passenger seat and sensed Gideon turn to her.

'This is what's going to happen next,' he said. 'The three of us are going into Dante's to collect Ellie. Once we have her, you're free to go. If you give us any trouble before or after we have her, the consequences for you and anyone you try to involve will be severe. Do you understand?'

She spun to face him.

'I won't let you hurt my friend.'

'I don't want to hurt her.'

'I don't believe you.'

Cain shifted in his seat and glared at her. Even in the darkness of the car's unlit cabin, she saw the colour of his eyes ripple from emerald to what looked like black, the change cascading outward from his pupils. And then she felt pressure inside her skull, just like she had in her apartment. It made her feel sick again, and she thought she could feel the blood draining from her face.

It doesn't matter what you believe. It only matters that you do as you're told.

She heard the words, but not out loud. They were in her head. How was that possible?

'What are you?' she asked, on the brink of throwing up again.

'Cain,' Gideon said, 'she vomited in her apartment when I *pushed* her. So go easy. We don't want her doing that in here.'

The pressure disappeared almost immediately, and her nausea subsided along with it. She wondered how Gideon knew she was about to retch, then figured he was probably inside her head, too.

Who the fuck were these people?

'How the hell did you do that?' she asked.

Magic.

'You're fucking insane.'

'What does she look like?' asked Gideon.

'What?'

'Ellie. Tall? Short? Blonde? Redhead? What does she look like?'

'You don't know? You *don't* know. Ha!'

She felt a heaviness inside her head again, like someone was pressing through a hole in her skull, right onto the soft tissue inside.

You can show us of your own free will, or I can make you show me. If I force you, it'll be more uncomfortable than you can bear, and you'll spew your guts all over this car. But you know what? It's not my car, and I'll happily drive around with the windows open until the stink disappears if it means we get what we need from you. So, it's your choice.

Zindy spat into Cain's face and tried to resist the pressure. She strained to ignore the weight on her brain, to resist his voiceless words, but it was impossible. Eventually, the pressure became too intense, and an image of Ellie started to materialise in her mind's eye. Blurry at first, it then burst into stunning clarity.

'Enough, Cain,' Gideon said. 'We have enough.'

Cain wiped his face with the palm of his hand and left the car. As he did so, the heaviness inside her head receded once more. She flung her door open, leaned out of the vehicle, and projectile vomited over the pavement. She didn't think it possible to have anything left in her stomach, considering what she'd brought up in her apartment earlier, but enough came up to make an odd-looking puke emoji a foot wide.

She went to sit back up, and a hand gently but firmly took her arm. It was Cain's. He'd already made his way around the car and was now at her door, presumably to make sure she didn't try to run for it. He half-helped, half-pulled her out of the car and held on to her as she regained her composure.

Gideon got out, shoved his door closed, and came around the back of the car.

'Now that you've emptied your stomach contents for a second time tonight,' he said, 'I'm hopeful that won't happen again.'

'No fucking way. You're not going to do that weird Jedi mind fuck on me again. No. Fucking. Way.'

'Just a gentle reminder of whom you're dealing with so that you'll behave yourself.'

He stared at her, his eyes grey pools of tranquillity. Then, ever so slowly, almost as if he didn't want to frighten her, they became a bright, warm amber.

She glanced at Cain, whose eyes were still the colour of dried blood. The sight of them and his fangs peeking out from behind his dark grin brought her back to a harsh reality—these *things* would almost certainly kill her if she warned Ellie and kill her friend if she didn't.

'Holy God,' she said. 'What the hell are you?'

'Which one is Dante's?' Gideon asked.

She ignored him. If he refused to answer her question, she wouldn't answer his.

'Which one?' he pressed, his canines visibly lengthening.

'The church. You go in through those doors to the side. The ones with the two bouncers outside.'

'Thank you. Now, we're going to walk over there, we're going to enter without alerting the two gorillas, and we're going to look for Ellie. Is that understood?'

She remained silent.

Cain growled. It was deep and feral, like a lion or some other large predator.

'Zindy?' Gideon pressed.

'Alright!'

They walked around the fountain, passed through a pair of concrete bollards, and headed across the square for Dante's. Gideon took the lead. Zindy followed, and Cain walked beside her, firmly grabbing her tricep. She hadn't heard him speak yet. Not out loud, at least. Maybe he couldn't. Maybe that was why Gideon was in front. It made sense for the one who *could* talk to go first.

The two oversized doormen stood like sentries at the gates to a citadel. Ellie had introduced them to her once, although she'd been half-drunk then, so while she miraculously remembered Torben and Victor's names, she had no clue who was who. She wondered whether they'd be able to overpower her captors so she could flee into the bar and find her friend and escape. Probably not. If these men could read her mind and speak to her telepathically, God knew what else they were capable of.

Cain tightened his grip on her arm as if he'd heard her thoughts, even though she sensed no one poking around inside her head and felt the distinct absence of nausea. She understood the message.

Be cool.

Ingmann had parked twenty metres up the road, on the other side of the street to Gideon's car. His camera rested on the steering wheel, and through its viewfinder, he watched the two Sicarii take a young woman toward Dante's, a place with which he was familiar. Cain was gripping her arm, so she wasn't there voluntarily.

He hoped the doormen would see them as potential trouble. Gideon wasn't the prettiest of people, Cain just looked like a thug in a suit, and both were overdressed for Dante's. Plus, the woman probably wouldn't look too happy being there against her will. Maybe she'd shout for help or make a run for it.

He thought his prediction had come true when they stalled at the door for almost half a minute. But then, with a swift turn of his lens, he zoomed in and saw that one of the bouncers was speaking to the woman. Rather than scowling or showing concern for her, it looked like he was sharing a joke with her. Finally, he opened one of the doors, and the trio disappeared inside.

'Damn it,' he muttered.

He put down his camera, tapped the screen on the dashboard, and called Thomas.

'*What have you got for me, Neils?*'

'We're at a new location. A nightclub called Dante's, on Vesterbros Torv. They've gone in. And they've got a woman with them.'

'*A woman? Do you know who she is?*'

'No, but I don't think it's Ellie. I don't think they would've found her and brought her here. Maybe a sister or flatmate. Or girlfriend. Someone who can identify her.'

'*Okay, we're about... eight minutes out. Hang on until we get there. Do not engage.*'

'Understood.'

The line went dead.

To hell with this, he thought. He needed to talk to his immediate supervisor about a change in direction. Sure, receiving a call directly from Cardinal Barjona had given his ego a boost, but being a glorified watchdog was not what he'd signed up for. He wanted more action. To be at the tip of the spear. He wanted a permanent place with the Vatican's Rapid Intervention Group.

He grabbed his packet of Princes from the passenger seat and removed a cigarette and a small plastic Bic lighter. He lit up, replaced the lighter, and tossed the pack back onto the seat, irritated. Then, as he blew rings of smoke out the open window into the cold night air, he waited and watched.

Like a good little dog.

40

With the adrenaline of their altercation with Knud Frandsen and his friends having dissipated, Ellie had relaxed again. She stood next to Goat, leaning on a wall-mounted shelf, cradling a clear plastic cup of off-brand dark rum and Coke Light, watching Natasja crush Chewie in a game where she'd sunk all but one of her spotted balls, and he still had five stripes on the table. Jakob and Suzi stood on the other side of the table. She took a sip of her drink and watched Chewie's impending defeat with amusement.

'I don't think he knew she was this good,' she said to Goat.

'What?' he yelled.

She repeated herself, shouting because the band, Hellenbach, had come on a minute earlier for their second set and had turned up the volume.

'Oh. That's how she got me,' he said.

'What do you mean?'

'Haven't I told you this story?'

She shook her head and shrugged.

'Back in Perth, she'd had her eye on me for a while. She asked me out a few times, but I wasn't interested. So, she made a bet with me.'

'What kind of bet?'

'That if she could kick my arse at pool, I'd have to take her out. For a proper dinner, mind you. Not just to the pie wagon after a night at the pub. I was a bit full of myself back then, so I couldn't see how I'd lose.

And I wanted her off my back. So, I took the bet. And Ellie, I tried my fuckin' hardest to win. A proper dinner meant trousers and a shirt, not jeans and a leather jacket, and there was no fuckin' way I'd let my mates see me in town wearing that kind of tackle.'

'And?'

He held up his ring finger and smirked.

'Poor woman,' she said.

'Poor woman, indeed,' laughed Goat. 'That beautiful soul is lumbered with me for the rest of her earthly days. What the hell she saw in me, I do not know.'

'Probably the beard. Us chicks do love manly beards.'

He chuckled and nodded to the pool table.

Chewie had lined up on the cue ball and aimed off-centre at his orange number thirteen, which lay a few inches from a corner pocket. He thrust his cue forward but fumbled the shot. The orange careened off the cushion and rolled to the far end of the table, and the white ball came to rest behind his number ten, giving Natasja no clear line of sight to her remaining ball. He straightened and looked smugly at her as if it were what he'd intended all along. She paced around the table, bending here and there to check angles and lines of sight.

'You look worried,' he said.

'You shouldn't talk to yourself like that, Chewie. Negative self-talk is a terrible thing.'

'Yeah, whatever.'

Natasja chose her place, leaned over, then drew back her cue behind the white ball and aimed for a cushion on the opposite side of the table.

'Good luck,' he said sarcastically.

She slid her pool stick back and forth to get her aim in, then drove it forward. The ball rebounded off the cushion and struck her last spotted ball dead centre, which then flew toward one of the centre pockets, rolled around the rubber liner, and disappeared out of sight.

Chewie watched dumbfounded and saw that the black ball—

Natasja's final target—was wide open and perched adjacent to a corner pocket. She bent over the table and aimed. She made a show of sliding her cue back and forth several times, then looked up at him, blew him a kiss, and thrust her stick forward while looking into his eyes. As the black dropped, so did his jaw.

'Fucking ringer,' he said.

Everyone laughed, and she gave him a conciliatory pat on the cheek. Jakob came around the table and kissed Ellie on the forehead. She looked at him quizzically. He smiled and winked, then walked away toward the staircase and disappeared downstairs.

Zindy couldn't believe how busy Paradiso—Dante's main floor—was. A wall of revellers, four bodies deep, swarmed near the bar in the east alcove. Most waited patiently for their turn to order. Some not so much. They all seemed to pulse back and forth in time with the music. It would be impossible to push through to the other end of the bar, especially with Gideon holding her back. After they'd entered the club, he'd taken over from Cain as her captor, and his grip was vicelike. Despite her promise to behave, he wasn't taking any chances. A gap appeared in front of her, so she wormed through it to the dancefloor, full of bodies buzzing with drink and drugs and the feel-good factor of being at a live gig with what sounded like a decent band.

She slowly worked her way along the edge of the dancefloor, being jostled on all sides as she went. She emerged from the crowd at the staircase to the pool tables above. Thankfully, she hadn't seen Ellie or any of the others yet. But she now had a choice—go upstairs or head past the booths to the bar on the far side of the room. If Ellie were likely to be anywhere, especially now the band was on, it would be the ground floor, so it was the last place she wanted to be. She didn't dare look around any more than she already had, in case she spotted Ellie, or worse, she saw her and came over. She made for the staircase, but

Gideon pulled her to a stop.

'No,' he shouted, his face close to hers. 'We don't go upstairs yet. We need to check this floor first. There.'

He nodded to the booths.

Shit!

The music throbbed in her head and bones. She felt sick. She couldn't believe she was here, having to track down her friend for some demonic thug. She breathed in and out deeply, then reluctantly went toward the booths. In the first were two women who were chatting animatedly. Neither of them was Ellie. She sighed with relief and went to carry on, but Gideon held her back and checked the booth for himself. He stared at the women in turn, which she thought odd because he'd asked her earlier what Ellie looked like, so obviously, he didn't know and wouldn't be able to recognise her even if she were staring right at him.

And then she remembered that, in the car, Cain had done that weird thing in her head and made her visualise Ellie.

Balls, she thought. Shit fuck balls!

In the second booth were four men who looked completely out of place, with the pampered faces, haircuts and expensive clothes of the trust fund crowd. One had a large stain on his shirt and looked angry. Another looked like he was in pain. The other two were gesturing exaggeratedly and talking loudly. One of them was holding up a phone for the others to see. She managed to catch a glimpse of the screen. They were watching a football match.

Idiots.

There was little space between the front of the booths and the backs of the mob on the dancefloor, so making her way to the next stall was hard work. At one point, there was a surge in the crowd, and she thought she might be able to lose Gideon, but he reminded her he was there with a tug on her arm. Damn it, she thought. There seemed no chance of escaping him.

She turned to the next booth, and her heart thumped in her chest. Despite the band's volume, she could hear the boom of her pulse in her ears. She felt her palms get hotter. She curled her fingers against them and could feel them slicked with sweat.

Standing outside the booth with her back to her was Ellie.

Zindy stiffened.

Gideon must have sensed her pause because he shoved her out of the way and spun the woman around. She almost cried with relief. It wasn't Ellie. Same height, same hair, but not her. The woman glared at him, swore at him, and shoved him in the chest. He raised his hands.

'I'm sorry,' he said. 'I thought you were someone else.'

Two of the woman's friends, both men, stood up and edged out of the booth. They were taller than Gideon and looked like they spent most of their time in the gym.

'You need to watch where you put your hands,' one said.

In her mind, Zindy urged the man on. All she needed was for him and his friend to start a fight with Gideon and Cain and maybe get the bouncers involved, and it would give her the chance to get away, find Ellie, and get the fuck out of there.

'You're right,' said Gideon. 'Again, I'm sorry.'

Cain stepped forward. The guy who'd spoken glared and puffed up his chest. His friend did the same. Gideon glanced at Cain, and he stepped back.

'I thought so,' the man said.

Gideon turned to Zindy and gestured for her to keep moving. She walked past the next booth—occupied by two men and a woman who looked stoned—and headed into the west alcove toward the bar. The wall of people in front of her wasn't as deep as it was at the bar on the other side of the room, so she had an easier time working her way through it. As she went, she checked people's faces, but none were Ellie or the others. Which left three likely options. They were either on the far side of the dancefloor somewhere, downstairs in Inferno, or on one of the two upper balconies.

As she turned back to the dancefloor, she glanced up at the east balcony and spotted Chewie through an arched opening. If Ellie hadn't yet picked up her garbled voicemail message, the chances were that she was up there, too. Zindy couldn't lead Gideon there. She had to take him somewhere else. Anywhere but upstairs. If he got up there, Ellie was trapped.

If she could lead the men down to the basement bar, her friend could leave safely. But how would she know to go? How in hell would she warn her without putting her in harm's way? It wasn't like she could wave her arms at Chewie, get him to bring Ellie to the archway, point at Gideon and Cain, and then wave her away again. And with her phone in Gideon's pocket, she couldn't even pretend to need the bathroom to send a text. And what difference would a text make anyway, if Ellie wasn't checking her phone?

Fuck!

All Zindy could do was lead Gideon through the dancefloor and downstairs. She aimed for the bar on the far side of the room and prayed he would forget about going upstairs.

Ellie and the others had given up their pool table again, this time to a group of women who appeared to be celebrating a divorce. As she talked with Suzi—thankfully not about her dreams or marital status— she glanced over at Chewie, who stood at the edge of the group, listening to everyone talk but not joining in. A casual observer might have thought he was despondent after his defeat at the hands of Natasja, but she suspected more was going on inside his head. She knew he wasn't overly competitive, nor was he one of those misogynistic dicks who'd be upset about a woman beating him. She guessed he was unhappy at his lack of success with Suzi and thought he could do with cheering up. With Jakob not having returned from wherever he went—

the bathroom, she presumed—that job fell to her, so she patted Suzi on the arm and circled to Chewie.

'You okay, big guy?' she asked.

'Yeah. Why?'

'You know it's not you, right?'

'Huh?'

'Suzi. Her not being into you has nothing to do with you.'

'I know that.' He took a large gulp of his Tuborg. 'Doesn't make it any easier, though.'

She nodded, sipped her drink, and thought for a moment.

'Why does it bother you so much?' she asked. 'Earlier on, you were chatting up that chick with the dreads.'

'So?'

'So, to the outside world, it looks like you'll go after anyone with tits. You're pretty relentless, actually, and playing the odds like that will get you lucky at some point, so why get so hung up on Sooz?'

He considered this for a moment.

'I dunno. There are plenty of women around who aren't rug-munch —'

'Easy, Chewie,' she said, smiling but using a cautionary tone.

'Sorry. I just mean that I know she swings the other way and that I don't stand a chance with her, and I shouldn't waste my time or hers, but I can't help myself. She's fucking gorgeous.'

Ellie laughed.

'That she is, my friend.'

She raised her plastic cup and tapped it against his. She was about to ask him whether he'd got the phone number of the dreadlocked woman when he looked distractedly through the archway they stood beside.

'What's up?' she asked.

'I think I might've just seen Zindy.'

'What? Where?'

'Down there, by the other bar.'

'Really? That's weird. She said she wouldn't be coming tonight.'

She scanned the crowd. After a few seconds of searching, she spotted her flatmate. Zindy looked upset. No, not upset—afraid. She went to wave, but Zindy caught her eye, raised her eyebrows, and slowly shook her head. Ellie questioned her with a frown, and then saw the two men behind her. They looked entirely out of place. And the one closest to her friend, with an ugly scar running down his face, was gripping her arm.

'What the hell?' she murmured.

She looked from Zindy to the two men again. They weren't cops. That much was obvious. Doctors from the hospital where Zindy worked? Maybe, but doubtful. No, the way that guy was manhandling Zindy indicated she wasn't there by choice. Ellie knew her friend was acquainted with a few unsavoury types, but so was she. And they were generally bikers and local pot dealers. These two guys looked serious— like proper gangsters. The thought distracted her for a moment. When she refocused, she looked back at the guy holding Zindy. He was looking directly at her, and even with the distance between them, she could see that his eyes glowed like embers.

As if sensing her shock, the man smiled.

Zindy tried to steer the men away, but the guy holding her, having already pinpointed Ellie, forced her toward the stairs up to the balcony.

At that moment, the music died, and almost without pause, a drum machine began a slow, quiet riff. Chewie fell in beside Ellie.

'You know that guy?' he asked.

'Nope.'

When Zindy reached the top of the stairs, she was visibly distraught. Ellie rushed over.

'Zin? What's going on? You okay?'

'I'm so sorry, Ells. I—'

The man holding Zindy released her and stepped forward. 'Ellie Hansen, I need you to come with us,' he said in English. 'Now.'

The voice of the band's singer came quietly over the speakers.

'I can feel it... coming in the air tonight... oh Lord.'

Someone behind Ellie lightly touched her shoulder. She glanced sideways and saw Goat ready to back her up.

'And who are you?' she asked.

'My name is Gideon. That,' he said, gesturing with his head behind him, 'is my associate, Cain. We need you to come outside.'

She looked at Zindy and then back at Gideon.

'I'm not going anywhere with you,' she said. 'And *you* need to let my friend go.'

He reached for her arm, but she pulled away before he managed to take hold. Goat came forward and placed a hand on his chest.

'Back off, pal.'

Goat shoved him, and he barely moved. Confusion and annoyance clouded Goat's face as he swayed backward, the force of his thrust returning to him off Gideon's chest. Cain stepped forward and seized Ellie's wrist. She cried out, and Chewie responded with a punch to his face. He dodged the blow, thrust out his hand and struck Chewie in the chest with the heel of his palm. Chewie flew backward over the pool table, crashed into the wall behind it, and landed in a heap on the floor.

'It's all been a pack of lies,' sang the band's vocalist.

Goat took a fast, brutal swipe at Gideon with the thick end of a pool cue. He deflected the blow with his forearm, then slid his arm around and under Goat's. He locked the Scot's arm in his own, then pushed his elbow the wrong way. Goat howled, his legs almost buckling underneath him. Then Gideon chopped him in the larynx with the edge of his hand, and he collapsed to the floor, gulping in air, his face a vivid crimson.

'Motherfucker!' screamed Natasja. She charged at Gideon with her pool cue. As she swung it, he dodged under it, grabbed her by the throat, and slammed her down onto the pool table. She howled as pool balls dug into her back and legs.

Terrified and enraged by what these two strangers were doing to her friends, Ellie flew at Cain. She landed a solid punch to the side of his temple and an uppercut to his chin and then went in with a kick to his knee, hoping her steel-toed Doc Martens would do some immediately crippling and permanent damage.

He buckled and went down on one knee. She went to slap him on both ears with cupped hands, intending to puncture his eardrums and cause him some severe pain—a move Lars had taught her—but as her hands were millimetres from connecting with his ears, he caught her wrists so firmly it felt like he was going to crush her bones. He glared into her eyes, and she watched in horrified confusion as his irises turned a dark crimson and his canine teeth extended.

'What the fuck?' she yelled.

She tried to retreat, squirming in his grip, but his strength felt superhuman.

'*It's no stranger to you and me!*' screamed Hellenbach's singer.

Cain stood unhurriedly as if teasing her, making her wait for further pain. Then, as the deep, resonating sound of heavy drums and distorted guitars brought the band's song to its climax, there was an explosion of wood and glass around his head. He roared and whirled around. There stood Jakob, who'd jumped in to protect Ellie and help his friends with the closest weapon he could find—a framed photograph he'd taken off the wall. Cain brushed a hand through his hair and over his scalp. When he drew it back, it was covered in blood and glass.

'You don't get to touch her,' raged Jakob, pointing at him and circling to Ellie's side. 'Ever.'

Cain bellowed, his eyes almost black with fury. As he lunged at Jakob, he was grabbed from behind and hauled backward.

'Du er ude!' said his assailant. *You're out!*

It was Victor, one of the doormen. He attempted to drag Cain toward the staircase, but Cain spun his body in a graceful twirl, spiralled underneath the bouncer's arm, and got free of his grip. Victor reached out again, but Cain managed to evade him, seize and twist his wrist, and wrench his fingers backward. When he let go, Ellie could see they were all bent at an unnatural angle, failing to return to their normal position. He then heeled the side of Victor's knee. The doorman went down hard, incapacitated and howling like an animal refusing to die.

Ellie looked on helplessly, her hands covering her mouth and tears streaming down her face. What the hell was happening? Who were these… whatever they were? And why did they want her?

Her attention turned to Gideon. He was now contending with Torben, the other doorman, who was about to suffer the same fate as his colleague. Rather than breaking the poor man's fingers, Gideon snapped one of his elbows the wrong way and then kicked the front of his knees, which she guessed would have shattered his kneecaps. She screamed. Jakob took her hand. With both bouncers writhing on the floor in agony, Gideon and Cain turned back to her and Jakob.

'We're going to have to take them both,' Gideon said.

Cain nodded and lunged for Jakob. He seized his jacket's collar and forced him toward the stairs. Ellie tried to fight him off, but Gideon grabbed her tricep and clamped down hard.

She howled in pain.

As he dragged her away from the pool tables, she managed to survey the damage he and Cain had inflicted on her friends. Goat was on the floor, still struggling to breathe, but his face was now almost back to its usual Scottish paleness. Natasja was twisting in pain atop one of the pool tables. Chewie was in a crumpled heap on the other side of the tables but, thankfully, moving. And Zindy and Suzi stood in the corner, hugging each other, too petrified to do anything else.

Her strength left her, so she gave up fighting Gideon and let him haul her toward the stairs.

41

Ellie burst through the fire exit—once the entrance doors to the church—at the top of some stone steps that led down to the public square, with Gideon beside and slightly behind her, gripping the collar of her top and half-pushing, half-lifting her forward. Without her coat, which was still in Dante's cloakroom, she felt the cold bite immediately. Her whole body shook. It had started snowing since she arrived at Dante's, and a thin blanket of white powder now covered the square and everything else in sight except the main roads of Vesterbrogade and Gasværksvej. The snow was still coming down softly, and a large flake gently kissed her face. She shivered again. Gideon urged her on. She stumbled on the edge of a step and jarred her ankle. Before she could fall, he steadied her and kept her moving.

'Why are we moving so fast?' she asked.

'I hate churches.'

'It's not a church anymore.'

'Churches are always churches. Only their congregations and the gods they worship change.'

A stream of thoughts flashed through her mind as they reached the bottom of the steps. Maybe this guy did just want to talk to her. Maybe he'd say whatever he needed to and then let her go. Maybe, in about ten minutes, she and Jakob would be back inside, getting warm and drunk and laughing with the others about what a fucked-up night it had been.

'Okay, so we're outside now,' she said. 'You said you needed to talk to me, so talk.'

'Not here. Our car's over there.'

He nodded to a black car parked on the pavement on the far side of the square. She tensed up. Being dragged outside for a chat by an aggressive stranger who'd just hurt her friends was one thing, but getting into a car with him could only end badly.

'There's no fucking way I'm going anywhere with you until you tell me what this is about.'

Gideon continued to direct her toward the car in silence.

'What do you want with me?' she screamed.

She flashed back to his strange eyes and Cain's fang-like teeth. Whatever the hell these guys were, they weren't there to talk. And they were not going to let her go. That he seemed intent on getting her into his car convinced her of that.

She regained her will to fight. She squirmed and heaved away from him, and she got free. For a split second. He grabbed her wrist and her neck and reeled her back in. When he touched her bare flesh, she felt him flinch as if a jolt of electricity had passed between them. Her eyes met his, which burned bright orange.

'It *is* you,' he said.

'What? What do you—'

'Get the fuck off me!'

It was Jakob. She peered around Gideon, back toward Dante's, and saw that Cain was shoving him onward, one hand gripping his upper arm and the other planted firmly against his back. She glanced beyond them and saw patrons and staff from Dante's spill out after them at the top of the steps, most no doubt out of plain old curiosity, but probably some were hoping to see the violence continue. A bouncer she didn't know shouted and ran down the steps toward them. When he reached the bottom, he called out again.

Cain stopped and turned to face the man, one hand still on Jakob's arm, his free arm stretched out toward the bouncer, palm out, fingers splayed. The man was over three metres from him but stopped as abruptly as if he'd run into a wall. Suddenly, his hands flew to his own throat, his face turned crimson, and veins rose in thick lines across his forehead and temples. Cain lowered his arm, and the man dropped to his knees, gasping for breath like a fish plucked from its bowl. As he fell forward onto the snow-dusted ground, the mob, now at the foot of the steps, became silent. Then murmurs of disbelief and amazement rippled through the bystanders, and faces became masks of horror, shock, and bewildered amusement.

'Holy shit,' said Jakob.

'Keep moving, Cain,' Gideon ordered.

There was a commotion deep within the crowd. Goat was pushing his way through the front line of the mob, dragging Natasja behind him. Still clearly in pain but wearing a look of determination and holding the thick end of a broken pool stick, he charged at Cain.

'Leave it, Goat,' Jakob yelled.

'Jakob. What the hell is going on? Who are these guys?'

'Fuck knows. Just call—'

'Ellie!'

It was Suzi. She'd skirted around the backs of the onlookers and now stood out in the open. Ellie pulled against Gideon's firm grip, stopping him from taking her further.

'Suzi, call the police!' she shouted.

As she watched Suzi reach into her jeans pocket, an object blurred through the air toward Gideon, who seemed to notice it at the last second but moved too slowly to avoid it. He roared as it struck his head and opened a gash above his left eye. He gingerly ran his fingers across the cut and snarled, wolflike, when they came away bloody. She looked at the floor around his feet and saw that the object which had struck him was a black eight-ball.

With blood seeping from his forehead and running down his face, he scanned the crowd for the person who threw it. At the back, a head taller than everyone else and looking immensely smug, stood Chewie. He pointed at Gideon and then showed him his middle finger.

'Jesus, Chewie,' Ellie muttered.

Gideon bellowed with fury and raised his hand at him as Cain had done with the bouncer.

'No,' Ellie cried out. 'Please. He's just trying to help us.'

Gideon glanced sideways at her, and she saw his canines had lengthened, and his eyes were a furious amber again. He waved his arm, and half of the bystanders flew backward with such force that they pushed Chewie and four others back up the steps and over one of the stone walls that ran up the sides. It must have been a twelve-foot drop on the other side.

'You fucking animal,' she screamed, ignoring the implausibility of what he'd done.

'We don't have time for this, Ellie,' he said, wiping blood from his eye with his free hand. 'Please stop fighting us. And tell your other friends to back off, or what just happened to the tall one will happen to them, too.'

She looked over at Jakob, who'd collapsed to the ground. He stared without focus at the legs in the crowd, almost as if he were looking through them. Her heart wrenched for him. Had he just watched his best friend die?

Cain hauled him to his feet and marched him toward the stone fountain near the road. Ellie felt herself move in the same direction as Gideon guided her, albeit less forcefully than he'd done earlier. When they were halfway to the fountain, she looked over at Jakob.

'Babe, are you—'

She was interrupted by the thundering roar of a dark Mercedes SUV speeding through the four-point intersection thirty metres to her right. It braked hard, crossed the oncoming lane, slid sideways as it mounted the pavement, and stopped, facing the square at forty-five degrees.

'Damn it,' Gideon muttered.

Ellie could vaguely see two men in the SUV's front seats. For a few seconds, they remained still. Then all the doors opened, and the occupants climbed out—the two men from the front, a woman, and a third guy who looked even larger than Cain. The man from the front passenger seat wore jeans and a leather jacket. The others were dressed just as casually. They didn't look like police, but she didn't care. Whoever they were, their timing was perfect.

The driver disappeared to the rear of the vehicle, then returned holding a large black shotgun with a pistol grip. The guy in the leather jacket took out a black pistol. He pulled the slide on the top of the weapon, tucked the gun into the front of his belt, and began slowly walking forward. The others walked with him. Movement across the street caught her eye. There was a man leaning on a dark blue Audi. He pushed himself off the car and began walking in her direction, matching the speed of the four who'd arrived in the Mercedes. Five of them against Gideon and Cain. Good odds. She prepared herself to either run or fight.

'Help us,' she yelled to the group from the Mercedes.

'Keep moving,' Gideon ordered, pushing her toward the fountain.

'Ellie?'

It was the man in the leather jacket. How the hell did he know her name? Maybe they *were* the police, and one of her friends had called them.

'Yes! Please! Help us!'

'Gideon,' he shouted.

Gideon ignored him and continued guiding her to his car. The man called out again. This time, he stopped and turned to face him.

'Give us the woman, Gideon,' the man said, his voice raised but calm and even.

'You know I can't do that, Thomas.'

'This will not end well for you if you don't hand her over.'

'It won't end well if I do.'

'Help us,' Ellie pleaded again. 'He's just killed our friend.'

'Come on, man,' said Thomas. 'Don't make this diff—'

Suddenly, the hulk who'd arrived with him slammed into him, knocking him to the ground front-first and pinning him down. He looked over his shoulder and said something to the man. Ellie guessed it wasn't complimentary. The big man removed himself from Thomas and offered him his hand. He took it, then brushed himself down and glared at Cain, who scowled at him and showed him his middle finger.

Ellie realised that Cain must have propelled the big man in the same way that Gideon had swept the crowd up the steps moments earlier, with some form of telekinesis.

Which her brain told her was impossible.

Wasn't it?

Other than appearing pissed off at being knocked to the ground, Thomas seemed otherwise unfazed by Cain's magic trick, as did the woman and the big man, like they'd seen it before. Their driver, though, looked as unsettled as she felt.

The giant reached into his jacket, pulled out a large silver pistol and held it up.

'Cain,' he said, calmly but loud enough for Ellie to hear, 'I'm going to shoot out your fucking eyes and take your head off with the blunt end of this.'

'Okay,' shouted Thomas. 'Let's not all get too excited.' He looked at the giant's gun and motioned with his head. The man let his arm drop to his side but didn't put the weapon away. Thomas turned back to Ellie and Gideon and continued walking toward them. His colleagues kept pace with him.

'Just hand her the fuck over, Gideon. Before this gets messier than it needs to be. I won't ask again.'

Gideon turned back to the fountain. Before he could pull Ellie another step toward it, there was a thunderous crack, and something metallic pinged off the stone pavers in front of them. Panicked screams and shouts came from the crowd at the foot of Dante's steps, most of whom were now holding their phones, filming or taking photos of the bizarre scene before them. Thomas's head whirled toward his female companion. Her gun raised in both hands, she paced toward the street side of the brick wall that separated the road from the public square.

'Ellie?'

'I'm okay, Jakob.'

'He's serious, Gideon,' the woman said. 'And we've got the numbers.'

Gideon looked back at Cain, who shoved Jakob forward. Gideon caught him roughly on the arm and dragged him and Ellie toward the parked Jaguar. As they neared it, the rear door closest to them swung open, pulled by an invisible force.

'This is fucking crazy,' Jakob said.

'Get in.'

'No fucking way,' Ellie said. 'We're not going anywhere with you.'

'C'mon, man,' Thomas shouted. 'Just give them over. Rebekah's right. You can't win this one. We've got superior—'

There was a snap from Ellie's right, like someone had flicked a metal ruler against a table, and the man from the Audi stumbled and fell to his knees. A small red patch appeared on his chest and began to spread. Then he flew backward with such force that his body bent in the middle as if he were trying to touch his toes. He struck the metal doorframe of a high-end homewares store and fell soundlessly to the ground, blood flowing out of his mouth and down his chin.

She spun her head and saw that Cain had both his hands raised. One hand was open, his fingers splayed like when he'd throttled the bouncer. The other held a black pistol with a long tube attached. She'd seen enough films to know it was a suppressor, meant to make a weapon quieter. He fired again and put a bullet in the middle of the man's forehead as accurately as if he'd been standing a metre away instead of almost thirty. A cloud of red and pink sprayed out behind the man onto the glass of the shop's door, and a split second later, his head snapped back, and his body slumped sideways to the pavement.

Thomas's driver called Cain a bastard and let off a slew of shots in his direction, frantically shucking the shotgun's sliding fore-stock. Cain drew a second weapon with almost immeasurable speed, fired a hail of bullets at Thomas's team, and bolted for cover behind a low wall. Meanwhile, Gideon shoved Ellie and Jakob onto the rear seat of the Jaguar.

'If you want to live through this, stay down,' he said.

He slammed the door, which immediately locked. The sound of gunfire reverberated through Ellie's ears, the glass and aluminium shell around her doing little to dampen the noise. She swore and squeezed down, knees first, onto the floor behind the driver's seat, her back to the door.

'What the hell is going on?' Jakob asked, forcing himself down behind the other front seat, facing her, and visibly in as much shock and fear for their safety as she was. 'Who are these guys?'

'I don't know.'

'What the fuck do they want with—'

'Jakob, please! I've got no fucking idea. I've never seen them before.'

'We need to call the police.'

'Those other guys probably *are* the police. They knew my name. How would they know my name unless one of our crew called them?'

He patted his pockets for his phone and found it in the back of his jeans. As he shakily pulled it out, something slammed into the front passenger door outside, followed by a flurry of metallic pings against the car's exterior. She screamed, and he dropped his phone, which slid off his knees and under the front seat.

'Fuck,' he said.

She peered over the shoulders of the front seats and saw Gideon slide down the car's door and out of view, leaving a streak of blood down the glass.

'They didn't show any badges,' said Jakob, fumbling for his phone.

'They could be a rival gang or something.'

'Gang? This isn't Sons of fucking Anarchy, Jakob.'

'No, but the woman and that guy Thomas both sound American, and I'm pretty sure that Desert Eagles, G-Wagons, and giant fucking shotguns aren't standard police issue in Denmark. So they are not the fucking cops.'

He retrieved his phone, unlocked it, and dialled. As he held it to his ear, there was a screech of tyres, the blare of a car's horn, and the crack of a single gunshot. Ellie peeked over the seat in front again and saw a red Honda parked in the middle of the road. A woman was running away from it, hysterical, toward the opposite side of the street.

'Hello,' Jakob said into his phone. 'I need—'

Suddenly, Gideon's head and shoulders appeared beside the rear passenger door. Ellie jumped, then watched as he twisted quickly and moved to the front of the car. He fired a shot over the car's bonnet with a silenced pistol and slid out of sight again.

'Sorry. I need the police... Yes... We're being abducted... Yes, abducted... People are shooting... Yes... No, we're not hurt... My name's Jakob Nørgard... Yes... Vesterbros Torv... How long? Okay.'

As he hung up, Ellie heard the scuffle of someone working their way around the car toward its rear. She guessed it was Gideon, trying to reach safety.

'What did they say?' she asked.

'She said they'll have someone here ASAP. I'm not sure she believed me, though.'

'We have to get out of here, Jakob.'

She twisted around and tried the door handle closest to her. She expected the lock to disengage when she pulled the lever, but it didn't. She kept rattling the door handle, but the door remained closed, so she fumbled with the lock itself.

'It won't open,' she yelled. 'Try yours.'

He turned as much as he could and complied, but the door and the lock stayed shut.

'Nope,' he said.

'Shit.'

There was scraping on the back of the car on her side, then the persistent metallic sputtering of what she supposed was Gideon firing multiple shots at someone. Almost simultaneously, she heard glass shatter and a muffled cry from whom she guessed was the woman, Rebekah.

After half a minute or so of more sporadic gunfire, alternating between the coughs of suppressed weapons, cracks of unsilenced pistols and the boom of the shotgun, they were suddenly in a cocoon of silence. No shouts, no scuffling outside the car, and no more gunshots. All she could hear was the sound of her and Jakob breathing.

A shadow passed across the window behind her. She tensed up. Gideon and Cain had somehow beaten Thomas and his people and were going to whisk her and Jakob away. Probably without further interference unless the police arrived before they managed to leave. Suddenly, the small window panel in the door beside her exploded inward, showering the back seat and her hair with chunks of glass. She screamed involuntarily. Then the door opened with a tearing screech as if the force of it had sheared off the lock. The shadow grew darker, and a hand appeared to the right of her face, which she flinched away from instinctively.

'Come with me,' a calm voice said.

She glanced over her shoulder and saw Thomas, hand outstretched. She wanted with all her heart to take it, but she was too petrified to move. He hunkered down so that his eyes were level with hers.

'Hey,' he said quietly. 'You need to come with me. Do you understand?'

She could feel tears streaming down her face. She'd heard him and understood what he'd said, so she nodded, but her limbs wouldn't move.

'Are they dead?' she asked.

'No,' he said, dropping his hand. 'And they won't be down for long. So we need to move. Now.'

'Babe,' said Jakob, his voice calm but his eyes betraying his fear. 'We need to go.'

She knew he was right. She knew that if they stayed and Gideon and Cain weren't dead, she and Jakob could soon be. Thomas held out his hand again, and she took it, her grip light with trepidation at first, then tightening as her self-preservation instincts kicked in. Thomas smiled down at her, but as she took his hand, she thought she saw his eye twitch slightly. Maybe that was just how he smiled.

'Let's go,' he said.

He helped her out of the Jaguar. She took a few steps to give Jakob room to get out and saw that Rebekah stood behind the car's rear, pointing her gun at Gideon. He was sitting on the road, his legs stretched out in front of him, his back against the car's bumper. His torso, which leaned slightly to the right, was a red, sticky mess. There was a hole in his chest, above his heart, and another in his left shoulder. His head flopped to the right, and she could see through a patch of dark, congealed blood that the gash on his forehead from Chewie's pool ball looked like it had already healed. His eyes were closed, and he looked dead. Thomas had said he wasn't. With a rage building inside her, she wanted to repeatedly kick him in the head to find out.

Jakob took her hand. Nothing they could say to each other would make any of this better. All she had were questions, and he would be the same. She looked at Thomas and hoped he'd be able to explain what the hell was happening. Before she could ask him anything, the big Mercedes pulled up sharply beside them, its engine growling like some angry predator. He opened the closest rear door.

'Get in,' he said.

In the distance was the faint wail of police sirens.

'Seth,' he called. 'Rebekah. Let's move.'

Before climbing into the SUV, Ellie glanced at the big man Thomas had called Seth. He was halfway between the Jaguar and the stone fountain, holding the shotgun their driver had been using. There was a dark red hole in the top of his right thigh, and he had the foot of the same leg on the blood-soaked chest of Cain, who was lying flat on his back. Cain's left forearm curled limply over his boot.

She climbed inside and slid across to the far door. Jakob got in beside her.

'You alright?' he asked.

She wasn't, but she nodded. There was nothing he could do for her, so why deliberately make him feel useless? She watched through the windshield as Seth walked backward to the G-Wagon, keeping the shotgun pointed at Cain. He went to the SUV's rear, opened the tailgate, and heaved himself inside. As he pulled the door closed, Rebekah left Gideon, climbed in next to Jakob, and slammed her door shut.

Thomas stood beside Gideon and pressed the tip of his gun against his forehead. He held it there briefly, then climbed into the Mercedes.

'Everyone okay?' he asked, twisting in his seat.

'What the fuck is going on?' Ellie demanded.

'Rasmus, get us out of here.'

The driver floored the accelerator. As the big SUV's spinning wheels fought for traction, Jakob glanced out of Rebekah's window.

'He's alive,' he said to Ellie. 'Chewie's alive.'

She leaned forward to look past him and Rebekah. At the foot of Dante's steps, she saw Suzi and Natasja. They were hugging each other. And behind them, using Goat as a crutch, was Chewie.

'Oh my God,' she said, bursting into tears.

She hugged Jakob tightly and then turned to Thomas.

'Hey!' she said, striking him in the shoulder.

He held up his hand and pulled a large black flip-type wallet from his jacket, which he opened and showed to her.

'The Vatican?'

'What the hell is a Rapid Intervention Group?' asked Jakob.

'It saves people like you from people like them,' Seth quipped.

'My name is Thomas. The large gentleman in the back is Seth, and the young woman beside you with the gaping wound in her shoulder is Rebekah.'

'Okay,' said Jakob. 'So, what the fuck are those guys, why do they want Ellie, and why would the Vatican send you to save her from them?'

42

With the blood loss from the bullet wounds in his chest and shoulder and the mental fatigue of needing to focus on both Thomas and Rebekah as separate targets and on telekinetically keeping the Jaguar's doors locked, Gideon had passed out from exhaustion. Now, loudening police sirens and the indistinct murmurs of voices roused him. He cracked open his blood-crusted eyes and found himself surrounded by a semi-circle of onlookers. Someone moved toward him, and through blurry vision, he vaguely saw a leg swing backward. It sped forward, the biker's boot on the end of it travelling straight for his face.

'Wake up, fucker,' the boot's owner said.

He tilted his head far enough to narrowly avoid a kick to the face and fully opened his eyes. The leg swung away, and the boot came toward him again with more speed. Focussed now by anger and adrenaline, he grabbed it with both hands and glared up at its owner. It was the bearded man who'd shoved him inside. He remembered that Jakob had called him Goat. He snarled and twisted the man's foot, pushing it away as he did so. Goat spun in the air, collided with some bystanders, and landed awkwardly and painfully by the howl he let out.

'Jesus forbandet Kristus.' *Jesus fucking Christ.*

It was the woman who'd attacked Gideon with a pool cue. Before she or anyone else could take a swipe at him, he sprang to his feet. The woman and the rest of the spectators—whom he could now see included all the people Ellie had been inside with—swiftly took a few steps backward.

'Cain,' he called out.

His chest and shoulder ached. He pulled his shirt open and saw that the wounds were already healing. If either of the rounds he'd taken were still inside him, he'd need to remove them now or surgically extract them later. Pulling the rounds out now would hurt, but surgery would be more painful as he'd have to reopen the wounds, and his metabolism would burn up any anaesthesia before he'd feel its effects.

'Cain!'

He reached over his left shoulder with his right hand and felt for exit holes. He could feel one at the back of his shoulder, but the round he'd taken in the chest was still inside him. As he mentally prepared for what he had to do next, a loud snarl behind the onlookers made them part abruptly and chaotically. Cain appeared in the middle of them. Black, sticky blood covered his jaw, and there was no white left on the front of his shirt except for the higher parts of the collar. He walked through the crowd cradling his right arm across his chest.

'What's the damage?' Gideon asked.

Cain dipped his head.

A compound fracture of my radius, a few bullets to remove later, and an overwhelming need for payback.

Gideon breathed in and out sharply several times and, with the wail of a wounded animal, squeezed the tips of his thumb and forefinger into the hole in his chest. Some of the bystanders gasped, while others swore. One man whirled and vomited on the pavement. After half a minute of probing, he pulled out the small silvery-grey head of a bullet, which he dropped to the tarmac.

The volume of the sirens increased. He estimated they had perhaps thirty seconds before the police arrived. Cain pointed at the crowd, many of whom were still holding phones. Gideon knew what he meant.

'We don't have time to take their phones. We'll just have to take our chances.'

Cain grunted, tossed him the car keys and eased himself into the Jaguar's front passenger seat. Gideon climbed into the driver's seat, fired up the engine, and put the car into gear. He spun the steering wheel to the left as far as it would turn, then released the parking brake and slammed the accelerator. The Jag leapt forward into a tight left turn. He kept the wheel locked until the car spun a one-eighty and pointed away from where the police sirens were coming. He checked the rear-view mirror to ensure the police weren't following them, then glanced at Cain, who'd reclined his seat and laid back with his eyes closed and his shattered arm resting on his bloody, punctured chest. He wasn't concerned. The bone, although painful to reset, would heal quickly enough. And if any of the bullets in Cain's chest had pierced his heart, it would continue, albeit labouredly until its wall repaired itself, to pump his lifeblood around his body and keep him alive.

As Gideon noticed the flash of blue lights in the mirror, a curve in the road began to put them and the public square out of sight. The onlookers by the road and outside Dante's vanished like matches blown out by the wind. All that remained for the police was a red Honda riddled with bullet holes and the body of a man slumped against the broken door of the homewares shop, with dark, bloody holes in the middle of his chest and forehead and his chin a tacky crimson mess.

43

As the big Mercedes SUV thundered through the city, Ellie felt relieved yet still tense and afraid. Adrenaline coursed through her veins, her heart pounded, and questions remained unanswered. Who were the men who attacked her, and what did they want with her? She risked a sideways glance past Jakob at Rebekah, who was shuffling around, poking a finger through the bloody, frayed bullet hole in her jacket, her face appearing to show annoyance at the state of the garment more than concern or pain from the injury she had suffered. Seth made noises in the back, which sounded like grumbles of frustration more than groans of pain. She wondered who these miraculous saviours were. Not bulletproof, but not dead either. Not even seriously hurt. Mostly just pissed off. Finally, she turned her attention back to Thomas, who was staring dead ahead.

'So, come on,' she said, pushing the back of his shoulder again but with less force than before. 'What the hell's going on?'

He remained stoically silent.

'Where are you taking us?' she asked.

'Roskilde,' he replied without turning around.

'Roskilde?' echoed Jakob. 'The airport? We're not going to the airport. We're not going anywhere with you until you explain all of this. Stop the car.'

Ellie bent forward and slapped Rasmus hard on the side of the head.

'Hey,' she said. 'Pull over!'

She caught his eye in the rear-view mirror. He glared at her, then glanced at Thomas, who continued looking forward. After receiving no instruction from him to stop the car, his eyes returned to the road.

'Fuck!' she said, thumping the back of Thomas's seat.

'Well, this jacket is definitely ruined,' said Rebekah, pulling her finger from the bullet hole. 'Thomas, we need to discuss a clothing allowance at some point.'

'Okay,' Jakob said to Thomas. 'You need to start giving us some answers. What's the Vatican's Rapid Intervention Group? Some kind of religious police force? Are we under arrest?'

'No. You're not under arrest.'

'So, what is all this?' asked Ellie.

Thomas turned in his seat.

'You recently had a meeting with a priest. Father Frederik Sigv—'

'How do you know that?'

'After your meeting, Sigvardt called a colleague of his in London. Bishop Leonard Byrne. A specialist in—'

'Again, how the hell do you know that?'

'We intercepted the call.'

'What? How?'

Thomas inhaled deeply.

'Without boring you with the details,' he said, 'the Vatican uses some very sophisticated software to monitor all communications that go through its email servers and telephone accounts. That software searches for keyword combinations that may indicate a threat to the Church or may be of interest to it, such as in your case. And we work for a group governed by the Vatican which—'

'Which what?'

He rubbed the bridge of his nose and exhaled heavily.

'Ellie, you'll never have a question answered if you keep interrupting,' he said. 'And, you know... gratitude.'

She looked blankly at him, unfazed. He was right, of course, that she should be grateful. But this was all some serious shit, and it was freaking her out.

'May I continue?' he asked.

'You don't need to be a facetious prick,' she said. 'Just get on with it.'

'Which, among other things,' he continued, 'is searching for people with dreams and visions like yours.'

'Why?'

'I'm not at liberty to say at this stage.'

'You're not at liberty to say?'

'No.'

'Why not?'

'I report to a higher authority which—'

'And who's that?' asked Jakob. 'God?'

Thomas chuckled.

'Ultimately, yeah,' he said. 'But on a day-to-day basis, someone a little closer to home. A cardinal named Peter.'

'So, he gives you orders, and you just follow them?'

'That's usually the way it works, yeah.'

'This is a complete joke,' said Ellie.

'Hang on,' Jakob said. 'You just said you work for a group the Vatican *governs*. What does that mean? That you're not actually a part of the Vatican?'

Seth sighed audibly from the back of the Mercedes.

'He doesn't miss a trick, this one.'

'No,' said Thomas. He looked at Jakob for a few seconds, appearing to consider something. 'We—'

'Don't do it, man,' Seth said.

'They'll be told eventually, and frankly, if getting them on the plane without a fight means answering their questions, I'd much rather do it the easy way.'

Seth chuckled. 'It's your funeral.'

'We work,' Thomas continued, 'for a group known as the Elyonim, led by Peter. Its existence is kept under wraps for several reasons. The RIG does legitimately exist, but our membership of it, for want of a better term, is a cover put in place by Peter and used mainly to help us get around bureaucratic obstacles and that kind of thing.'

'Of course it is,' Ellie said with a laugh. 'Because nothing says Catholic Church like a good cover-up.'

'That all sounds pretty fucking ridiculous,' said Jakob.

'Maybe,' Thomas said, turning back to face forward. 'But it doesn't make it any less true.'

'So, what exactly are the El-whatever?'

Thomas hesitated.

'Let me guess,' said Ellie, 'You're not at liberty to say. Jesus, you guys are a pain in the ass.'

'And, like he said, we just saved *your* asses,' said Seth.

'So, if we're heading to the airport,' she said, ignoring him, 'where are you taking us from there?'

Thomas turned back to her.

'London.'

'London?' said Jakob. 'That's where this Bishop Byrne is, right?'

'Yes.'

'We don't have our passports.'

'We'll take care of that,' Rebekah said.

Ellie looked at Jakob, uncertain of what to think of it all. A secret organisation within the Vatican whose mission was to track down people like her, whatever that meant? And those men at Dante's. Gideon and Cain. Those *things*. It all seemed too farfetched to comprehend. He took her hand, squeezed it twice, and winked. She knew he probably was as freaked out as she was and that he was putting a brave face on it for her sake.

God, she loved him.

There was silence in the car for the rest of the journey to the airport. There was too much spinning around in her head to make sense of, and the answers to any more questions she wanted to ask would probably add to her confusion. She exhaled deeply and realised she was exhausted. And hungry. She looked over at Jakob again, who'd laid his head back against the headrest and had closed his eyes. Probably he felt the same.

When they arrived at the airport's security gate, a female immigration official exited the hut and approached the driver's side. Rasmus slid his window down, collected passports from Thomas, Rebekah, and Seth, and handed them to the woman along with his own Vatican credentials. She pointed to Ellie and Jakob. Thomas leaned across and explained they wouldn't be travelling. After a few seconds of peering at each occupant, she took the passports into the hut, stamped them, returned to the car, and gave them back to Rasmus. She waved lazily to the guard in the hut, and the fence wheeled open with a squeal. Rasmus put the G-Wagon into gear and rolled the car forward. After a minute and a half of driving around a tarmac ring road, they crossed onto the apron where their jet was parked.

The SUV pulled up to the aircraft and came to a jerky halt, for which Rasmus apologised. He stepped out onto the apron and went to the rear to open the tailgate for Seth, who grunted his thanks and made straight for the plane. Ellie opened her door and slid out, and Jakob sluggishly followed her. She supposed the adrenaline flowing through him probably had subsided, and he was now crashing. It's exactly how she felt. Her limbs felt like lead weights, and she could barely keep her head upright. Rasmus helped Thomas guide them to the jet's stairs, where Rebekah was waiting.

'Thank you, Rasmus,' Thomas said, shaking the driver's hand.

'No thanks necessary.'

'I'm sorry about Ingmann.'

Rasmus nodded and returned to the Mercedes without speaking to either Ellie or Jakob. As the Mercedes drove away, Jakob turned to Thomas, his face sombre.

'So, are you going to tell us what exactly those freaks are, and what they want with Ellie?'

'Why would you call them freaks?'

'Oh, you mean apart from the super strength and being able to choke and throw people with a wave of their hands, and the fact that you said they're not dead, even though they were full of bullets? Apart from all of that?'

'You saw them use their abilities?'

'No, I just made that up.'

'Well, I can tell you they're not entirely human.'

'No fucking shit,' quipped Jakob. 'So, what? Super soldiers?'

'You think super soldiers can move things with their minds?'

'I think they're vampires,' Ellie said.

Thomas raised his eyebrows and tilted his head.

'Huh?' asked Jakob.

'When I first saw Gideon in Dante's, his eyes were glowing. Then, when Cain grabbed me, his eyes changed colour. They went to such a dark red they were almost black. And I'm pretty sure he grew fangs right before my eyes.'

'Is that why you're not supposed to tell us what *you* really are?' Jakob asked. 'Because you're a bunch of vampire hunters?'

'No,' said Thomas, motioning for them to climb the steps. 'They're not vampires.'

'What are they, then?' Ellie asked.

'Something else.'

'What something else?'

Thomas sighed.

'Get on the plane, and I'll tell you,' he said.

'Tell us, and we'll get on the plane.'

'Don't be a child, Jakob.'

Ellie looked at the jet. None of this felt right to her. A knot began to form in the pit of her stomach, and tears started to well in her eyes.

'I don't think I can do this.'

'Do what?' asked Thomas.

'Any of this. Get on that plane. Go to London with you.'

'Okay, so here's the thing. Those men back there? If they had to mobilise on as little notice as we did, which I'm sure was likely, there's no way they would've been able to secure a landing slot at Kastrup, which means it's almost guaranteed they landed right here at this facility. Now, I can promise you, despite how badly they were hurt, it won't take them long to recover, and knowing that we're probably going to whisk you away to someplace safe, where do you think they're likely to head next?'

Ellie remained silent.

'Correct,' Thomas said. 'Right here, so they can fly the fuck out of here. So, you have two choices. You can stay here on the tarmac and wait for them to arrive and find you here, or you can get on that plane, stay safe, and find out what all of this is really about.'

She glared at him and clenched her fists, feeling rage burn inside of her. She wanted to kick him in the balls to put him on his knees and then punch him in the face, maybe knock out a tooth or two. Rebekah, who seemed to have sensed her anger, touched her shoulder.

'What's it going to be?' Rebekah asked. 'You gonna take the blue pill or the red pill?'

'Funny,' Jakob said.

Ellie felt the dam break, and tears streamed down her cheeks. She swallowed a sob and inhaled deeply.

'Fuck it,' she said.

44

As Ellie took the first forward-facing seat she came to, another wave of exhaustion hit her. Jakob went to fasten her seatbelt—either to be helpful or feel less help*less*, she supposed—but she pushed him away. She was tired but not incapable. He looked slightly wounded, so she threw him an apologetic smile, which he acknowledged with a tired wink as he took the seat across the aisle. There was a jolt as the aircraft's brakes disengaged. As it taxied along the runway, she looked out of the small porthole window at nothing, took in a lungful of air through her nose, and blew it out through pursed lips. The whine of the jet's turbine engines built to a roar, and within seconds it was airborne. Her stomach lurched as the black ground fell away. When she turned back to the cabin, Thomas was looking at her intently from the rear-facing seat opposite. As she stared back at him, a thought wormed itself into her mind.

'What?' he asked.

'Where do I know you from?'

'What do you mean?'

'Have you been on TV or something?'

'I don't think so. I hope not, at least. My secret identity in the RIG would be shot to shit if I had been.'

'You seem very familiar to me.'

'Maybe I just have one of those faces.'

'I—'

'So, what are they?' Jakob demanded from across the aisle. 'Gideon and Cain, I mean. If they're not super soldiers or vampires, what are they?'

Rebekah appeared from the narrow galley between the cockpit and the main cabin and leaned against its doorless frame. She'd removed her jacket and held a wad of gauze against the wound in her shoulder.

'I can explain it,' said Thomas, 'but it's not something you will likely believe.'

'You sure about this, man?' Rebekah asked, taking the seat opposite Jakob.

He shrugged.

Ellie had already lost patience with his evasiveness, and her frustration with being kept in the dark was edging closer to anger.

'Give it a try anyway,' she said.

'Alright,' he said, taking in a deep breath. 'They're Nephilim.'

'Which are what exactly?'

'The offspring of angels and humans. The females are called Anakim, although the terms Nephilim and Anakim are often used interchangeably regardless of gender.'

'The offspring of angels,' Jakob echoed. 'Seriously?'

'More accurately, of what we call the Grigori. What you would probably know better as the fallen angels.'

'Oh, okay,' said Ellie. 'So, they're not vampires. Just evil angels.'

'Come on, babes. Didn't you hear the man? They're only *half* angel.'

'Of course. How stupid am I?'

Thomas smiled.

'Okay,' she said. 'Not that I believe in angels and all that shit, but let's just say they do exist. Aren't they supposed to be, like, spirits or something? You know, not made of solid stuff like us. How could they possibly have children?'

'I suppose some background would be useful,' Thomas said. 'Humans as a species have evolved from—'

'Uh, hang on. Aren't you supposed to lead with the whole God-created-Adam thing? Because you know...' she said, pointing at both him and Rebekah, '...the Vatican.'

They both smiled, and she heard Seth either chuckle or grumble from a sofa at the back of the jet he'd sprawled out on.

'While it's true that God created all life on this planet,' Thomas went on, 'it's also true that almost all life has evolved. Adam *wasn't* the first man. He wasn't even one of the first generations of humans. Far from it, in fact. He was simply a convenient starting point for the record of human existence. Back then, humans had no concept of evolution. No archaeology or carbon dating or DNA tech. By the time written language had developed enough for them to start recording their history, all their predecessors—Homo erectus, the Neanderthals, the Denisovans, and so on—had disappeared without anyone ever knowing they existed. All early humans knew of were themselves and perhaps a few generations before them, passed down in stories around communal cooking fires.

'Now, thanks to science, we know better than they did. But religions can't exactly go and rewrite their scriptures, as that would damage the very foundations of those faiths.'

Ellie rubbed her eyes. If he didn't get to his point soon, she knew she'd lose interest fast.

'Shall I go on?' he asked.

She puffed out her cheeks, exhaled heavily, and nodded.

'So, as I was saying,' he continued, 'humans evolved from earlier hominins who, until then, had fumbled around in Africa with stone tools and weapons and had even discovered and learned how to control fire. Then Homo sapiens arrived a quarter of a million years ago, and these guys were different. Their brains were capable of doing and understanding so much more than the Neanderthals and the other Homo sub-species ever could.

'Eventually, all hominins except Homo sapiens died out. Partly because they were bred out, but mainly through their inability to learn and adapt even the most basic technologies that would help them survive as a species. Then, around ninety thousand years ago, human migration exploded out of Africa in a big way, and shortly after that, populations began rapidly expanding. And there were basic advancements in their technologies along the way—the bow and arrow, weaving, ceramics and pottery, basic astronomy, and even primitive ocean-going boats.

'But while their mental capacity was developed enough to comprehend spoken language, culture, civilisation, new technologies, and so on, they weren't making the leaps necessary to survive as a species. Especially as the planet was still in the grip of the last ice age. Harsh conditions everywhere, even in those areas not covered by ice, would have resulted in declining birth rates and a higher death toll.'

Oh my God, she thought. Kill me now!

'So, about twenty thousand years ago,' Thomas went on, 'when humans' survival had become at risk, God decided to send angels to guide them on their developmental journey. But there was a catch. To coexist with humans, they had to blend in—to appear human. Now, in their true form, they're eternal beings of pure energy. Asking them to give that up was a big deal, so God decreed that all angels who came would have a choice—they could age as humans do and return to their true celestial forms upon their physical deaths, or they could live immortally at the age of their choosing. Almost all chose immortality.'

'Of course they did,' Jakob said sardonically.

'What do you mean the age of their choosing?' asked Ellie.

'Having observed humans for millennia, they'd learned that some people follow youthful ambition, while others prefer to be guided by those with a few more miles on them, with greater life experience and the wisdom that comes from it. So, God let each angel decide which physical age would best help them fulfil their role here, with the warning that those who'd chosen immortality would be locked into that age for their entire existence here.'

Ellie began to feel lost and wasn't sure she wanted the history lesson to continue. She'd never paid much attention to religious studies in school, for the reason her attention was beginning to fade now—it was mind-numbingly dull. Couldn't Thomas just have agreed with her and said they were vampires, even if they weren't? It would have been so much easier. She could deal with that. Everyone knows what vampires are, and she wouldn't have to listen to a history lesson that made her want someone to put a bullet in her brain to save her from it.

'They went to every continent except Antarctica,' Rebekah said from her seat opposite Jakob, 'and to wherever there were human communities large enough to which they could pass on knowledge. The rules were simple. They were to provide only the knowledge God permitted them to pass on and only when told to do so. Otherwise, they were not to interfere in human affairs.

'For the first few millennia, everything went great. Humans advanced, generally in line with the pace their brains were naturally developing, but when necessary, and only with God's permission, the angels helped them take some hops forward. Construction, written language, the wheel, agriculture, plumbing, cartography, time measurement, the mass production of materials, medicines, and so on. And as humans migrated further, taking their knowledge, social structures, and technologies, the angels travelled with them. The six cradles of civilisation—Mesopotamia, Egypt, the Indus Valley, China, the Andean coast, and Mesoamerica—directly resulted from angelic integration. And after those, Rome, Greece, and so on.'

'Around twelve thousand years ago,' Thomas continued, 'before any of those civilisations appeared, a seraph named Sammael came to believe that God had no real love for angels, valued them less than humans, and tricked them with the reward of immortality into coming here to serve humans, basically as slaves. Given how superior angels are to humans, you can understand their perspective.'

'Superior, how?' Jakob asked. 'Other than the energy thing and the immortality, obviously.'

'For a start, they're much stronger and faster, and their senses are heightened way beyond those of humans. Their brains are like supercomputers, able to process information immeasurably quicker than you, which means they can react faster in any situation. Those slow-motion scenes in superhero movies and such where people can move fast enough to dodge bullets? That's how they can see things. Some can also move objects by thought alone, others can read minds, and some can project their thoughts into the minds of others. Some can do all three, which is why, in stories and scripture, they appear out of nowhere, float with or without wings, have a halo of fire around them, and so on. They can influence the thoughts of those they communicate with and so control how they're perceived.'

'Those with telekinetic abilities we call *movers*,' Rebekah said. 'Those who can read minds, we call *readers*. And those who can implant their thoughts into others, we call *pushers*.'

'Catchy,' said Jakob.

'There's no disputing,' Thomas said, 'that angels *are* superior to humans in every way, and because of that, Sammael believed they were fit for a higher purpose.'

'Which was?' Ellie asked, already guessing the answer.

'To rule,' Rebekah responded.

'Sammael spent a millennium or so seeking out other angels who felt as he did,' Thomas went on. 'Eventually, support for him and his ideals grew to the point where he believed he could stage a coup. And that's precisely what he did.'

'The archangel Michael and those loyal to him battled with Sammael and his followers,' Rebekah said. 'Here, on Earth. There was no great insurrection in Heaven, no casting out into Hell. It all happened at Har Megiddo, in what used to be ancient Palestine, now northern Israel'.

'Har Megiddo,' Jakob said, 'sounds a lot like—'

'Armageddon? Yeah. Har Megiddo means Heights of Megiddo in Hebrew, but the New Testament was originally written in Greek, and the Greek translation of Har Megiddo is... anyone?'

'Michael was based at the city of Megiddo,' Thomas continued, 'so Sammael summoned his forces and took the fight to him. He took close to a legion. Almost six thousand warriors. Some were angels, but most were just men, irrelevant and expendable as far as he was concerned. But Michael had received intel on his intentions, so he gathered an army. Each side took heavy losses, but Sammael's army was half the size of Michael's and was ultimately defeated. He and his cohorts who survived were cast out into the wilderness. They became known as the Grigori. The fallen angels. And, because of name-calling and various translations and whatnot, you'd probably know Sammael better as—'

'Lucifer,' Ellie said.

'Lucifer,' echoed Thomas. 'At the time, it was thought that he would rebuild his army, retaliate at some point in their not-too-distant future, and do so at Har Megiddo again. So, the Bible's one reference to Armageddon is to the specific location of a war to come, but at some point, it became synonymous with a global, catastrophic, humanity-ending war between good and evil.'

'One of the first things the Grigori did when Michael banished them,' said Rebekah, 'was to mate with any humans they came across. Partly to rebuild their numbers with as much angelic blood as possible, regardless of how diluted. And partly because angels had been forbidden by God to breed, either among themselves or with humans. It was the ultimate act of defiance and revenge. Both male and female Grigori did this. Their offspring were the Nephilim and Anakim who, like their angelic parents, have almost superhuman speed and strength and have senses far superior to humans. They have perfect night vision, can hear your blood pumping through your veins, and can literally taste the fear in the pheromones your body releases when you're afraid. Some of them were giants, such as Goliath, although there aren't so many of those around anymore.'

'They're virtually immortal,' said Thomas. 'And, like angels, they're *readers*, *pushers*, and *movers*. Most only have one, maybe two abilities. A rare few have all of them. As for the eyes and the teeth, those are just physical quirks that usually only manifest when they're either enraged or using one of their abilities.'

'There were female angels?' Ellie asked. 'I thought all angels were male.'

'I thought you didn't believe in angels.'

'Humour me.'

'Like God, angels in their true form are sexless,' Rebekah said. 'So God allowed them to pick their genders as well as their ages. Some became male, some female. It was around a seventy-thirty split in favour of the male form. Unfortunately, one of the many negative side-effects of patriarchal societies, especially those controlling the formation of religions, was that beings of power and strength were typically only ever shown to be male, while women were cast as either subservient, wicked, or sinful. Think Delilah, Jezebel, the witch of Endor, Mary Magdalene, and, of course, the original sinner... Eve. So, those in charge recast female angels as male. Gabriel was a prime example.'

'Gabriel was female?' asked Jakob.

Rebekah nodded.

'Gabriella.'

'And God is sexless?'

'Yep. That whole old-man-on-a-cloud thing was invented to give humans something they could relate to instead of just being expected to believe in some faceless thing that has the power to create and, if it so wished, destroy entire worlds, which is a lot scarier. And again, the patriarchy. If anything, God is closer to being female than male.'

Ellie closed her eyes and inhaled deeply. Everything these people were telling her seemed ridiculous. How was it even possible this was happening to her? What was so special about her that those men, whatever they were, wanted her so badly? Badly enough, it seemed, to be prepared to die to keep her in their possession. She was just a tattooist from Copenhagen, for fuck's sake.

'Do you have anything to drink on here?' she asked no one in particular.

Rebekah smiled and went into the galley, reappearing a moment later with four cut-glass tumblers, which she handed out. She reached back into the galley, produced a bottle of Jack Daniel's, and poured generous measures into the glasses.

'So, what do you think so far?' Thomas asked.

'To be honest,' said Ellie, 'I think it's all crap. Angels and half-angels? Come on, man.'

'You're happy to believe they're vampires but can't accept they could be something else just as supernatural?'

She shrugged, knowing that Gideon and Cain being vampires was just as implausible as them being the half-human offspring of angels. Maybe her reluctance to accept them as part-angel was due to her general lack of faith.

'In the early days,' Rebekah said, 'the Nephilim and Anakim abused their power without fear. They roamed in gangs, conquering or destroying every settlement they came across. They'd kill anyone who opposed them and enslave those who didn't. They offered human sacrifices to Sammael. At first, they burned those sacrifices, but at some point, they started eating them.'

'Jesus Christ!'

'Eventually, human communities banded together and formed hunting parties to find and kill them,' Thomas said. 'While they were powerful, they were always fewer in number than humans. So, they went into hiding. Ultimately, they realised that to survive, they had to adapt their behaviour. They had to blend in. And they had to stop preying on humans in broad daylight. So, now and then, in the darkness, humans would disappear. More often than not, and even if it weren't the case, those disappearances were blamed on the Nephilim and Anakim—the superhuman cannibalistic creatures of the night. And so, the vampire myth was born. In the Middle East, thousands of years ago.'

'You said they're virtually immortal. What does that mean?'

'They age at a normal rate until their mid-twenties. After that, they still age, but it'll take them roughly four centuries to look like they've aged a single human year. They're completely immune to disease. They can survive almost any injury. Drowning, burning, impaling, you name it. They can heal from even the most horrific wounds over time, although evidence of the injury may always exist in the most severe cases. The two you met tonight both being prime examples of that.'

Thomas ran a finger down his face to emphasise his point.

'Other aspects of their physiology which helped to perpetuate the vampire myth,' said Rebekah.

'If they suffer enough injuries over time,' Thomas continued, 'and depending on the seriousness of those injuries, they age faster—a consequence of the use of angelic energy within their DNA to heal themselves.'

'So, unstoppable machines that feel no pain,' Jakob said. 'If you tell us they've come from the future to kill Ellie so she can't give birth to the saviour of humanity, I'm going to smack you in the face with that bottle of Jack.'

'No, Jakob. They're not Terminators. They're very much flesh and blood from the past. And the present. And they feel pain, just as humans do. And heat and cold. As do the angels. They just heal better than humans. And faster.'

'So, they can't be killed?' Ellie asked.

'The only known way to kill them,' said Rebekah, 'is to decapitate them.'

'Which you didn't do back in Copenhagen,' Jakob said. 'How come?'

'We didn't have the right tools with us. We weren't expecting them to be there.'

'How many are there?' Ellie asked.

'We don't know. For reasons we don't understand, not all angels were capable of reproduction, but if we assume that even half of every surviving Grigori could breed with a human and had just one offspring, there could easily have been fifteen hundred Nephilim and Anakim initially. Perhaps more.'

'What we do know,' Thomas said, 'is that only the Nephilim and Anakim who carried the blood of the most powerful of the Grigori—Sammael, Azazel, Lilith, and a few others—were known to be able to reproduce. And if their offspring had children, and they had children, and so on, the angelic blood within each new generation would be diluted, making them less powerful and, importantly, closer to being mortal. So, you effectively have a race that's unable to propagate itself or at least perpetuate the strength and longevity it started with. Combine that with the loss of those killed in battle or otherwise since then, and it could be anywhere between five and five hundred. It's impossible to know for sure.'

'So, why are they after me? What do they want with me?'

'The two you encountered earlier—Gideon and Cain—work for an organisation called the Sicarii. A group of assassins who carry out the more gruesome work the Grigori don't like to get their hands bloody with. We believe the Sicarii might have intercepted Father Sigvardt's call to Bishop Byrne in London.'

'How?'

'We don't know that yet, but we suspect they've somehow hacked our servers or embedded spies within our organisation. Probably both.'

'Okay, so what do they want with Ellie?' Jakob asked, his irritation at asking the same question yet again clear to her.

Thomas sighed heavily.

'They believe she may be a lost descendant of someone important,' he said.

'Who?' she asked.

'All I can tell you right now is that the Sicarii are hunting you, and, for now, we've stopped them. I know that might not be enough of an answer for you, but believe me, all will be properly explained to you once we reach London.' He looked at his watch. 'We've got close to an hour and a half until we land, and there's nothing they can do while we're airborne, so I suggest you flip your seats back and get some rest.'

'That's it?' she asked. 'That's all we get?'

'For now, yes.'

'Unfuckingbelievable.'

45

Gideon eased the Jaguar to a stop at Roskilde's chain-link entrance gate and lowered his window as the immigration officer left the security hut. He glanced down at himself and then at Cain's bloody, bullet-ridden torso and then remembered the broken rear quarter-pane in the door behind him and the streak of bullet holes in the car's right-hand side, but he considered none of that problematic. Nonetheless, to avoid telegraphing their appearance to the guard in the hut, who was already watching them with a keen interest and could easily use the radio to call for reinforcements, he kept the cabin light off and waited for the woman to approach.

As she stepped to the open window, her eyes widened. She quickly stepped away and straightened, but before she could retreat or signal to her colleague in the hut, he snared her with his burning amber gaze.

'There's no need to do anything stupid,' he said. 'Just tell your friend over there to open the gate and let us through.'

She stood motionless for a second as if she were either struggling to comprehend what he'd said or deciding to defy him. He knew neither would be the case, but he applied further force to his *push*.

'Do it now,' he said.

She nodded dumbly and signalled to the guard with a circular motion of her arm like she was whirling a lasso. After a second, the gate rattled open.

'If anyone asks, you'll tell them we're your superiors conducting a routine inspection of all border crossing procedures and that we'll return shortly through this same gate. Is that understood?'

She nodded again. Satisfied his command would be obeyed, he drove through the open gate and onwards to where their jet waited. In the rear-view mirror, he saw the gate skitter back into place and the woman stroll back to the hut, scratching her chin and frowning as if attempting to work something out.

On the drive from the city, he'd called their pilot, Enrique, and instructed him to prepare their plane for an immediate departure. While he couldn't be sure that Thomas had left the country with Ellie, it was the most likely scenario. The only question was where he would take her. Probably back to Peter in Rome, but that wasn't guaranteed. If he *had* left Denmark, he wouldn't have too much of a lead yet, and if Simon's spy, Mercury, could somehow communicate his intended destination to Gideon quickly enough, they may even have a chance to catch up.

As Gideon pulled the car to a screeching stop next to the Bombardier, he could hear that Enrique already had the jet's engines running, and he hoped the man had also obtained clearance from the tower to depart quickly. He turned off the car's motor, pulled the release for the boot, climbed out, dropped the key fob on his seat, and closed the door. Then, he went to the car's rear and retrieved the box of grenades, shut the boot lid, and approached Cain's open door.

During the journey to the airport, Cain had, with much growling, pushed his broken radius bone back into his forearm. While the torn flesh was already healing, the bone itself would take longer to reset, so Gideon offered his hand. Cain pushed him away, heaved himself out of the car with a grunt, and made his way to the plane. He understood Cain's frustration. If they'd pulled Ellie out of Dante's thirty seconds earlier, the confrontation with Thomas and his team would never have occurred, and they'd still have her. He closed the door and headed for the jet. As he entered the cabin, Enrique was waiting for him.

'I've put out some clean clothes for you,' he said, motioning to a black suit carrier on one of the two tables nearest the front of the plane.

'Thanks,' Gideon replied, handing him the grenade box.

As Enrique went to the storage area at the back of the aircraft, Gideon glanced at Cain, already shirtless and seated at a table. The four bullet holes in his chest had closed to less than half their initial diameter, and extracting the rounds would be almost as painful as when they'd first pierced the flesh. A medical kit was open on the table. In Cain's right hand was a pair of long-nosed, scissor-handled forceps, and in his left was an open but full bottle of The Dalmore, which Enrique must have left with the kit. He gulped down half the whisky. While alcohol had the same immediate effects on them that it had on humans, those effects wore off within seconds, so he would be able to drink the entire bottle without his senses or judgement being impaired or otherwise affected. He pressed the curved end of the forceps into one of the holes in his chest and opened it to twice its size, snarling as he did so. The growl became louder as he did the same with the other wounds.

'You alright?' Gideon asked him.

He grunted.

Gideon took the whisky, some disinfecting wipes, and three patches of self-adhesive gauze from the medical kit, then went to his seat, removed his jacket, shoulder holster, and shirt, and laid them on the table next to the suit protector Enrique had put out. He sat down and examined the bullet holes in his chest and shoulder. They were almost closed. Then he ran a finger across the back of his shoulder. The hole was still wide open, which made sense, given how much flesh a bullet takes when it passes through a person.

He took a long draw from the bottle, then cleaned around all three wounds with the wipes and applied the gauze patches, more to keep his new shirt free of blood than to disinfect and protect the wounds, which would heal soon enough. Then he stood again, took the clean shirt and trousers from the garment carrier, and pulled them on. At that moment,

Enrique reappeared.

'Where to?' he asked.

'We're awaiting further information.'

'What?'

Gideon exhaled forcefully.

'We don't know where they're going,' he said. 'We don't even know if they've left Copenhagen yet.'

'Three private aircraft took off from here in the last seven minutes. We can't know with any certainty that Thomas used this airfield, but it's a safe bet he did. International airports like Kastrup aren't conducive to making quick getaways, which he'd want. And even the Vatican would've had difficulty securing a landing window there on short notice for their arrival. So, it's likely he's onboard one of those jets.'

'Agreed. Can you obtain any details from the tower?'

'No. That information will be classified unless we can provide credentials with enough authority to demand an override, and I don't think even Jacques could get those on short notice. Besides, without knowing which aircraft Thomas may have been on, I couldn't even guess which to enquire about. We could risk a departure without knowing our destination, but if we tail the wrong aircraft, we'd be chasing vapours to who-knows-where.'

Gideon nodded, buttoning his shirt. He'd need to be patient and trust that their spy would be able to provide the required information without too long a delay. He motioned over at Cain.

'Give him a hand, will you, Enrique.'

I'm fine.

Cain clicked his fingers twice and motioned to the whisky, which Enrique took from Gideon and passed across. He took a large mouthful, reclined his seat, closed his eyes, and started taking slow, deep breaths. Then, with a grunt that quickly became a bellow, he tensed the muscles in his chest. The others looked on as bullets came to the surface of the four holes in his chest. One by one, they popped out and rolled down his torso.

'That never gets old,' said Enrique.

Cain moved his seat back to an upright position, then swabbed and covered the wounds on his chest. Enrique passed him his suit carrier from the chair behind him and headed for the cockpit. After a few moments, he stood and unzipped the garment protector. As he removed the clean clothes from it, he looked across at Gideon.

So, what now?

Gideon reached over to his ruined suit jacket, pulled out his phone, and put it on the table.

'Now we need to find out where the fuck we're going.'

And you need to call Simon.

'I know.'

You've been putting it off.

'I know.'

He's going to be pissed.

'I know!'

He growled, and his eyes burned amber. Cain raised his hands in surrender, but Gideon knew he was right. Simon wouldn't be pleased. He picked up his phone and made the call.

46

Within fourteen minutes of the Embraer taking off, Ellie was asleep. The adrenaline of the night's events had worn off quickly once Thomas had explained what was happening and who Gideon and Cain were. She'd reclined her seat and fallen asleep almost as soon as she'd closed her eyes. Jakob couldn't sleep, nor did he want to. Anger, more than adrenaline, still coursed through him at what those men—those *things*—had done to them and their friends. Rebekah had gone to the back of the plane, and he was thankful he didn't have to avoid her gaze by looking out of the window into darkness or pretending to sleep only to really fall asleep. He glanced over at Ellie again and noticed that Thomas, still seated across from her, was looking at him.

'You okay?' Thomas asked.

'It doesn't make any sense.'

'Which part?'

'All of it. Why Ellie's on some Vatican watchlist for reasons you apparently can't talk about. Why she's being hunted by... whatever they are. It all smells like pure bullshit.'

'Then how would you explain everything that happened earlier?'

Jakob sagged. It was a question, much like many rushing through his brain, to which he had no answer.

'I have no fucking clue,' he murmured.

'Well, you saw what Gideon and Cain are capable of with your own eyes. I have no other way of explaining it because what I've told you is the truth.'

'Yeah, well, everyone's truth is different.'

'That's an interesting point of view. Why do you put it like that?'

'Like what?'

'That everyone's truth is different. It implies there could be innumerable truths for any one specific event or thing.'

'Of course there could. You see things one way. I could see things completely differently. Same situation, different truths.'

'Okay, so what's *your* truth about all of this?'

'As I said, I have no fucking clue.'

Thomas smiled.

'Look, we're going to be in the air for another hour or so. There's not much we can do while we're sitting here, so why don't you try and get some rest?'

'I still don't believe a word of this, and I absolutely do not trust you.'

Thomas nodded.

'I can understand that,' he said.

'So, what happens next?'

'When we get to London, we're going straight to Westminster Cathedral to see Byrne.'

'At this time of night?'

'Let's just say this is important enough to get him out of bed. Hopefully, he'll be able to determine what Ellie's dealing with. Peter, my direct superior, will also be there, and he'll be able to shed more light on what's going on.'

Jakob frowned. So far, none of this made any sense to him, and he was unhappy with the lack of any further meaningful explanation from Thomas or his colleagues. They seemed to think this was some game, but they didn't understand that you don't fuck with people's lives.

'I know you're frustrated, Jakob, but that's all I can give you for now.'

Before he could respond, Seth and Rebekah appeared. Rebekah

slumped into the seat opposite him again, and Seth went into the galley, grumbling under his breath.

'Everything okay there, big man?' Thomas asked.

'Hungry.'

'Hulk no smash,' Jakob said, hoping Seth could take a joke. 'Plane fragile.'

'Hilarious, *little* man,' he replied, taking a large packet of salted potato crisps from an overhead cupboard and the bottle of Jack Daniel's, which was now almost empty, from a lower one. 'Well, thanks for leaving me a mouthful, you greedy assholes.'

'You're welcome,' Rebekah answered, flashing a grin. 'Oh, by the way,' she said, swiping a finger at Jakob and Ellie, 'there *are* people here who needed that more than you do.'

'There better be a fresh one on here, or Hulk *will* smash.'

He opened the bottle and emptied it in one large gulp, pulling a face as he swallowed. He put the empty bottle into the galley's sink, then looked in the low cupboard for a replacement and pulled out a bottle of something dark, which Jakob couldn't identify.

'This'll do.'

He opened the bottle, and as he placed it on the counter, a pocket of turbulence shook the jet. Rather than its flat underside gently meeting the countertop, the bottle landed at an angle. The weight of his hand forced its base to slide away from him, and as its spout became horizontal, its contents spilt over his jeans, which, although black, now had a darker stain on the crotch.

'Shit,' he said, grabbing a hand towel from a drawer and wiping himself down.

'Oops,' said Rebekah, chuckling. She curled her feet underneath her, turned to the window, tucked her hair behind her ear, and then said over her shoulder, 'Remember, man, if you rub it more than three times, it's a wan—'

'Thank you, Rebekah,' said Thomas, reaching into his jacket and pulling out his phone. 'I need to let Peter know we're on our way.'

As Seth returned to his seat, grumbling and still trying to soak up whatever drink had drenched his jeans, Jakob glanced over at Rebekah, who, after a few seconds, realised he was looking at her.

'What?' she asked.

'You don't seem like church people.'

'In what way?'

'In every way. How you dress, all the swearing, the fact you carry guns.'

'Faith doesn't have a dress code, Jakob. And I like to swear. It's the sign of a superior intellect. As for the guns, they're... you know... like condoms.'

He chuckled, knowing what she meant.

'Better to have them and not need them,' he said, 'than need them and not have them.'

'Exactly.'

'And why exactly would a Vatican operative need condoms?'

'Do I need to draw you a picture?'

He laughed again but quietly, not wanting to wake Ellie.

'I meant, isn't that banned for you guys by the Ten Commandments or something? That and, you know... killing people?'

'The commandments forbid adultery, Jakob. Not fornication. There *is* a difference. I'm not married, and I don't knowingly screw people who are. So, not an adulteress. As for the killing, we obviously try to avoid that at all costs, but I'll refer you to Exodus twenty-one, twenty-three— take life for life. You saw back in Copenhagen what we're up against. Those things are real, man. So, if they shoot at us, we shoot back. If we don't, *we* die.'

He mulled this over for a moment, then nodded. He couldn't fault her logic. She and her colleagues had saved his life and Ellie's and had to defend themselves to do it. Evidently satisfied that her response had placated him, she turned and stared out of the window, and drummed her fingers against her thigh as if she were listening to music in her head.

Conversation over, he thought.

He looked back at Thomas, who, after a few seconds of speedily thumbing his phone, put the device back in his jacket, stood up, and went to the rear of the plane. He wouldn't likely get anything more out of him, either. He yawned, blinked twice with wide eyes, and gazed at Ellie, who was quietly snoring. As exhausted as he was, and despite these people saving their lives, he wouldn't be letting his guard down while she was asleep.

As he stared out at the cloudless black of night, an encoded message left the Embraer, headed for Chicago via a privately owned communications satellite. It contained only one word.

London.

47

Gideon, impatient and irritated and already tired of watching his phone lie mutely on the table, gently turned his tumbler back and forth. He glanced at Cain, who was intently cleaning, checking, and reloading his pistols on a white towel spread across his table. Suddenly, his phone vibrated. His hand shot out for the device like a striking snake. The message preview confirmed it was from Mercury and displayed a single word.

London.

He opened the text to check whether it contained any additional information, such as the airport where Thomas would land. It didn't, but it was of little consequence. His final destination would likely be somewhere central, so he'd fly to either City Airport or Northolt, each roughly forty-five minutes from the heart of London. Gideon could issue instructions for Sicarii personnel to watch both airports, but if the Elyonim spotted them, he could lose Ellie again—possibly permanently, depending on where Thomas would take her and despite Mercury's inclusion in the Vatican's team. The only viable course of action was to trust that Mercury would communicate their destination in London without much further delay and for himself and Cain to make their way there, infiltrate the location, and reacquire her.

He rose from his seat, strode to the cockpit, and gave Enrique their destination, knowing the man would do everything necessary to obtain swift departure clearance from the airport's control tower. As he returned to the cabin to the scream of jet turbines, Cain looked up.

'We're heading back to London.'

Cain grunted and finished reloading the last of his guns' magazines. Gideon checked the time. Enrique had told him that three aircraft had departed from Roskilde airport in the seven minutes before he and Cain returned from Copenhagen. If Thomas was aboard one of those jets, he had a head start of between fourteen and twenty-one minutes. Even with City Airport's arrival procedures to navigate, that would give him plenty of time to get Ellie to wherever he intended to take her, which, hopefully, would be neutral ground rather than a Vatican-owned stronghold.

While the thought of being so far behind frustrated him, he knew Enrique would do his best to reduce Thomas's lead. He also knew nothing he could personally do on the ninety-minute flight to London would contribute to that effort. As the Bombardier began its taxi to the main runway, he reclined his seat, closed his eyes, and accepted that matters were out of his control.

For now.

48

SATURDAY

Half an hour past midnight, the Vatican team's Embraer jet landed at City Airport in London. The jolt of the landing and the screech of brakes jarred Ellie awake. She stifled a yawn and looked across the aisle at Jakob, who looked like he'd also been asleep and seemed surprised and angry about it. Perhaps he'd meant to stay awake to watch over her, but she was glad he'd managed to get some rest. There was no telling how long this ordeal would last, and they couldn't run on adrenaline for much longer.

The rear-facing seats in front of them were empty. A news broadcast was quietly playing on a small, flat television hanging from the cabin's ceiling over the opening to the galley. She looked over her shoulder. Thomas was sitting in one of four chairs around a rectangular table, watching the news. Beyond him, at the back of the aircraft, Seth and Rebekah were having a conversation she couldn't hear. They all looked wide awake and alert. Thomas caught her glance and pressed a button on the side of his seat. The television turned off, smoothly retracted upward, and disappeared, its underside flush with the ceiling. He looked disturbed. Was it something he'd seen on the news or something else? She realised she didn't care. She just wanted this craziness to be over.

'Okay,' he said, standing. 'Let's go.'

As everyone rose from their seats with various grunts and moans, he went through the galley and disappeared out the aircraft's door, which the co-pilot had opened. Rebekah gestured for her and Jakob to follow, which they did. By the time she reached the door, Thomas was already on the apron with his phone pressed to his ear and making his way purposefully toward the first of two dark grey Range Rovers parked ten metres from the bottom of the jet's stairs.

As she stepped out, biting wind and icy drizzle grazed her face. She retreated momentarily, rubbing her arms and chest. In her hasty, unplanned exit from Dante's, she'd been unable to retrieve her coat. She shivered, then felt a tap on her shoulder.

'Take this,' Rebekah said, holding out her jacket. 'Don't worry about the blood around that bullet hole. It's already dried.'

'You don't need it?'

'I'll be fine.'

She thanked Rebekah, then shrugged on the jacket and headed out and down the stairs, followed closely by Jakob.

'I'm still not sure about this, you know,' she said to him as they reached the tarmac.

'Me neither, but what choice do we have but to go with them?'

'It'll be okay,' Rebekah said from behind them.

'So *you* say,' Jakob replied, 'but you're not the ones with superpowered killers hunting you.'

Seth appeared at her side and gestured toward the vehicles.

'Shall we?' he asked.

Still bone tired despite sleeping almost the entire journey from Copenhagen, she exhaled heavily and set off for the Range Rovers. Jakob was beside her. Seth and Rebekah followed like red-carpet bodyguards. Or like jailers ready to beat them down if they tried to escape. She reached the first car and drew up next to Thomas.

'Around forty-five minutes,' he said into his phone before ending the call.

'Where are you taking us?' she asked him.

'Westminster Cathedral.'

'Wh—'

331

'Please,' he said, quickly raising a hand. 'For now, no more questions, okay?'

He got into the car and slammed his door. She understood that he was probably as tired and wired as she and that perhaps he really couldn't give her any more answers, but he didn't have to be rude about it, and he could have shown a little more empathy.

Rebekah touched her elbow and guided her toward the car's rear seats. 'You two are in here,' she said, opening the nearest door and flashing a smile she supposed was meant to reassure them.

She hesitated and then felt Jakob's hand on the small of her back. It wasn't a shove or even a gentle push. It was just there. To let her know *he* was right there with her. She climbed in and slid over to give him room. When he was on board, he closed the door, and she watched through the window as Rebekah turned to Seth, nodded at the car behind, and enthusiastically shouted, 'Shotgun!'

Seth, unhappy with Rebekah taking the second car's front seat, opened his mouth to protest, but she winked at him cheekily before he could speak.

'Back of the bus, big man,' she said.

'You can be a real asshole. You know that?'

'Every single day.'

He grunted and got in behind the driver's seat. Rebekah climbed in next to their driver, who put the car into gear and waited for Thomas's vehicle to set off. When it did, it moved quickly, taking an immediate and tight left turn. He floored the accelerator to keep with it, and Rebekah, who hadn't yet buckled her seatbelt, lurched sideways.

'Easy man,' she said.

'My apologies,' he replied.

Seth chuckled.

'Yeah, it's hilarious,' she said, pushing her hair behind her ear and resting her hand on her thigh.

'Why d'you do that?' Seth asked.

'I'm sorry,' said the driver. 'I had to—'

'I wasn't talking to you, man.'

Rebekah half-turned her head.

'Do what?'

'That thing with your fingers. The tapping. You seem to do that a lot.'

'Anxiety.'

'You? Anxious? About what?'

'Oh, you know. Bad driving,' she said, glancing at their driver. 'And that I'm an attractive woman in her prime, who earns great money and can take care of herself, yet is still single.'

'Uh-huh.'

'Oh, and this nasty twist-in-my-gut feeling that we haven't outrun Gideon and that this is all going to get real messy, real quick.'

'Yeah,' he said, pulling out his phone. 'You could be right about that.'

49

As Enrique smoothly guided the Bombardier to the Sicarii's leased area at RAF Northolt, Gideon checked the time. It was ten minutes to one in the morning. Eighteen minutes earlier, he'd received a text from Mercury containing only two words.

```
Westminster Cathedral.
```

His assumption about Thomas's destination being in central London had proved correct. Familiar with the cathedral, he considered that it wasn't the ideal location for them to retake Ellie, but it wasn't the worst either. It wasn't an Elyonim stronghold impossible to access or even get close to—it was a public place with several potential entry points, and any Elyonim presence was likely to be restricted to Thomas's team and perhaps a few foot soldiers. Their biggest problem would be travel time—a drive of roughly forty-five minutes, barring unfavourable traffic. By the time they arrived, Thomas could already have left, and Ellie with him.

He stood holding his weapons case, impatient for the opening cabin door to lower enough to exit the plane. When it had, he moved. Cain was close behind, carrying his case and the box of grenades. As they descended the stairway, he noticed the immigration official from the previous evening, standing between the aircraft and Cain's car, parked fifteen metres away. When they reached the tarmac, Cain gave him his passport and continued to the Mustang, leaving him to deal with the official—a task he didn't have time for but couldn't avoid.

'Good morning, sir.'

'Good morning.'

'Transit or final destination?'

'Final,' Gideon said, handing over the passports.

The man inspected each document, scanned them with his handheld device, and returned them.

'Thank you,' he said. 'The airport's immigration system has been updated, so just show your passports again at the exit gate, and security will let you through.'

Enrique appeared at Gideon's side as the official returned to wherever he'd come from.

'I'll refuel the jet and lodge a flight plan with the tower for a short-notice departure for Chicago.'

'Thanks, Enrique. And see what you can do about getting hold of that, and getting it flight-ready for a potential pickup in central London.'

He motioned to a black, shark-like helicopter sitting outside a hangar sixty metres away. Enrique whistled.

'A Bell five-two-five Relentless. Basically, an executive jet with rotors. It might be a tough ask, but I'll see what I can do. If I can't, I'll come up with an alternative.'

'Noted. If our plans change for HQ, I'll let you know.'

The pilot nodded distractedly, his attention drawn by something beyond the helicopter.

'What?' Gideon asked.

'It's nothing. Just...'

Enrique refocused, shook his hand, and returned to the plane. Gideon walked to the Mustang, loaded his case, closed the boot's lid, and climbed into the passenger seat. Already in the driver's seat, Cain started the car, and it rumbled to life. He revved the engine hard, and his scowl became a wide grin.

'Time is not our friend, Cain.'

Cain grunted. His grin faded to a slight smirk and he tapped the steering wheel like the car was a pet, then shifted in his seat, getting himself comfortable and ready to drive. He put the car into gear, released the handbrake, spun the wheel to the left, and floored the accelerator. The car slid around in a tight circle, its tyres screeching until he loosened his grip on the wheel and the car straightened out.

As they approached the gatehouse, one of the two guards staffing it came outside and stood in the car's path. She wore the patch of the Military Provost Guard Service—a branch of the British military that provided security to army, navy, air force, and Ministry of Defence bases across the country. She motioned for them to stop, then approached Gideon's window, which he wound down. She stood far enough from the car to see his face without bending or squatting, held out her left hand, and asked for their passports. Her right hand remained firmly on the grip of her rifle, her finger resting on the trigger guard.

He still had both passports and gave them over. The guard returned to the gatehouse, flipped the first open, and held it to the glass. Her colleague inside pointed a handheld device at it, then looked at something out of sight, which he supposed was a computer monitor. The man nodded, and the two guards went through the same routine with the second passport. Satisfied that he and Cain had completed the necessary immigration procedures, the guard outside returned to the car and handed the passports back. The whole process took under thirty seconds.

'You're clear to exit,' she said as the security gate swung smoothly and silently open. 'The roads are greasy as hell tonight, so drive safely.'

He'd barely thanked her before Cain floored the accelerator. The engine snarled, and the wheels spun briefly, then the car leapt forward, sliding right and then left before straightening out. He looked at his watch again. Traffic permitting, they would reach Westminster Cathedral at roughly one thirty. He hoped they wouldn't be too late.

50

Ellie glanced at the clock on the Range Rover's dashboard screen as it pulled to the curb next to a large public space. It was seven minutes past one. Her body clock was still on Copenhagen time, which was an hour ahead. No wonder she was having trouble keeping her eyes open. The drive from the airport had taken thirty-seven minutes—marginally less than she'd heard Thomas predict when he was on the phone, but she wasn't surprised. Their car had travelled at speeds that had seemed too fast to be legal through a city centre, rarely slowing and doing so briefly and jerkily, which she suspected was to avoid triggering whatever speed cameras they'd passed.

Thomas left the car first. He opened her door, and she wearily stepped out. Jakob scooted across the back seat and got out behind her. She glanced at the second Range Rover. Rebekah and Seth were already on the pavement. Rebekah held a black canvas duffel bag.

'You're not going to be able to leave the car here,' Thomas said to the driver, 'so head around the back to the car park. Then join us inside.'

The driver nodded and pulled away when he shut the door. The second car immediately followed. It had stopped raining, but the air was still bitterly cold, so Ellie drew her borrowed jacket tightly around her. Jakob noticed and pulled her close to him so they were chest-to-chest.

'You know, I still don't fully trust these guys,' he said, 'but now we're here, maybe we'll get the answers and the help we need. And as soon as we're done, we'll have these idiots take us straight home.'

She wasn't so sure.

'Let's go,' said Thomas, heading off across the piazza.

'Where?' she asked.

He pointed.

'That's it?' asked Jakob. 'That's where all the British royals get married? It's not as fancy as it looks on TV.'

'Westminster *Abbey*,' Thomas said, 'where members of the *Anglican* royal family get married, is down the street. This is Westminster Cathedral, and it's Catholic.'

'And this is where this Byrne guy is based?'

'I believe so.'

'You believe so?'

'Look, man. All I know is that I'm to bring you here to meet my superior.'

'Cardinal whatever-his-name-is.'

'Peter.'

'So—'

'Jakob,' said Thomas, wheeling around, 'I'm freezing my balls off out here. Let's go inside, where hopefully it'll be a damn sight warmer, and all will be explained.'

'He's right, Jakob,' Ellie said, a shiver jolting her body. 'It's freezing. Can we just go in?'

Jakob nodded.

When they reached the cathedral's main doors, Thomas tried to open one, but it didn't move. He twisted the handle and pushed again. The door remained in place. Ellie couldn't see his face, but she sensed he was frustrated from the set of his shoulders and the drop of his head. He turned toward a smaller doorway to the left, but a metallic grating sound stopped him. One of the main doors opened into darkness, and then a tall man in a dark blue suit and matching shirt appeared, gripping the doorframe with one hand, barring their entry.

When the man recognised him, he immediately stepped back, his face devoid of warmth or welcome. Thomas stood to one side, gestured for everyone to enter the cathedral, then fell in behind them. When they were all inside, the man who'd blocked their way closed the door, locked it, and whispered something to him.

'He's in the cathedral's admin offices out back,' he told Seth and Rebekah, tilting his head toward the altar.

'Who is?' asked Ellie.

'Peter. He's with Byrne.'

She peered into the cathedral. The place was almost entirely dark, and it reminded her of pictures of underground caves she'd seen, the columns on each side of the central aisle like conjoined stalagmites and stalactites. The only light in its cavernous belly was coming from the far end. Lights mounted high on the walls on each side cast a soft, eerie glow on an image of Christ painted on a gigantic blood-red crucifix edged elaborately in gold. Another shiver trickled down her back, but this time it wasn't the cold. It was this place. It unsettled her.

Thomas took out his phone and wandered away to make a call. She listened hard and heard him say, 'We're here,' and, 'Yes, and the boyfriend,' and, 'Understood.'

When he returned, he faced the man who'd let them into the cathedral, whom she guessed to be the driver or the bodyguard of Thomas's boss, Peter.

'Markus, our drivers are parking out back. I've told them to join us. Let them in and have them take defensive positions up here, then stay at the back door.'

'You're expecting trouble?'

'It's unlikely, but it doesn't hurt to be prepared.'

Markus nodded and walked away.

Thomas turned back to the group.

'Alright, Ellie. Peter and the bishop will be joining us shortly. Time to find out what all this is about.'

They made their way down the central aisle. She walked beside

Jakob, bookended by Thomas in front and Rebekah and Seth behind. Her insides felt twisted. None of this seemed right to her. Surely they were safe now they were out of Copenhagen, so why the rush to get here, to this place, tonight? Why not get some sleep first and do whatever they were here to do in the morning?

As they reached the front row of pews, Thomas motioned for her and Jakob to sit, which they did without hesitation. They were both exhausted, and she knew there'd be no point in arguing about it. Rebekah sat on the front pew across the aisle and put her bag on the ground. Thomas and Seth remained standing.

They waited quietly for almost a minute. The silence was broken by the bang of a heavy door and footsteps approaching them from beyond the choir. They belonged to the two Range Rover drivers, who walked up the central aisle to the front doors. A minute later, the door thudded again, and two more men came out of the shadows behind the massive crucifix. One was a tall, overweight, redheaded man wearing black trousers and a blue cardigan with what she thought was a kind but sad face. But the man in front of him grabbed her attention the most.

He was tall, with silvery-grey hair and olive skin, and he gazed directly at her. Despite his smile, there was a stern look in his eyes. This had to be the man in charge.

Peter.

Thomas approached him and spoke quietly. Without taking his gaze from her, he listened, nodded, and stepped toward her. She made to stand, and he motioned for her to stay seated. Fuck that, she thought. She wouldn't be talked down to, literally or figuratively. She didn't care who this man was or how much power he had—she was a person just like him, and she needed answers.

She stood, and Jakob rose with her. Peter smiled, unperturbed by her defiance.

'So, you're Ellie,' he said. 'I hear you've had quite the evening.'

'You could say that. Are you going to tell me what the hell is going on?'

The *hell* was instead of a *fuck*. While she wanted answers, being too impolite to this man was probably not the best way to get them.

'And you must be Jakob,' he said, ignoring her question. 'I see Thomas couldn't convince you to stay in Copenhagen.'

'Fucking right, he couldn't.'

Seemingly unfazed by Jakob's strong language, he looked back at her.

'My name is Cardinal Peter Barjona. This,' he said, motioning to the man behind him, 'is Bishop Leonard Byrne. I understand you're aware of who he is.'

She nodded.

'A pleasure,' said Byrne. He gave her an apologetic look. 'I had hoped that if we met, it would be in more comfortable surroundings and a little earlier in the day.'

She smiled and was about to respond, but Peter interjected.

'How much has Thomas told you of this... situation?' he asked her.

She summarised everything she'd learned on the flight from Copenhagen. Sammael's rebellion, Sammael being Lucifer, the Nephilim. Everything she could remember hearing. He listened without interrupting.

'To be completely honest,' she said, 'I think it's all crap.'

'Why would you think that?'

'Come on. You all work for a super-secret group within the Vatican, and supernatural assassins are hunting me because I'm supposed to be some long-lost descendant of some bigshot in history? None of it's very believable. Except maybe the secret group thing. Everyone knows how you Catholics like to keep secrets.'

Peter smiled.

'It's all quite true,' he said. 'I can assure you of that. Your own eyes ought to have convinced you of that when Gideon and his associate confronted you. I understand they gave you a glimpse of their true selves.'

'I'm not sure what I saw,' she lied, uncertain why. 'I'd already had a few drinks by the time they turned up.'

'Even so, there's more to the story than Thomas has given you, as I'm sure you've guessed. It's all as unbelievable as everything else you've heard tonight, but it's also quite true.'

'Okay,' said Jakob. 'Why don't you fill us in?'

Peter gestured to the pews they'd been sitting on.

'Why don't you both sit back down? Granted, they're not comfortable, but you've had a long day, and they're better than standing.'

Ellie looked at Jakob, who shrugged and did as Peter suggested. Before she could sit, her body stiffened. A vision flashed through her mind's eye. It lasted only a split second, but she knew it wasn't something new. It was a flash of Yehuda's abduction from Shimon's house and was over as quickly as it had come. Her body slumped. Jakob bolted off the pew and grabbed her shoulders to stop her from dropping to the floor.

'Help me,' he shouted.

Rebekah rushed forward and slid her hands under Ellie's armpits. She gently lowered her to the pew, then stepped back. Jakob knelt beside Ellie.

'Are you alright?' he asked.

She nodded and took a deep, calming breath.

'I'm fine.'

'What happened?'

'A vision. One of the old ones.'

'They're usually that quick?' Peter asked.

She looked at him. There was something niggling at her. Something about him she couldn't quite put her finger on.

'No,' she said. 'They're usually much longer. It wasn't a full vision. It was just a flashback.'

'Of what?' asked Jakob.

'It doesn't matter.' She looked at Peter again. 'So, what are all these other unbelievable truths, then?'

He took off his overcoat, folded it over the back of one of the pews, and sat down next to her.

'As Thomas told you on your flight here, we belong to a group known as the Elyonim. I'm responsible for its day-to-day operations. Our existence is largely a secret within the Vatican—not even His Holiness is aware of us. We have people in key positions in the other major faiths and a few lesser ones. We also have ties with several governments and almost all the European royal families. Originally, our purpose was to spread the word of God. Eventually, our mission evolved to protect Christ and what he stood for.'

'To protect him?'

'Of course. He had enemies on all sides. The Romans. The Orthodox Jews. There were even snakes within his inner circle.'

Byrne cleared his throat.

'Elyonim,' he said. 'That's—'

'An old Hebrew name,' said Peter, giving him a frosty glare at the interruption, 'which took hold in the beginning and which no one has ever bothered to change.'

'Why do you have people in other religions?' Ellie asked.

'One of our primary concerns, and one to which the Vatican itself is largely and regrettably indifferent, is the continued existence of the bloodlines of those in Christ's inner circle. Some of those bloodlines we're aware of, some even remain within our group, but others were lost over time. With factors such as migration, dilution of lineages, and so on, it's entirely possible their descendants now belong to other cultures and religions. The only way to be alerted to their existence is to have people within those faiths.'

'Are you saying I could be from one of those bloodlines?'

'Yes.'

'Whose?' asked Jakob.

'When you've had your dreams,' Peter said to Ellie, 'they've been from the perspective of a woman named Marta, correct?'

'Yes.'

'They've shown you scenes in her life, through her eyes.'

She nodded.

'What if I were to tell you that everything you've seen happened? The abduction of Judas. His death at the hand of Christ. All of it is true.'

'Your Eminence,' said Byrne. 'Might I have a word with you in private?'

'No, bishop, you may not. You asked me earlier for an explanation, and now you will have it. You're about to hear things that will make you question your faith and what you believe in, and with which you will no doubt disagree. If you think yourself unable to handle that, you're welcome to leave and continue your tenure none the wiser, blind to truths veiled for millennia. Otherwise, stay and become enlightened, but please remain silent.'

Byrne's shoulders fell, and he looked like a scolded child.

'Okay,' Ellie said. 'Let's say I believe you. Let's say it's all true. Why am I seeing it? *How* am I seeing it?'

'Thomas told you of the angels and their offspring,' Peter continued. 'The offspring inherit the memories of their ancestors in the angelic line, irrespective of how diluted the bloodline becomes. A child with even a trace of angelic blood will inherit the memories of everyone in the bloodline who came before it. Typically, the ability to recall those memories fades with each new generation as more human genes pollute the bloodline, but it can remain relatively strong in descendants of the more powerful angels.'

'What are you saying?'

'We believe you're experiencing these visions because you have genetically inherited the memories of your sixty-seventh or sixty-eighth great-grandmother, Marta.'

'Marta had angelic blood?'

'No. She was human. Her offspring carried the angelic blood of their father.'

'Their father?'

'Yehuda Sicarii.'

'Are you suggesting Ellie is a descendant of Judas Iscariot?' asked Byrne. 'And that he was an angel?'

'Correct. We believe Marta was pregnant when these events occurred. That child would not only have inherited Iscariot's genetic memories to the point of its conception but would also have absorbed everything Marta experienced while in her womb. Those memories were passed down through the generations and now rest with Ellie.'

'Wait,' Jakob said. 'You're saying that Ellie's the part-angel great-something granddaughter of the guy who sold out Jesus?'

'That, and, regrettably, more.'

'How much worse can it be?' she asked. Her pulse raced, and her skin became hot. She could feel the prickle of sweat on her forehead.

'When Sammael—Lucifer—discovered that God had sent His only son to guide humankind, he paired with a female angel named Lilith and had his own child. Not a Nephilim, I should add, but a pureblood angel. One whom Sammael sent to subvert Christ and his mission. That child was Yehuda Sicarii.'

'*What?* But that would make me—'

'A descendant of Sammael,' Peter said gravely.

'Of Lucifer?' Byrne said, bristling. Evidently, Peter's version of history did not reflect his understanding of it.

'That's impossible,' Jakob protested.

Ellie's stomach turned, and she suddenly felt so disoriented that she would have fallen over if she weren't sitting down.

'I'd be prepared to wager,' Peter continued, 'that you've never been ill, and any injury you've sustained healed abnormally quickly.'

'As a matter of—'

She was unable to finish her sentence. Her body shook violently, and her eyes rolled back into her head. Everything went black. Suddenly, she was Marta again. She was on the edge of the clearing outside the city walls. Shimon was at her side. In front of her, in the middle of the clearing, on his knees, was Yehuda. Yeshua stood before him with his sword raised above his head. Kepha was beside him, his left ear wrapped in a blood-soaked bandage.

And then there was a blinding white light.

She gulped air like she'd been underwater for too long. Confusion fogged her mind, and her eyesight was blurred. She looked at the faces around her as they came back into focus: Jakob and Byrne, then Rebekah, Thomas and Seth.

And him.

Peter, with his expensive overcoat, his impeccable suit, and the thing that bothered her.

His cropped left ear.

'You were there,' she said to him.

'Who was where?' asked Jakob.

'Yes,' said Peter. 'I was there.'

'Where?' Jakob asked again, his voice rising.

'You were Christ's right-hand man. You're Kepha.'

'Hang on,' said Jakob, confusion warping his face. 'Are you saying this guy was in your dreams? He was actually there, with Jesus?'

'Yeah,' she said, staring at Peter. 'He was there when they kidnapped Judas. Shimon gave him that clipped ear. And he was there when Jesus executed Judas.'

'Okay, I'm calling bullshit on this whole thing,'

'It's entirely true, Jakob,' Peter said.

'But that would make you over two thousand years old, which is impossible. Unless you're one of them. A Nephilim.'

Peter chuckled.

'A Nephilim? No, Jakob. I'm not a Nephilim. And I've been around for a lot more than two millennia.'

'What the hell are you, then?'

'I'm what you'd call a pureblood.'

'A what?'

'He's an angel, Jakob,' said Ellie. 'He's saying he's an angel.'

Jakob shot up from the pew and thrust his hand at her.

'Come on, Ellie. I've heard enough. These people can't help you. They're fucking crazy.'

Instead of reaching for his hand, she stared past it at Peter's face, puzzled by something elusive on the periphery of her consciousness.

'She's correct, Jakob,' he said. 'I am an angel. More specifically, an archangel.'

Jakob whirled and stepped toward him, stopping when their noses were only inches apart.

'How fucking stupid do you think we are?' he asked, his voice calm and quiet. 'First, you'd have us believe that half-angel assassins are chasing us and that Ellie's related to the Devil, and now you're telling us *you're* an angel? You're insane,' he said, pointing at Peter's face, 'and we're leaving.'

'Jakob,' Thomas said quietly. 'Sit down and *calm* down, man.'

'Fuck you, Thomas,' he said, pointing at him but maintaining eye contact with Peter. 'This whole story is fucking ridiculous. Ellie, are you buying any of this?'

She wanted to believe he was right. That this was all bullshit. But the evidence—Gideon's and Cain's eyes changing colour, the psychokinesis they'd used, and that she recognised Peter as Kepha—told her these people were telling the truth.

'I would have to agree with Jakob,' Byrne said, stepping to Peter's side. 'Your Eminence, it's painfully obvious to me these young people are confused and terrified for their lives, and adding to their confusion with extravagant tales of angels and half-humans and Christ executing Iscariot isn't helping.'

'Why would you think them extravagant, Leonard? Granted, the Bible is conveniently vague, misleading even, on Iscariot's fate, but the existence of the angels and their offspring is well-documented in its scriptures. Upon which, I would remind you, you've built a very comfortable life. Surely, you're not telling me that you question their veracity?'

'Frankly, I've always considered the more fantastical aspects of the Bible to be figurative. I don't doubt that messengers of God existed but in the form of human prophets spreading His word, not spiritual beings. As for the Nephilim, they were most likely just bands of wandering, bloodthirsty thugs that became a convenient foundation on which to build the myth of the evil offspring of fallen angels.'

'And who do you think gave the word of God to those human prophets?'

Byrne looked blankly at him.

'Perhaps a brief demonstration would help.' he said.

Peter pointed to the adjacent column of pews and made a slow sweeping motion toward the back of the cathedral. One by one, and at the precise moment his fingers pointed at them, the pews tilted backward and balanced on their back legs as if invisible ropes held them up. Ellie watched wearily, Jakob scoffed and shook his head, and Byrne made the sign of the cross in front of himself.

After a few more seconds of his magical balancing act, Peter lowered his arm, and the benches returned almost silently to their original positions. Byrne continued to look at them open-mouthed as if they still teetered in mid-air, but Ellie turned her attention back to him. Something still bothered her. Something she still couldn't quite work out.

'I presume that will be enough to satisfy your doubts, Leonard,' he said, his eyes locking on to Byrne's. 'Let's keep that to ourselves, shall we?'

Byrne remained silent but nodded robotically.

'Now,' Peter said to Ellie, 'I'd like to know more about these dreams of yours. If you permit me, I'd like to see them myself.'

She remembered what Thomas had said earlier about angels' ability to read minds.

'Will it hurt?'

'You'll feel a slight pressure in your head and may experience some mild queasiness, but it won't be painful, and it will be significantly faster than you trying to explain them to me.'

She pondered this for a moment. While she was wary of an intrusion into her mind, she considered it could be the only way to find out why she was having the dreams. She took a deep breath and nodded. Peter smiled warmly.

'Ellie, you can't,' Jakob protested.

'It's okay, Jakob. I've seen and heard enough to convince me that at least some of what they're telling us is true. I just want this done with now. I want the dreams to stop. And if this is how I do that...'

Peter sat down next to her. He removed the glove from his right hand and stretched out his hand toward her face. As she looked into his eyes, they turned black. She gasped and withdrew on reflex. He paused, his eyes never leaving hers. She inhaled deeply again and leaned forward. This time, when his hand approached, she remained still.

As he touched her forehead, his eyes widened, and his body jolted as if she'd passed on a static charge picked up by walking on carpet, only much more potent. His reaction was like Gideon's when he'd grabbed her wrist outside Dante's. As his expression went from surprise to concentration, she felt a heaviness inside her head, and a wave of nausea swept over her, just as he'd predicted. Her head was spinning like it did whenever she drank too much cherry wine or when she had vertigo that one time. Everyone and everything around her began to blur. She closed her eyes to stop the swirling, but it didn't help.

Suddenly, an explosion of imagery flooded her mind's eye. Memories long-forgotten, deliberately or otherwise, sped through her brain.

Her fifth birthday party.

Being told two years later that her parents had died in a train crash in Finland.

Going off the rails herself at thirteen.

Her first boyfriend three years after that.

Meeting Jakob.

And then the dreams came. One by one, in the order she'd experienced them. They flashed by, there and gone in an instant. But she relived the pain, fear, and grief as much as she first had. Her heart thumped, and she could feel her forehead tingle with sweat.

And then everything went black.

It was over.

She felt Peter's hand leave her head. She resisted the urge to vomit and opened her eyes. Everyone stared at her. Jakob and Byrne wore looks of concern. Oddly, so did Rebekah. Thomas and Seth appeared unmoved.

'Did you see?' she asked, willing her heart to stop racing.

'Everything,' Peter said, replacing his glove.

'And?'

He smiled, but there was no warmth in his eyes this time. There was something else there. Something darker.

'You do, indeed, carry the blood of Sammael.'

She felt the cathedral's walls close in on her and crush the wind out of her lungs. She gripped the edge of her wooden seat because if she were to let go, she'd fall a thousand metres into blackness and would be unable to climb her way back out.

'This cannot be real,' said Jakob, sitting beside her. He rubbed his hands over his face and ran them through his hair. 'It can't be.'

'It's as real as it gets, dude,' Rebekah said.

'I'm guessing you three are special, too,' he said sarcastically, looking at her, 'given how, you know... *you* got shot and seem fine, and none of you freaked out when Gideon did his magic trick with the car door back home.'

She nodded.

'So, what are you?' Ellie asked, desperate for her thoughts to be occupied with something other than painful memories and the revelation that she was apparently the great-something granddaughter of fucking Satan now.

'Nephilim,' said Seth.

'Angels,' Rebekah said, pointing to herself and Thomas. 'But just the bog-standard kind. Not the special kind, like Peter.'

Both Thomas and Peter gave her admonishing glances.

'Oh, just *bog-standard* angels,' said Jakob, making quotation marks in the air. Then he looked at Seth. 'I thought Nephilim were the children of fallen angels. Are you one of those, or are you, uh—'

'My mother was one of the fallen, yes.'

'So how come you're here with these guys?' Ellie asked.

'Like everyone else, we have free will. I recognised a long time ago whose side was the right one, and I made a choice. Simple as that.'

She thought that seemed reasonable enough. She had friends who had terrible parents but were kind, generous, warm-hearted, beautiful people, and she knew others with great parents who were absolute assholes, so why wouldn't it be the same for the children of fallen angels? After another moment of processing everything, she looked more closely at Thomas and finally understood why she recognised him.

'You're Taoma,' she said to him. 'You helped Peter carry Jesus to Golgotha.'

'Yes.'

'You were both Christ's apostles,' she said, looking from him to Peter.

He nodded.

Her mind was wracked with confusion. The niggle in the back of her head pushed its way forward. While she now believed it possible that these people, and the two men who came after them in Copenhagen, could be angels and Nephilim, she felt there was something not quite right about the story they'd given her. There was a gaping hole, but she couldn't figure out what it was.

And then she had it.

She knew what had been gnawing at her.

51

'What I don't get,' Ellie said to Peter, 'is why they want to kill me. Gideon and Cain. If, as *you* say, I'm some long-lost descendant of Sammael and they're the offspring of the fallen angels, why were they trying to kill me? What possible threat could I be to them?'

'They weren't there to kill you,' Thomas said.

'What?' said Jakob. 'Are you joking? They dragged her flatmate out of their apartment to find her, attacked us in Dante's, and had a fucking gunfight in the street with people—sorry, *angels*—from the Vatican, who they clearly knew. What part of any of that makes you think they weren't there to kill her?'

'They're hunting her because they want her in their ranks. They likely believe that, as a descendant of Sammael, she could be useful to them. They want her for whatever power runs through her veins.'

'Which,' Peter said, 'could be substantial if what I felt when I touched you earlier is any indication.'

'What you felt?' she asked.

'There's an energy in angelic blood. We can sense it when we touch someone who carries it. Humans, however, cannot. Its intensity varies, depending on how diluted the bloodline is. I felt it in you. It courses through you, stronger than I've felt in any others who aren't purebloods and stronger even than some who are.'

'Okay, so if they don't want to kill her, why all the aggression back in Copenhagen?' Jakob continued. 'Why not just ask to have a conversation?'

'Because they're the bad guys, man,' said Seth. 'You think they're going to sit her down over tea and cake and ask her if she wants to join their club in exchange for a cool membership badge and a mention in their monthly newsletter?'

Ellie's head spun. Ignoring the stuff about angels and half-angels and considering only the facts of what had happened in the past few hours, what she was hearing made perfect sense. A good person asks for your help. A bad one coerces you. Then, she was struck by a thought so absurd it couldn't possibly be true. To voice that thought could be dangerous. But if she were right, she was in danger regardless.

She had to know.

'They behaved that way because they wanted to make sure you didn't get your hands on me, didn't they? All of their violence, their hostility, their impatience. They wanted me out of there before your team arrived.'

'Of course they did,' Thomas replied. 'Like we said, they—'

'No. Not just because they want me on their team. It's something else. Something worse.'

'What do you mean?' Jakob asked.

'Think about it, Jakob. These guys turned up in force to stop those other two from carting me off somewhere? Why? Why am I so important to them? To the Vatican, or the Elyonim, or whoever these people are? Why would they want to get to me first?'

He looked at her blankly, for which she couldn't blame him. Nothing made sense, and if even half of what she'd learned in the last few hours was true, her life had changed irrevocably. She took a deep breath and prepared herself to say aloud what the growing knot in her stomach was agonisingly trying to convince her was the truth.

'Christ and Lucifer were enemies,' she said. 'The Vatican and the Grigori or Sicarii or—Jesus, this is so confusing—are still enemies. One side, evil or not, wants to bring me into the fold. Which means the other side, their enemy...'

She raised her eyebrows and opened her hands, inviting him to take the leap and finish her sentence.

'Wants you dead?'

'Wants me dead.' She looked at Peter. 'They weren't just in Copenhagen to get me to join them, were they? They were trying to protect me from you.'

Peter smiled wolfishly, then began to clap his hands slowly. He chuckled briefly, deep and full of menace.

'You're brighter than you look.'

'Fuck you!'

'Is this true, Cardinal?' asked Byrne.

'I think I've had enough foul language, Ellie.' Peter said.

'Like I said. Fuck you!'

Peter lashed out and struck her across her face with the back of his right hand. The blow was hard enough to knock her out of the pew and to her knees. She gingerly touched her face, and her fingers came away bloody. Despite being covered by his glove, Peter's signet ring had caught her cheek and torn the skin.

'You fucking asshole!' Jakob roared.

'Jakob, no!' Byrne shouted.

He ignored the bishop and launched himself at Peter, who calmly grabbed him by the throat and lifted him off the ground as easily as if he were a child's doll. Ellie picked herself up from the floor and saw that Peter's eyes had become ovals of solid black again. Jakob thrashed his arms and legs, either because he wanted to strike Peter somewhere with enough force to make him relinquish his grip or because he was about to pass out from a lack of oxygen, and panic had set in. Or both. She didn't care which. She just wanted him set free. She raised herself to full height and commanded Peter to put him down. He smiled and raised Jakob higher. Drawn by the noise in the cathedral, his driver, Markus, returned to the group from his post beyond the choir.

'Cardinal Barjona,' said Byrne. 'Put that man down right now. This is completely unacceptable.'

Peter ignored him and looked at Ellie.

'Cardinal,' the bishop said.

'Let him go!' she ordered.

'Cardinal!' Byrne shouted.

'Seth.' Peter said quietly, his eyes still locked on Ellie's.

Seth approached the bishop, grabbed his head in both hands and sharply twisted it to the left. There was a sickening crunch, and then the light left Byrne's eyes, and he dropped to the cold floor.

'You bastard!' Ellie yelled.

A gurgle from Jakob brought her back into focus. She looked from his frightened eyes to Peter's pitch-dark ones and back. Despite the rage burning inside her, she knew there was nothing she could do to help him. He was going to die, right then and there, in front of her.

'Jakob,' she said with hot tears streaming down her cheeks. 'I'm... fuck! I love you. I'm so sorry. Fuck! Fuck!'

As he tried desperately to respond, the two drivers stationed at the cathedral's large front doors fell silently to the ground, almost simultaneously. For a fraction of a second, everyone looked on in silence, wonder and disbelief. Thomas drew his weapon and lunged for Ellie. He grabbed her hair, stepped behind her, pulled her against his chest, and placed the tip of his pistol against her temple. Rebekah moved toward her duffel bag, which was on the ground behind Markus, who now stood next to Seth. Both men had drawn their guns. Peter maintained his grip on Jakob's throat and snarled.

There was a clatter of metal on stone in front of the altar.

Then the world went white, and Ellie's eyes burned.

And then darkness fell.

She was blind.

A nanosecond later, a shockwave of sound assaulted her ears as if one thousand starter pistols had been fired around her head. It took all her effort not to hurl her guts out onto the stone slabs.

And then she was deaf.

She screamed but couldn't hear herself—not even inside her own head. Then, almost as soon as the deafness began, it subsided and gave way to an excruciating, high-pitched ringing, underneath which she could make out the dull murmur of voices. She tried to blink away the burning tears in her eyes. As the blackness dissipated, she could make out the rough shape of Peter, who looked like he was still holding Jakob by the throat. The explosion of light and sound had affected him, too, even with his angelic strength, because he'd dropped to his knees, taking Jakob to the floor with him.

She caught the blur of movement in her peripheral vision, in the shadows toward the back of the cathedral. She could make out a body-shaped outline. As her vision cleared further, so did the blurred figure. A man with one arm oddly longer than the other. No. A gun. He was holding a gun. Her pulse raced, and tears streamed down her face, no longer from the sting of the flash grenade but from relief.

It was Gideon.

A tidal wave of relief crashed over her, almost sending her to her knees. At that moment, she didn't care what he was or whose side he was on. All she knew, if Thomas had been telling the truth, was that he didn't want to kill her. And, right then, that was good enough for her.

'Help us!' she screamed.

'Shut the fuck up,' said Thomas, knotting his fist even tighter into her hair and smacking the butt of his pistol into the side of her head.

Standing again and still gripping Jakob, Peter snarled ferociously. She glanced at him, ignoring the pain shooting across her scalp. His canine teeth had extended as Cain's had in Copenhagen but seemed longer and dripped with a thick, milky liquid that reminded her of snake venom she'd seen on nature documentaries. Thomas kept his gun pressed against her temple. Standing beside each other, Seth and Markus aimed at Gideon but held their fire. Rebekah remained behind them, fumbling through her bag.

'Let them go, Azrael,' Gideon commanded. His voice was firm, with no hint of fear or reverence for Peter's angelical nature.

'You made a mistake coming here, Gideon,' Peter said. 'The girl is going to die, there's no question of that, but the boy doesn't have to. Walk away now, and he'll live.'

'That's a lie.'

Peter smirked and tightened his grip on Jakob's throat, causing him to wheeze.

'He doesn't have long, Gideon. Make the right choice.'

'We can't stand here all night, Azrael. I just want them. I don't want to kill you for them, but I will. All of you if I have to.'

Seth pulled the slide on the top of his weapon.

'Let's just kill this motherfu—'

Before he could finish his sentence or pull the trigger, a cloud of red mist sprayed across his face. He spat it from his mouth and rubbed it from his eyes just as Markus fell to his knees. As the driver's body slumped forward to the ground, his head tipped the other way and rolled down his back, and when his chest struck the floor, blood sputtered from his headless neck across the stone slabs.

Ellie screamed, and then her stomach churned, and she felt bile rise in her gut. She closed her mouth, and it filled with hot, bitter liquid. It leaked out of the sides of her mouth, and when she tried to swallow it back down—a reflex more than a conscious decision not to defile the cathedral—it caught in the back of her throat and made her gag, and she vomited the entire load of it over the stone floor.

Peter, Thomas, and Seth stared in shock and confusion at their colleague's lifeless body, blood flowing freely from where his head should have been. And then they looked to Rebekah, whose face, spattered with arterial spray, was a mix of delight and rage. She held a bloodied machete and stood with one foot on Markus's head. She stamped on it and it collapsed, sending bloody chunks of pinkish-grey tissue and shards of bone in all directions.

She shook blood and brain matter from her boot, stepped away to put distance between herself and Seth, and turned her head to Gideon while keeping her eyes fixed on her colleagues. 'About time you showed up. I thought I'd have to deal with all these fuckers on my own.'

'She's with the fucking Grigori!' Seth spat.

'What the fuck?' asked Thomas. 'You're working with *them*?'

'I know, right!' she said, her eyes glowing bright violet. 'You're thinking this is one monumental catastrofuck. And I *am* a Grigori, you dumb shit, but you stupid motherfucking assholes are all so arrogant and blinded by your superiority and your belief that you're untouchable, you never saw it. Not even the mighty Azrael,' she said, looking at Peter.

'I'm gonna take your fucking head off, bitch!' Seth bellowed.

As he stepped forward, a thunderous roar erupted from behind him, and a large, heavy wooden pew slammed into his back. He crashed chest-down to the floor, headbutting it as he landed. A figure came out of the shadows behind him.

Cain.

Before either Thomas or Peter could react, Rebekah drew her gun and fired two shots at Thomas. Both missed, but he released Ellie to find cover and protect himself. With nowhere to go, she tucked herself against the side of a pew. Gideon fired a single shot at Peter, his bullet piercing the cardinal's shoulder. He howled and dropped Jakob, who crawled to a bench and pulled himself to his feet, gasping, desperate for breath.

Seth, who'd been knocked out cold, came around. Blood poured from a two-inch gash on his forehead, blinding his right eye. He wiped his face and cleared away enough blood to see again, then tried to stand. He only made it to his knees. Holding a large knife resembling a boomerang, Cain leapt at him. He landed on Seth's back and knocked him back to the ground. Seth bellowed—a yell that became a bloody gurgle as Cain thrust his long knife through the back of his neck and out through the thyroid cartilage in his larynx with such force that it penetrated the stone floor, pinning him to the ground. Cain roared and sunk his teeth into the back of his neck. Seth howled, blood bubbling from his mouth and the wound in his throat.

Peter lunged for Ellie. She scrambled away, but he managed to grab her ankle and pull her back to him. He seized her throat and stood up, lifting her with him, then tucked her in close to his body, her back to his chest.

'Get your fucking hands off me,' she shouted, writhing to break free.

Gideon grabbed Jakob's collar and pulled him out of the way, then glared at Peter and shot him in the knee. He roared and released Ellie, and as Gideon put a bullet in his other knee, he bellowed again and collapsed to the floor.

Crouching between two pews, Thomas leaned around the corner of the forwardmost bench and fired three shots at Rebekah, who remained out in the open. The first struck the stone floor, the second tore through her jeans into the flesh of her right thigh, and the third pierced her right arm. She yelled out in pain, and before she could salvage her composure, he telekinetically swept her into the air with a flourish and cast her toward the cathedral's main doors.

'Traitorous cunt!' he yelled.

She twisted her body mid-air and landed on her feet, facing toward him, her gun raised. Before he could get another shot off, she fired twice, the bullets striking him in the chest. As he fell backward, she thrust her hands out in front of her as if pushing something away from her, and the column of pews he lay within shifted forward, a tsunami of heavy wood trapping him underneath. Then, she swung her arms from left to right, adding the adjacent benches to the pile that already covered him.

Meanwhile, Cain placed his foot on Seth's back, then took hold of his wrists and wrenched his arms backward, dislocating them. Seth, still conscious, cried out. Cain then withdrew his knife from Seth's neck and throat and sliced the backs of his legs from his knees to his glutes, severing his hamstrings. Seth let out a sickening, raspy moan, seemingly empty of the energy to do anything more.

Gideon moved to Ellie's side and pointed his gun at Peter, who lay on the floor, propping himself up on an elbow. As Rebekah joined them, the cardinal looked at her with undisguised contempt.

'You're a traitor and a fool,' he spat.

'No, Azrael,' Gideon snapped, his eyes burning amber. 'You were the traitors. You, Michael, them,' he said, nodding toward Thomas and Seth. 'And the others who joined you. You betrayed Sammael. You betrayed Judas. You—'

'And *you're* guilty by blood, you fucking half-breed. Every Nephilim. Every Anakim. Every last one of you abominations.'

'Tell him he can't win,' Gideon said quietly.

He raised his gun and put two bullets into Peter's chest and a third into his forehead. Peter's elbow gave way, and he slumped heavily backward. He pointed his weapon at the cardinal's head for another second, then grabbed Ellie's wrist. As his hand encircled her bare flesh, she felt the same jolt of electricity as when he'd seized her in Copenhagen and when Peter had touched her earlier when he'd seen her thoughts. He seemed to ignore it and, pulling her behind him, guided Jakob to Cain, who took his arm and kept him moving.

Rebekah half-ran, half-limped over to Markus's headless body and rummaged through his clothes. A second later, she stood up, dangled a set of keys and motioned toward the rear of the church.

'The cars are parked back there.'

When they reached the door that led to the car park, Gideon kicked it open, almost breaking it from its hinges. It had started to rain again since Ellie had entered the cathedral, and now it was pelting down. In the parking area sat a dark green Bentley, beyond which were the two Range Rovers that had brought them from the airport. The noses of all three vehicles pointed inward at the cathedral's wall. Rebekah moved alongside him and pressed the button on the key fob she'd taken from

Markus. The indicators on the Bentley flashed, and there was a quiet clunk as the doors unlocked.

'Peter's,' she said. 'It's virtually bombproof.'

She passed the keys to him, went to the car's back door on its far side, opened it, and got in. He threw the keys to Cain.

'Get it started. It won't take them long to recover, so I need to take care of those.' he motioned to the Range Rovers.

Ellie followed Jakob to the near-side rear door, behind the driver's seat. She opened it, opting to sit in the middle, but when she ducked her head into the cabin, she saw the bulky centre console that divided the rear bench into two separate seats.

'Shit,' she said.

'Looks like you two will have to double up,' Rebekah chirped from across the console.

She huffed and, being lighter than Jakob, let him get in so she could sit on his lap. She gave him a few seconds to settle and then climbed in. He grunted as she tried to get comfortable.

'No more curries for you,' he said wryly.

'Screw you and your bony legs.'

Cain slammed their door shut, got into the driver's seat, started the engine, and selected reverse gear. She watched through Rebekah's window as Gideon stood between the two Range Rovers, drew his gun, and fired it twice at each vehicle. The nearest one shuddered with each shot. He returned to the Bentley and climbed into the front passenger seat, and Cain released the parking brake and floored the accelerator before he'd closed his door. The Bentley shot backward onto the street. He spun the steering wheel to the left, pointed the car up the road, and slammed on the brakes.

'We can't risk going straight to Northolt,' Gideon told him. 'This thing probably has a tracker. They'd locate and pick us off before we get halfway.'

He glanced wordlessly at Gideon.

'Head for the junction of Queen Street and Cheapside. We'll dump the car there and then run for safe ground.'

Cain nodded, put the car into drive and stomped on the accelerator. The car surged forward, and instead of taking the right-hand bend at the end of the street, he tugged the wheel to the left and jumped the curb, taking the car onto the piazza in front of the cathedral. Few people were in the square, so they had a clear run across it.

When they reached the end, he aimed the car between a pair of chunky, low-level concrete bollards set marginally wider apart than the car's width. The Bentley shot through them and across the pavement, causing the few pedestrians in the area to stare in disbelief or sprint away to avoid being flattened.

As the car joined Victoria Street, he aimed it at a traffic-light-controlled pedestrian crossing, took the car over it, then spun the steering wheel to the right and headed east.

52

Peter hauled himself off the cathedral floor and sat on one of the front pews. Dark crimson ringed the bullet holes in the knees of his trousers and the shoulder of his suit jacket, and the front of his white shirt was slick and almost black. Blood seeped from the hole in his forehead and flowed into his eyes. He took a pale grey handkerchief from his jacket, wiped his brow, and tossed the bloodied cloth onto the pew beside him, then rested his elbows on his knees and allowed his head to drop into his hands.

Eventually, he leaned against the pew's backrest, opened his shirt to his belt, and closed his eyes. He took two quick, deep breaths and tensed every muscle in his body in preparation for what came next. Then, through sheer force of will alone, he began to dislodge the six bullets Gideon had fired into him. He roared as each round moved through flesh, bone, and cartilage. Each misshapen, blood-covered bullet tip oozed out of him and landed on the stone slabs with a clink.

Rage coursed through every vein and artery, his temples throbbed, and while he could not see them, he knew his eyes were as dark and lifeless as twin black holes.

A scuffing noise behind caught his attention. He glanced over his shoulder and noticed Thomas approaching. He'd dislodged himself from the pile of heavy benches Rebekah had buried him under and was walking awkwardly. Sticky blood, already congealing and turning black, covered his chin, and his breathing was laboured. Peter guessed the impact of the pews landing on him had broken at least one leg and some ribs, which had punctured one, if not both, of his lungs.

'What the fuck happened, Peter?'

Re-buttoning his ruined shirt, Peter looked blankly back at him.

'How could they have infiltrated us like that without us seeing it? Without you seeing it? Without—'

'I don't have an answer to that, Thomas.'

'You need to find one.'

The words were gurgled and rasping and had an odd whistle to them. They had come from Seth. He sat on the floor with his legs stretched out before him. The gash on his temple had closed, and the hole in his larynx had almost mended, but the damage to his vocal cords had not yet healed.

'It won't just be Rebekah,' he continued.

'He's right,' said Thomas. 'She won't be the only one.'

'No,' Peter said. 'Just as we have ours in their ranks.'

'Which ain't doing shit for us right now,' Seth replied. 'Might I refer you to one Katerine Clément, for example.'

'Her intelligence on Sicarii armament requirements proved invaluable.'

'Until she fucked up and they found out.'

'We need to find out where they're going,' said Thomas.

Peter pulled his phone from his jacket, thumbed the screen a few times and opened an application the Vatican's technical wizards had developed to track Church-owned vehicles. It was accurate to within five metres.

'They've taken my car.'

'Of course they fucking have,' Seth said, not bothering to hide his frustration.

'If you have something to say, Seth, please just say it.'

Seth unsteadily got to his feet with a loud grunt, then turned to face the stone column he'd been leaning against, inhaled deeply, and slammed his right shoulder into it. He roared, took another breath, and did the same with the other shoulder, bellowing again. With both shoulders relocated, he shrugged his jacket, brushed down his trousers, and then turned to face Peter.

'Spies within our ranks, a lack of backup here, human operatives who soak up bullets like fucking sponges, informers who spit out our name all over TV. Peter, I don't know what the fuck is going on with you at the moment, but this—'

'You forget your place, Nephilim.'

Seth snarled.

'Okay, let's stay focussed, said Thomas, stepping between them and taking out his phone. 'We need to figure out where they're going. Peter, what's your car's registration number?'

He dictated the car's licence plate number showing on his screen. Thomas typed it into his phone.

'I have them,' he said after a few seconds. He paced to the front of the cathedral, kneeling and disappearing from view when he got there. He returned holding a set of car keys he'd lifted from one of the dead drivers and headed for the door to the car park. Seth watched him go, then looked at Peter.

'This conversation ain't over, Peter.'

'No. It's not.'

He scowled and turned to follow Thomas out.

'Thomas,' Peter called. Thomas stopped and looked back. 'Kill everyone but the girl.'

53

After a brief silence, Gideon turned in his seat and looked at everyone in the back. Ellie and Jakob were visibly shaken and exhausted. Unfortunately, what had already been a long night for them wouldn't end any time soon.

'Everyone okay?'

'Yeah, we're peachy.'

He ignored Jakob's sarcasm and glanced at Rebekah.

'What about you?' he asked.

'Had to be done.'

He nodded. Her decision to take the head of Peter's driver would have been difficult. Maintain her cover within the Elyonim as she'd done for millennia, and continue to provide the Sicarii with valuable intelligence, or break it to save her colleagues and, crucially, Ellie and Jakob.

'Well, as someone who isn't leaking like a sieve again,' he said, 'and whose head remains attached to his neck, I think you made the right decision.'

'You're welcome.'

'And I'm glad to see the implants did their job.'

Ellie looked at her chest.

'Not those kinds of implants,' she said, laughing and tapping her temple. 'Prototype subdermal communications system, linked by a permanent 5G connection to the Sicarii's comms servers. All nanotech, hard-wired to my optical nerve. When I switch it on, I see a virtual keyboard. I can send a message via email or text just by tapping my fingers on any surface.'

'Okay,' said Ellie.

Rebekah laughed again.

'Too much info, huh?'

Ellie raised her eyebrows and nodded.

'Gideon, you need to start explaining all of this,' Jakob said.

'We're heading to a safe place. Once we're there, you'll get all the answers you need.'

'Yeah, we were fed that bullshit in Copenhagen, too. The whole blue-pill red-pill thing from Morpheus back here.' He looked over at Rebekah, who shrugged and attempted to look suitably apologetic. 'So, we trusted Thomas and got on a plane with him, and look what happened after that. I get that you probably saved our lives back there, but if you want us to trust you, you need to start talking.'

He appreciated Jakob's concerns and could admit that how he and Cain had approached Ellie and removed her from Dante's wasn't the best way to engender trust. Regardless, the only answer he was prepared to give at that moment was silence.

'I'm serious,' Jakob said. 'If we don't get some answers, we're getting out of this fucking car.'

He maintained eye contact with Jakob for a couple of seconds and then looked at Cain, who gave him a sideways glance and then pushed a button on his armrest. There was an audible clunk. He'd locked the doors.

'Fuck you,' Jakob said.

Gideon faced forward in his seat, pulled out his phone, scrolled his contacts for an entry listed simply as L/O—an abbreviation he used for the Sicarii's London office—then thumbed the screen and put the device to his ear.

'This is Gideon,' he said when the call connected. 'We have a Black

Alert scenario. Arrival within fifteen minutes. I want all on-site security personnel to be armed and on station, including those currently off-duty but still in the building. I want any on-call security staff currently located within a five-minute travel time of the building called in. And I want the conference room made available and a video link to Chicago initiated.'

He hung up without waiting for a response.

They passed Westminster Abbey. Ellie pointed it out to Jakob. He responded sarcastically that it was great. As they drove around Parliament Square, past the statues of Gandhi and Churchill and the Houses of Parliament, Gideon called Simon.

'We have them,' he said quietly. While Cain and Rebekah could hear every word, not only of what he said but also of Simon's end of the conversation, he considered it unnecessary for Ellie and Jakob to be privy to the discussion.

'*Unharmed?*' Simon asked.

'They appear to be.'

'*What do they know?*'

'I'm not sure yet. I'm guessing—'

Before he could go on, he felt pressure in his skull and heard Rebekah's voice inside his head.

She knows who she is. Azrael confirmed it.

'Rebekah tells me,' he continued, 'that Azrael told Ellie who she is, although I suspect that was accompanied by half-truths and more than a few outright lies.'

'*Rebekah?*'

'I'll explain later.'

'*What have you told Ellie?*'

'Nothing yet, but she does need an explanation, and I think you ought to be the one to provide it.'

'*Why?*'

'Credibility through familiarity.'

369

'The dreams.'

'Yes.'

'How long until you're somewhere I can talk to her?'

'Twelve minutes, give or take. I've got a video link being organised as we speak.'

'Understood. I'll be ready.'

Gideon hung up and made yet another call, this time to Enrique, who answered the call almost immediately. He bypassed pleasantries and got straight to it.

'Enrique, we're going to need a pickup. Did you manage to acquire that helicopter?'

'I'm working on it. When do you need me?'

'Forty-five minutes or so.'

'Where?'

'The Bank.'

'Gideon, that's central London.'

'I know.'

'I mean, built-up central London. The middle of Hyde Park it is not.'

He understood Enrique's apprehension about bringing a helicopter into an urban area without the proper clearance, but he had more pressing concerns at that moment.

'Enrique, can you—'

'Leave it with me, Gideon. Just be ready. There's only so much time I'll be able to hang around before a police chopper shows up.'

'Understood. Thank you, Enrique.'

He put the phone back into his pocket, and the car fell silent. It remained that way as they drove up Whitehall, past the Cenotaph on the right, then the closed black gates of Downing Street on the left. Cain took a right after the Ministry of Defence building. On the opposite side of the river, motionless and illuminated in vivid Coca-Cola red, was the London Eye. They turned left onto Victoria Embankment, barely slowing through the green-lit junction, then continued in silence until they reached Blackfriars Bridge, where Gideon half-turned in his seat.

'What else were they told?' he asked Rebekah.

'Pretty much everything. How Ellie's having the dreams, what *we* all are, plus the usual crap about Sammael's rebellion and subsequent banishment.'

Cain grunted and swung the car north on Puddle Dock and then east onto Queen Victoria Street.

'Did Azrael say what he intended to do with her?' Gideon asked.

'He didn't at the cathedral, and if Thomas knew, he never told me.'

'Azrael is Peter, right?' Ellie said.

Rebekah nodded. 'The Rock of Christ and the Angel of Death are one and the same. Azrael is his true angelic name.'

'And you two are Nephilim,' she said to Gideon, pointing at him and Cain.

'Yes,' replied Gideon, facing forward again. 'Two of the first.'

'And you're an angelic spy,' Jakob said to Rebekah.

'Yep. I even have a codename. Merc—'

'Rebekah,' warned Gideon.

She raised her hands in mock surrender.

'It's obsolete now anyway, probably,' she said. 'I can't see Simon assigning it to anyone else.'

'Nonetheless.'

'Jesus, I can't get my head around any of this,' Ellie said. 'What are you going to do with us?'

'That will depend on you,' Gideon replied.

'What does that mean?' asked Jakob.

'There's a lot you need to know, all of which you'll be told shortly. I can promise you that. What happens once you have the full story—the truth—will be entirely down to you. But, for now, all you need to know is that you're in no danger from us.'

'Because you want to recruit Ellie into your army, right? So you can use whatever residual angelic power she has. And when you say that what happens next is up to her, you mean that she joins you or she dies, right?'

'No, Jakob.'

'So, you don't want to kill us?' she asked.

'We don't want any harm coming to you at all.'

'Please tell me you're the good guys.'

'Well, *good* is subjective. We're capable of terrible things when they are necessary.'

'That's comforting,' Jakob said.

'But we're not naturally evil in the way that Azrael and Thomas probably described us to you. You have nothing to fear from us, Ellie.'

She said nothing. He could work his way into her mind to see what she was thinking and persuade her to believe him, but he figured he'd let her get to wherever she needed to get on her own.

'You could've told us who you were when you turned up in Dante's,' she said finally, 'instead of dragging Zindy there, coming over all psycho-kidnapper, beating the crap out of everyone, and sending Chewie over a wall.'

'That tall dude's name was Chewie?' said Rebekah. 'That's hilarious.'

'Frankly,' Gideon said, 'and thanks to Rebekah's intel, we knew Thomas was coming for you, so we didn't have time for politeness. We had to be quick and clinical, for which I apologise.'

'And then,' said Rebekah, 'there was the whole gunfight-in-the-street thing.' She tapped Cain on the shoulder. 'By the way, you owe me a new jacket, Silent Bob.'

'Watch out!' Ellie suddenly shouted.

As they approached a junction, the traffic light facing them was red. He ignored her warning and floored the accelerator. The Bentley surged forward and sped through the red light, narrowly missing a car coming from the left. Its driver blared its horn.

'Are you crazy?' shouted Jakob. 'Jesus fucking Christ!'

Cain whirled and grinned, then returned his attention to the road.

'You think that's funny? You could've killed us and whoever was in that car.'

Cain grunted.

'Hey,' Ellie said, poking his shoulder.

'He doesn't talk,' said Rebekah.

'What?'

'No tongue. Seth took it in a fit of sibling rivalry.'

'Seth's his brother?'

'Yeah. Seth killed their father. And then he killed Abel. When Cain—'

'Wait,' Jakob said. 'Cain and Abel? Not *the*—'

'*The* Cain and Abel, yeah. Crazy, right? Seth's their younger brother.'

'Seth said his mother was a fallen angel. That means Eve—'

'Was that angel, yes,' Rebekah said. 'She was their mother, and Adam was their human father.'

'Holy shit,' said Ellie. 'So, the story of the serpent in the garden—'

'Was bullshit. Casting Eve as the original sinner—a *human* sinner—was payback for her siding with Sammael and taking a human husband. And Cain was cast as Abel's killer.'

'Wow.'

'Yeah. The Elyonim like to tell it their way to make the story sound better. And it was... look; there's a lot you still don't know, and you need to hear the big stuff first. Then, if you want, we can come back to this. Besides, I'm thinking maybe Cain can tell you himself when, you know, he's not busy driving you to safety.'

'I thought you said he can't talk,' Jakob said.

'He's a telepath. A *pusher* and a *reader*.'

'Of course he is.'

'So, why didn't his tongue grow back?' Ellie asked. 'I thought you guys heal.'

'We heal in the same way humans do,' said Gideon. 'In all but the most extreme cases, your broken bones mend, and your cuts heal, even if they leave scars. With us, the process is quicker, and there's usually less lasting damage for all but the most severe injury, as in my case. But you can't regrow a limb or a finger or a tongue, and nor can we.'

Cain ran another red light at the junction with Cannon Street and accelerated hard for roughly a hundred metres, and as he swung the big car through a sharp left onto Queen Street, Gideon turned back to the others.

'We're going to be stopping two about hundred yards from where we need to be. I have no idea how close Thomas or any of his people might be, but we don't want to get caught out in the open, so you'll need to run fast.'

There were nods of assent from the back seat.

Cain skidded the Bentley to a swerving stop halfway up Queen Street. As he unlocked all the doors, Gideon unbuckled his seat belt, opened his door, and issued his instruction without looking back.

'Move fast.'

54

As Thomas reached the cathedral's car park, he clicked the key fob he'd taken from his dead driver. The indicators flashed on the furthest Range Rover, and its horn chirped. He strode over to it, Seth close behind him. As he reached the car's front bumper, he saw the front tyre was flat. Then he noticed the rear tyre had also deflated. And then he saw the bullet holes.

'Damn it!'

Seth pointed to the tyres on the adjacent car. They had also been shot.

'Clever fucks,' he said.

'We don't have time for this crap.'

'Nor do we have time for calling in another car. We need to change out those wheels. You grab the spares from each car, and I'll get the nuts off.'

Thomas went to the rear of their car, opened the boot, and removed the spare wheel and a cross-shaped wheel brace, which he tossed to Seth. Then he went to the boot of the other car and tried the handle. It was locked. He pulled harder but ripped the handle mounting from the metal instead of opening the boot.

'Fuck!'

He punched down on the car's rear bumper, detaching it, then wedged the fingers of both hands under the lip of the boot and heaved it toward him with a grunt. The locking mechanism snapped with a metallic clang, and the boot opened. He quickly grabbed the spare wheel, dragged it out, and placed it on the ground beside their car's rear wheel.

'Okay, let's get this fucker jacked-up,' Seth said, taking the last nut off the back wheel.

He went to the middle of their car, crouched down with his back against it, and grabbed its underside with both hands. Then, with a groan, he stood up, the strain of lifting the two-and-a-half-tonne vehicle barely showing on his face.

With the car tilted on two wheels, Thomas slid the unbolted wheels off and replaced them with the spares. Once they were on, he quickly reattached the wheel nuts with his fingers. When they were all on and tight enough to keep the wheels in place, Seth lowered the car to the ground, and Thomas gave all the wheel nuts a final twist with the wheel brace.

He tossed the keys to Seth, went around the front, and got into the front passenger seat, then checked the tracking application on his phone again. Seth climbed in and started the engine.

'They've stopped.'

'Where?'

He showed his phone to Seth, who looked at the screen and huffed, then he thumbed the phone's screen again, brought up his contacts list, scrolled to the entry he wanted, and pressed it. The call connected on the first ring.

'*Logistics.*'

'Jäger, Thomas. RIG.'

'*Identification code, please.*'

'Tango kilo four two one.'

'*Identity confirmed. How can I assist you?*'

'Can you remotely access the device I'm calling you on?'

'*Yes, sir.*'

'I need you to access the London traffic camera system and run a facial recognition scan of the photos I'm about to pull up.'

He took the phone away from his ear, brought up the photograph library, and then selected pictures of Ellie and Jakob he'd taken on the flight from Copenhagen while they'd been asleep. He waited a few seconds to give the operator time to transfer the photographs to her system, then returned the phone to his face.

'You get those?'

'Yes. Are you able to narrow the search area?'

'Within five hundred metres of the junction of Cheapside and Queen Street.'

'Timeframe?'

'The last ten minutes.'

'Understood. Hold on.'

The operator went silent, and Thomas heard the tapping of computer keys through the phone. The Vatican had no ongoing connection to the city's numerous camera systems, nor was it authorised to use them without a lengthy process of obtaining consent. The operator would need to break her way in with a brute force hack, a dictionary attack, or whatever the hell the crypto specialists used these days. He wasn't surprised, though, that she hadn't baulked at either the legal implications or technical difficulty of his request. The people the Elyonim used were the best at what they did—even if most were human.

After a few more moments of silence, however, he grew impatient.

'Is this going—'

'I have one of the targets. The woman. A camera at the intersection above Bank tube station caught her going into a building on Poultry. Number eighteen.'

'I need two tactical units prepped for full assault at that location.'

'Timing?'

'Immediate.'

'We can have personnel on station in... nineteen minutes.'

He sighed, knowing there'd be no point in demanding a quicker response time. The tactical units were experts in rapid response and could deploy within minutes, but they could do little to overcome the traffic between their destination and their base near Regent's Park.

'Understood,' he said. 'Be advised that their vehicles must park at least fifty metres from the building. I do not want anyone in that building alerted to the team's presence. Is that clear?'

'*Affirmative.*'

'And I want an exfil chopper standing ready at ground level.'

'*One moment.*'

More tapping of keys.

'*There's a Blackhawk available at City Airport, but—*'

'But what?'

'*It's the Square Mile. Landing anywhere in that area will be practically impossible.*'

'What's the closest clear area large enough to land a chopper on?'

'*There's a bowling lawn in Finsbury Circus, roughly a three-minute drive to the north.*'

'Not good enough.'

'*The only space large enough to accommodate a landing any closer than that would be the junction above Bank Station, but that's right in the—*'

'Perfect. Get it done.'

'*Sir—*'

Thomas disconnected the call and put the phone away.

'So?' asked Seth.

'Twenty minutes, give or take.'

55

Ninety metres west of the junction above Bank underground station was the front door of an imposing Grade I listed building that used to house the headquarters of Midland Bank, once the largest deposit bank in the world. The building was gradually vacated after HSBC acquired Midland in 1992. It stayed empty for eight years until it was purchased in 2012 by a high-end leisure operator, converted into a five-star hotel, and renamed The Bank. The leisure business was one of many legitimate enterprises owned by the Sicarii.

The hotel had two hundred guest bedrooms, five meeting rooms, a gym with an indoor training pool, a spa, and six restaurants. One of them, named The Vault, sat behind a large, circular, twenty-tonne steel door in the basement.

The two uppermost floors and the roof were off-limits to hotel guests and staff alike. On the lowest of these were thirty-two luxury suites. On one half of the next floor were administrative offices, a conference room, and meeting rooms. On the other half were two lounge bars, a restaurant, a small cinema, and a gym. And on the roof were two small bars, a restaurant, and a heated open-air swimming pool. While accessible via the hotel's elevators, entry to those floors was restricted exclusively to employees and associates of the Sicarii.

The conference room was dimly lit by tiny LED bulbs embedded into the ceiling, giving off a warm white glow. Ellie sat on a comfortable leather-clad swivel chair at a long, dark wood table, in the middle of which was a frosted crystal pitcher of water and six matching glasses. She could tell that every fixture, fitting, and piece of furniture was expensive.

Jakob sat to her right. Cain and Rebekah sat on the other side of the table. Gideon's chair, directly opposite hers, was empty. He was standing at a waist-height cabinet against the wall facing her, his back to the room. He and Cain had removed their shoulder holsters and placed them on the cabinet, and he was now clattering with something she couldn't see.

On the wall directly to her left was a gigantic ultra-thin television screen, which was on and showed the top of an empty chair, similar in style to the one she sat in, in a room more brightly lit than theirs. She reached for the pitcher, filled a glass, and took a long gulp. The water had a hint of lemon taste to it.

Gideon walked to the table with a silver tray carrying five tumblers and a crystal decanter containing a dark amber liquid. He'd already poured measures of the drink into the glasses.

'You're going to need these,' he said, putting the tray next to the water jug.

Jakob immediately took one of the tumblers and downed its contents in a single gulp. He pulled a face and held out his glass to Gideon, who smirked and poured him another measure.

'That's a seventy-year-old Glen Grant,' he said, taking his seat. 'Not some cheap tequila. You might want to take it easy with that.'

'Why? I'm not paying for it.'

'Jakob,' Ellie murmured.

She could understand his fractious attitude. It had already been a long, incredibly shitty day, which didn't look like ending soon. She reached for the tumbler nearest to her and took a sip. The whisky warmed her lips and burned as it went down. As she placed the glass on the table, movement on the television attracted her attention. She looked at the screen, and her breath caught in her throat. In front of her, wearing a navy suit and a dark blue shirt, was a forty-something man with salt and pepper hair and tanned skin.

'Shimon?' she asked.

The man's face lit up with a smile.

'I haven't heard that name in a very long time,' he said. 'I go by Simon these days.'

'Wait,' said Jakob. '*The* Shimon? From your dreams?'

She nodded, dumbfounded.

'How is this possible?' she asked.

'He's like us,' said Rebekah.

'Thank you, Rebekah,' Simon said. 'Incidentally, it's nice that you could join us.'

Ellie noted his sarcasm and detected a hint of irritation in his voice, no doubt because Rebekah, now looking sheepishly back at him, had broken her cover.

'I didn't have much choice, Simon. I—'

'She did the right thing, Simon,' Gideon said. 'After I'd put down two of their people, we were still outgunned two-to-one, even without her engaging us as one of them, misleadingly or otherwise. If Cain and I had been killed or incapacitated, Peter would have abducted Ellie and possibly Jakob, and there's no guarantee he would've kept her in the loop after that as to their whereabouts. He may even have executed them right there. Rebekah blowing her cover created some confusion and gave us a tactical advantage. Yes, she's burned now, and we're a Messenger down in their ranks, and that may have worse implications in the long term, especially for the others still embedded with them or elsewhere. But, in my opinion, she was correct in her assessment that our need to secure Ellie's safety was of greater importance at that moment.'

Simon looked thoughtfully through the screen momentarily and then nodded, accepting the explanation. Rebekah visibly relaxed.

'Are you a Nephilim or an angel?' Ellie asked him, hoping to ease the tension. 'Or something else?'

'An archangel. One of the first. My true name is Azazel, although using that in public tends to draw unwanted attention, hence Shimon and now Simon.

'And you're in charge of the Sicarii?'

'I am. For the last two millennia, in addition to having overseen its general operations, I have commanded it in its mission to protect Sammael's bloodline.'

'Which now includes me,' she said, barely more than whispering.

'It's not as bad as you think, Ellie.'

She gazed at him through the screen. She had memories of this man. Good memories, it seemed. This was a man she felt she ought to trust. Inhaling deeply, she decided to do that.

'Peter told me about the whole memory inheritance thing,' she said, 'but he didn't explain why they've surfaced.'

'Most inherited memories, particularly those from generations ago, stay well-buried. Only the most traumatic or otherwise significant memories surface, but even then, it's usually only fleetingly. I've heard the phone conversation between the priest in Copenhagen and the bishop over there in London, so I'm aware of the nature and content of some of your dreams. For a person to experience memories with the force, vividness, and regularity you have is uncommon. And to be perfectly transparent with you, I'm not sure I understand why this is happening now, or in the way that it is, other than, and you'll forgive my poeticism, it's simply because within you shines the light of the Morning Star.'

'The what?' asked Jakob.

'I'm a descendant of Sammael,' she said, recognising the reference to one of the angel's many other names.

'Right,' he said quietly.

'One, potentially, of many others we hope to find,' Simon said.

'You said the Sicarii's job is to protect the bloodline,' she said, 'but Thomas said you're just a bunch of assassins who do the Grigori's dirty work. Peter even referred to Judas as Yehuda Sicarii, so I'm guessing he was an assassin too, right?'

'Once again, more half-truths. The Sicarii were originally a group of Jewish extremists who ideologically and physically opposed Rome's invasion of Judea. They were also against Christ's teachings, claiming he was perverting the core ideologies of Judaism. The Romans named them after the Latin word for dagger-men because of the small knives they concealed beneath their cloaks called sicae, and yes, they were assassins.

'But, as you're probably starting to appreciate, not everything in the Bible is as it truly was. We were never affiliated with the Sicarii while Judas was alive, but what better way to reinforce the image of him as a betrayer than to cast him as Yehuda Sicarii, a reformed mercenary and assassin who, as it would turn out, never reformed at all?'

'I guess so,' she agreed.

'Judas was my closest friend, and when Christ executed him, I wanted revenge. There weren't many of our kind in Jerusalem I could call allies, and I needed numbers, so I joined the Sicarii and, thanks to my abilities, quickly took over. I intended to strike out as hard as I could. I didn't care that the Sicarii were all human or that most if not all of them would likely die for a cause not their own. In fact, their hatred of Christ and his ministry made it easier for me to deal with.

'Before we could attack, we learned that Christ's people had somehow discovered Marta's pregnancy. So, I took her across the Mediterranean to southern Europe to give birth safely, and I took most of the Sicarii with me to protect her child. The child grew and had children of her own. As the bloodline flourished, I recruited Nephilim, Anakim, and my kind into the ranks.'

He paused, and Ellie wondered whether retelling this story was hard for him, even now. She supposed the pain of losing your best friend, much like losing a family member, dulled but never truly disappeared, and talking about Judas could only bring the grief back to the surface.

'The human Sicarii that remained in Jerusalem,' he continued, 'carried on against the Romans for a while but eventually disbanded and were consigned to the history books. Our organisation, however, has grown in relative secrecy, and keeping the bloodline safe remains its core purpose. It has been necessary for our people to kill in carrying out that duty, and no doubt that will continue to be the case, and if that makes us assassins, so be it. But we're not mercenaries, and we rarely kill for the sake of it. We take lives only to defend our own and those we protect.'

'So, how come no one knew about me?' she asked.

Gideon exhaled heavily.

'Because we lost a branch of the bloodline in the eighth century,' Simon said. 'And despite our best efforts, we've been unable to recover any of its members since then. Until you.'

'You lost the bloodline?'

'Not all of it. Three children. Siblings.'

'How did you lose them?'

'They were travelling in southern France. A caravan of four wagons. They were attacked, and their Sicarii escorts sought refuge in a monastery. Regrettably, they weren't safe even within the compound's walls.'

'A monastery? I thought you guys were anti-church.'

'Fundamentally, we are, but those with the children would've put their safety above all else.'

Ellie realised that Gideon was staring into his whisky. He seemed unhappy. Or perhaps it was something else. Guilt? Shame, maybe? Had he been escorting the children and failed to protect them?

'You were involved,' she said to him, feeling tears begin to well. 'That's why you were so full-on in Copenhagen. This is personal for you. You're trying to put it right.'

He nodded.

'I was meant to escort the caravan, but I was called away temporarily. By the time I caught up, the monastery was a smouldering wreck, the children were gone, and the Sicarii escorts—all but one of whom were human—were dead.'

'The Elyonim?' Jakob asked.

'I thought so when I arrived. Those days, they masqueraded as Charlemagne's paladins and could've demanded the monastery open its gates, which the abbot would've done without argument. But the Elyonim would've decapitated all four escorts to be sure they were dead. When I found the bodies, three were intact. Only one of them—a Nephilim named Saul—was headless. I found a young monk buried under some rubble, barely alive. He told me that bandits had been chasing the caravan. They attacked the monastery, took the children, and killed everyone else.

'No one travelled with four wagons unless they had money, so the bandits must've thought it a prize worth the effort. They wouldn't have known who or what the children were, but all children in those days were commodities, so we suspect they took them to put to work or sell into slavery. My guess is that Saul wouldn't stay down, and the bandits took his head because they were out of other options.'

Ellie burst into tears.

Jakob placed his hand over hers.

'It wasn't Gideon's fault,' said Simon. 'It was mine. I'd called him away. Yet he still blames himself. And if the Elyonim *had* been responsible, the children would either have been killed or kept, which means Ellie would either not exist or would've grown up within their ranks. So, we're thankful for small mercies.'

'If it was that long ago,' Jakob said, 'there could be hundreds like her around now. Possibly even thousands.'

A pained smile crossed Simon's face.

'Yes,' he said. 'All of whom we're desperate to find and protect, but until we do, there's always a risk of their discovery and capture by the Elyonim. We'll stop at nothing to ensure their safety, which is why Gideon and Cain had to act quickly and, regretfully, so aggressively in

Copenhagen.'

Ellie sniffed, wiped her face, and nodded. She now understood.

'And which is why we need to move quickly now,' Simon continued. 'Before I provide you with answers to the many more questions I know you must still have, I need to know everything. What you've seen in your dreams and what Peter and his sycophants have told you.'

'There's a lot to go through.'

'Pictures tell a thousand words.'

'Huh?'

'I want to see, Ellie, not hear.'

'Oh, right,' she said, realising what he meant.

'There's no lasting damage from the mind thing, right?' Jakob asked, coming to the same realisation. 'Peter went inside her head earlier.'

'None at all, but it can be a little nauseating. Try to relax, Ellie, and open your mind.'

'You're going to do it from there?' she asked. 'Through Skype? Is that possible? Peter had to touch my head. It was all very Vulcan mind-meld.'

'Peter's always had a taste for theatrics. All that's required is a line of sight.'

She closed her eyes, inhaled deeply, then opened them and signalled her readiness with a single nod. Simon's expression changed to one of focus, and she saw the colour of his irises ripple from the colour of chocolate to bright gold. She was instantly mesmerised, even before he began delving into her mind.

The pressure inside her head was instantaneous. This time, though, it seemed gentler and less invasive than when Peter had read her thoughts as if Simon were taking care not to probe too forcefully. Her mind, though, remained blank.

'Is this going to work? I'm not—'

Her body stiffened as if an unseen force had gripped her, and she felt paralysed. Images came at her as if she were on one of those virtual helicopter rides through nature where trees, mountains, and waterfalls rush at you from screens on all sides, inches from the cabin, making you think you'll crash at any moment.

Only, this wasn't trees and mountains and waterfalls.

This was her entire life.

Everything she'd ever seen or done, and things she hadn't, but which she somehow now remembered, flooded her consciousness. Her memories intertwined with those of other people who were clearly from different periods in the past. Visions of battles and great wars became those of boyfriends and getting her first tattoo. Images of her parents and grandparents merged with one of a mother holding an infant in a darkened, cave-like room. A replay of her mugging melted into Judas's abduction and execution.

And more.

So much more.

Too much to comprehend.

And then it was over as suddenly as it had ended when Peter had been inside her mind. But now, she felt more at peace than she had in months. She felt like she'd been cleansed from the inside out. She kept her eyes closed, knowing what awaited her—expectant faces, just like before, wanting to know what she'd seen and what answers she could give them.

She wasn't sure she had any to give.

She composed herself, opened her eyes, and reached for her whisky. She downed what was left in a single gulp and put the tumbler back on the table. With a wry smile, Cain refilled it for her, and she swallowed the entire measure.

'That was... intense,' she said.

Rebekah and Cain both chuckled. Gideon's face didn't give much away, but she thought she saw something in his eyes. Relief, maybe?

'Well?' Jakob asked Simon, taking her hand. 'Did you get what you needed?'

Simon frowned and nodded slowly. It didn't seem like his expression was one of anger but rather one of puzzlement as if he were thinking something over.

'I did,' he said. 'It was… enlightening.'

'So, is this the part where you say, 'Surprise!', throw up jazz hands and tell us that you're really, and always have been, the bad guys, and fuck-us-very-much for giving you whatever it is you needed to win Armageddon or take over the world or something?'

'No, Jakob, it's not. It's where we correct the lies Peter and his people have told you. It's where you learn the truth.'

'About what?' Ellie asked.

'Everything.'

56

As they turned onto Queen Street, Thomas saw Peter's abandoned Bentley parked haphazardly halfway up the street. They drove past it and turned east onto Cheapside, and he immediately spotted a black Mercedes panel van ahead of them in a side street, one building between it and The Bank, its rear doors facing the street.

He grinned.

The assault teams had arrived earlier than anticipated, which was a good sign. As he'd instructed, the van was parked far enough from the hotel to remain undetected by the building's curb-side security staff and its external CCTV cameras. There was no sight or sound yet of the helicopter he'd ordered, but that wasn't necessarily a bad thing. The noise of a chopper would only alert The Bank's occupants to their presence—something that would inevitably happen but better to be done later rather than sooner.

Seth pulled the Range Rover into the side street and parked a few metres in front of the van. He applied the parking brake but kept the engine running. As both men opened their doors and climbed out, the front passenger door of the van opened, and a tall, bearded man wearing black assault gear stepped out. A squat-looking assault rifle hung on its sling across his torso, which Thomas recognised as the RIG's standard issue American-made Bushmaster Carbon 15 SBR. The man's backup weapon was a semiautomatic pistol carried in a quick-draw holster on his right hip.

'Sergeant Major Harris,' he said, neither saluting nor offering a hand for shaking.

'Sergeant Major, my name is Thomas. This is Seth. You now report to me.'

Harris nodded curtly.

'What are we dealing with?' he asked.

'Is your phone set to receive data?'

Harris lifted his right forearm. Attached to it, under a protective plastic sheath, was his phone. He tapped a gloved finger on the plastic, then typed a six-digit passcode on the device's screen to unlock it, the protective pocket and his tactical helmet rendering the phone's facial recognition software useless. He navigated to its settings list when the phone unlocked and tapped again.

'It is now.'

Thomas pulled out his phone and unlocked it, then pulled up the photograph of Ellie he'd provided to the logistics operator earlier and touched his phone against Harris's.

'She's your target. She's likely to be on an upper floor, and she's to be captured alive and unharmed. Anyone who tries to prevent you from acquiring her is expendable. Is that understood?'

Harris looked at the screen on his phone as the photo appeared.

'Yes.'

He was impressed that Harris had neither asked for further details nor flinched at the instruction that he could freely kill anyone but Ellie. Such was the power of being under the orders and protection of the Vatican and, ultimately, the Elyonim.

'How many people do you have?'

'Eighteen. Nine here, including myself, and nine in a van parked on Princes Street, one building away from the hotel on the other side. All prepped and awaiting your green light.'

'Let's get 'em out, shall we? But maintain a discreet position for now. I don't want to alert those door guards until absolutely necessary.'

Harris pushed a black button clipped to his armoured vest and ordered his teams to dismount, the order transmitting through a tactical microphone he wore around his throat. The van's front and sliding side doors opened and within seconds, eight people, all dressed identically to him, stood in the side street. Like him, their goggles were raised, but unlike him, balaclavas covered the lower halves of their faces. He tapped his phone's screen a few times, thumbed the button on his chest again, and addressed the team.

'This is your target. Her name is—'

He looked at Thomas, who said, 'Ellie Hansen.'

'Ellie Hansen. She is to be unharmed. Weapons-free on all other parties who offer resistance.'

When he released his intercom button, Thomas pointed down the street.

'We've ordered a Blackhawk for extraction, which will land on the junction above Bank station. Once that's here, we're good to go.'

Seth pulled out his phone, unlocked it, and moved his thumb and forefinger on its screen.

'Do you carry RGR gear?' he asked Harris, using their shortcode for a rapid ground-to-roof assault.

'In the van parked on the other side of the hotel.'

'I'll take four men from that team and go in from the roof. It looks like a leisure deck or something, so we should be able to access the building from there.' He turned his phone and showed Harris a zoomed Google Maps satellite image. 'There's a loading dock on that side of the hotel and what look like stepped levels up to the roof, which should make the ascent easier and keep us out of sight.'

Harris thumbed his mike button again and called out four names.

'You four,' he said,' will be joining a very large man called Seth on a climb up the side of the hotel. You report directly to him until he cedes command back to me. Prep your grapnels and ascenders and stand by.'

'You'd best drive over,' Thomas said. 'No point in giving the game away by getting picked up by their cameras or spotted by someone who recognises you.'

'I'd say the big loud helicopter will probably do that, but what the fuck do I know?'

'True, but we'll all be inside before they have time to get their shit together.' He turned to Harris and motioned to his assault rifle. 'You have a spare couple of those, about twenty mags, and some mikes?'

'Baby,' Harris said, pressing his intercom button, 'bring me a couple of fifteens, as many spare mag belts as we have, and two tac-com rigs, would you?'

Baby was six-foot-six and as wide as the average doorway. He went to the van and returned with the weapons, four ammunition belts, and two throat mikes wired to digital radio handsets. He silently handed them over to Harris, who gave Thomas and Seth the throat mikes and radios first, and waited for them to clip the gear to their belts and necks before passing over the weapons and ammunition.

Thomas pulled the slide of his rifle a few times to ensure the chamber was clear, then released the magazine, checked it was loaded, replaced it, and slung the rifle across his chest. Then, he quickly checked every magazine in his two ammunition belts to ensure they were also full. While these operators were professionals, he preferred to trust his own eyes rather than make assumptions. Seth mirrored his movements.

'We'll hold back until you're in position on the roof,' he told Seth. 'As soon as you're up there, let me know.'

Seth climbed back into the Range Rover and slowly backed his way out of the side street. The driver of another car blared their horn when he reversed onto Cheapside. He waved the driver around him and then disappeared from view.

Thomas pulled out his cigarettes and his lighter. He lit up, took a long, deep pull, and offered the pack to Harris, who declined.

'That shit'll kill you.'

'Says the man about to walk into a shitstorm of bullets and blades.'

Harris looked thoughtful for a moment and then took a cigarette. 'Thought so,' said Thomas.

57

Ellie watched Simon on the television screen and waited expectantly for the answers he'd promised her. She felt her focus drift, not for the first time since she'd arrived in the conference room. Despite her head feeling clearer, it still felt like a lead weight on her shoulders, and she could barely keep her eyes open. She was drifting off at the wheel, but Simon's voice drew her back like the horn of a juggernaut coming at her from the other direction.

'Truth is almost always the basis of the greatest lies,' he said, 'so, unsurprisingly, much of what you already know is accurate. Many angels did become disenchanted with their lives on Earth and the roles God gave them. They saw humans as weak and unimportant. The lie, or rather the most significant one, is that Sammael rebelled. He was God's firstborn. A seraph. A Burning One. He was the brightest of all of us. He was the first to volunteer to come here and was granted leadership of all God's angels on Earth in return. He was firm but fair and, for many millennia, a well-loved leader of the angels and had nothing but respect for humans and our role in guiding them.'

'So, what *did* happen?' she asked, reaching for her glass of water, her throat becoming dry again.

'Sammael's younger brother, Michael.'

'The archangel?'

'A venomous snake and the worst kind of traitor,' Gideon said.

She saw his eyes briefly burn amber when he said the word *snake*.

They changed back to their usual hue before she could blink.

'Michael, like many others, grew to believe that angels were superior to humans,' Simon continued. 'Physiologically speaking, of course, he was correct. We are stronger, faster, have abilities humans don't, and we're immortal. He became disillusioned with the notion of spending an eternity in servitude to lower beings, even though he, like the rest of us, had volunteered to come here.'

'And that was a bad thing, why?' Jakob asked.

'Because he wanted to take the forbidden fruit and ram it down humankind's throat,' said Gideon.

'It was never God's desire to be known of,' Rebekah said. 'Humans were meant to draw their own conclusions about their place in the universe. To have the freedom to believe what was right for them. We were forbidden from speaking about God or our own celestial origins. We had to appear as normal people who showed wisdom and had flashes of inspiration that helped the people around us.

'Now, pulling off normal ain't easy when you're immortal, as we can't hide that we don't age as humans do, but it worked. Mostly. But Michael became consumed by the idea that humans should learn of us, their creator, and their proper place in the universe—serving us. So, he went to Sammael with it, who was less than impressed and forbade him from doing anything.'

'So, Michael ignored his order and the rebellion kicked off,' Jakob said, shifting in his seat.

'No. It took about three thousand years for Michael to get the balls to stand up to him properly. Three millennia and the persuasion of almost eighty-five per cent of the angels on Earth.'

'Michael summoned Sammael to his stronghold at Har Megiddo,' Simon said, 'to discuss what he called an aligned future. He agreed to the meeting and took some of us with him for company, moral support, and security.'

'Not the six thousand warriors that Thomas said he had,' said

Rebekah.

'When we arrived at Har Megiddo,' Simon continued, 'Michael was sitting in a tent half a mile outside the city walls with his army on display. We went into the tent, and he laid out his grand plan. He had enough support and geographic reach by then that Sammael couldn't stop him. We were only there so Michael could gloat and see the look of defeat in his eyes.'

'How did Michael convince so many to join him?' Ellie asked.

'The promise of power and wealth,' said Rebekah. 'We have free will, remember. And we're not infallible nor incorruptible. It was too tempting for them.'

Gideon stood up and refilled everyone's whisky tumblers.

'So, Sammael didn't fall? He wasn't one of... what did Thomas call them? The Grigori?'

'No, Ellie, he never fell,' Rebekah replied. 'He stood fast.'

Ellie had been suffocating under the weight of the revelation that she carried the blood of what almost the entire world considered a being of pure evil. Suddenly, though, she could breathe again.

'But he *was* a Grigori,' Simon said. 'We all were in the beginning. Every angel who came here. It simply meant Watchers, as that was our primary purpose. To watch and, when necessary, to teach. But after the revolt, Michael and his allies used the term Watchers as a slur because, in their eyes, all we could do was watch them carry out their crusade, powerless to fight against them. So, they called us the Watchers—Grigori if they wanted to insult us, although I've never been sure how that's an insult—and they called themselves the Elyonim.'

'I'm guessing that doesn't mean anything good,' said Jakob.

'Its literal translation is The Upper Ones,' Gideon replied.

'Sounds like angel-speak for Master Race.'

'Indeed.'

'And you guys?' Ellie asked him. 'Thomas said the Nephilim and Anakim were some kind of revenge act by the Grigori—a big fuck-you to God because angels weren't allowed to reproduce.'

'Again, more half-truths. God didn't condone angels breeding with humans, but never forbade it either.'

'That's quite the grey area,' Jakob said.

This raised chuckles from the others around the table and even from Simon.

'And what about the prophecy of Armageddon?' she asked.

'What's in the scriptures is not, strictly speaking, a prophecy,' Simon said. 'It's more of an open threat against the Grigori, making it clear that, regardless of who starts the war, Michael will ensure countless human lives will be lost as collateral damage.'

'But clearly, that hasn't happened.'

'Yet,' Gideon replied.

For a few seconds, the room was silent, the enormity of that single word sinking in.

'So, how come you were with the Elyonim?' she asked Rebekah.

'Every army needs good intel.'

'How long were you with them?'

'Eight thousand and something years. Since Michael first went to Sammael with his idea for domination.'

'Eight thousand years?'

'When Sammael forbade Michael from acting on his desire for dominion over humans, he knew it was unlikely he would obey his orders. So, he asked some of us to volunteer for spy duty. What Michael had suggested went against our entire reason for being here and was a huge middle finger to the being that gave us life. Plus, I never liked him. He was such a self-important asshole. I was happy to do it.'

'How did you keep it secret?' Jakob asked. 'They can read minds, for fuck's sake. You didn't slip even once?'

'Rebekah is one of the most powerful, most skilled angels I've ever known,' Simon said with a look of pride. 'She belongs to the angelic order of Cherubs. She and others who do what she's done are the best of us.'

Rebekah grinned widely and winked at him.

'And often the most infantile, unruly, and disobedient,' he said. The trace of a smile edged onto the corners of his mouth and his eyes.

Now Ellie grinned.

'And Michael was so arrogant back then,' Rebekah continued, 'that he didn't even consider he might have a mole problem. So, once I was in, I was in. Not being found out was easy. The hard part was just being around those assholes, listening to their bullshit about Sammael, and going along with their crap. And, of course, having to fight my friends and colleagues and not kill them.'

'Okay, so can we finally deal with the elephant in the room?' Jakob asked. 'Why exactly do they want Ellie?'

'Either they want to exploit her abilities,' Gideon said, 'which I can't think would be worth their time, given how diluted her angelic blood will be, or they want her as a bargaining chip, or...'

He didn't need to finish his sentence. It was plain to Ellie that there could be only one reason the Elyonim came for her.

They wanted her dead.

At that moment, there was a roar overhead as if thousands of birds had flown by outside. Cain stood and walked to the window behind her, which, like the others, was covered by blackout blinds. He fingered a blind open a couple of inches and peered out, then looked up and down, scanned left and right, let the blind fall back into place, and returned to his seat. Gideon gave him a look, and he shrugged and shook his head.

'Okay, so why didn't God just wipe out Michael and the rest of the rogue angels?' asked Jakob.

'Because God believes in free will,' Rebekah said. 'And in not taking lives. How could It destroy the things It created and loved, even if they had rebelled?'

'Yet we have war, starvation, drought, and disease on a global scale, and God does nothing about any of those things.'

'It's one thing to allow such things passively, Jakob,' Simon said, 'and I admit it may appear cruel to do so, but it's another thing entirely to extinguish a life, especially one you've created.'

Ellie considered that, but she wasn't sure she understood or agreed with it. Allowing people to die when you have the power to stop it was as bad as killing them yourself, wasn't it?

'So, everything we've been taught about Lucifer. About Sammael. It's all—'

'Propaganda,' Simon replied. 'Fabricated by the Elyonim to further their campaign for power over humans.'

'History's written by the winners, right?' Rebekah remarked.

'If Michael hated Sammael that much, he would've wanted to make sure nothing of Sammael survived,' Ellie said. 'No wonder they want me dead.'

Nobody spoke. She wondered what would have happened to her if Gideon and Cain hadn't saved her back in the cathedral. Suddenly, she couldn't breathe. As if sensing this, Jakob took her hand, and she gulped in a lungful of air.

'What I don't get,' he said, 'is if Christ was God's son on Earth, why did he surround himself with the Elyonim, and why did he execute Judas, the son of God's most loyal angel?'

'Because, Jakob,'said Simon. '*Michael* was Christ.'

'What?'

'When you come to Chicago, you'll learn everything—about the Fall, and Sammael, and Michael and his quest for power. Right now, you don't have the time.'

'Chicago? We can't go to Chicago.'

'Well, you certainly can't go home, Jakob. And you're probably not safe where you are now.'

'But—'

Ellie laid her hand on his arm, and he fell silent.

'Okay, so what did you see when you walked around my mind?' she asked. 'Is it true? Am I the descendant of Sammael you all think I am? Do I shine with the light of the Morning Star?'

'Ellie, I'm—'

Suddenly, the conference room door burst open. A blonde woman in a dark business suit stood in the doorway.

'What is it?' Gideon asked.

'We've just had a report from the security desk downstairs. A large, heavily armed force has just stormed the lobby.'

'Fuck!' Rebekah said.

'It's them,' said Simon. He stared out from the screen at Gideon. 'Please tell me you have a contingency in place for this.'

Gideon nodded, then stood up and looked at the faces around the table. His irises glowed like fire.

'Let's go,' he said.

58

Ellie heard gunfire from somewhere below. Most people go their whole lives without seeing a gun in real life, let alone being in a gunfight. But, if they got caught up in whatever was happening elsewhere in the building, which was entirely probable, this would be her second or third in one day. Or fourth? She'd already lost count and found it challenging to keep it together.

Her mind was a mess of racing thoughts. Despite everything Simon and the others had said and all the supernatural things she'd seen in the past few hours, it felt like an unbelievable dream she would eventually wake up from or a virtual reality from which she could unplug herself.

More gunfire brought her back into focus. It was louder than before. Closer. The invaders were making their way up to them, and quickly. Jakob clamped his hand around her wrist, hauled her out of her chair, and headed toward the door where Gideon, having already slung on his shoulder holster, stood with his pistol drawn. Cain had grabbed his weapons rig and had already left the room. Rebekah took up the rear.

'Jesus, Jakob, that hurts,' Ellie said.

'Sorry, babes, but there's no way I'm going to let them get their hands on you again.'

The building shook with a loud boom on a lower floor. A large picture fell off the wall. Not gunfire, she thought. An explosion. What the hell was going on down there? A moment later, the building's fire alarm system activated. The siren emitted a piercing, high-pitched, dual-tone noise that immediately nauseated her, and strobe lights in the corridors alternated between a three-flash burst and a one-second pause. Luckily, the ceiling-mounted sprinkler system hadn't yet kicked in.

Jakob looked at Gideon.

'I don't suppose you have a spare gun, do you?' he shouted.

'Jakob!' Ellie said.

'Do you know how to use one?' Gideon yelled back.

'Point and shoot, right?'

Gideon huffed.

'Right, but—'

'Oh shit,' someone shouted.

It was the blonde woman who'd alerted them to the attack. She stood motionless, staring toward the end of the wide hallway beyond the open-plan waiting area outside the conference room. There was the sound of a single gunshot, and her head snapped back. She fell to the ground without so much as a whimper.

Ellie peered around Gideon and saw what looked like a SWAT team member half-crouched by the open doorway of an emergency stairwell ten metres away. Using the doorway as cover, the shooter swung his shoulders and aimed toward them, but before he could get a shot off, the left eyepiece of his goggles shattered. Blood and shards of clear polycarbonate poured out of the goggles' frame, and he fell backward into the stairwell.

She heard swift, heavy footsteps approaching them from a hallway opposite the stairwell. It was Cain. He frowned at Gideon, who nodded.

'What was that?' she asked. 'What did he tell you?'

He ignored the question and handed his gun to Jakob, then drew his second pistol and picked up his sword from the cabinet against the wall.

'Take your time with it,' he said. 'Squeeze the trigger, don't mash it. And for fuck's sake, don't shoot any of us.'

'I'm not an idiot.'

'Let's hope not.' He looked at the others. 'Let's get to the roof.'

'What?' Ellie asked. 'What are we going to do up there? Have a party? We'll be trapped up there. We need to go down.'

'Ellie, they're making their way here, floor by floor. No doubt they'll also use the lifts, or at the very least, lock them off so we can't. Our only chance of surviving—*your* only chance—is to head upstairs. Trust me.'

A shuffling sound behind him caught his attention. He turned as the lower half of the man Cain shot was dragged into the emergency stairwell. A black snake-like device appeared in his place. It curved around the doorframe, its head pointing in their direction. He fired his gun, barely aiming, and the device shattered.

'Camera,' he said. 'Let's move.'

Cain led them to the opposite end of the hallway, toward another emergency stairwell. Jakob followed him, then Ellie, and then Rebekah. Gideon took up the rear, keeping his gun locked onto the stairwell the attackers were using.

Cain raised his hand as a signal to stop, and everyone complied. He quietly opened the stairwell's door, crept onto the concrete-floored landing, and quickly looked over the staircase's railings, first down, then up. Satisfied, he made his way upward, and the others followed.

Thankfully, it was much quieter in the stairwell. Maybe the fire alarm system was designed to get people out of their rooms and into the emergency stairwells, and once they were on the stairs, the forward pressure of people behind them would keep them moving without the need for a blaring siren. Suddenly, there was a loud bang from above and feet stomped on concrete. Cain motioned for everyone to flatten themselves against the wall, and he raised his guns toward the return landing of the stairwell.

Black high heels, sparkly black sandals, and black leather brogues. Not the footwear of an assault team. Ellie's heart pounded with relief. Cain quickly lowered his weapons and hid them behind his back as two women and a man, all similarly dressed in black shirts and black trousers, came down the stairs toward them. Bar staff, she supposed.

The first woman stopped.

'What the hell are you all doing?' she asked. 'You can't be here. You need to evacuate the building immediately.'

'Cain?' asked the second woman. 'Is this you?'

He grunted.

'Yolanda, is there anyone else upstairs?' Gideon asked the woman who'd spoken to Cain.

'No.'

'Nobody that shouldn't be there?'

'No. We closed thirty minutes ago. The three of us were just clearing up and came straight down when the alarm went off.'

He stared intently at her and then her two co-workers.

'You need to get out of here,' he said. 'Do not stop. And none of you has seen us. Do you understand?'

The three bar staff agreed in unison, made their way past everyone, and carried on down the stairs. Cain raised his guns and started moving again. He paused when he reached the door to the next floor.

'Why here?' asked Jakob. 'I thought we were heading to the roof. That sign says this is a restaurant.'

Cain turned around and locked his blood-red eyes onto his. He raised his empty hand in a gesture of apology and took a step backward. Cain flattened himself against the wall, grabbed the doorknob and twisted. He turned back to the others and put his forefinger to his lips, then slowly pulled the door open half a metre, wedged it open with his foot, and gingerly peered around the doorframe.

As he opened the door, the blare of the fire alarm hit them again. A couple of seconds passed, and then, without looking back to the others, he motioned for them to follow him and led them into the restaurant.

59

The flashing strobe and scream of the fire alarm assaulted Ellie's senses again. The noise and the pulsing light must have annoyed Cain as much as it irritated her because he swiftly brought up his gun and shot the strobe, which went dead immediately. He scanned the room for the siren, found it within one second, and put a bullet in it in the next. Like the strobe, it died instantly.

She glanced around the restaurant. The bar was along the right wall. On the patrons' side was a line of tall, wicker-backed chairs. Twelve square tables took up the main space, aligned in two rows of six, each surrounded by four chairs identical in all but height to those at the bar. Above the room were glazed ceiling panels, half-covered by retractable shades.

The entire left wall was glass. Beyond it was a large, dark, rectangular void that appeared to be lit from below. Parallel to the restaurant on the other side of the dark space was a dimly lit terrace with a domed structure at its midpoint. Running perpendicular to both at the far end of the roof was an open-air swimming pool illuminated by blue spotlights under the water and surrounded by what was probably a sundeck. At the closest end was an external walkway leading to the terrace.

She peered through the windows. While the lights inside and subdued illumination outside made it difficult to see anything clearly, she could make out a broad, black form thirty metres away on the pool deck. Slowly moving toward her, the shape split in two, and those parts then divided. Four black objects were now approaching the restaurant. As they came closer and her eyes adjusted, she began to pick out details on the four skulking forms—black clothing, helmets, ski goggles, and guns. It was an assault team. And from behind them stepped a giant of a man.

Seth.

'Oh my God,' she said, her breath catching in her throat.

Cain glanced at Rebekah. Ellie felt pressure within her skull and heard his voice in her head.

Rebekah, you take these two that way, find cover, and hold tight. Gideon and I will take those fuckers head-on. All of you, keep low.

He motioned with his head to a sliding glass door to their left that led to the external walkway. Before anyone could argue, he turned to face the attackers and fired two shots from each of his guns. One of the large windows shattered, and two members of the assault team simultaneously grabbed at their throats and dropped to the floor. They didn't get up. Gideon joined him, a gun in one hand and a sword in the other. Seth roared at them from across the roof. He wedged the butt of his rifle into his shoulder and fired a torrent of bullets toward the bar, bellowing with rage.

Everyone inside the restaurant ducked for cover behind the tables. Gideon and Cain responded with rapid barrages, forcing the remaining two assault team members outside to take cover. Seth remained defiant and stood his ground. A bullet grazed him between the shoulder and neck, but he barely flinched.

'I'm going to tear your fucking heads off,' he yelled.

Cain slammed one of his guns on the table before him, then raised his empty hand. He closed his fingers in a pincer-like movement as he'd done with the bouncer outside of Dante's, and Seth gripped his throat with both hands. He pulled his arm back, and Seth stumbled forward. Then he thrust his arm away from himself, and Seth flew backward, disappearing into the swimming pool.

Gideon turned to Rebekah.

'Go! Now!' he yelled.

Rebekah squeezed past Ellie and then Jakob.

'Come on,' she commanded. 'Keep your heads down and stay close.'

She led them through the sliding glass door, her pistol raised. A low wall topped by glazed safety panels separated the walkway from the void, which Ellie discovered was a deep lightwell to the hotel lobby's glass skylight a few storeys below. They descended a short set of steps, where the wall became high enough to crouch against without being seen.

'Stay put and stay calm,' Rebekah said. 'I'm going to try and draw their fire.'

'This is fucking crazy,' Jakob said.

The walkway dog-legged to the right, onto the terrace. Rebekah snuck forward and rounded the corner. Ellie watched her disappear and tried to peek over the wall, but Jakob pulled her back down.

'Are you mental?' he said. 'You'll get your head blown off.'

'We need to see what's happening, Jakob. What if those guys take everyone down and make their way over here? We need to be ready for that.'

'To do what? Take them on hand-to-hand?'

She didn't know, but if the Elyonim managed to overcome the Sicarii, and if she *were* a descendant of the most powerful angel that ever existed, surely she'd be able to do *something*. She peeked over the lip of the wall, keeping as low as possible, and saw that Rebekah had stopped short of the domed structure—which she now saw was another bar—and was peering over the wall toward the pool deck.

Seth had dragged himself out of the swimming pool and engaged Gideon and Cain with the remaining two attackers. Rebekah must have seen a chance to move because she made for the dome. Before she got there, she came under fire. One of the two black-clad assailants had spotted her and advanced to cut her off. She flipped a table over, crouched behind it, and fired off a couple of rounds but missed her target. She fired again, forcing the man to duck behind the low wall that separated the deck from the lightwell.

Then she stood, aimed, and waited.

A few seconds later, the gunman appeared a metre from his last position. She fired. The back of his neck exploded in a cloud of red mist, and he fell out of sight. She returned to Ellie and Jakob, and they crouched against the wall, keeping their heads low for safety.

'You guys okay?' she asked.

'Yeah,' Ellie said. 'If you can call being trapped on a roof in the middle of a blazing gunfight *okay*.'

'We need to get out of here,' said Jakob. 'Can't we just try and make our way down? Isn't there an external fire escape or something?'

'No. We're stuck up here until we kill those motherfuckers.'

'Seth is here, so Thomas will be, too. He's probably inside, making his way up here with more of those SWAT guys. You think you'll be able to take them all out?'

They glanced over the wall. Cain and Seth were fighting in close quarters, each with short swords. They had nasty-looking gashes on their faces and bodies, their clothes drenched with blood. Gideon had lost or put away his weapon and was pacing toward the last member of the assault team, who was struggling with his rifle.

Suddenly, Ellie was in mid-air and flying backward to the restaurant. She screamed.

'Ellie,' Jakob yelled.

When she stopped, it felt like she'd flown into a steel vice. She turned her head enough to see the clamp around her neck was on the end of someone's arm.

It was Thomas.

He sneered, and her heart thumped.

Behind him were more black-clad figures with their weapons raised and, for now, holding their fire. Jakob raised the gun Gideon had given him and took aim at Thomas. She knew he wouldn't take the shot. She obscured too much of him, and he wouldn't risk hitting her. Despairing at being powerless to help her, he lowered the gun. He tried to stand up and run to her, but Rebekah held him back.

They began to argue loudly enough that she could hear them.

'Jakob, you can't,' Rebekah yelled. 'They'll kill you.'

'We can't just let them fucking take her. We have—'

Suddenly, she felt a searing pain in her shoulder as if someone had thrust a hot poker into it. She screamed and saw blood pouring from a hole at the top of her right arm. Then, glancing at movement on the pool deck, she noticed through watering eyes that Gideon's opponent, whom he gripped by the throat, was flailing his pistol around. He must have fired a shot at Gideon, which went astray and struck her instead. The hot metal burned inside her flesh, and the pain was unbearable.

Thomas raised his free arm alongside her face, thrust it toward the man Gideon held, then closed his fist and pulled his arm toward himself. Both the gunman and Gideon crashed through one of the glass panels at the lightwell's edge and disappeared into the void below.

'Gideon!' she screamed.

She looked at Jakob, who glanced from her to where Gideon had fallen. She could see the anger rising in him, his insides likely a cauldron of searing molten rage. He clenched his fists and roared with fury.

And then she saw fire.

Real fire.

Bright flames of electric blue neon engulfed his entire body. They began in his chest and burst outward, toward his hands and feet. What the hell was happening?

'Jakob!' she screamed, clawing at Thomas's fingers, trying to prise them from her neck. 'Jakob!'

She watched as he gulped air in huge mouthfuls, no doubt trying to tame the panic, but when the fire reached his neck, he started hyperventilating. Then, as the flames enveloped his head, he shrieked, overwhelmed by fear, rage, and pain.

Then he stopped screaming.

He looked down at his hands and then at the rest of himself. The flames weren't burning his flesh or even his clothes. Instead, the blue inferno surrounding him expanded until it burned a foot thick around his body, its brightness intensifying.

His head came up, and he looked straight at her, his face serene.

And then he rose off the floor.

60

Gideon gripped the ledge and heard almost nothing. No gunfire, no sounds of combat, no groans of pain. Only the strange rush of what sounded like a raging fire. Having saved himself on a windowsill within the lightwell, he'd climbed back up, driving his tanto knives like pitons into the cement between the brickwork. He hauled himself up and over the edge and onto the deck, then got to his knees, and with his back to the void, he glanced to his right. Cain and Seth were no longer fighting each other. They were facing the lightwell, motionless. Confused about why the two brothers had ceased trying to kill each other, he turned and saw Jakob floating in mid-air, consumed by a violent blue fire.

Jakob's head swivelled in his direction, and he saw that his irises were now the same neon blue as the fire that consumed him. Rebekah stood on the terrace next to the dome. He jumped, clearing the gaping corner of the lightwell easily, and thudded down beside her.

'What the fuck is going on, Gideon?'

'It's not Ellie,' he said. 'It never was. It's Jakob.'

'But how's that possible? *Ellie* has the memories. *She's* had the dreams.'

'I think—'

Before he could finish verbalising the thought forming in his head, Jakob roared. The blaze surrounding him suddenly expanded rapidly across the entire roof like a neon supernova, shattering the restaurant windows and the glass panels around the lip of the lightwell and striking everyone with such force that not a single person remained standing.

Apart from the fire alarm blaring from lower down in the building, the only sound on the rooftop was the roar of the blue fire engulfing him. It continued to rage for a few seconds and then disappeared like a blown-out match. He dropped to the floor and almost collapsed, but he grabbed the side of the wall and kept himself upright.

Everyone on the roof was motionless, watching for what would happen next. Even Ellie, whom Thomas had unintentionally released, hadn't yet tried to run.

Then, chaos.

Seth bellowed and charged at Cain. He thrust his blade into Cain's chest and out through his back and then stamped on his knee from the side, rupturing ligaments and shattering the cartilage. Cain roared, blood spewing from his mouth, and fell to the ground.

'Payback, motherfucker,' he growled, then bolted past Thomas into the restaurant.

Gideon and Rebekah aimed their guns at Thomas, who'd recaptured Ellie and held her in front of him again. While Jakob had feared shooting him in case he hit her, Gideon didn't have that apprehension, and neither, he knew, did Rebekah.

But then Jakob stumbled forward and unwittingly placed himself in the line of fire.

'Jakob,' he shouted. 'Get down.'

Jakob regained his composure, ignored him, and ran at Thomas, who grinned and backed into the restaurant, holding Ellie up as a swinging shield. An intelligent play, Gideon thought. Thomas knew neither he nor Rebekah would risk shooting while Ellie was moving in and out of their line of fire.

'Damn it,' he murmured, keeping his gun trained on a line through her to Thomas's head.

Seth vanished into the stairwell, followed by the remaining assault team members. Thomas, now the last Elyonim operative on the roof, held Ellie up as a taunt, then disappeared, too.

'Ellie!' Jakob cried out.

He ran for the restaurant. Gideon leapt over the gaping lightwell, caught up to him, and grabbed his arm to slow him down. Before they reached the restaurant, the door to the internal stairwell exploded toward them, the force of the blast knocking them backward.

Gideon got to his knees, ignoring the high-pitched ringing in his ears, knowing it would fade quickly enough, and glanced around. Rebekah was on one knee, shaking off the effects of the explosion but otherwise unharmed. Cain was sitting on the floor, attempting to realign his knee. The blast had knocked him back with such force that the impact with the floor had pushed Seth's sword from his chest. Jakob was on his back, his debris-covered face blank and his wide, unblinking eyes streaming with tears.

He doubted Ellie had been hurt in the explosion. Thomas wouldn't have risked that. He'd merely intended for the blast to prevent the Sicarii from following. But Jakob might not necessarily realise that. He went to him and gently pulled him to his feet.

'I'm sure Ellie's fine, Jakob. You saw what Thomas did to the guy who accidentally shot her. If death is the consequence of harming her, they want her alive. She wouldn't have been anywhere near that blast. Thomas using her as a shield had nothing to do with protecting himself. It was about keeping us at arm's length so he could trap us up here and get away without interference.'

'How could you possibly know that?'

'It's what I would have done. Can you walk?'

'Yeah.'

'Okay. We need to get moving.'

'How? To where? Like you said, we're fucking trapped up here. And, what the *fuck* was that with the blue fire?'

'I have a theory about—'

Suddenly, there was a deafening howl, and a black-and-white form loomed overhead. It was an odd-looking vehicle, part helicopter and part aeroplane. Gideon was familiar with the Bell V22 Osprey tiltrotor aircraft used primarily by the United States Marines, but those aircraft were grey, fat and ugly. This looked like a sleek private jet. The tiltable propellers on the tips of its wings pointed skyward, and the vehicle came to a hover above the lightwell, facing the domed bar. It spun slowly until its nose pointed toward him and the others. There were two people in the cockpit. The first wore a flight helmet equipped with night vision goggles. The second was their pilot, Enrique, who waved.

'He's not going to be able to land here, Gideon,' Rebekah shouted.

'He won't need to. Let's get over there.'

He motioned to the pool deck, then looked at Enrique and pointed, making his intentions clear. As they made their way along one side of the lightwell, Cain limped around the other. The sleek craft hovered and spun slowly until its cabin door was directly above the deck. Enrique disappeared from view, and a moment later, the door opened and folded downward.

'Rebekah, help me with Jakob, will you?' Gideon said.

'I don't need any help.'

Rebekah laughed.

'How you gonna get up there, Human Torch?' she quipped. 'That thing isn't landing.'

'What? It's got to be four metres off the ground. At least. There's no way—'

Before he could finish, Gideon and Rebekah crouched behind him. They each placed a shoulder behind his buttocks and grabbed his ankles.

'Woah, wait. Hang on!'

'Buckle up,' Rebekah said, grinning widely.

They gave him no countdown or time to prepare. One second, he was standing firmly, if not all too steadily, on the pool deck, and the next, he was reeling backward at the edge of the aircraft's doorway. Enrique grabbed his jacket, hauled him to safety, guided him inside, and stepped back from the door. Rebekah jumped in, then Cain. Gideon took a final look at the devastation on the roof and then leapt into the strange craft.

'Welcome aboard,' Enrique said, extending his hand.

Gideon took it, grateful that his friend had managed to acquire the strange vehicle and come to their aid. He pointed toward the front of the aircraft.

'Get us out of here.'

Enrique returned to the cockpit, and he followed, exhaling heavily.

'Tough night.' Enrique said.

'Somewhat,' he replied, deadpan. He looked back into the cabin. It was almost as luxurious as the Sicarii's Bombardier jet. 'Where did you get this thing? More importantly, *how* did you get it?'

'It's a Leonardo AW609. A prototype. They're testing it out of Northolt. It was behind that fancy chopper you wanted. I couldn't find anyone responsible for that, but then I saw this thing's pilot conducting pre-flight checks, and—'

'What sort of fallout are we looking at for this?'

'There'll be no fallout, Gideon. Long story short, let's say it was a happy coincidence that I know the pilot, and she owed me a favour, so...'

'She?'

Enrique nodded.

'Owed you a favour?'

Enrique shrugged.

'So, what now?' he asked. 'Northolt then Chicago?'

'Back to Northolt, yes, but given what just happened, I suspect it'll be Madrid rather than Chicago.'

Enrique whistled.

'Yeah,' Gideon said gravely.

He returned to the cabin, leaving Enrique to instruct the pilot to return to Northolt, where they would exit the Leonardo and board the Sicarii's jet. Cain had taken one of the cabin's front seats. Despite his dedication to the mission of finding and protecting those of Sammael's bloodline, he could easily have gotten caught up in exacting revenge on his brother—one of few opportunities in the millennia since Seth's betrayal of their family. Gideon was grateful that his friend had remained focused, understanding how difficult that would have been. As he passed him, he briefly rested his hand on his shoulder and nodded.

Cain gave him a single nod in return.

Rebekah, sitting further down the cabin, caught Gideon's eye with a subtle wave of her fingers. She raised her eyebrows and jutted her chin at Jakob, who sat across the aisle, hunched over with his head down, his hands rifling through his hair. She patted the air softly twice with one hand.

He got the message.

He needed to handle this carefully.

The seat directly in front of Jakob faced backward, so he sat down in it and waited for Jakob to look up at him. When he didn't move, Gideon opened his mouth to talk. Jakob must have sensed it because he spoke first.

'What the fuck just happened to me?' he asked quietly, not looking up from his feet. His voice was shaky and hoarse.

Gideon leaned forward in his chair, ready to put his earlier thought into words.

'I don't know. I've never seen anything like it. But if I were to guess, I'd say you have some angelic blood in you, and whatever that was, it was brought on by your rage over Ellie getting shot or of being powerless to help her.'

Jakob slowly lifted his head. His eyes were bloodshot and glazed over with tears.

'Angelic blood?'

'How else would you explain it?'

He shrugged and shook his head.

'So, Ellie and I are both descended from angels? She from Lucifer, and me from whoeverthefuck? How does that happen?'

'Sammael. Not Lucifer. Lucifer is what the Elyonim called him.'

'Whatever the hell his name was, Gideon. You think I give a shit about what to call him right now?'

Gideon reminded himself that Jakob needed support rather than criticism.

'It's possible,' he said, 'that you're descended from two different angels, yes. Although I think you both having angelic blood and ending up together is highly improbable. I suspect it's something else.'

'Like what?'

'Do you remember, back in the conference room just before the attack began, Ellie asked Simon if she's Sammael's descendant?'

'He didn't say anything. That woman interrupted him.'

'True, but I think he was about to say that she doesn't carry Sammael's blood.'

'Why do you think that?'

'Because I think he was going to say that it's you. That *you* are Sammael's descendant.'

'That's ridiculous,' Jakob said softly.

'As ridiculous as levitating in a cloud of blue fire that didn't burn your clothes or leave a mark on you?'

Jakob didn't answer.

'And, if that's what he *was* about to say, he may have been right. I think it's you.'

'But how could he know or think that? It wasn't my head he went into. And what about her dreams?'

'I think she's having those dreams because she's carrying your child.'

'What?'

'It seems the most likely scenario.'

'How could she be pregnant?'

'Well,' said Rebekah, 'the man puts his—'

Gideon shot her a look that cut her off.

'Not helpful, Rebekah,' Jakob said. 'I know how a person gets pregnant. I meant, I didn't know Ellie's pregnant. I don't even think *she* knows. So how the fuck do *you*?'

Gideon sat back.

'Those with angelic blood give off this kind of energy that—'

'Yeah, yeah, the energy thing,' Jakob said irritably. 'Peter told us about that. So?'

'It's like electricity. I felt it in Ellie when I took her to the car outside Dante's. It coursed through her. That's why I was initially so convinced she was the one. But her being pregnant with a child of Sammael's bloodline would also explain the strength of the surge I felt and why she's having the dreams.'

'Why haven't I felt this energy in her, then, if I've got angel blood and *our kind* are supposed to be able to sense it?'

Gideon spread his hands and shook his head. It was a question to which he had no answer.

'That, I don't know.'

'So why is she having the dreams and not me?'

'You ever been pregnant?' asked Rebekah.

'Twice,' he said sarcastically.

'My point is that Ellie's hormones are not only all over the place due to the pregnancy generally, but probably especially so because... you know... the baby's part-angel. Maybe that's it.'

'You may be right,' Gideon said.

Jakob fell silent. There was a lot for him to process, and Gideon didn't want to push him. He'd just discovered that the life he thought he had was over, and an entirely new, frighteningly different one had taken its place.

'So, you think that's where they took her?' he asked after a long silence.

'Where?'

'Madrid? I heard you tell that guy we're going to Madrid.'

'No, Jakob,' Gideon replied softly. 'That's not where they took her.'

'Then why are we going there? Why aren't we going after her? They're going to kill her.'

'We thought that might be the case initially, but now I doubt that.'

'That's what they've been trying to do all night. That's what *you* claim you've been trying to save her from.' He jabbed his finger at Gideon's chest. 'And now you're saying they're *not* going to kill her.'

'No, I don't believe they will.'

'Why not?'

'As I said on the roof, if they wanted to harm Ellie, Thomas wouldn't have taken her, and he wouldn't have killed that member of his team who shot her. And...'

'And what?'

'They saw what we saw, Jakob. You, consumed by fire. They'll draw the same conclusions we've drawn. There is now a strategic advantage to them keeping her alive.'

'And that would be?'

'To raise her child—*your* child—within their fold. To guide it, to teach it to hate the Grigori and the Sicarii and everything we stand for, and to train it to fight against us.'

'You think that's what they'll do?'

'It's what I would do.'

Jakob half-laughed, rubbed his hands across his face, and exhaled deeply. Gideon sympathised. He had lived so long that he'd forgotten how he felt when he discovered he was half-angel despite having grown up surrounded by others of his kind. He couldn't begin to guess how Jakob was feeling now, having learned he could be the descendant of an entity he'd been brought up to believe was the Devil, that he'd now be hunted by a group that would want him dead, that his girlfriend was pregnant with his child, and that the child would be raised to hate him.

Jakob took his hands away from his face and looked sternly at Gideon.

'So, what's in Madrid?'
'Not what, Jakob. Who.'

61

Located at the edge of Madrid's city centre was El Retiro Park. Filled with galleries, sculptures, monuments, and a lake, the park covered over three hundred acres and was said to have over fifteen thousand trees. Initially owned by the Spanish monarchy, it became a public park in the late nineteenth century. Jakob and Gideon walked east along the Paseo Fernán Núñez, a thoroughfare that ran east to west through the park. While the mid-morning sun warmed Jakob's face, he was still cold. It must have been around nine degrees, but it still beat Copenhagen for a winter's day. He thrust his hands in his pockets and exhaled a cloud of misty breath.

They passed runners and people on pushbikes, bundled-up locals out for a stroll, and what he guessed, judging by their guidebooks and unfolded maps, were off-season tourists, there for the culture more than the sun. A pack of unruly dogs, led by a large white Swiss Shepherd eager to get to the next tree, bush, or water bowl, was dragging their young walker along. Her ponytail bounced frenetically behind her as she tried to restrain and keep up with them.

Up ahead, the avenue met a large circular space. In its centre was a stone fountain bounded by a low stone wall. Water flowed from the mouths of ugly figureheads set into the fountain's tall pedestal, and on its top was a statue of an angel looking to the sky and shielding his face. When they reached the junction of the path and the circle, Gideon stopped, observed the statue for a moment, and then looked at his watch.

Jakob pinched the bridge of his nose. Despite himself and his worry over Ellie, he'd slept on the short flight from London, but it hadn't been enough and he could feel exhaustion creeping in.

'What are we doing here, Gideon? We're wasting time when we could be going for Ellie.'

'All good things come to those who prepare for them, Jakob. And preparation requires knowledge.'

He nodded past the fountain. On the other side of it, at the junction of two more avenues that led to the circle, was a café kiosk surrounded by chairs, tables, and large umbrellas on three sides.

'You want to get a coffee?' Jakob asked. 'Are you serious?'

Gideon smiled and began walking toward the café. Jakob saw that its blinds were down, and the umbrellas were closed.

'I think we're too early,' he said, with as much sarcasm as he could muster.

Gideon opened his mouth to respond but became distracted by something. Jakob turned to look at whatever it was he'd spotted.

A man was approaching from the south. He looked around forty, give or take a couple of years, although he now knew that looks meant nothing when it came to the true ages of these people. The man was Gideon's height and had a mop of thick, curly black hair, olive skin, and a neatly trimmed beard. He was dressed casually in a khaki sports coat over a V-necked sweater of the same colour, dark jeans, and beige suede boots.

When the man reached them, he smiled warmly at Gideon and offered his hand. He hesitated briefly before taking it as if he were meeting royalty and was unsure of the etiquette.

'Good to see you, Gideon,' the man said.

Jakob couldn't place his accent. He could have been a local, but he suspected he was from somewhere else, far from Madrid. His voice was quiet and soft, and he had an air of authority but didn't come across as self-important or arrogant.

'You too,' Gideon replied.

The man grasped his forearm with his free hand, left it there for a moment, then let go and turned to Jakob, extending his hand. There was something about him that, for an instant, made Jakob forget his rage and his anxiety over Ellie. He had a kind, friendly, welcoming face, and he smiled so broadly that the outer corners of his dark brown eyes creased deeply.

'Jakob. It's a pleasure to meet you. I wish it could've been under less grave circumstances.'

'Yeah.'

Jakob took his hand. As their palms touched, the man's irises rippled and became the same colour as the flames that had engulfed him on the rooftop in London. The man smiled again and motioned to the fountain.

'It's called the Fuente del Ángel Caído,' he said. 'The Fountain of the Fallen Angel. It's supposed to depict Lucifer as Michael cast him out of Heaven. You can see the anguish on his face as he hides it from God in shame. Those gargoyle-like things spewing out water are his demons, I suppose.'

'Who are you?'

'It's bronze. Cast by a man named Ricardo Bellver in the late eighteen-hundreds for the third World's Fair in Paris, then bought by the Museo del Prado and brought here in eighteen eighty-five. It sits at exactly six hundred and sixty-six metres above sea level. A clever little nod to that whole Number of the Beast thing, I suppose. What most people don't realise, though, is that the biblical number relates to man, not to a devil of some sort—that man himself is the beast. Of course, neither is true. It's just fearmongering.'

Jakob sighed inwardly but said nothing. He realised that pushing the man wouldn't get him anywhere. The guy had something to say and evidently wouldn't be rushed to say it, as frustrating as that was.

'I've never liked it,' the man continued. 'The statue, I mean. Apart from being aesthetically and anatomically incorrect, it's a completely inaccurate depiction of what happened to him.'

'Aesthetically incorrect? Are you saying you actually know—'

Jakob cut himself off, rubbed his hands over his face, and changed his mind about letting this guy ramble on.

'You know what, I don't want to be rude, but I really don't care. My girlfriend has been spirited away to fuck-knows-where. Every bone in my body aches. I've been abducted, caught in the middle of three gunfights, and almost choked to death. Oh, and I can now apparently surround myself with bright blue fire that doesn't burn me. It's been one serious fucking day, and I really don't have the energy for stories about statues, okay? And, regardless of what Gideon thinks, Ellie certainly doesn't have the time for it, so why don't you tell me who the fuck you are and how you can help her.'

The corner of the man's mouth creased with the hint of a smile.

'To answer your first question, I, like Simon and Peter, whom I understand you've met, have had many names over the years, some more creative than others.'

Great, Jakob thought. More cryptic clues.

'So you're another one of them? An angel, or a Nephilim, or something?'

'I'm an angel, yes. A seraph.'

'And you're what? Simon's boss?'

'It's probably more accurate to say that we're more like a family that works together, and I sit at the head of the table.'

Jakob was struck by a realisation.

'You're Sammael.'

'I go by Samuel these days, but yes.'

'But that would make you...'

Samuel nodded and smiled warmly.

'It's not the name of which I'm most fond, Jakob, but yes. I am also Lucifer.'

Jakob blinked several times quickly, then scoffed.

'You expect me to believe that?'

'I am who I am, Jakob. You can choose to believe it or not.'

'I don't.'

'But you're happy to believe that I *am* an angel, that Gideon here is what he is, and that you can spontaneously ignite with blue flame?'

'Good point.'

He took a large, heaving breath and ran his hands through his hair. Samuel motioned with his head toward the café.

'It's been a long night for you,' he said. 'Why don't we take a seat?'

They walked toward the kiosk, leaving Gideon where he was. As they neared the closest table, a white-haired elderly man came through the kiosk's swing door, approached the same table, hauled up its umbrella, and disappeared back into the café.

'He one of yours, too?' Jakob asked.

'Him? No. The timing of him starting his shift is entirely coincidental.'

There was a glint in Samuel's eyes as he spoke, and Jakob realised that everything happening around them in the park was a charade. Everyone he'd seen—and, more importantly, those he hadn't but who were undoubtedly there—were there to protect Samuel and, probably, him too. He imagined that all the guy had to do was rub his eyebrow, tap his finger on the table, or cross his legs a certain way, and a hundred armed Sicarii would rapidly surround them. He laughed at that.

'It's good that you can still laugh, Jakob.'

'If you don't laugh, you'll cry, right?'

'Indeed. And yes, Matthias is one of mine.'

When they reached the table, Samuel gestured for him to sit down, which he did. Rather than sit opposite him, Samuel took the chair to his left, and the old barista appeared with a small rectangular silver tray carrying two small white espresso cups, a few sugar packets, and two glasses of water. Samuel looked at him and winked. Matthias winked back and returned to the kiosk.

'Don't drink the coffee to the end,' Samuel said. 'It's unfiltered and has a layer of silt at the bottom of the cup.'

'Yeah, Turkish style. I know. I have a friend who drinks this stuff. Is he really a barista?'

'Not everyone who works for me is a hunter, Jakob.'

'No?'

'He used to be, though.'

'Human, right?'

'Nephilim.'

'But he looks... old. Older than Gideon and Cain, and I thought they were two of the first. How's he so different?'

Samuel sighed deeply.

'Matthias has seen many battles, but he's not as skilled or as fortunate as others such as Gideon and regrettably has suffered many injuries, some so severe that healing himself aged him more quickly. So, about two hundred years ago, I decided he deserved a quiet life, and I retired him.'

'So, people only get to leave if you say so?'

'On the contrary, Jakob. They can leave whenever they wish to. I'm a great believer in free will. Matthias's problem was that he didn't want to leave, and he took much persuading to do so. And now, even though he might complain about it if you were to ask him, he finds great enjoyment in life. And peace. I'm happy for him.'

Jakob scoffed.

'You don't believe me.'

'There's a lot of what I've seen and heard in the past few hours that I'm having trouble believing, and an old man being a supernatural ex-assassin is the least of them.'

'I know I'm often called the Father of Lies, Jakob, but I never lie.'

'That's what a liar *would* say.'

Samuel laughed heartily, and despite his reservations, Jakob found himself warming to this man who, if Gideon was right, could be his great-something grandfather. He took a sip of his coffee. It was hot and bitter. He opened a sugar packet, emptied it into the cup, and looked toward the fountain.

'You want answers,' Samuel said.

'You may not be the Father of Lies, but you're the master of understatement.'

'Before I give you them, Jakob, I need to know—'

'Whether I am actually Neo.'

'Who?'

'The One. The Chosen. Full of the light of the Morning Star that Simon said Ellie was and that Gideon thinks I am.'

'There is no doubt you possess angelic ancestry, Jakob. That much is clear. But we need to establish from whom you descended. To do that, I need to see the memories your angelic ancestors passed to you. Do I have your permission to do that?'

'You're asking?'

'As I said before, I believe in free will. I have never coerced anyone.'

He glanced at the fountain, but Jakob sensed he wasn't looking at it but rather through it, unfocused.

'What about Judas?'

'It wasn't what I wanted, and I never made him go to Michael. It was his choice.'

'Kids can be stubborn.'

Samuel smiled sadly, and his eyes welled up.

'Okay,' Jakob said. 'Let's get on with it.'

62

Jakob's mind flooded with a kaleidoscope of colour and, strangely, sound. It was like rushing toward an edgeless cinema screen of memories stretched to infinity in every direction. Instead of crashing into it, he went through it like a wormhole. Its sides wrapped around him and almost instantaneously showed him, in reverse, every sight and sound of his life—even those he would ordinarily not have consciously remembered.

His pulse raced, his breathing quickened, and he thought he might hyperventilate. Suddenly, the wall of colour turned black, but only for a microsecond. Then more imagery assaulted him, in full technicolour, like a time-lapse film being played backward at incredible speed. There was too much happening and too quickly for him to focus on anything. Everything was a blur.

And then it ended in an explosion of pure white light.

He stared silently into the distance at nothing, contemplating that what had just flashed through his mind's eye were the memories of every one of his angel-blooded ancestors and, according to Peter, those of every human woman in his line who carried a child of angelic blood. He sipped his coffee, put the cup down in front of him, fiddled with its handle, pointed it away from himself, and looked at Samuel.

'Are you alright?' Samuel asked.

'Yeah, although if I lose my breakfast, it'll be your fault.'

'I'm sorry about that. I tend to forget how intense that can be, even for purebloods.'

'So, what's the verdict?' he asked, running his hands over his jeans. 'Am I...?'

Samuel grinned widely. His eyes lit up in electric neon blue, and water began to well up in them again.

'Yes, Jakob. You are.'

His heart pounded. How was it possible that the man beside him—created an angel, sent to Earth millennia ago, apparently betrayed by his own kind, and falsely cast as the embodiment of evil on Earth—was his own flesh and blood?

'Does that make me a Nephilim?'

'No. Only the direct offspring of angels and humans are Nephilim or Anakim. But that doesn't mean you're not special, Jakob. You are extraordinary.'

He stared at the fountain again.

'How do you feel?'

'Totally overwhelmed. And I don't mean that whole head-rush thing. Just knowing what I am... It's a lot to get my head around.'

Samuel nodded but said nothing. At that moment, Jakob could think of nothing to say either, so they sat quietly, their silence disturbed only by birdsong, the distant hum of traffic, and the whisper of wind through the park's trees.

'What happened between you and Michael?' he asked eventually.

'What do you want to know?'

'If I'm to stand any chance of helping Ellie, I think I need to know everything.'

'Everything? That's a very long story.'

'Well, I know I won't be going for her without your help, and I'm guessing you'll tell me that won't happen any time soon, so I suppose I have time for a story, don't I?'

'Perhaps I could, you know...' Samuel pointed between his temple and Jakob's. 'Just give you the highlights.'

'Uh, no thanks. One light show is enough for now.'

Samuel smiled and then sat quietly. Jakob guessed he was trying to decide where to start.

'Michael and I were created within... well, there is no human word for the unit of time that existed between our both coming into being, but it was almost instantaneous. Me first, then him. We were beings of pure energy, conscious and sentient and curious, and we were the only two for a long time. We helped our creator—who you call God—mould life on this planet and others. We were content. Even after the rest of our kind were created, our bond was stronger than with any other. And we loved humankind. They were as much our children as they were God's.'

'And all that went to shit when you came here,' Jakob said, thinking that when things calmed down, he might return to Samuel's comment about life on other planets.

'Not at first. But, as you already know, Michael did eventually become dissatisfied with our angelic lot on Earth. He came to me and proposed that we rise above humankind to become their masters. He knew God wouldn't intervene and that I was his only obstacle. He claimed he would've been happy for me to remain in command if I consented to his wishes, as all he wanted was for us to elevate ourselves above humans.

'But I wouldn't do it. I couldn't. It went against our entire purpose for being here. So, he went away and, over the next few millennia, convinced thousands of our kind to join him. Once he'd built a strong enough following, he summoned me to Har Megiddo. I took a few angels with me, and he, with an army at his back, told me of his intentions, which by then I already had a fair idea of, thanks to angels like Rebekah, who'd managed to get close enough to him or those within his inner circle.'

Jakob took another sip of coffee and sat back in his chair. Again, the story of Michael as the rogue angel and Samuel—Lucifer—as the innocent party. Could it be true? He usually had a pretty good bullshit detector, but Samuel seemed just as sincere and as emphatic about his side of things as Peter and Thomas had been when they'd told theirs, and he was finding it difficult to even want to believe any of it. But then he remembered the look on Thomas's face when he'd grabbed Ellie on the roof back in London. His grin. It was one of pure menace.

No. Everything Samuel was telling him now was true.

He exhaled heavily.

'So, what was his grand plan?'

'He wanted supremacy over humans, but he knew that physically enslaving them would eventually lead to revolution. As powerful as we are, humans vastly outnumbered his angelic forces even in those days, and he would've risked being overthrown. But in those days—and, frankly, even now—humans had primitive mentalities, and he realised there was a solution that suited his needs and put him right where he wanted to be.'

'Which was?'

'Organised religion.'

'Organised?'

'Humans have worshipped in one form or another for hundreds of thousands of years—tribal religion, shamanism, ancestor worship. Most were not linked to deities but were related to nature or to venerating the dead. At some point, spiritual beliefs emerged, possibly because of humans' early interaction with our kind and exposure to our abilities. Perhaps we weren't as careful as we ought to have been. But for the most part, those early beliefs were disparate, lacked structure, and were not overly common.

'Back then, people believed primarily in what they could see—the sun and moon, thunder and lightning, abundance and famine, and so on. Michael thought he could construct a system of control by harnessing those beliefs—and, importantly, the superstitions linked to them—by attributing personae to the subjects of those beliefs. By deifying them.'

'And you couldn't stop him?'

'No. Globally, we were outnumbered almost nine-to-one. Had I tried to kill him at Har Megiddo, it would've resulted in the deaths of everyone with me, and retribution against those loyal to me elsewhere would have quickly followed, regardless of whether I'd been successful. I couldn't allow that. There was nothing I could do, and he knew it. So, he let me leave, but not before telling me that I didn't have to join him, but if I tried to stop him, there would be severe consequences.'

'So, I'm guessing you just stayed out of his way.'

'Yes. Even though we remained in many of the same communities as Michael's allies, particularly in the Fertile Crescent, northern Africa and southern Europe, we left them alone, and they us. But then he had a change of heart and ordered the Great Purge.'

Jakob shook his head, the term unfamiliar to him.

'You would know it as the Great Flood of the book of Genesis.'

'You're kidding. Michael could control the weather like that?'

'It wasn't a real flood, Jakob. It was simply a campaign to exterminate us and our bloodlines. It started in the Levant and swept outward. Many of us died. Those who survived the initial attacks fled in any direction they could. I and some others went west, first to Cyprus and then to an island called Thera—what is now Santorini—to a small settlement the humans who inhabited the island called Atalanteides.'

A thought crept into Jakob's mind.

'You're talking about Atlantis. I thought that was supposed to be a myth.'

'No, it was real. It grew into a beautiful city of culture, art, innovation, and free-thinking on the site of a place historians and archaeologists now call Akrotiri. Before it was decimated three and a half thousand years ago by the Theran volcanic eruption, that is. The only records that survived its destruction were stories from the few human inhabitants that managed to survive or those who'd previously been there, passed down to others. Nothing tangible. Hence the myth.'

'Fuck! So, Michael tried to get you out of the way so he could carry out his campaign without challenge.'

'Yes, and he began with the polytheistic belief systems.'

'You mean like the religions of ancient Rome and Greece?'

'Exactly. Rome, Greece, Sumeria, Egypt, Scandinavia, India, the Americas, and even Australia. He created gods, spirits, and devils to represent each of those things in nature that early humans already worshipped. Eventually, in some areas, people's belief in deities linked to galactic bodies, nature, fertility, and so on, began to wane. They started to see, for example, that Ra would not shroud them in darkness or kill their crops one day if they hadn't worshipped him the day before, or bless them with bountiful harvests or children they prayed for if they'd been good followers. So, Michael needed a new plan and a fresh start, and he came up with monotheism.'

'The belief in a single God.'

'Precisely. A single, all-powerful creator, wrathful and vengeful. And—crucially for his ability to control the masses and grow his power and wealth—not one who'd inflict immediate, visible repercussions on you for lack of worship and obedience, but one who would, on your death, banish your soul to an eternal afterlife in a fiery underworld as the plaything of a callous, evil, spiteful demon. Superstition and imagination can be powerful, and Michael used them to his advantage. He fashioned his one true God, needful of reverence and vengeful against those who weren't worshipful, on an entity that never wanted to be known to humankind and made his own brother the Devil.'

'He sounds like a real asshole.'

'That's an understatement.'

Jakob finished his coffee and gulped some water to wash the silty residue from his mouth. As he put down his glass, Matthias reappeared and placed what looked like an egg cup in front of him, which contained several raspberries.

'For the palette,' he said in accented English.

'Uh, thanks.'

The old man spoke to Samuel in a language he didn't understand. It sounded like Arabic but was probably angel-tongue. Samuel replied in the same dialect. Matthias started to cry, briefly placed his hand on Samuel's shoulder, and returned to the kiosk.

'What was that about?'

'He just asked who you are, and I told him.'

Jakob nodded gravely, then plucked a raspberry from the egg cup and ate it. A shock of sharp sweetness exploded in his mouth.

'In each religion through the ages, Michael and his cohorts became the earthly representatives of the deities he created,' Samuel said. 'Prophets, messengers, high priests and priestesses and, of course, angels. In some cases, such as in Egypt, the personification of the gods themselves. He was never brave enough to portray himself as the god above all other gods, though. As one would say here in Madrid, he didn't have the *cojones* for that.'

Jakob chuckled, recognising the Spanish slang for testicles.

'So, he was behind Judaism and Islam, too?'

'Eventually, yes. He started his single-god cult in Persia around two thousand BC. He took on the name Zoroaster and peddled himself as a prophet for a creator deity he named Hormazd. He devised the notions of heaven and hell, judgement day, an evil spirit, and even a saviour. When the Persian empire expanded, his new religion—Zoroastrianism— grew with it, eventually spreading back along the trade routes from China to Europe and the Middle East. With the concept of monotheism taking hold, he went to what is now Iraq, called himself Ab-Raham, fine- tuned Zoroastrianism, and laid the foundations of what became Judaism, Christianity, and Islam.'

'Holy shit!'

'Quite. Then, around fifteen hundred BC, he went back into Egypt where his cults of Amun and Osiris were struggling, gave himself a new name, brought together those disillusioned with polytheism, introduced them to the one true God, and led them out of the country where, on their journey east, he devised the idea of holy laws which he as God's envoy on Earth would dictate and enforce.'

Jakob put together the pieces of what Samuel was telling him.

'The Ten Commandments. You're telling me the guy was also Moses?'

'Yes. And as Moses, he became a prophet for his future arrival as the messiah of the Jews.'

'He set *himself* up to become Christ?'

'He did. Michael was the original narcissistic sociopath. He was entitled, arrogant, and superior. He was a master manipulator, was preoccupied with attaining power, and needed excessive amounts of praise and adulation. His ego was huge. He needed to place himself at the centre of worship or as close to it as possible without claiming to be God. So, in creating and preaching almost all his religions, he devised saviour prophecies that *he* intended to eventually fulfil.'

'Prophecies plural?'

'Over the three thousand years before he appeared as Christ, he made and fulfilled several of them. Horus of Egypt, Attis of Phrygia, Crite of Chaldea.' Samuel counted on his fingers as he reeled off names. 'Thammuz of Babylonia, Chrishna of Hindustan, Heracles of Greece, Mithra of Persia, Budha Sakia of India, Dionysus of Greece. Some born on the twenty-fifth of December. All crucified or slain. And almost all had a miraculous birth, came to prominence in their thirties or early forties, and were resurrected in some way. Some, like Christ, even had a divine father. And before you say it, no, that's not a coincidence. That's a pattern. He would test out different angles each time to see what worked best.'

Jakob inhaled deeply and breathed out heavily through his nose. He was aware of the theory that Christ's birthdate was pegged to the pagan celebration of the winter solstice to appease and convert the pagans in the early days of Christianity, but he hadn't realised there were so many other cultures and religions to which that date was significant. Nor had he known there were so many other messianic prophecies or that they were all linked to one person.

To Michael.

At that moment, Matthias returned with two silver teaspoons and two small glasses filled with what looked like a dark chocolate mousse.

'An indulgence of mine,' Samuel said, picking up a spoon and one of the glasses. He scooped up some mousse, swallowed it, and stared at the fountain, smiling.

Jakob did the same. The dessert was good. Not too bitter, not too sweet, not too heavy. As he looked at the fountain, he realised Gideon had disappeared. Probably to give them some privacy. He wondered how far he'd need to go for his superhuman hearing not to pick up any of their conversation. He guessed it was easily thirty metres from his chair to the fountain's centre, and he wasn't visible on this side of it or the other. So, at least sixty metres. Unless he'd gone to the bathroom—presumably, Nephilim had to urinate just like anyone else.

'So, what happened with Judas? How did he manage to get anywhere near Michael? Surely, with the energy that flows through you guys—through us, I guess—wouldn't Michael have known that he was your son and killed him straight away? Or ransomed him back to you in exchange for you joining him?'

'Are you aware of the story in the Bible about Christ's time in the Judean desert? When he fasted for forty days and nights and had to suffer Satan's temptations?'

'Vaguely.'

'There is a grain of truth to it. Michael and I did meet in the wilderness, shortly before he went to Galilee and began marketing himself as Christ the Messiah. He sent word to me that he wanted peace between us. We were each to bring just two companions. I took Azazel—Simon—and, against my better judgement, Judas. Michael took Gabriella, and Azrael—Peter.'

'Sounds like a fun party.'

436

'To say it was tense would be an understatement. The short of it is that Michael claimed he was remorseful for everything he'd done to us and wanted to reunite the Grigori and the Elyonim. So, I gave him three conditions.'

He raised three fingers, one by one, as he recounted his demands. Considering everything Michael had allegedly done, Jakob thought they were more than reasonable and privately wondered why Samuel had given him such an easy way out.

'Michael agreed that neither he nor his cohorts would make or fulfil any saviour prophecies from that point on. And he consented to allow all Grigori, Nephilim and Anakim to return, without harm, to all lands they'd fled during and after the Great Purge. But he refused to discontinue his campaign to spread his new religion. He claimed Rome's occupation of Judea brought with it its polytheistic religion—one, ironically, *he* created—and he felt it necessary to right all the wrongs of his earlier actions and teach humans there was only one God. The only concession he would make on that condition is that he'd do so simply as Christ the man—an identity he'd already established—and not Christ, the messianic and divine son of God.'

'So what? No deal?'

'While I couldn't condone the continuance of his religious campaign, I was powerless to stop him. And more than anything, I wanted peace between us, however fragile that would be. I was desperate for it. I wanted our people to be able to live without constantly looking over their shoulders and wondering when their lives would end. So, I told him he had to prove his intentions to honour the other conditions.'

Jakob straightened in his chair.

'Judas went to make sure he kept his promise,' he said.

Samuel bowed his head.

'As I said before, it wasn't what I wanted. Countless angels would've volunteered, but Judas was insistent that he be the one to go. We argued about it for hours. Ultimately, I agreed, on the condition that someone went with him and with the private hope that perhaps between them, he and whoever accompanied him might be able to persuade Michael to stop his crusade or at least influence how he delivered his message to the masses.'

'It was Simon, wasn't it? That went with him.'

'My most loyal friend, yes. And for a time, Michael let them believe he was keeping to his promise. But then...'

Samuel's eyes filled again, but this time, he couldn't contain his tears. Jakob almost felt his pain and needed to let him have that moment. Samuel withdrew a handkerchief from a pocket, dabbed his cheeks and face, and took a sip of water.

'I'm sorry about that,' he said. 'Even now, it's still a painful memory.'

'Did you go after Michael?'

'I wanted to. But he was too well-protected for me to get close to personally, and I didn't want others to risk their lives doing what I couldn't. And then, not long after his glorious resurrection as the earthly son of God, he left Jerusalem with Azrael and a few others and disappeared for a time. They moved around, planting the seeds of their newest religion. Every thirty years or so, they either reinvented themselves or slunk back into the shadows. Roman emperors, rulers of the kingdoms of Britain, Frankish royalty. Even Asian warlords for a time, if you can believe that. A never-ending quest for power, wealth, and above all, veneration.'

'So, everything in the Bible is a lie?'

'Part lie, part allegory, part truth, with the truth being the smallest part. As with almost all other scriptures and much of history that involved Michael. All written to serve his purpose.'

Jakob scoffed, lowered his head, and shook it.

'The greatest trick the Devil ever pulled...' he murmured.

'Was convincing the world he didn't exist.'

His head snapped up.

'Don't be so surprised, Jakob,' Samuel said with a chuckle. 'I watch movies, too, and that's one of my favourites. Although, I think, in Michael's case, it would be more appropriate to say that he convinced the world he was someone he wasn't.'

'Did you ever try to reconcile with him?'

Samuel's expression became even more solemn.

'No,' he said.

'I'm sorry.'

'It's alright. A lot of blood has passed under the bridge since then.'

Jakob sat back in his chair and rubbed his face. Exhaustion began to weigh him down again like a large, heavy blanket.

'You don't believe any of this, do you?' Samuel asked.

'I do, actually. It's just a fuckload to process.'

'It is. And I'm sorry you have to deal with it this way. I truly am.' He placed his hand on Jakob's shoulder. 'I'd hoped that, whenever we were to find anyone from the lost branch of my bloodline, they could gradually learn what they are—and who I am—in their own time and on their terms. Not as you've done, on the run and under threat from the Elyonim.'

Jakob nodded. It would be a lie to say that learning of his ancestry in the manner he'd done wasn't jarring, but he wondered whether it would have been different under less life-threatening circumstances. Was there a good time to discover you were the Devil's kin? Even if the Devil was the good guy? Probably not.

'Gideon thinks the Elyonim will raise our baby as theirs. Teach it to hate you.'

'If Ellie *is* pregnant, then yes, Jakob. I suspect that will be the most likely scenario.'

'Why? What possible benefit would that be to them other than pissing you off?'

'Well, if that is their goal, they've certainly succeeded. But, I believe everything the Elyonim currently do, and have done for some time, is designed to bring them closer to the Parousia.'

'Which in normal language is what?'

'The return of Christ at the battle of Armageddon.'

'You're kidding, right?'

'Jakob, you are only the second person I know of to burst into flame like you did in London. I am the other and have done so only once—when I learned of my son's death. If your child has anywhere near the power I think *you* might have, it will be a valuable asset to the Elyonim in the coming war.'

'Hang on, are you saying they're going to weaponise my kid to help bring about the end of the world?'

'It won't be the end of the world, but it *will* be a war for domination of the planet. And depending on when that war begins, they'll use your child, or those in its future bloodline, to kill anyone who stands with us or against them. It won't matter to them either way.'

'And Ellie?'

'They'll either threaten or brainwash her to make her compliant, keep her hostage to control your child, or...'

'They'll kill her.'

'Let's not think about any of that,' Samuel said, reaching for his water and finishing it with a small gulp. 'There's an African proverb which says that tomorrow belongs to the people who prepare for it today.'

'And what the fuck does that mean?'

'It means we regroup, put our heads together, and figure out how to recover Ellie and your child.'

63

Ellie woke curled up on a soft brown leather sofa. It took a second for alertness to reach her, and when it did, it felt like a punch in the stomach. She pushed herself upright, which made her head throb. Her mind flashed to Jakob, on the hotel roof, engulfed by blue fire. What the hell *was* that? Was he okay? Was he even alive? Her head swivelled left to right. She was somewhere unfamiliar, and she was alone. Panic set in. She gulped air, dug her fingers into the sofa's leather, squeezed her eyes closed, and tried to calm herself.

When she was ready, she opened her eyes again. Three metres in front of her was a solitary chair made of light wood and grey fabric. From the back, it looked like one of those low-slung pieces from the sixties or seventies. A metre or so beyond it was a glass wall the width of the room, and past that was nothing but blue sky dotted with wispy white clouds. She looked at her watch. It showed the time as just past one-forty in the afternoon. It would be accurate if she were still in the UK, but after Thomas had taken her from the hotel, she was bundled onto a jet and not told their destination, so now she was fuck-knows-where, and it was highly likely her watch was wrong.

She pushed herself off the sofa and walked to the glass. As the view beyond it revealed itself, she felt a lump grow in her throat. Hundreds of metres below stretched a rectangular expanse of woodland that was easily five hundred metres across and at least a few kilometres long. It was crisscrossed with pathways and tracks, dotted with green open spaces and small bodies of water, and just over halfway along, there was a massive lake. It was a view she recognised from TV and films.

It was Central Park.

She was in New York.

'Oh my God!'

She stood for a few moments touching the glass, which was warm from what she guessed was the morning sun. She inhaled deeply, composed herself and turned to look at the room she was in. It was square, roughly fifteen metres across. The floor was cherry-red hardwood, and positioned centrally on it was a square rug that looked old. Not decades old. Centuries old.

The two flank walls were all glass until about two-thirds of the way back, where they became panels of wood that matched the floor. Hanging on each panel was a large rectangular piece of abstract art—one was deep reds, oranges and blacks, and the other was all blues and purples. They looked like Rothko pieces, but she couldn't be sure.

Beyond the glass of the side walls were the tops of adjacent buildings, all lower than her. She thought the apartment, or whatever this place was, was probably the equivalent of a shiny red sports car—a status symbol for the self-important, an overcompensation for something, or both.

The entire rear wall was a floor-to-ceiling bookcase made of the same dark wood as the floor and walls, filled with books whose spines all appeared to be neatly aligned to the shelves' outer edges. Whoever owned this place had major OCD, she thought. Between the bookcase and the sofa were two rows of display cases—six cabinets spaced evenly across the room, all containing artefacts.

She suddenly realised there was no door, staircase, or other obvious way to get into or, more importantly, out of the room. She felt a sweat break out on her forehead, and her heart pumped a little faster, but then it struck her that there must be a way in and out. Otherwise, she wouldn't be there.

A trapdoor? Possibly. A secret bookcase door? Probably.

So, that was it. All she had to do was find the bronze bust that tilted to expose a big red button, the piano with the out-of-tune keys, or a lever behind a painting that swung open on hinges, and she could open the hidden door and get the fuck out of there.

There was no piano in the room.

She scanned the bookcase. No bust either.

She went to the painting with the reds, oranges, and blacks, grabbed one side of its frame, and tugged. It remained in place. She grasped the other side and pulled. Nothing. She ran to the other painting and performed the same test. Again, nothing. So, what was the alternative? Pull out every book on the shelves until a door swung open or popped up from the floor? Fuck it, she thought. It wasn't like she had anything better to do. She'd already established that someone had taken her phone, and no phone was visible anywhere in the room, so calling for help was out, even if she knew exactly where she was being held.

She looked at the bookcase. There must have been hundreds of books on it, so where to start? The most obvious place would be between her waist and eyes, easily reached. But wouldn't that be *too* obvious? Probably. So, she'd start at the top left and work along and down each section.

As she made her way to the far end of the bookcase, her eyes were drawn to the nearest display case in the first row. It had a tall, dark wooden plinth that came up to her chest and a glass casing that ended just above her head. Within the case were two stone tablets standing back-to-back, each the size of a large paperback novel. Their edges and surfaces were rough, worn, and uneven like they'd been hewn using blunt tools. They were mottled with age, and horizontal lines of scratch-like engravings covered the front of each.

Her interest piqued, Ellie glanced at the first cabinet in the second row. It was almost all glass, with a shallow plinth. The casing ended at the same height as the first, and inside it, held vertically by some unseen apparatus, was a long piece of wood, knotted and twisted in places, like the branch of a tree. It was as tall as her and as thick as her forearm, and it looked old.

She looked at the other cabinets. Their glass housings ended at the same height as the first two, but the tallness of the plinths differed according to what they contained. She walked between the two rows to inspect the artefacts. A metal helmet shaped like an upside-down funnel and wrapped in leather with long leather flaps at the sides. A stunning golden statuette of a falcon wearing what appeared to be a conical crown. Three black iron spikes, each roughly eight inches long, tapering gradually from the points up to square heads an inch across. They looked like gruesome torture implements.

The last case contained a sword that, from hilt to point, was slightly longer than her arm. It was made of bright metal that shone as if under direct sunlight, even though it was in shadow. And it was immaculate. There were no nicks, mottling, or stains on it. It looked like it had never been used.

'Do you like it?'

She didn't have to turn around to know who spoke to her. It was Peter. Given what she'd learned over the last few hours, it didn't surprise her that he'd survived Gideon's bullets.

'You steal it like you stole me?' she asked, her back still to him.

'It's a memento, actually. Legitimately owned, like the other artefacts. Not mine, though, regrettably.'

Ellie sighed and wearily turned to face him. He'd changed into fresh clothes and there was a faint ring in the centre of his forehead, but otherwise, no one would know he'd been shot to shit a few hours earlier.

'Secret bookcase door?' she asked.

He chuckled and nodded.

'Where am I?'

'New York.'

'Yeah, I figured that much out for myself,' she said, gesturing toward the glass. 'I meant where exactly?'

'Somewhere safe.'

'You fuckers and your *somewhere safe* bullshit. You mean I'm somewhere I can't be rescued from.'

'If you'd prefer I put it like that, then yes.' He motioned to the sword. 'It's made to a particular metallurgical recipe, known coincidentally as angelic steel.'

'I really don't give a shit, Peter. I want to get out of here. How long have I been here?'

'Two days.'

'*Two days?*'

'We gave you a sedative before leaving London, and we've given you electrolytes and more sedatives intravenously since then.'

She vaguely remembered Thomas telling her to calm down as he dragged her into the hotel's elevator, then giving her a bottle of water when he put her back on the plane at City Airport, but not much else after that.

'Fuck! You fuckers *pushed* me, roofied me, and then injected my body without my consent? Rape much, you Catholic fucks?'

'It's had many names over the years,' he said, ignoring the barb. 'The sword of Attila, Durandal, Joyeuse, Kaliborn.'

His last word struck a familiar chord with her.

'Kaliborn? You mean Excalibur?'

'You know your legends.'

'I know my crappy films. And, at this point, I don't give a fuck what it is or what it's called. Why am I here, Peter?'

'Why do you think you're here?'

'Don't get cryptic, you asshole. This isn't a therapy session. I'm exhausted, and I don't mind admitting I'm fucking terrified. Why am I here? Why am I still alive? I thought you wanted me dead.'

'Who says we don't still want you dead?'

She opened her arms and gestured to the room.

'Keeping someone in a fancy penthouse library is a strange way to kill them,' she said.

'Thomas told me what happened on the roof in London. Specifically, what happened to Jakob. It's shed... no pun intended... a new light on things for us. On what we need from you.'

'What you need from me?'

'Why fight the line of Lucifer when you can use it?'

'You're going to use me? For what?'

'Not you, Ellie. Your child.'

'What child?'

'The one you carry in your belly.'

Her lack of comprehension must have shown on her face.

'You didn't know that you're pregnant?'

Her stomach lurched, and her mouth became dry. She felt her forehead prickle and become hot. She staggered, but Peter caught her elbow and steadied her.

'We have a sonogram to prove it. I can show it to you if you wish. I didn't realise it when I read your memories, but it's why you've been having the dreams. Your child carries the blood of Lucifer. Inherited from its father. From Jakob.'

'That's impossible.'

'As impossible as me standing here after being shot in the head? Or as Jakob being consumed by blue fire?'

She thought about what he was saying. Of course it was possible. She'd seen enough strangeness since Dante's to accept that one of the most natural things in the world could have happened to her. And it made perfect sense. She *was* already late by a few weeks. She *had* been nauseated. And if she *was* pregnant, then her baby *would* carry the same blood.

Jakob's blood.

Lucifer's blood.

Peter smiled. He must have seen the realisation in her. The

resignation to a situation she had no control over.

'You'll have your child,' he said, 'and it will be raised with us, as one of us. We have no specific reason to see you dead now, as you're no longer the threat we perceived you to be, so whether you live or die after the child is born will be up to you.'

'Up to me?'

He stepped closer. He was so close that if he breathed in deeply, his chest would touch hers.

'Well, we'll send you back to Copenhagen, where you'll choose either to forget everything that you've witnessed and live to continue your small, unimportant life there or—'

'Or?'

'Or, you'll run your mouth off about us,' he said, cupping her jaw and rubbing his thumb over her lips, 'and meet with an untimely end, like your parents.'

'You killed—'

'Of course not.' He smiled, evidently amused by her pain. 'We've only recently become aware of you, so why would we have? But I saw what happened to them when I read—'

Ellie lost control and slapped him across the face. He barely moved, so she struck out again, but he caught her wrist. His grip tightened, and she thought he might break bones. She cried out, twisting her arm to try and escape his grasp. He let go, and her arm snapped back, almost catching her in the face.

'Why can't you just blank out my memories?'

'And make it easy for you? Where would be the fun in that?'

'Fuck you, Peter.'

She whirled and stormed back to the glass wall. Peter touching her made her stomach churn. As she stared out over Central Park, her eyes glazed over, and she began to worry about Jakob and whether she and her child—if Peter hadn't lied about her being pregnant—would be safe. Hushed voices behind her drew her attention. She turned. Peter had his back to her, obscuring her view of whoever had joined them. When he eventually moved, her breath caught in her throat.

In front of her stood a man who looked only a few years older than Jakob and slightly taller. He had thick, dark hair and light olive skin that seemed to glow. She'd never seen his face with her own eyes, but she recognised him immediately.

'Hello, Ellie.'

'Jesus!'

'Once,' he said with a chuckle. 'But these days, I'm known by my true name.'

She looked at him impassively. She didn't want to give him the satisfaction of appearing curious. He smiled at her. There was no warmth to it. It was false and smug and unkind. Her grandmother would say he looked like the cat who'd got the canary. He began walking toward her, and as he did so, the air around him shimmered like a heatwave in the shape of six gigantic wings. He got to within inches of her and stopped. She could feel his warm, fresh breath like a gentle breeze on her face.

'Call me Michael.'

AUTHOR'S NOTE

First and most importantly, I want to thank my wife, Caroline, without whose love, patience, and support this book would never have been written. Caroline, I love you. I promise the next one won't take as long.

Second, I'd like to thank my beta readers (Caroline, Tess, and Genevieve), who provided valuable feedback on my first draft. Thank you.

And third, thank *you* for taking a chance and reading this book, whether you bought it (thank you again) or borrowed it.

It took me over twenty years to write this book. Due to academic commitments, work responsibilities, and life generally, it was shelved and revisited countless times. In 2016, I was made redundant for the third time in five years. I was living in the Middle East then, and after six months of unsuccessfully looking for another job in real estate, my wife (a banking lawyer at the time) encouraged me to return to writing the book. For that, I will be forever grateful.

Now, a few points to separate fiction from fact.

The Vatican's Rapid Intervention Group does exist, but it's an anti-terrorism unit and does not, as far as I'm aware, include angels and part-angels in its ranks.

Interpol does indeed share floorspace with the Vatican's Gendarmerie. Vatican City has been a member state of Interpol since 2008.

The Leonardo AW609 aircraft that Enrique commandeered in London does exist. Its first flight was in 2003, and at the time of writing (2022), it was expected to go into production in the mid-2020s.

As far as I know, Rebekah's sub-dermal communications implant is pure science fiction and not yet a *thing*, but I suspect it's not too far away. For example, Neuralink Corporation, founded in 2016 by Elon Musk (yes, of Tesla fame), is developing brain-computer interfaces that will restore vision and motor function in disabled people, allow them to communicate with electronic devices, and potentially link their brain function to artificial intelligence. It wouldn't be too much of a stretch to see such technology advance to allow people to communicate as Rebekah did.

The Fuente del Ángel Caído (statue of the Fallen Angel) in Madrid's El Retiro park really does sit at 666 metres above sea level. I'm sure that was intentional, but if not, it's the greatest coincidence ever.

Regarding the saviours Samuel tells Jakob of—born on the 25th of December, miraculous births, killed in their thirties, resurrected—I didn't make those up. You'll find references to them in the histories of their respective cultures.

For the record, I'm not anti-God or against the idea of a supreme, all-powerful force (whether God or energy that binds all living things or whatever). I believe something *could* exist out there, which, I hope, is evident in the book. Neither am I against the notion of personal faith. Everyone is entitled to their beliefs. It's organised religion I disagree with. It has been (and continues to be) the root cause of many conflicts in the world. And if you were to list institutions that thrive on amassing power and wealth through control and fearmongering (don't sin or you'll go to Hell—instead come to church and give us your money), Religion Inc. would be at the top of the list.

However, it seems the tide may be turning against organised religions—certainly the Christian ones. European churches are closing each year. An article published by *The Wall Street Journal* on 2 January 2015 (entitled *Europe's Empty Churches Go on Sale*) claimed that the Church of England was shutting roughly twenty churches a year, Germany had closed around five hundred and fifteen churches in the previous ten years, approximately two hundred churches in Denmark had been considered "non-viable or underused", in the Netherlands, seven hundred Protestant churches would close by 2019, and in the same country, Roman Catholic higher-ups had estimated closure of roughly one thousand of its churches. Some of those buildings continue to be in community use, but others have become florists, supermarkets, bookstores, gyms, and even bars. The article states that a former Lutheran church in Edinburgh became a Frankenstein-themed bar.

So, there may be hope for a world without Religion Inc.

I loved almost every minute of working on this book. I hope you enjoyed it. I know it's unconventional. It may even have upset or angered you. I'm sorry if that's the case. At the very least, I hope it opened your mind to the possibility that just because the Bible, the Tanakh, or the Quran (or whichever religious text you read) tells you something, it doesn't necessarily mean it's true. Like this book, it could just be an excellent story.

Finally, a few words on music. When I wrote the book, I did so with the dream of it reaching the silver screen at some point (Netflix / Prime Video, do you hear me?) As I worked through each chapter, I tried to imagine which songs would work best with certain scenes on screen. Some of those tracks are only hinted at, while others made it into the book explicitly, but it's incumbent upon me to credit those responsible for all of them, as they're all great tracks. There are fourteen in total, and they are:

Immortality by Pearl Jam
Angel by Massive Attack
Eternal Life by Jeff Buckley
God's Gonna Cut You Down by Johnny Cash
Crucify by Tori Amos
Devil's Dance by Metallica
Devils & Dust by Bruce Springsteen
Everybody Wants to Rule the World by Tears for Fears
Antichrist Superstar by Marilyn Manson

Personal Jesus by Depeche Mode
Neon Angels on the Road to Ruin by The Runaways
In The Air Tonight by Phil Collins
Cherub Rock by Smashing Pumpkins
Sympathy for the Devil by The Rolling Stones (end credits)

Once again, thank you for reading this book. Now, I'm going to take a short break before starting my next novel (for which, yes, I have a few ideas).

LEAVE A REVIEW

If you would like to review this book, please scan the QR code below. Thank you.